Sybil Stone scanned the group of twenty already boarded on the flight. "No press or nonessential staff on this flight. Skeleton crew only. Get them off fast and get the press and staff separated, Agent Westford." Worry clouded her eyes, turning her irises midnight blue. "Delay their return to the States until Monday."

Monday? But it was only Wednesday. "Staff and press, Vice President Stone?"

She nodded. "Yes, Agent Westford. Let's get going. We have seventy-two hours, and we're going to need every minute, 'Hail Mary,' and scrap of luck we can scrounge up."

"I'll have to bring in the CIA," he reminded her, an accompanyimg chill crawling up his backbone. Liberty wasn't prone to exaggeration, and only once, during a crisis in the Middle East that had threatened to rip open barely healed wounds, had he heard her resort to a verbal "Hail Mary" pass. "The press will scream bloody murder."

"I look forward to hearing it."

That baffled him. "Ma'am?"

"They'll be alive to scream."

LADY LIBERTY

Vicki Hinze

BANTAM BOOKS

LADY LIBERTY
A Bantam Book / November 2002

ISBN 0-553-58352-2

Published simultaneously in the United States and Canada

Bantam Books are published by Bantam Books, a division of
Random House, Inc. Its trademark, consisting of the words "Bantam
Books" and the portrayal of a rooster, is Registered in U.S. Patent
and Trademark Office and in other countries. Marca Registrada.
Bantam Books, 1540 Broadway, New York, New York 10036.

PRINTED IN THE UNITED STATES OF AMERICA

10   9   8   7   6   5   4   3   2   1

OPM

Acknowledgments

An idea does not a novel make. If a writer is extremely lucky, she encounters a generous soul along the way who is willing to share her time, expertise, and insights. This novel made that difficult transition blessed by many generous souls:

My amazing agent, Helen Breitwieser, who said, "Vic, write me a story about a woman VP," and then not only loved it, but wholeheartedly supported it. My team at Bantam—a warm and enthusiastic group of professionals who always get what I mean—and when I get mired, explain it to me: Kara Cesare, Beth de Guzman, Anne Bohner, Nita Taublib, Wendy McCurdy, and Liz Scheier. Ladies, the depth of your caring and commitment humble me.

My family, who knows *everything* about me and loves me anyway. My friends, fans, and fellow writers, particularly those upon whom I constantly rely: Lorna Tedder, Elizabeth Sinclair, Teresa Hill, Susan Wiggs, and all my RomEx sisters.

Special Thanks

To Eliza for her sharp eye and insights, and to my research sources, who for reasons of their own choose to remain nameless, yet graciously gift me with technical support, insights on policy, procedures, and probabilities. You guys are terrific, and any errors are definitely mine.

From the bottom of my heart, I thank you all.

LADY LIBERTY

Chapter One

"Lady Liberty is on the move."

Agent Jonathan Westford stilled. The message had transmitted through his earpiece clearly, but what he had heard couldn't be accurate. Three agents had been assigned to the security detail guarding Sybil Stone, the Vice President of the United States. Three. Westford as mission chief; Harrison, an old-timer; and Cramer, who was new to working Special Detail Unit's international details. Right now Liberty was supposed to be sequestered, having dinner in a private dining room with the other dignitaries, and Harrison was supposed to be standing watch. *So why the hell was* Cramer *calling in her moves?*

Forgetting his half-eaten dinner of steak and potatoes, Jonathan snatched his napkin from his lap and left the sanctuary of the Grand Palace Hotel's dining room, silently damning budget cutbacks, reduced manpower, and Home Base for allowing itself to be forced to assign a rookie like

Cramer to any Level-Five SDU mission, much less to one involving Liberty.

The main lobby was littered with guests, many of whom had been identified as press and more who had not been identified. The hotel was far too public, in Jonathan's opinion, but it had been the one place Peris and Abdan's leaders had agreed to meet, and when the president of the last superpower in the world employed you and he said go, you went or you resigned. Since Jonathan hadn't been ready to resign, he'd gone.

Keeping a sharp watch for oddities, he strolled across the expansive lobby, longing for the days of summit meetings at Camp David or places equally secluded and less complicated to secure. *Why was Liberty on the move? And why were Harrison and Cramer not reporting?*

As soon as he cleared the watchful eyes of the press, Jonathan broke into a full run, hurdled the velvet-rope barrier restricting public access to the diplomatic wing, then barreled down the deserted hallway leading to the conference room where Liberty had spent the last four days trying to broker a peace agreement between the leaders of two of the former Soviet nations, Abdan and Peris.

She alone had succeeded at getting them to the negotiating table. So far, she had managed to keep their tempers simmering, though threats of eruptions hung as heavily in the air as their threats for war. Fired up over a mineral-rich land dispute, both countries had been stockpiling arms for months, and in the past few weeks, they had escalated their purchases significantly.

Both had nuclear weaponry in their arsenals. Both had demonstrated the will to use them.

Vic Sampson, the hotel's chief of security, intercepted Jonathan at the mouth of the corridor. Years of hard choices seamed his lean face. "What's up? Why is she off-schedule?"

"I don't know yet." Admitting that grated at Jonathan, and he sniffed. *Citrus?* "What am I smelling, Vic?"

"Air freshener. It's in the climate-control unit."

Bad news all around. "Lose it." Jonathan doubled his pace.

Vic lifted his walkie-talkie to his mouth, then issued the order. Seconds later he issued another. "I don't give a damn how you do it, just shut down the unit and get rid of it—now." He slid the device back into its case at his belt. "Why did I do that?"

"Fragrance can mask contaminants." Jonathan spared him a glance. "Maybe lethal contaminants."

Vic paled.

It was a serious mistake, and Vic had made it. No more needed to be said. He hadn't been crazy about taking on the elevated risks of terrorist attacks or any of the other thousand extra challenges that came with hosting the summit, but he and his staff had been professional and extremely accommodating. To minimize security risks, they had blocked off an entire wing and had provided each of the peace-seekers and their staff suites, conference rooms, and offices with comfortable salons. All in all, the message to the peace-seeking entourage was unqualified, clear—and mirrored unilaterally throughout the world: *Be successful.*

No one in power wanted these negotiations to fail.

No sane person wanted war.

"Clear behind us." Vic reported a rear check. "Potential attack?"

"It's possible." Before Liberty's plane had left D.C., two groups of terrorists, Ballast and PUSH, had threatened attacks. Vic had been warned and the Grand Palace had quietly given its employees "heavy-traffic" bonuses for working during the summit. But anyone with half a clue would know that this was "hazardous-duty" pay. Unfortunately, it was justified.

Jonathan rounded the corner and spotted Liberty walking toward him. Flanked by the other leaders, their guards, three Russian translators, and Cramer, she looked tiny—a blue-eyed blonde, about five-five in pumps, with a pretty girl-next-door face and a trim body polished by nature and healthy habits. Typical confident stride, purposeful yet not overbearing. No obvious distress. Actually, the woman was smiling, amused by something the Peris leader had said.

"She looks okay." Vic summarized his visual check. "But I'll hang close, just in case."

Jonathan nodded and continued with his own assessment. Though dwarfed by the tall, thick-shouldered men surrounding her, Liberty had a presence that had nothing to do with her navy power suit or her political clout. It signaled to even the most casual observer that she was in charge, which of course she was. In many ways, she was a remarkable woman: classy, competent, and cool but not distant. She had presence; he knew it, and others knew it. That was enough.

He stopped in the hallway in front of the office door, just steps away from the conference room they had been using for negotiations, and lifted a hand to snag her attention.

"Excuse me a moment please," Liberty told the others, her voice soft and husky.

She walked over, stopped beside Jonathan, and smoothed back her pale, chin-length hair.

A Band-Aid on her finger? His breath locked in his lungs. *What the hell was she doing with a Band-Aid on her finger? And why the hell hadn't he been notified?*

"Agent Westford?" Her brow furrowed, puzzled. "Is everything all right?"

"I need a moment, ma'am." He had to work at keeping his voice level.

She had to work at holding her smile. "Of course," she said, then stepped into his office.

He followed her to the doorway, stared Cramer to a

stop outside, and then spoke into his transmitter. "Harrison. My office. STAT."

"On my way, sir."

He turned to Cramer and ordered, "Do not move." When he nodded, Jonathan entered the office, shut the door, and then flipped the switch to activate the electronics installed to create white noise and keep conversations private. Between satellite and high-tech surveillance equipment, few places existed where sound waves couldn't be intercepted. White noise minimized the risks. That was important. If overheard, this conversation would have immediate international repercussions.

Liberty stood waiting in front of his desk. "Is something wrong?"

He glanced down at her hand. "What happened to your finger?"

"I hope, nothing." She frowned. "The waiter slipped and the edge of his tray cut me. It bled a ridiculous amount."

"He gave you the Band-Aid, then?"

She nodded. "Waiters always carry Band-Aids."

The hell they did. Jonathan grabbed a pair of scissors and then cut off the bandage, careful to use the scissor tips to grasp the bandage and not contaminate it or himself. "Don't touch that wound."

Rounding the corner of the desk, he removed an evidence bag from the bottom left drawer, dropped the blood-soiled Band-Aid inside, and then seamed the bag shut. The scissors went into a second sealed bag.

Liberty looked at him with pure dread. "Why did you bag that?"

He held up a finger and again spoke into his transmitter. "Harrison, get a Band-Aid from Grace, alcohol and peroxide, and get the mobile lab on site." Grace, Liberty's personal assistant, was the consummate professional and always prepared. "Possible Code Red."

"On my way."

"Agent Westford." Liberty reclaimed his attention. "It's a scratch from an ornate silver tray, not a mortal wound."

He raised her hand and examined her finger. "Was the waiter holding any cutlery?"

"No, just the tray. Why?"

"This isn't a scratch, ma'am." He lifted his gaze to meet her eyes. "It's a knife wound."

"A knife wound?" Her shock was evident. "I didn't see a knife."

Must have been hidden beneath the lip of the tray. "Clean. Deep. No jagged edges." He glanced up from her hand to her eyes. "Definitely a knife wound, ma'am."

Her expression soured. "Even so, calling a Code Red, summoning the mobile lab—isn't that a little overkill?"

The incident had occurred in the presence of Peris and Abdan's leaders and security staff. Either could claim it an attack by the other side and end negotiations. Obviously, she was worried that they would. "Not if the knife blade was contaminated."

"Listen, I appreciate your diligent attention to details, but the waiter wasn't a terrorist. The poor man was eighty years old. He just slipped while carrying a large tray." She was deliberately minimizing the gravity of the situation; he read it in her face.

"And he apologized profusely for it, and you accepted the Band-Aid from him to avoid hurting his feelings."

Resignation that he knew what she was doing settled in, and a steely look glinted in her eyes. "An overt reaction on my part would have given Peris and Abdan's premieres an excuse to halt the talks and leave the table. That would have meant war."

Vintage Liberty. "So taking the Band-Aid was a calculated risk and not a synapse misfire?"

"Of course."

He cocked his head and raked his lower lip with his teeth. "High risks."

She hiked her chin. "High stakes."

Too high. Jonathan put a hard edge in his voice. She'd heard it before and would know what it meant. "Please refrain from accepting aid, assistance, or anything you ingest from anyone except me, members of my team, or approved hotel staff. Anyone—even an eighty-year-old waiter—can be a terrorist. And even a seemingly innocent incident can be a third-party terrorist attack."

"But I explained why—"

"No buts, ma'am," he interrupted. "We're in Gregor Faust's backyard and a stone's throw from PUSH. We know they're hostile and they want you to fail here. We'd be foolish to forget it, and we are not foolish people."

"Of course not." She had the grace to blush but neglected to promise it wouldn't happen again. Odds were, it would. First time Liberty deemed it necessary, she'd put herself right back in the line of fire.

Unfortunately, she was right about Peris and Abdan. Both premiers felt that being together made them more vulnerable to attack and their meeting increased the possibility of danger to their own lives. They *could* have blamed the incident with the waiter on each other and walked away. Still, Jonathan felt duty-bound to remind her of the terrorist threats. "With Gregor Faust at the helm, Ballast has become one of the most feared international terrorist groups in the world—and if the CIA's suspicions are accurate, he's also the arms dealer supplying Peris and Abdan with weapons." Less intelligence had been gathered on PUSH, or People United, as it was sometimes called. "And it's true that PUSH operates mostly in Western Europe and North Africa, but that doesn't mean it can't pull an attack here."

"I've read the reports, Agent Westford," Liberty said.

"And I've heard the rumors that PUSH has developed ties to China."

"Whether or not the rumors are true, PUSH has been pumping out strong signals to the terrorist community that it's eager to expand its arms sales and take down Ballast's stronghold in Eastern Europe. That's significant, ma'am." It was. The simple mention of Faust's name sent shockwaves through more countries than were members of NATO—and ripples of terror through the heart of every man or woman responsible for the safety of the people in those countries.

"I've been thinking about that." She lifted a finger. "To take on Ballast, PUSH has to be formidable. Far stronger than we believed."

"Formidable, or suicidal." He waited for the analogy between PUSH's behavior and her own to occur to her.

When it did, she frowned. "You're right, okay? You're right." Liberty stepped back and rested a hip against the desk. "I—I'm sorry." She looked down at her fingertip. "I will try not to do it again."

"I appreciate your consideration." He took the compliment that she trusted him to do his job as such, but it fell short of a promise. Still, it was the best he was going to get, so he had to object. "It isn't in your best interest to take risks right now. Particularly not here."

Worry darkened the irises of her eyes to a smoky blue. "Do you think one of the terrorist groups contaminated the knife blade?"

"Maybe. But don't discount Peris or Abdan." In the past, the warmongers had committed worse acts. "We'll check with the lab to be sure."

A rap sounded at the door and Jonathan called out, "Come in, Harrison."

Flustered and tense, he entered with the requested first-aid supplies. "I take full responsibility—"

Jonathan silenced him with a look, cleaned Liberty's

wound, and then applied a new Band-Aid. "There you go, ma'am." He backed up and forced a smile to ease her mind. "Sorry for the interruption. Harrison will escort you back to the conference room. I'll take over momentarily."

"Thank you, Agent Westford." She turned for the door and paused, dipped her chin. Sleek and smooth, her hair swept forward and brushed against her jaw. "You'll let me know—"

"It'll be a while, but when I know, you'll know." When she nodded, he added, "Gabby called. She needs to talk with you ASAP." Gabby was Sybil's oldest friend, the closest thing to family she had left, and from his days on her detail, Jonathan knew Gabby often called Sybil to chat, though she rarely interrupted Sybil's missions unless she had information that was of vital interest or bad news.

"I'll call her now."

"Yes, ma'am." Jonathan watched Liberty go. Harrison followed her, his concern burning through his masked expression.

Jonathan motioned Cramer inside and closed the door. The man was good at general domestic details, which made him a strong candidate for Special Detail Unit and international details. He was thin and wiry but fast, sharp-minded, a master marksman and—judging by the look in his brown eyes and the rigid tension in his stance—appropriately worried right now. Since he was new to international and to working Jonathan's SDU details, he supposed he would have to cut the rookie a little slack even though his natural inclination was to cut the idiot's throat for allowing this to happen. "Why were you standing watch?"

"Harrison got the runs, sir."

"Why wasn't I notified?"

"I would have had to be obvious. You ordered us to be discreet when the other guards were present, and one was posted on either side of me. I thought Harrison would brief you, but I guess he was preoccupied with making it to the rest room."

"Fine." Jonathan would take this up with Harrison. He was an old hand and damn well knew the only excuse for not reporting was to be dead. "What about Liberty's injury?"

"The waiter slipped. I was posted on point, sir. Before I could get to her, she had accepted the Band-Aid from the waiter. I couldn't say anything without making a production out of it and embarrassing her."

"Next time, embarrass her." She might take calculated risks with her life, but he wouldn't. "If you have to physically get between them, then do it, but you intercede, Cramer."

"Yes, sir."

"Did you observe my intercept in the hallway?"

"Yes, sir."

"Learn from it." Jonathan frowned. "I realize you're new to international and to me, but Vice President Stone can't afford to be your training ground on this mission, and I won't tolerate it. She's trying to prevent a war that could destabilize an entire region, one vital to our interests—and she's committed to succeeding. It's our responsibility to see to it she survives to have the opportunity."

"I know, sir."

He *knew*? Cramer had no idea she had been taking a calculated risk. "Right. And you also know she's under heavy threat from Ballast and PUSH and there are no excuses for screwing up, so don't insult either of us by making any."

Cramer blinked fast, swallowed hard. "No, sir."

Sweat beaded on the man's forehead, and Jonathan was glad to see it. Obviously he needed the hell scared out of him to gain his edge. That edge was often the only thing that kept Special Detail Unit agents alive. Considering SDU didn't overtly exist, the agents' assignments typically didn't officially exist, and Commander Conlee, who ruled Home Base's highly specialized division of the Secret Service with an iron fist, didn't exist, the sooner Cramer locked onto his edge, the better for all of them.

"Listen, Liberty is carrying a lot on her shoulders, and she's got even more on her mind. The welfare of millions around the globe rides on her decisions. That doesn't leave her much time to think about mundane security matters like keeping herself out of the line of fire—and she damn well shouldn't have to think about them. That's my job as her mission chief and your job as a detail member assigned to protect her. You screwed up, which means *we* screwed up." He narrowed his eyes, deepened his voice and, he hoped, Cramer's fear. "We don't screw up, Cramer. It's not professional, and being unprofessional is not conducive to staying alive. I'm not ready to die. Are you?"

"No, sir." Unable to hold Jonathan's gaze, Cramer focused on his tie.

Well, that was something. "Did it occur to you that the waiter could be a plant?" He'd been briefed on the threats, for God's sake. He'd been told they were credible. "Or that the wound isn't consistent with a tray scrape?"

"I didn't see her wound, sir."

"No, you didn't. If you had, you would have seen that it was a knife cut. And you would have suspected the knife that made the cut could have been laced with a biological or chemical contaminant." Jonathan's voice elevated an octave. "Has a warning signal started flashing in your head yet?" He tapped his temple twice, more to distract himself from the clenching in his gut than to cause clenching in Cramer's. His next statement was one he didn't even want to think about. "Liberty could already be dying."

The color drained from Cramer's face.

Jonathan shoved the evidence bags at him, again cursing Home Base for putting a rookie on a Level-Five SDU mission. "The mobile lab should be in place in five minutes.

Get this to it. I want a full-screen toxicology done—the works. Take the north exit from the building and walk four blocks south. Lab is in a black van. It'll be curbside, waiting for you."

He took the bag and started toward the door.

"Cramer." Jonathan frowned at the man. "Verify that you've got the right van *before* you hand over the evidence bags. And if you haven't already, start praying the sample tests are clean."

★ ★ ★

Moonlight slanted through slices of shadows and blended with the amber glow the street lamps cast on the wet concrete. The smell of rain hung in the air and thin streams of water clung to the street at the curb. Cramer rushed down the sidewalk toward the mobile lab.

Liberty could already be dying.

Westford's words haunted Cramer, and he blew out a breath heavy with fear.

Harrison met him at the corner. "I warned you not to screw up. Not on Westford's detail."

"I know. I blew it." Under normal conditions, Westford wanted excellence. But when Lady Liberty was involved, mere excellence wasn't good enough. You had to be God, or suffer Westford's wrath. And everyone with the agency knew that God showed mercy; Westford did not. "He'll definitely put me on report," Cramer said. "Probably have me yanked off SDU details and dumped back into domestic grunt work, too."

"I hate to break it to you, kid, but odds are better than fifty-fifty he'll get you canned."

Fired? He'd lose his job, his gun, and his credentials: the things he had wanted and worked for his entire life. Cramer's insides hollowed.

"That's *if* Liberty survives this fiasco without injury. If she doesn't . . . well, I'd say your long-range planning doesn't look good."

Even a rookie understood the rage in Westford's eyes. "If Liberty dies, he'll see to it that I join her."

"That pretty much sums it up." Harrison stuffed his hands in his pockets, tucked his chin against the misting rain. "I don't mean to sound cold, but facts are facts. You've got to understand how things are between Westford and Liberty."

"Are they involved?"

"Yes." Harrison looked torn. "No."

"Thanks for clearing that up."

"It's complicated." Harrison shoved out a sigh. "Do you remember when she won over the NRA?"

The law she pushed through that forced prosecution on existing gun laws. "HR 855, right?"

"Yeah. She was just a junior congresswoman back then, but she caught Westford's eye. He's walked a lot of miles with her since."

Then they had walked a lot of miles together. Through child welfare issues, laws to keep pedophiles locked up, and ones to keep deadbeat dads paying support. A lot of miles.

"She wins, and he's downright giddy."

Shocked, Cramer did a double take at Harrison. "Westford, giddy?" Cramer couldn't imagine it. The man was as serious as a heart attack—and just as opinionated.

"Amazing, huh?" Harrison smiled. "But true. When she walked through the bill reorganizing protective services for neglected and abused kids, you should have seen him. He was so proud, I thought he'd bust a gut."

Cramer had heard about that success in the unit. The operatives all sang her praises, though not for the legislation itself. Because she'd covered her ass so well that Senator Cap Marlowe and his cronies—who had reputations for spinning in fault on issues where Liberty had none—

had tried and failed to trip her up. The guys at SDU were pro-anything that was anti-Marlowe, who tried to control them to the point of stifling them in doing their jobs. Even Sybil Stone.

A light went on in Cramer's mind. "Westford brought her to President Lance's attention."

Harrison nodded. "He denies it, but I was there and saw it."

"So it's like a proud-parent relationship between them?" Cramer asked.

"Hell no, kid. It's a lot more earthy than that."

Westford and Liberty weren't twisting the sheets. Cramer might be the new kid on the block, but he wasn't unconscious, and he hadn't picked up on any romantic vibes between them. In his book, that was a good thing. Liberty made a fine vice president, but she had a history as a lousy wife. A year ago, she'd just walked out on a fifteen-year marriage to Dr. Austin Stone, shocking everyone on the Hill. Stone wasn't some loser. He was an engineering genius—CEO of the kick-ass Secure Environet that had been tearing up Wall Street for the past two years—and he hadn't wanted the divorce. She'd pushed for it. Westford might be a hard-ass, but he deserved a better wife than that.

"Marlowe wanted her job," Harrison said, recapturing Cramer's attention. "He swears if he'd been a woman, Lance would have offered it to him."

"Would he?"

"Liberty could have been the purple people eater, and Lance wouldn't have given a damn. He chose her as a running mate so he wouldn't have to compete against her. She's that good."

"So she's special to Lance and to Westford."

"Special enough that when she took office two years ago, Westford left covert ops to head up her guard detail."

"That's a whale of a demotion." Cramer couldn't figure

it. Westford was the hottest operative in SDU, the logical choice for plum covert operation assignments.

"No demotion. The president handpicked him for the job. Officially, he had 'special concerns' for her safety, but if he had his way, he'd have Westford and Liberty joined at the hip."

"So why did Westford bail out?" Word around the unit was Westford had demanded reassignment.

"Some say he fell in love with her—complicated because at the time she was his boss and she was married. Others say he couldn't stomach working for a woman."

"What does he say?"

Looking pleased that Cramer had asked, Harrison shrugged. "He doesn't, and no one's had the guts to ask him directly."

Cramer thought through it all. President Lance could tag his "special concerns" any way he wanted, but underneath the politically correct facade, he was afraid she would be at greater risk than previous veeps because she was the first woman to hold the office. She did get at least a dozen death threats a week from hotheads, disgruntled citizens stuck in sixties' mentalities, and hostile foreign entities—especially those actively engaged in oppressing women. "Harrison, do you think it's true that some of the death threats are coming from her colleagues?"

"No hard evidence, but it's possible. There's a lot of resentment against her on the Hill."

That frustrated Cramer. "Then I don't get it."

"What?"

"When her colleagues need credibility or clout to push their pet projects through the process, they come to her first. If she can, she supports them. Why does she do it?" Cramer couldn't figure it. "She's got to know that once the project's a done deal, they're going to slide right back into resenting her. Most of them act as if the White House is the last 'For Men Only' club in the country, and their main mission in life is to act as armor and shield to keep their sacred space safe from her."

"Damned pathetic, isn't it?" Harrison grunted. "But it's telling, too, kid."

Cramer wasn't tracking, so he kept quiet and waited for Harrison to explain.

"They feel confident she *can* take the White House. No one around here wastes energy defending something not at risk."

"Politics." Cramer grunted. In the next block, a black van pulled up to the curb and killed its lights.

"Politics." Harrison clapped Cramer on the shoulder. "Verify the van, kid. I'll see you back at the hotel. I need to walk off some steam. Westford's going to be wired for sound and breathing down our necks for the rest of this mission."

Shivering with dread, Cramer hunched his shoulders and started watching the sidewalk, but he saw no sign of a U.S. penny. Panic set in. He couldn't pass the evidence bag to the lab without it. *Couldn't he get one break on this damn mission?*

Finally he spotted the coin, glinting heads-up on the sidewalk. He stooped down, pretending to tie a shoe, scooped it up, and then rushed his steps. Odds looked slim, but he had to perform at optimum level from here on out to save his backside and, if possible, his job.

A gust of cool wind tugged at the tail of his coat, and a fresh burst of rain blew in with it, soaking his suit. Cramer kept moving, pinning the coat with his arm to protect the evidence bags, though they were waterproof. He was in enough trouble already for screwing up after being warned Ballast and PUSH stood primed for attack with Lady Liberty fixed in their crosshairs. He couldn't afford to botch this up, too.

A bull of a man dressed all in black stepped out from behind the van. He was in his forties, and his most remarkable feature was having a face people would forget in ten seconds or less. Cramer envied him that. Average looks were a hell of an asset to an agent working in the field. The tip of his cigarette glowed red and, supposing smoking would be banned inside the van, Cramer nodded.

"Only lab personnel allowed inside." The man exhaled a stream of smoke that fogged the night air and opened his fist, palm up. A second penny gleamed in a streak of light.

Verified. Their van, their man. Cramer showed the agent the penny he had lifted off the walk. "No problem." He passed the evidence bags, and, as Westford had suggested, he prayed the Band-Aid tested clean.

★ ★ ★

In her salon, Sybil dialed Gabby's number and then glanced down at her freshly bandaged finger, hoping she hadn't made a mistake that would cost her her life.

Gabby answered with a gruff, "What is it, Lisa?"

"It's not Lisa, but if I had the misfortune to be your assistant, and you talked to me in that tone, I'd quit."

"She does. At least once a week. Usually on the days I haven't fired her."

Sybil smiled. Those two would be going at it when they died of old age. "You sound riled." That concerned Sybil. Gabby didn't do riled. She always had been passionate about her work, but she usually kept exasperation private.

"You on a secure line?"

"Yes." Not an uncommon question. Gabby had been a covert operative for years.

"It's this mission, Sybil. It's making me crazy."

"Do you need to pull out?"

"I can't. We have too much invested. It'd take a year to get back to where we are now."

Gabby's "where" was deeply entrenched in a corporate

espionage ring that had hooked into the judicial system and was suspected of selling reduced or suspended sentences to North Korean spies.

"So what are you going to do?" Sybil asked.

"The same thing you do when your work makes you nuts. Suck it up, and press on." She heaved a sigh Sybil felt down to her bones. "But I swear it'll be a cold day in hell before I go deep cover again."

"Of course." Gabby had sworn that same thing on her last five missions.

"I mean it. I'm burned out."

Sybil sat down on a lush sage-silk sofa and stared at a painting of magnolias hanging on the wall. "I know." She did, and she resented that.

"Is Jonathan behaving?"

Here she goes again. The self-appointed matchmaker from hell. "Agent Westford always behaves."

"Too bad." Gabby's deep breath crackled static through the receiver. "You could fix that with a little encouragement. It wouldn't take much."

"I'll pass." Sybil crossed an arm over her chest. "When it comes to men, my judgment leaves a lot to be desired."

"Austin doesn't count."

At least Gabby hadn't called him by her usual pet name. Sybil supposed she should be grateful for that small mercy. "I was married to the man for fifteen years. He counted." She swiped an irritated hand over her forehead. "Is there anything else, or did you just call to bitch about work and butt into my love life?"

"You don't have a love life."

"And I'm happier than I've been in years." She'd loved Austin, had given him everything she'd had to give, including the money to fund Secure Environet, and he had become her Achilles' heel. The *last* thing she needed was another love in her life. "Leave it alone, Gabby. Please."

"All right, but you're letting a winner slip through—"

"I said *please*," Sybil insisted. "If there's nothing else, I'd better get back." With no one running interference, the premiers were apt to kill each other.

"There is one thing," Gabby said, sounding hesitant. "It's the reason I called."

"Yes?"

"Be careful, okay? I woke up this morning with a really bad feeling about your whole peace-seeking mission."

"Have you had word from the commander?" Normally, Commander Conlee routed intelligence updates to Westford. But he had used Gabby when he'd deemed regular channels less secure.

"No, no. Nothing. It's just a gut feeling." Gabby paused a beat, and her voice took on a jagged edge. "Take no risks, Sybil. None."

Too late. Sybil looked down at the Band-Aid circling her finger, and an icy chill crept up her spine. She stiffened, determined not to give into fear, gave Gabby her promise, and then wondered. How was she going to keep Westford from telling Gabby about the Band-Aid incident?

For the first time in her career, Sybil Stone considered offering a man a bribe.

★ ★ ★

One should never underestimate the impact of a bribe.

Alexander Renault had learned that lesson the night he had been dubbed "Patch." It had been his ninth birthday, and to celebrate, his father had stabbed his mother to death. A patch of Alexander's hair had turned albino-white—from the trauma, the doctor had said. But what had traumatized Patch most was his father bribing his way out of ever being arrested, tried, or convicted. The official consensus? His mother had *fallen* onto the knife.

That night Patch had learned to hate: his father, for what he had done; his mother, for dying and leaving him;

his government, for being corrupt. That night he had also sworn to do something about it. And he had done plenty.

Sizing up the rookie agent, Patch surmised that Westford had already done a fair amount of ass-chewing. Cramer looked pale and shaken. At least he'd remembered the penny and its significance: *You're among your own.*

Their SDU secure-system communications had been nearly impossible to breach—once. Amazing what a healthy contract could do to a designer's sense of loyalty. But it made no difference now. Things had gone too far to do anything but play out. Millions would live or die, and their fate rested solely in the hands of Sybil Stone.

From the moment she cut her finger, she must have known it hadn't been an accident. But it was hoped that she would conclude it had been an attack rooted in the peace talks and not look beyond that. If she did, and she convinced Westford of it, yet another challenge for Ballast could be shifted to PUSH and avoided, and neither Lady Liberty nor Westford would be on the defensive for what lay ahead.

Grinding his shoe against the concrete, Patch stomped out his cigarette and then took the evidence bag from Cramer. "You'd better double-time it back to the hotel. Harrison is waiting for you in the bar."

Looking resigned, Cramer made a U-turn and headed back. Patch kept him in sight until distance obscured him, and then he pulled an identical Band-Aid filled evidence bag from his raincoat's inner pocket. He tucked Cramer's bag in its place against his chest, then tapped at the side door of the van.

It slid open about six inches. Patch flashed the penny, passed the substituted bag through the crack, and then walked away. He had seen no one inside the van and no one inside had seen him: a strictly professional transfer.

The van pulled away from the curb and headed down the street, its tires spraying through puddles of water.

Patch walked toward the hotel until the van hung a left onto a side street and vanished into the night.

Making a one-eighty, he hustled to his car. Cramer had made two new critical errors. He'd seen Patch's face during a professional transfer, and he hadn't so much as flinched at the discrepancy between Harrison saying he was going for a walk and Patch telling him Harrison was waiting in the bar. The rookie would have reason to regret both errors—though not because of Westford.

Relief at having avoided that personal encounter swam through Patch's stomach. Inside Ballast, Westford was known as the Widow-maker, and his reputation was nearly as daunting as Gregor Faust's. Overtly Westford had been with the Secret Service on general assignments for thirteen years. Covertly he had been assigned to the nonexistent SDU for the better part of a decade. Only the best agents made it to SDU, and Westford headed the list. He was sharp, judiciously ruthless, and didn't perform missions, he attacked them, using whatever means necessary to reach his objective. In a one-on-one conflict, he and Faust would be a close match, but Westford had a conscience and loyalties and that made him more predictable.

Faust wasn't troubled with either. That gave him the upper hand.

Patch opened his car door and its hinges squeaked. When he settled inside, he lifted his digital phone. His calls were as secure as money and technology could make them, every transmission scrambled. He double-checked his rearview mirror—nothing moving—and waited for the high-pitch beep to signal that the scrambler was operational. Finally hearing it, he spoke into the receiver. "ET calling home."

"Go ahead, ET."

"Interception complete."

Chapter Two

Wednesday, August 7 ★ Local Time: 22:17:12

"It's delivered. I'm in the bar with Cramer."

Positioned outside the conference room, Jonathan heard Harrison's transmission and considered it probable that Harrison was sharing a club soda with Cramer, reminding him why the rookie was lucky to still be breathing. Jonathan rubbed at his temple, stepped away from his Peris and Abdan counterparts, and deliberately lowered his voice. "Screw Cramer. Watch that waiter."

"He's in the bar, sir."

Jonathan was glad to hear it. Until the lab results came in, he wanted an agent Super-Glued to the man. He moved back into position outside the conference room door.

Peris's agent slid him a knowing glance Jonathan ignored. The rapport between them had been amicable enough, though they hadn't conversed beyond acknowledging nods. If the situation deteriorated and the need arose, killing the man would come easier if he hadn't shown Jonathan pictures of his kids.

Taking the at-ease stance, he laced his hands behind his back and scanned the long hallway from sculptured ceiling to marbled floor. At the north end, two women wearing hotel-staff badges stood near a potted ficus talking. Their laughter echoed down the empty corridor, grating at his ears. They had no idea how lucky they were to be unaware of what was going on in the conference room.

Peris and Abdan were at this summit solely because they trusted Liberty. She was here solely because President Lance trusted her. None of them trusted easily, but Liberty had earned it, as well as the respect of the international community. "Say what you mean, and mean what you say" was more than her political slogan, it was her way of life. Everyone, including key reporters—with the exception of that bastard Sam Sayelle from the *Washington Herald*—recognized her as the real thing and made sure everyone knew it. At least they had before her divorce.

Feeling a stab of guilt because he might have played a part in that divorce, Jonathan shifted his feet and his thoughts and dared to hope that she could make this summit work.

Judging by the occasional elevated voices inside and the moods of the leaders when they surfaced, the talks had been passionate and progressive, but he'd been through this too many times to not know negotiations could turn on a dime and end either way.

Something rustled. Cellophane. Glancing left, Jonathan watched the Abdan agent pop a peppermint into his mouth. Fifteen minutes passed. Then thirty.

At midnight, Liberty's personal assistant, Grace Hall, appeared at the mouth of the corridor and walked toward Jonathan. She wasn't smiling.

Grace was a twenty-year veteran, and regardless of what was going on, she always smiled in the presence of outsiders. Seeing her grim-faced now set Jonathan's teeth on edge and his nerves on alert.

She tapped at the bridge of her nose. Light from the chandelier overhead reflected on her glasses; a fingerprint smudged her left lens. "The president needs to speak with Vice President Stone, Jonathan."

Now? The president had been fully briefed during the dinner break, less than three hours ago. Had the lab reported her test results directly to him?

"He's holding." Grace's tension crackled between them. She thrust out a single finger and again tapped the nose bridge on her glasses.

A Code One. Urgent. His heart rate kicked up another notch. In all his years with the agency, he had gotten four Code Ones. All of them had been notifications of disasters. If this disaster informed them Liberty had been infected, he would kill Cramer with his bare hands. "Just a moment."

Jonathan turned, knocked on the ornately carved wooden door, and then opened it. "Excuse me, Madam Vice President." He waited for her to look at him. When she did, he added, "The call you expected at dinner has come through." He swept a single finger across the tip of his nose and sniffed, signaling the Code One.

"Ah, finally. Thank you." Liberty scooted back her chair and smiled at the men seated at the table. "Sorry for the interruption. This will only take a minute."

Smoothing the edge of her navy suit jacket, she swept by Jonathan, stirring the subtle scent of her perfume, then entered a private office abutting the conference room where she'd take the secure-line call. He waited outside the door, cautiously relieved. She wasn't exhibiting any negative symptoms.

Grace joined him, and their gazes met. Two decades of experience couldn't hide the anxiety in her eyes.

Minutes later Liberty emerged, her skirt swishing

against her calves, her pumps clicking on the marble floor. Far more rigid and formal than before she had taken the call, she dropped her voice so only they could hear her orders. "We're going home immediately. Notify the plane"— she shifted her gaze from Jonathan to Grace—"and have my things packed. I'll meet you at the concierge's desk in ten minutes."

"Are you all right?" He looked deliberately down at her bandaged finger.

She nodded. "Different matter, Agent Westford," she said, then walked back into the conference room.

Jonathan shut the door. The woman never lost her composure, but she was rattled now. Why would the president interrupt talks on a mission he had ranked as top priority?

Fortunately, it wasn't a contamination confirmation. Unfortunately, only the president and Liberty knew what it was and, rattled or not, they weren't talking. Jonathan flattened his lips. *Definitely a major disaster.*

Ten minutes later he stood beside Liberty as she addressed the young woman working as concierge. "I understand you have a case for me."

"Yes, ma'am." She reached down then lifted a new black briefcase to the desktop. A silver bracelet cuff dangled from its handle.

Liberty reached for it at the same moment Jonathan saw the device. "No!"

She blocked him. "It's okay. I know it's wired."

"No, ma'am." He shifted his body, positioning himself between her and the case. "It's not okay."

Liberty looked him right in the eye and spoke softly. "Mission necessity. Presidential orders."

He couldn't let her do this. Her safety was his responsibility. "Put it on me instead." He swore responsibility was the reason he had insisted, but he knew it was more. She was more. If anything happened to her . . .

The look in her eyes softened. "We both know I can't do that."

"You wouldn't even if you could." They both knew that, too. Her devotion was but one of the things he admired and resented about her.

She didn't respond to his challenge, just held his gaze and waited.

Jonathan grimaced and stepped aside. She shackled the cuff to her left wrist. When the lock clicked into place, his stomach knotted and a bitter taste filled his mouth. Couriered matter was seldom cuffed to anyone anymore. Liberty was well known and easily recognized, but the cuff and device made her an even more exposed target.

The desk clerk stammered, clearly unnerved. "W— will there be anything else, Vice President Stone?"

"Just one thing. I want you to deliver a glass of warm milk and two—no, three—chocolate-chip cookies to each of the leaders with a note from me every night for the rest of their stay here."

"Yes, ma'am." The woman looked as skeptical about the request as Jonathan felt. "What should the note say?"

"The children are counting on you."

Tension tightened in Jonathan's chest, and he rubbed at his neck. Her approach might be simple, but the emotional response it evoked was damned complex. And it would carry the weight of other nations, including the people of Peris and Abdan. The premiers wouldn't dare leave before reaching an agreement.

"Is the limo ready?" Liberty headed for the lobby, moving at a brisk clip.

"Yes, ma'am." He fell into step beside her. "But we're not clear to leave yet. It'll be a few more hours."

"Impossible," Liberty said in a firm tone. "We don't have a few hours."

"We're not leaving until the lab report's back."

"I'm overriding that order, Agent Westford."

"No, ma'am, you're not," he said, seeing her jaw tighten. "Before you get hostile, let me explain. Running the panels on your blood takes time."

"I just told you, we don't have any spare time."

"We can't afford to get out over the Atlantic and then find out you need immediate medical attention. I have ultimate authority on matters of your welfare, ma'am, and I say we're staying put until we get an all clear from the lab."

Liberty looked torn. "I wasn't exaggerating, Agent Westford. We're under an extremely important, time-sensitive deadline."

"Obviously, ma'am." Code Ones always had been both. "But dead women can't meet deadlines. Not even important, time-sensitive ones."

"All right, we'll wait," she said as if she had a choice in the matter. "But only until dawn. Then, either way, our plane takes off."

"Agreed." Jonathan felt safe in complying. The test results would be in before then.

"We'll wait for the results on the plane."

"Yes, ma'am." He notified Home Base, the staff, and then Captain Ken Dean, who was already on the plane, thanks to a call from Grace.

Soon they were in the limo and Liberty sat staring at the briefcase. More than a little regret burned in the depths of her eyes. Jonathan could tell that whatever had created the Code One crisis disappointed and frightened her—as much if not more than the potential for contamination from her knife wound. Instinct warned him that her fear wasn't rooted in her carrying a wired case. It ran deeper. How deep, he didn't know, since she did not utter another word on the twenty-minute ride to the airport.

When she crossed the threshold and entered the plane,

her confidence returned. Near the galley, she snagged an orange off the food cart and pulled Jonathan aside.

"No notice, diversionary route three." She looked up at him. "Get Grace, Rich, and Charles off this flight—and anyone else we do not have to have with us to get home." She scanned the group of twenty already boarded. "No press or nonessential staff. Skeleton crew only." She looked back at Jonathan. "Get them off fast and get the staff and press separated." Worry clouded her eyes, again turning her irises midnight blue. "Try to delay their return to the States until Monday."

Monday? But it was only Wednesday. "Staff and press?"

She nodded. "If at all possible. We have less than seventy-two hours, and we're going to need every minute, 'Hail Mary,' and scrap of luck we can scrounge up to make it."

"I'll have to bring in the CIA," he reminded her, an accompanying chill slithering up his back. Liberty wasn't prone to exaggeration, and only once, during a crisis in the Middle East that had threatened to rip open barely healed wounds, had he heard her resort to a verbal Hail Mary pass. "The press will scream bloody murder."

"I look forward to hearing it."

That baffled him. "Ma'am?"

"They'll be alive to scream."

Definitely a disaster crisis. One with long arms and a lot of potential, considering she wanted everyone kept out of the country. He glanced through the cabin. That so many had boarded the plane on such short notice didn't surprise him. The press and staff knew Liberty's sudden departure signaled a major development, and no one wanted to miss being at ground zero. "Yes, ma'am." He passed the order to clear the plane to Harrison and Cramer, set up the departure delays through Commander Conlee at Home Base, and then turned his thoughts to the flight.

Liberty ordering no notice wasn't uncommon. She routinely required three sets of flight plans and often chose one at the last minute that she didn't want filed through regular channels. But her choosing route three probably worried Intel, who monitored SDU details twenty-four seven, as much as it baffled Jonathan. Since the president's call, Liberty's every move had been swift and efficient; the woman clearly wanted to hurry. So why divert to Miami, then go north to D.C.? The captain had vetoed route one due to a line of severe thunderstorms, but route two was still open and definitely faster. If in a hurry, why add unnecessary hours of flight time? "Request for verification, ma'am," Jonathan said. "Diversionary route three?"

"Route three verified."

Static crackled in his earpiece radio—weather challenging communications. As chief, he could override the order, as he had the one on their departure. From Liberty's tense expression, she feared he would. Should he override or relay?

Jonathan silently debated. During Liberty's two years in office, he had learned what made her tick and what ticked her off. He'd seen the tiny blonde go toe-to-toe with other powerhouses and hang tough until her opponents crumbled. She won and lost graciously. He had also witnessed secret moments of uncertainty in her. Moments when she agonized over complex decisions that affected people's lives. Moments like this one. But not once had Jonathan seen anything that had caused him to regret giving her his loyalty or admiration or—though only he, Commander Conlee, and President Lance knew it—his heart. "Diversionary route three, Captain." He transmitted the relay. "Proceed to the taxiway, secure the perimeter, and await further instructions."

"Roger. Orders are confirmed and verified."

Hearing the radioed response, Jonathan looked at Liberty. "Captain Dean has been notified, ma'am."

"Thank you." Looking relieved, she took two steps toward her seat, paused, and then glanced back over her shoulder at him. Her gaze drifted down his black suit to his shoes and a thin frown settled between her brows. "Agent Westford?"

Her hesitancy put him back on alert. "Yes, ma'am?"

She looked him straight in the eye. "When we take off, you might want to put on your sneakers."

He raised an eyebrow, then nodded. Few outside the agency knew that when he expected trouble he wore black sneakers. The other agents ragged him about it, and his supervisors wrote him up, giving him hell for it. But since the sneakers had been the only negative remark in his performance rating for years, he had gotten away with ignoring their reprimands.

On more than one intense occasion, Liberty had glanced down at his shoes to gauge the situation. His shoes had been their code. But he had left her protection detail eight months ago, right after his emotions had overridden his good sense and he had threatened to kill her sorry-ass ex-husband. Since most of her assignments carried high risks and global consequences, it was far too dangerous for her to have a distracted, lovesick security chief. Elevated to SDU or not, he wouldn't have agreed to take on this mission if the request had come from anyone other than President Lance.

"Specific or general?" Jonathan asked the nature of the threat.

Worry gleamed in her eyes. "I don't know."

Even she hadn't been told.

Jonathan nodded, and she walked on to her seat.

Hours crawled by, tense and expectant, but nothing remarkable happened and no word came from the lab. Jonathan leaned back against the wall and checked on Liberty. She sat midcabin, fidgeting and staring over an open file out the window, toward the terminal. She looked weary and worried. Lady Liberty wasn't just afraid.

She was terrified.

★ ★ ★

"This isn't right." Sitting in Ballast headquarters' underground bunker, Patch squirmed in his desk chair and took a look from the row of monitor screens to his boss, Gregor Faust. It had taken hours to work up the guts to voice his objection. Now, for better or worse, Patch finally said out loud what had been nagging at him for days. "It's like we're coming down on the Madonna."

Faust resisted the urge to sigh only because he understood exactly what Patch meant. "Sybil Stone isn't the Madonna. Hell, she isn't even a mother," Gregor reminded his second-in-command. "And if you think she would blink twice before issuing a kill order on either of us—or on anyone else in Ballast *or* PUSH, for that matter—you had better read her dossier again."

"Reading her dossier is why I would prefer not to hurt her." Patch glanced over at the screen monitoring her plane, parked on the taxiway at the Geneva airport. Half the force was out there, securing the perimeter, and for each officer identified, Patch knew there were three plainclothes cops and CIA agents who hadn't been identified. "She isn't a mother, but she watches out for all kids. She's predictable. You heard the concierge's report about the note she wants delivered with the cookies and milk." Patch couldn't get that out of his mind.

Hell, Patch had executed kill orders on dozens of women in his time, but this one . . . this one bothered him and he hadn't even killed her yet. Worse, he had no idea why the thought of killing her bothered him. Gregor was right. Lady Liberty would issue a kill order on either of them without blinking twice. Yet there was something innocent and pure about her milk and cookies. About her. And Patch flat-ass didn't want to muddy it up.

"PUSH, not you, is going to hurt her. You aren't involved,"

Gregor reminded him, then lowered his voice to feign compassion. "She's not your mother, Patch."

Patch looked over at Gregor. "I know that." He did know it, but he had grown up without a mother; he couldn't even remember what she looked like anymore. Maybe, in his head, he was using Sybil Stone as a substitute. Logically, she was far too young to be his mother—he had a few years on her, in fact—but this annoying attack of conscience had nothing to do with age or logic. It had to do with the woman and who she was inside. She protected kids. She was different from the rest of those corrupt bloodsuckers. "She's predictable," he repeated, "and sincere."

She was. In Gregor's fifty years, he had seen a lot of leaders with admirable qualities, but he had never known a leader with such a deep conviction to her principles and morals that she had to suffer from diver's bends.

According to his mole's deep-background research, Liberty hadn't had an easy life. Most people assumed she had, though, since she had been raised in privilege by an old-money, old-name family in Philadelphia. Her mother had never understood Sybil's need to help others, and her father had always made her feel she had disappointed him. She had been an only child, often more lonely than loved. Gregor supposed that's why she had risked wanting only two things in her life: a career in politics—which she had gotten—and a family to love who loved her—which she had *not* gotten.

His own early years hadn't been so different, though many swore he had been spawned by the devil, and to his way of thinking, Sybil's 50 percent success rate on her life goals made her luckier than most, himself included. "It would be a vast tactical error to underestimate the esteemed lady from Pennsylvania, Patch. Yet we shouldn't give her too much credit. Not until we know firsthand it is warranted."

"I'm not underestimating her, and I'm not questioning your authority or wisdom, but—"

"But," Gregor interrupted, "you don't understand my reasoning about her."

"No, I don't." Patch adjusted the contrast on one of the monitors and then stared back over his shoulder at his boss. "You obviously respect her as an adversary."

For as long as Faust could remember, his survival had depended on keeping his intentions and rationale to himself. He guarded both as voraciously as he guarded his identity, yet if Patch were ever going to command Ballast, he had to understand. "I respect any and all adversaries. Underestimating them is too costly."

"Why are you willing to kill her?"

"For the same reason one kills a rattlesnake poised to strike. Death, the devastation of assets—these penalties are too steep to pay." Gregor pulled a thin brown cigar from a wooden box on his desk, snipped its tip, and lit it. The scent of heated cherry tobacco filled the air. "Liberty is a powerful woman—rare really, because she doesn't demand support. People inexplicably volunteer their support to her."

"She wears power well."

"Unfortunately, too well." Gregor squinted against a spiral of pungent smoke. "She's doing her best to cost me a great deal of money, and she's having significant success." Her peace-making efforts in India and Pakistan had cost him millions in arms sales. He didn't need a repeat performance to recognize the risks she posed with Peris and Abdan. "I cannot permit that."

"You could have just sent her back to D.C. with an empty briefcase."

"An empty case wouldn't have gotten through their scanners or CIA agents, much less been delivered to Liberty. And it would have worked against our backup plan. That plan is critical, Patch. Without it we could lose mission control."

"And Ballast never forfeits mission control." Understanding gleamed in Patch's eyes. "Dr. Austin Stone."

"Exactly." Liberty's ex-husband wasn't reliable or stupid. "He would have known the case was empty before it left Geneva." Gregor rubbed at the tense muscles in his neck. "Dangerous business, considering he has the ways and means to manipulate us. If we put the screws to him overtly, he will go off the deep end and reduce this operation to his own personal mission."

"Screwing everyone who crossed him, including us."

"Screwing everyone he remotely *perceives* has crossed him, including us."

Which is why the briefcase wasn't empty and Gregor had enclosed copied contents, not originals—and why he had intercepted Lady Liberty's blood to get her DNA.

As if a key puzzle piece slotted into place in his mind, Patch blinked hard. "You're afraid Dr. Stone is going to manipulate the mission."

"I prepared for the possibility. But remember, PUSH pulled this attack. Ballast was not involved."

"Right." Patch slid Gregor a knowing glance that grew doubtful. "But she's leaving the peace talks. Peris and Abdan are more likely to kill each other than to continue negotiations without her. You've already won, so why does she have to die?"

"She could live." Gregor spared the monitor a glance, saw Liberty's plane still sitting on the taxiway. "Provided Westford's instincts are as keen as reported."

"But what if they're not?"

"Then she'll die, and PUSH will be blamed." Gregor shrugged his indifference on the matter and flicked his ashes into a crystal tray. "Such is the price for disseminating false information on Westford's abilities."

The fax line rang. Patch slid his chair over to retrieve the incoming pages and took a look. "Lab results are in."

Gregor smiled. The first obstacle Austin Stone had tossed in Gregor's path to gain mission control—obtaining Liberty's DNA—had been cleared with minimal effort, and neither Westford nor his staff had any proof they had been infiltrated. Oh, certainly Liberty and Westford suspected they had, but they lacked hard evidence and they wouldn't find any. Unlike Agent Cramer, Gregor's men were seasoned and professional to the core.

Dr. Austin Stone, however, was another matter. He stood heads above anyone else in the secure-systems design field, but he had a personal agenda in this operation that could be problematic for Gregor. The need for Liberty's DNA surfacing so early in the process indicated that he would be a challenge.

Agitated, Gregor stubbed out his cigar and dropped on to a seat. How had a leader on the world stage, who had been so successful at gauging the mettle of others, ended up married to a man like Austin Stone in the first place?

True, he was a genius, and he had repeatedly demonstrated it by creating impressive, innovative secure-system designs. Extraordinarily marketable, secure-system designs that Gregor had bought, used, and sold throughout the world. But Liberty, not her ex-husband, owned controlling interest in Secure Environet. That, coupled with his envy of her power, had made him a bitter man who warranted observation. And Gregor had observed Stone as closely as he had observed Liberty. Her ex-husband had cursed her power yet seized every opportunity to use it for his own gain. People seldom surprised Gregor, but Austin Stone putting his corporate interests in a blind trust the day she had taken office had stunned him. Why had he agreed to do it? And since he had done it, why had she divorced him?

Liberty never discussed her rationale for the divorce. It was the only subject she consistently refused to address with the press. That agitated Gregor more. He was a strategist.

Understanding players' motivations were vital to his success. Vital to his survival.

Patch cleared his throat. "Should we release the lab results to Westford now?"

"Not yet." Gregor checked his watch and converted the time. It was two in the morning in Geneva. "Wait until four." Everyone would be in place by four—in Geneva, in Washington, and in Florida.

Patch relayed the directive to the lab. "Release the report to the Widow-maker at four."

Gregor strolled over the thick Persian carpet to view the monitors. "Any movement on Cap Marlowe?"

"None. The senator hasn't been briefed on the Code One yet."

President Lance was playing this close. "Keep me posted on him." Gregor moved toward the door, ready to grab a meal before things heated up. Marlowe was going to be interesting to watch. Unlike Lance, who was predictable, Marlowe was a wild card, and wild cards were not welcome mission elements to strategists. Gregor wanted to know what reactions he could expect from the senator. If the rumor mill proved accurate—and it usually was at this level of infiltration—Marlowe had been slated by the Republicans to become President Lance's successor in the next election. Why the party intended to bypass Lady Liberty, Gregor couldn't imagine. But he was one lucky black-market arms dealer because it did—provided Westford's instincts proved to be as honed as reported and she survived the next seventy hours.

How many other men in Gregor's position had the ability to blackmail someone destined to become the most powerful man in the free world? And what exactly would that man do to keep his connections to Gregor secret?

The possibilities made for a good game.

Gregor's game had begun six months earlier, when

President Lance had announced he would keep his campaign promise and not run for a second term, and, two months ago, albeit unknowingly, Marlowe had become a player. No doubt his fear of exposing his past crimes, large and small, had already caused the good senator many sleepless nights. Nights of waiting for the proverbial ax to fall. What would he do when it became clear to him who held that ax that now hung over his head?

Of more immediate concern, what would be Jonathan Westford's next move?

Westford was a pro. Gifted and, particularly when an operation involved Lady Liberty, lethally dangerous. Others might speculate, but Gregor knew of only one emotion strong enough to provoke the depth of Westford's protective instincts toward Liberty—one emotion so intense that a man would forfeit being with her to keep her safe: love. Gregor also knew that no other emotion could make a man less predictable or more treacherous.

If there had been any way to avoid a direct confrontation with Westford, he would have done so. But destiny had issued its decree. Westford might initially blame PUSH for the coming events, but only for a short time. Gregor and Westford would eventually collide on this mission, and the projected outcome of the clash seemed inevitable. Only one of them would survive.

The question was: Which one?

Chapter Three

At precisely 4:00 A.M. the lab phoned. Jonathan took the report in the galley, staring blankly at his distorted reflection in the stainless coffeepot. "You're certain?"

"Positive," the lab tech said. "We ran dual panels to test and verify simultaneously and pulled a hundred-percent cross-check comparison on the results."

"Thank you." Jonathan ended the call and swallowed hard a couple of times, but the damn lump in his throat wouldn't go up or down, and his knees felt as weak as water.

Walking to midcabin, he tuned his earpiece radio to conference call the cockpit and Home Base. On international assignments carrying Level-Five SDU status, Commander Conlee monitored Liberty himself. He would report the results to the president.

Liberty looked down at Jonathan's shoes, saw his sneakers, and dragged in a sharp breath, reacting instinctively even though she had suggested he wear them. A moment lapsed, and then she forced her gaze to lift and meet his. Intense, but steadfast. She knew he had received news. "Are we leaving?"

He blinked hard. The woman had more courage than anyone he had ever met. She was terrified and yet she sounded calm, together. He was anything but. His nose stung, the backs of his eyes burned, and a boulder had homesteaded on his chest. Too emotional to trust himself, he stood near her and spoke into his transmitter. "Captain Dean, you're cleared for takeoff."

"Thank God." Dean expelled a relieved breath that hissed static through the earpiece.

Afraid to allow himself to feel it, Jonathan kept his relief locked inside. He hadn't cried since he was a kid, but he was damn close to it now. He could have lost her. *Lost her*.

She reached over, pressed a staying hand to his forearm. A flash of vulnerability flickered through her eyes. "So, I'm okay?"

"You're fine, ma'am." He nodded and dared to put his hand atop hers on his arm. "Just fine." The relief inside him swelled and filled his chest. He loved and hated it. Loved that he knew she would live and hated the way that knowing affected him. He should *not* be emotionally attached. Not to her.

"Good." Her worry left her eyes, then clouded them again. "We've lost a lot of time."

The Code One disaster was back in priority position in her mind, if it ever had slipped to second place. Jonathan patted her hand. They were down to sixty-eight hours on the phantom seventy-two-hour deadline she'd given him at the hotel, and again he wondered exactly what it meant. "Take a minute to enjoy the good news. It's a long flight."

"But I have a ton of work to do on it." She pulled her hand away and sat back on her seat. "It's our duty to change the world, if we can."

She was still quoting Mr. Tibbs. Jonathan rubbed at the tense muscles knotting his neck. *"To Sir with Love* had a powerful impact on you, didn't it?" After the first time she had mentioned the movie, Jonathan had watched it three times. He remembered the line.

"It did." A near smile curved her lips. "Mr. Tibbs is one of my all-time favorite characters. He had purpose, clear vision, and discipline."

"He also respected human nature. He would pause to celebrate."

"Ah, you're going to lecture me again, aren't you, Agent Westford?" She lifted her glass of cola in mock salute. "Stop and smell the roses."

"And their leaves and stems."

"What about the thorns?" Thoughtful and suddenly pensive, she thumbed the rim of her glass and her playful tone disappeared. "You never mention the thorns."

"Appreciate those, too."

Totally serious now, she looked up into his eyes, seeking something she needed. "Why?"

He debated brushing off the question, but then remembered asking her once why she helped fair-weather colleagues. She'd told him it was the work that mattered, not who did it. If it was good, it was good. Harrison had heard her response and later told Jonathan that was when he had decided Liberty had more class than anyone else he knew and bigger balls than 90 percent of the men on the Hill. Jonathan had drawn that conclusion far earlier in her career. And if she had the courage to ask about the thorns, he had the courage to answer her. "Because thorns are sharp and they prick."

She thought about that, then responded. "Only if you've felt the prick can you truly appreciate the softness of the petal."

Not exactly as he would have put it, but it would do. He nodded.

She tilted her head. "Do you ever wish you could push a button that would keep you on an even emotional keel, and then just stay there?"

He exaggerated a level look down his nose at her. "Every time you take a Band-Aid from a potential terrorist."

Not at all intimidated, she glared at him. "You're as irreverent as you were when we were together, Agent Westford."

They had never been together. They could never be together. Of course, she didn't mean it that way. She was referring to when he headed her guard detail. "Terrible character flaw, ma'am. I'll work on it."

That remark earned him a grunt, then a cautious "Don't."

He cast her a quizzical look.

"Don't work on it. It's honest," she said with a slight shrug. "In this job, I don't get a lot of honest reactions. I like them."

"Gabby always gives you honest reactions."

"And bad advice," she said, looking torn, a little confused, and maybe slightly wistful.

"Not intentionally. She just hasn't pegged how your mind works."

That comment surprised her; her eyes widened and then narrowed with suspicion. "And you know this because..."

"I have pegged it."

"You know how my mind works?" Disbelief etched her voice.

"Yes, I do."

"I'm not sure I like that."

"I know I don't. But there it is." Regret etched his tone. Honest remarks, but he wished they hadn't surfaced. Being near her was hard enough without adding new complications.

"Excuse me," Cramer interrupted. "Priority call from Senator Wade, ma'am."

Their private moment was over. Jonathan stepped away. Evidently Harrison had assigned Cramer to fill in for Grace. Wade was a Democrat; the House minority whip, not that party affiliation mattered to Liberty. The night she had accepted the nomination for vice president at the national convention, she had vowed not to represent Democrats or Republicans or Independents but to represent Americans. On discovering that she hadn't been spewing rhetoric, the party hadn't much liked it, but the voters had, so the members took her vow in stride—at least, publicly.

"Thank you." She lifted the phone and waited for Cramer to move out of earshot. "Hello, Martin. What can I do for you?"

She listened attentively, her head angled, her eyes focused on the briefcase. She asked several pointed questions and then listened again.

Stiffening, she set her glass down. The metal cuff at her wrist scraped against the tabletop. "I see." Her voice remained soft and steady, but she clearly didn't like what she was hearing; her fingers clenched her chair arm and her knuckles raised up like knobs. "I'd be delighted to support your bill, provided you're willing to include one minor addition. Since you're a father and grandfather now yourself, I'm sure you won't find it objectionable."

Here it came, Jonathan thought. Her classic setup. Bait and hook. Praise then shame. Liberty was about to dig in her heels for something that really mattered to her. The signs were all there: the setup, the clenched fingers, the set jaw and fixed stare. Oh yes, he knew how her mind worked.

Falling back into old habits, he settled on 70 percent odds that she would reel in Senator Martin Wade. If she toed her right pump, Jonathan would up the odds to 95 percent. She saved toeing the pump for issues near and dear to her heart, and few failed not to knuckle under to it.

"Child support." She disclosed the concern. "The current recovery program requires that all sums collected through government intervention from deadbeat parents be split fifty-fifty. Half goes to the child. The other half goes to the federal government."

She paused to listen. Wade was no doubt reminding her of the government's considerable costs in recovering delinquent support payments.

Undaunted, she persisted. "Martin, listen. We've got a stable budget with a sizable surplus, a strong economy with minimal risks of inflation, Social Security is secure, and we've finally got a good grip on healthcare. There is no reasonable justification for the most prosperous country in the world to take money from these kids." A skipped beat, then a second volley. "What if you were broke and Sarah's ex had skipped out on support payments for Beth? What if Sarah was struggling to keep a roof over their heads and food in their stomachs? I know your daughter has a great education and a promising career, but what if she didn't? What if that fifty percent going to the government meant Beth and Sarah didn't have grocery money? Your daughter and granddaughter would go hungry today. How would you feel about the current policy then?" A missed moment response, then she added, "But that's how we have to look at it. Most of these kids are borderline poverty and, Martin, they're all *someone's* grandchild."

Jonathan leaned back against the wall and crossed his arms over his chest. *Down and dirty tactic, Liberty*. Senator Wade had one daughter and one granddaughter. Beth had been born just two weeks ago, and Wade was still acting appropriately dotty. Amazing how a six-pound kid could take down a giant. While extremely vocal and strongly opposed to tobacco remaining legal, Wade had been so thrilled about Beth's birth he had passed around enough cigars to fund the tobacco industry's lobbying costs for the next six months.

Liberty again paused for Wade's response, and then it happened. The right pump came off and thumped against the carpet. "I'm a little fuzzy on a rationale that would sub-stantiate that position, Martin. Our courts established these funds as money due to the children—for their main-tenance and support. So it's their money, not the deadbeat parent's. Do we agree on that?" She waited for his response, and then went on. "Okay, fine. So if the money already be-longs to the child—let's say, to Beth—and the government recovers it for her, then isn't the government withholding half of Beth's money from her clearly a crime? We are de-priving her of the use and benefit of her own assets."

The senator said something she didn't like, and Lib-erty's jaw tightened more. "Well, since when does our judi-cial system charge victims a fee for being victims of a crime?" A half beat, and she interrupted. "No, Martin. That *isn't* the way it works now. The way it works now, the kids are victimized by their nonpaying parent and then victim-ized again by their government. Don't you consider that un-acceptable? Don't all of our Beths and Sarahs deserve better from us?"

Jonathan rubbed at his chin. If Martin Wade didn't consider the position unacceptable, Jonathan had the feel-ing the man was going to wish he had. Liberty now had toed off both pumps. Bare feet made the woman feel vulnerable, and when vulnerable, Liberty went razor-sharp, on guard, and straight for the jugular. *Odds? A hundred percent.*

She stiffened and narrowed her eyes, but her tone re-mained unchanged. "I'm sorry to hear that, Martin," she said, her disappointment in him obvious. "If you should change your mind, you know my door is always open." She lifted the orange and squeezed it hard, probably wishing it were Martin Wade's neck. "No, there's no need to send me a copy. I'd like to help you on this—the bill certainly has merit—but without the stipulation for the children, I can't endorse it, or even support it. Actually, I'll be ethically forced to oppose it. Strongly. Do give Sarah and Beth my best."

Jonathan wasn't buying it. Liberty hadn't given up. She had dug in.

Apparently the senator realized it.

A slow smile spread over her face. "That sounds excellent, Martin. Send the bill and its supporting documents to Grace, and we'll take it from there. It's my pleasure to help you whenever I can. And, Martin, thank you. You're doing a good thing for the children. This will literally change their lives."

She said good-bye, thumbed a phone button, and ended the call. "God bless bipartisan politics!"

Though her words had been whispered, her success sparkled in her eyes. Jonathan couldn't resist. "More good news, ma'am?"

Liberty smiled, soft and watery. "A rose petal, Agent Westford."

"Congratulations." He smiled back. When happy, Liberty was a sight to behold. One too potent for a man guarding her to behold. Needing a little distance, he nodded, then walked the plane.

Hours passed, yet Jonathan couldn't shake the feeling that they were swiftly approaching a significant brink. Having the lab results come back clear and verified had taken a load off his mind, but the incident itself gnawed at him. If not to contaminate her, why deliberately cut Liberty with a knife? There had to be a reason, and his not knowing what it was worried him.

About two that afternoon, Captain Dean eased the plane into a northerly heading over the Florida coast and made a descent so smooth it ranked barely noticeable. This was the last leg of the journey, and so far no problems had cropped up. Grateful for that but still wary, Jonathan scanned the plane then looked back at Liberty.

Somewhere over the Atlantic, she finally had dozed

off. An open file folder rested in her lap and she still held a pen in her hand. The pumps, of course, had been put back on her feet. She had a thing about shoes, as if bare feet somehow equated to a bare soul, and she defended her soul's privacy with passion. Yet she bared her soul when it mattered, as she had with Wade for the kids.

Women in general he understood fairly well, about as well as a man could understand women. But Liberty specifically? Even though he knew everything the best intelligence resources on the planet and personal professional observations could provide, in ways she remained a mystery to him.

Seated midcabin and taking their cues from the vice president, Harrison and Cramer appeared at ease now, too. A crew member napped. Cramer sat silently keying information into a laptop. The keys clicked steadily. He was preparing D.C. for their arrival at Andrews Air Force Base. Normally Grace would have handled that duty.

She had given Harrison hell about being ordered off the plane. That was the trouble with consummate professionals. They didn't appreciate being deemed "unessential" even if it spared them their lives. Grace was one woman who knew how to hold a grudge with conviction. Unfortunately, she would have plenty of hell-raising help from the other discontented staffers who had been bumped off the flight. Unlike members of the House who came and went, staffers tended to nest on the Hill until retirement. Being deemed unessential was telling them their lives were unessential. That kind of thing didn't slide like water off a duck's back. It soaked down to the bone.

When staffers returned to the Hill on Monday, Liberty would be doing hard time, soothing ruffled feathers. Staffers were a hard-nosed, jaded bunch and had pretty much seen it all. Few would be touched by knowing that, at the time the order had been issued, Liberty had had a bomb shackled to her wrist. And none would feel their removal had been warranted.

Tuning out the storm-induced static in his earpiece transmitter, Jonathan thought about her eviction order. She hadn't cleared everyone out because of the briefcase bomb. If it blew, it likely would destroy only the contents of the case and maybe her. Lance wouldn't have authorized it otherwise, unless he had no choice; and that was a possibility, considering the Code One. It seemed as if she were expecting a tragedy on this flight. Yet there had been no specific threat—there couldn't have been, or Jonathan would have been notified. Even if the storm had made it impossible for Home Base to contact him via transmitter, they would have done so through Captain Dean. So what had prompted Liberty to issue the skeleton-crew-only order?

Julie, a crackerjack navigator with a thousand-watt smile, took over the duties of the banished flight attendant and delivered a cup of coffee to Harrison.

"Thanks." He took the steaming mug. "Next run, forget the cup and just hook me up to a caffeine IV."

He was tired. They were all tired. During the last five days, there hadn't been much time for sleep.

"The IV will cost you," Julie warned in her thick Texas drawl. "One day when you least expect it."

"Always does."

"Dang right." On her way back to the galley, she stopped at Jonathan's side. "Coffee's fresh. Can I get you a cup?"

"No thanks." It smelled good. Rich and strong, but the last thing he needed was more caffeine. Everyone on the plane seemed relaxed except him. He was wired tight. Damn it, something wasn't right.

He bent down to look out the window and recognized the Florida Everglades, the thickets of woods and marsh and dense brush just to its north, then glanced at his watch and converted to Eastern Standard Time: 4:12 P.M. Right on schedule. To the west, lightning ripped through the sky. The band of thunderstorms that had originally diverted them from route one were now sweeping east and the plane would soon be right in the middle of them. The bad weather had to be screwing up Home Base's satellite observations. How could they continue to monitor and advise without accurate Intel?

His internal radar up, Jonathan walked the plane, looking for something—anything—to explain his discomfort. Nothing seemed amiss, yet each silent step he took reinforced his certainty that something serious was about to happen.

He burned. Down deep, in that secret place no one can define or describe or teach you exists, he burned, and he knew.

Then he smelled it.

Bitter as brine, more pungent than smoke, thick and heavy and consuming. The same sickly smell that had assaulted him right before he had taken the bullet for the former vice president. The same deep, dank stench that always warned him tragedy would soon strike.

The unmistakable smell of death.

Every time he had sensed it—every single time— death had followed.

Alert and wary, searching for anything out of the ordinary, anything the least bit suspicious, he noticed the scent fading and returned to midcabin to check on Liberty.

Still dozing. No longer fitful. Finally the tension had left her oval face. Something inside him went soft. When she relaxed, she looked more like a woman in her twenties than her thirties, pretty in a nonclassical, polished kind of way. A strand of blond hair caressed her cheek. His stomach clutched.

Grimacing, he looked away. He had been right to transfer off her detail. He still wasn't sure what had caused his admiration for her to change to something deeper. He didn't welcome or want it, but the change had happened. When he looked at her, rather than seeing the vice president, his assignment, he saw a leggy blonde with a crooked nose and deep blue eyes that could praise or flay with a flicker, and that had left him no choice. Emotional attachments colored judgment, and this could cost Lady Liberty her life.

Threatening Austin Stone had made Jonathan's lack of objectivity and professional distance glaringly apparent. The bastard had deserved killing, but losing control enough to threaten him made Jonathan dangerous to her. SDU missions were no place to be in when losing your temper. That aside, she had never looked at him and seen a man, only an agent. And she had never, not once, so much as called him by his first name.

The bottom line was that none of those things mattered. He loved her, which was no big deal. He loved most women he respected and admired. The difference was he could see himself falling in love with Liberty, and that situation Jonathan wanted to avoid.

The professional considerations were substantial. Even setting those aside, he understood too well the pain and destruction that could be done in the name of love. Personally, he'd suffered enough and wanted no part of it.

Considering his history and the odds, Jonathan would have to be nuts to buy into any part of the love-and-marriage package. After her experience with Austin Stone, Liberty surely felt the same.

Because that bothered him in a way it shouldn't, Jonathan again walked the plane. Near the galley, the death smell suddenly grew stronger, more potent, filling his nostrils, closing his throat.

So if everything is okay, why the hell are you smelling death, Westford? Why can't you shake it?

Desperate to find out what was wrong, he turned toward the rear of the plane. Harrison slumped against the wall, his eyes closed. The newspaper he had been reading hung limp in his hands, fluttering in the draft of an air-conditioning vent.

Jonathan rubbed at the tension knotting his neck. Harrison was sharp, intuitive, and he hadn't yet picked up on anything. Maybe Liberty's actions, the president's call, and Jonathan's own suspicions on the Band-Aid incident had caused a synapse misfire. Maybe nothing was wrong, and his expectation had triggered the scent. Maybe the sense the flight was doomed was all in his mind.

The plane dipped into a slow, gliding descent, and the captain depressurized the cabin. Jonathan's edgy feeling honed to cutting-edge worry. To depressurize, they had to be cruising at under ten thousand feet. Why had the captain breached high altitude, standard operating procedure? Ken Dean wasn't a rookie. He wouldn't open them up to low-grade, surface-to-air ground-fire threats for no reason.

Cramer perked up, set the laptop aside.

Harrison awakened and tossed the newspaper to the floor.

It isn't just in your mind, Jonathan.

He swallowed hard. The death stench grew heavier, more dense. The danger was real. Close. Inevitable.

Reaching up to the radio transmitter in his ear, he issued a warning to Home Base. "Heads up, Commander."

Shifting the channel, he tuned into the plane's cockpit. Ken Dean's voice piped through. He was engaged in a low-key conversation about Tiger Woods taking the Masters' Tournament lead in a big way.

"Seven under par," he said, sounding completely normal. "Seven. The guy's on a roll."

"Yeah. He's stomping some serious ass on his drives," another man responded. Jonathan didn't recognize the voice. "Cost me fifty bucks yesterday."

"I warned you he was hot, Mark." Julie was talking. The other guy, Mark, would be the relief copilot. "Didn't I tell you not to bet against him?"

"Yeah, yeah, you told me. Christ, woman, you sound like my mother. Stow it, okay?"

"No way. I'll leave being gracious to the veep. When I get a shot to say I told you so, I'm taking it and rubbing it in." The hint of laughter lingered in her voice. "Who's up for coffee?"

"I could use a cup," Ken said. "Toss in some extra cream, would you?"

Extra cream? First the shallow-descent SOP security breach and now *cream?* Fear slammed into Jonathan's gut. They were in serious trouble.

Silent and swift, he moved to Sybil, released the latch on her seat belt, and shook her arm. Harrison and Cramer brushed by, rushing to get on point.

Startled awake, she strained to focus on his face. When she did, she frowned. "What is it, Agent West—"

He silenced her with a steely stare, checked over his shoulder, and half shoved, half pulled her toward the back of the plane, not slowing down until they stood in front of the emergency exit. Harrison was on his feet, gun drawn at the foot of the corridor. Cramer stood six feet in front of Harrison, his gun aimed at the cockpit door.

Liberty's knuckles on the briefcase handle went white. "What the hell are you people doing?"

"Shh." Jonathan glanced past Harrison, past Cramer, to the front of the plane, shoved Liberty's sleeve down her arm, freeing her jacket from her shoulder and then wrapping it around her left arm, above the handcuffed brief-case. She had kept on her emergency chute. *Good. Good.*

Tension coiled through him like the lightning sizzling outside. He bent down and pulled a visual, checking out the window. Patches of heavy clouds but definitely below ten thousand feet. The cabin wasn't pressurized. Oxygen wouldn't be a problem. Rapid decompression shouldn't be too bad.

"Westford!" Liberty struggled to get out of his grip. "I demand an immediate explanation."

Three soft pops sounded at the front of the plane— *gunshots.* Jonathan stared at her but didn't answer; he was too busy trying to think. He'd opted for mobility over the remote risk of a forced evacuation so he wasn't wearing a chute, and there wasn't time to get into one now. Giving her a quick once-over, he estimated their combined weights. Roughly three-twenty. Her chute was certified to three-fifty. Too damn close, but he had to risk it.

Pop! Pop! Pop!

More gunfire. He doubled over and shoved a shoulder to her chest, pinning her to the wall beside the emergency exit. "Grab hold."

She glared at him. "What the hell for?"

"Just do it, Sybil!" he snapped.

Stunned by his using her first name as much as by his tone, she reacted automatically, grasping fistfull of jacket and shirt at his waist. Working around the dangling briefcase, he popped the emergency hatch then tossed it aside.

The drone of the engines elevated to a deafening roar. Wind gushed into the plane, plastering her hair against his face, torturing his eyelids, burning his eyes. Straining to hold her against the wall, he clenched his jaw, held fast and firm to the grips. Pain tightened her mouth and she cocked her head, hiked her shoulder to block the whistle from her ears.

Finally the air stabilized.

She narrowed her gaze and, nose to nose, shouted at him. "I am *not* jumping out of this plane, Westford."

Scuffling midcabin. Surprised cries. Confusion and chaos, and no time to argue. "No, ma'am," he said. "You're not jumping."

Praying they could get coordinated enough in the air to get the chute opened, that it would hold their combined weight and not rip to shreds before they could get down, he latched onto her and nosedived out of the plane.

Chapter Four

On Sam Sayelle's first day of work covering the Hill for the *Washington Herald*, he had reported to Marcus Gilbert, the retiring *Herald* veteran he was replacing, full of dreams and high hopes. The kind of dreams and hopes only a kid fresh out of the Midwest, who had climbed his way up through the ranks to Chicago and finally had gotten a shot at the big-time, dared to dream or hope.

Marcus hadn't bothered with a traditional welcome. Instead, he had issued Sam a warning—and strongly advised him never to forget it. "The Hill is hypnotic and as addictive as crack cocaine," he had said. "Once it gets into your blood, you're its victim for life."

It was hard to believe that had happened five years ago.

Back then Sam hadn't been able to imagine what Marcus meant. He had come to Washington with all the right credentials, the right attitude, and the right nose for hard-hitting news. He also had come with a healthy dose of idealism that had quickly been snuffed out. Marcus, well respected on the Hill by the members, staffers, and his peers in the press, had applauded the speed with which Sam's blinders had come off.

Now he knew exactly what Marcus had meant, and he swore daily he would give his eye teeth and his family jewels to once more be that idealist who believed in the dream of politicians who did the right thing for the right reason rather than to advance their own personal political agendas. But being an idealist was a lot like being a virgin. Once it was gone, it was gone for life. Familiarity indeed does breed contempt, and insider knowledge condemned him to cynicism and to intimacy with resentment.

The truth was, partisan politics reigned in all its glory as common practice on the Hill. Big business, lobbyists, and malleable politicians set policy, making deal on deal that lacked so much as a whiff of moral justification. Reelection was the main goal in town. The Hill was home to corruption and creative spin, and honest men and women who came to it with pure intentions and hearts, believing they could make a difference, learned quickly to wheel and deal and play the game as directed. Those who didn't took it in the shorts. The Hill closed ranks, chewed them up, and spit them out in the next election. For all the public claims of progress, in actuality, the good-old-boy network—which included a respectable number of artfully chosen women these days—was alive and well and thriving in Washington, D.C.

Sam knew all of this firsthand, and he was a survivor. That required him to be a realist and accept it. Yet even after half a decade of being frustrated and stonewalled, deep down, in places he didn't discuss at White House briefings, at social gatherings, or in his articles published by the *Herald*, he still harbored a hope of the idealist he had been when he had first come to the Hill as that fresh-faced kid. And despite his best efforts to kill that hope, he still believed that someone someday would appear on the Hill with pure intentions and the

courage to do the right thing for the right reasons. That someone would prove to the cynic Sam—and to the now-retired
cynic, Marcus Gilbert—that they had been wrong.

So far, it hadn't happened. And on sober days Sam accepted it wasn't likely to ever happen. But every now and
then even the most hardened cynic runs out of steam and
needs the fuel of dreams and that spark of hope to keep
trudging along. Especially when lying politicians like Sybil
Stone were enjoying success upon success by talking the
talk but never walking the walk.

She was the worst kind of hypocrite, publicly embracing kids' issues while lying to the American people, telling
them she was unable to have children of her own due to a
medical challenge. Since when did a husband's vasectomy—
an elective surgery—make a woman barren and medically
challenged? Only by the grace of Senator Cap Marlowe
had word of Austin Stone's vasectomy remained out of the
news.

Sam had managed to attack Sybil Stone publicly with
monotonous regularity on various issues—and he would
continue to attack her publicly as long as he remained on
the Hill and had access to the inside information Cap Marlowe provided him. According to Marcus Gilbert, Cap was
one of the good guys, who skillfully and strategically got
things done without stomping on any toes to do them. Cap
didn't use the public's emotions against the press. Sybil
Stone did. For that, Sam admired him and hated her.

He rocked back in his chair in the White House Press
Room. The place was crowded with reporters and corre-
spondents, all watching the clock hoping for something
newsworthy after such a long delay. The briefing had been
set for three, but it was now nearly five, and the press secretary, as well as the rest of the White House staff, was still
avoiding the room as if it had been quarantined. Something
serious was up. Sam sensed it in the staff's frenzied activity,
in the edgy expectation that hung like a pending execution

over the press corps. Even Barber, who typically would sell his soul to give Sam a scoop—provided it showcased the White House and Lance in a good light or made the opposition look bad—was in squelch mode.

The cell phone vibrated against his hip. Sam yanked it from its case. "Sayelle."

"We have assassinated your vice president. Other organizations claim credit, but they only seek recognition by your media. PUSH holds the honor of actually killing her."

Sam's throat went thick. "So why are you calling me?"

"Because you hate her."

A click and the line went dead.

White House Chief of Staff Richard Barber clipped the corner and nearly smacked into Sam.

"Hey, I just got a report that PUSH assassinated Vice President Stone."

"Not now, Sam." Barber spared him a rattled glance but didn't even break his stride before disappearing behind closed doors.

Barber was a genuine piece of work: a cynic's dream, a real American's nightmare. He stayed on alert, always vying for position and looking for ways to cement his future and advance his career. For some reason, he wasn't just making himself scarce right now, he was deliberately avoiding Sam. But there was one person Barber wouldn't dare try to avoid—not if he still had serious aspirations of being appointed to a key position in the future leader's administration: Senator Cap Marlowe.

Sam left the press room and headed to the senator's office. Odds were that he had already left for the day, though it depended on what had everyone in such an uproar. *Could Sybil Stone really be dead?*

As chairman of the Armed Services Committee, the senator kept a permanent finger on the Hill's pulse. Cap had been on the Hill as long as Sam had been alive. Fortunately, he had been a Marcus Gilbert fan, and Marcus had introduced Sam, suggesting he keep an eye on the senator. The introduction had given Sam a key contact.

Why Marcus had bothered, Sam had no idea. Maybe it was out of loyalty to the *Herald*, or maybe he'd just awakened feeling gregarious that morning. Hell, Sam didn't know. Gilbert was a crotchety old man who firmly believed women shouldn't hold public office. Until the day he retired, he refused to meet, interview, or write one word about any of them. None wasted her breath to complain. Marcus had a lot of friends on the Hill and a very long memory. It was highly unlikely he ever in his life had done anything out of the kindness of his heart. After thirty years on the Hill, he no longer had a heart.

Whatever the reason, Sam wasn't one to kick a gift horse in the mouth. He had nurtured the relationship since the beginning, and it had been beneficial to him and the *Herald*, and to Cap Marlowe.

Cap looked out for Sam, opened doors for him, and, on more than one occasion, leaked information he wanted the public to know—information the people had the right to know. The two men used each other for their mutual benefit and never had pretended otherwise. On their opinions of Sybil Stone, they were kindred spirits. They both felt Cap should have been offered the job as vice president and that he had been bypassed for the politically correct choice of the times: a woman. Yet Lance had said he would serve only one term, so unless Cap screwed up big time between now and then, he would snag the Republican Party's nomination for President. If and when that happened, Sam felt confident the first order of business on Cap Marlowe's agenda would be to send Sybil Stone packing back to her native Pennsylvania for good—as a private citizen. Provided, of course, the PUSH call had been a hoax and she was still alive.

Sam rounded the corner and entered Cap's office. Jean, his personal assistant, was seated at her desk, keying in something at her computer terminal.

Forty, bright-eyed, conservative, and razor-sharp, she glanced up and smiled. "Hi, Sam."

"Good to see you, Jean." She looked too cool and collected to know the veep was dead. The call had to have been bogus. He nodded toward the senator's private office. "Is he still in?"

"For the moment." She lifted the phone receiver and cradled it between her ear and hunched shoulder. The overhead light glinted on her red hair, twinkled on her gold earring. "Sam's here, Senator." She listened and then cradled the receiver. "Go on back. He's due at a fundraiser, but he can give you ten minutes."

"I won't make him late." Sam breezed past Jean's desk and opened the door to Cap's inner sanctum. The smells of old money, lemon oil, and rubbing alcohol surrounded him. Cap sat at his desk with his sleeve rolled up and his arm braced elbow down on the desktop. Holding a syringe in position, he injected himself. Sam swallowed a sharp breath. "What are you doing?"

Pushing sixty, white-haired, and still gifted with distinguished looks the camera loved, Cap laughed, crinkling the skin around his eyes. "Not what you're thinking, that's for sure. It's insulin."

Sam shoved his hands in his pockets to cover his surprise. "You're a diabetic?"

"Twenty-two years now."

How could Sam not have known that? And what did he say now? He couldn't deny that he'd thought Cap had been shooting up. "I'm—I'm sorry. I didn't know." Didn't most diabetics inject themselves in the abdomen or thigh?

"No problem." Cap blew off the apology. "I don't advertise it. People are ignorant and biased as hell. They perceive anything like this as a weakness." He rolled down his sleeve and slid the syringe into a red biohazard sharps waste box. "What can I do for you?"

"You can tell me what's going on at the White House.

Staffers are burning high octane, but none is talking. We're still waiting for the three o'clock briefing."

"It's been rescheduled for nine in the morning. Word came out about five minutes ago, with profound apologies for the delay."

"What's going on over there, Cap?" Should he mention the PUSH call? Probably not, until he had some kind of credible verification. If she were dead, Cap would know it.

"I haven't been briefed on anything. If I am, you'll be the first to know."

"Thanks." Still stinging and embarrassed about his re-action to seeing the senator inject himself, Sam made small talk for a few minutes and then left the office.

Cap had lied to him, of course. He knew exactly what was going on, he just hadn't wanted to share it at that moment. If running true to form, that translated to his having uncovered something interesting about Sybil Stone, though not her death. Cap wouldn't be able to contain himself on that. He guarded "deniability" with a vengeance that bordered on religion. He never relayed negative information on the veep or anyone else directly to Sam. He filtered it through Jean. So if Jean stopped Sam on his way out, then he could be sure that whatever was happening had Sybil Stone front and center in it.

She was on the phone in the outer office. Sam smiled and waved, then moved on. He was about to step into the el-evator when she called out from her office door. "Sam, wait."

Ah, a message from Cap. Pleased with himself, Sam walked back to her. "Did you need something?"

Jean dropped her voice. "There's an unconfirmed ru-mor going around you might want to check out." Fear burned in her eyes. "They're saying Ballast has jeopardized Sybil Stone's peace-seeking mission in Geneva."

Oh, man. The PUSH rumor wouldn't be far behind. If Sam sat on it, which he had to do until he'd checked it out, the terrorists would just phone other reporters until one ran with the story. PUSH was bad, but Ballast was a hundred times worse. Gregor Faust and his hired thugs just kept stacking up crises. No UN member could target him for assassination without committing an agreement violation, and, frankly, he greased too many political palms and financed too many campaigns for anyone legitimate to take him out. But why hadn't some zealot spared the world and killed the twisted bastard?

Jean lowered her voice to a whisper. "If what I'm hearing is right, Ballast is doing a lot more than making vicious threats this time, Sam. They think Faust himself has contacted the White House and blamed PUSH. He's predicted casualties."

That phone call was significant. No one knew exactly what Faust looked or sounded like, though several months ago PUSH had released an artist's sketch of a man purported to be he.

"How many casualties?" No wonder they had been frenzied, canceled the briefing, and Barber had been in squelch mode. Sam didn't like the sound of any of this. Faust had no scruples. He was loyal only to money and power; capable of doing anything to anyone, anywhere.

"Some say a handful," Jean hedged.

The White House wouldn't be in an uproar over a few casualties. Not even if the few were highly placed officials or one of them was Sybil Stone. There would be upset, but not like this. "What do others say?"

She blinked hard and whispered. "Millions."

The word ricocheted through his brain and echoed. His blood drained from his face, the heat seeped out of him, and he swallowed hard. "Damn, Jean. I need to talk to Cap."

"But his fundraiser—"

"Jean." Sam clasped her arm. "PUSH called me. They said they killed her."

"Killed whom?"

"Sybil Stone."

Chapter Five

Thursday, August 8 ★ First-Strike Launch: 55:05:21

She couldn't be dead; every bone in her body ached.

Unsure whether to curse or rejoice, Sybil lay sprawled atop Agent Westford in a patch of rain-soaked muddy ground. He lay motionless, his eyes closed, his breathing labored.

"Westford?"

Startled conscious, he gasped in a deep breath that rocked her and raised a hand that brushed against her breast. She instinctively slapped at it. "Have you lost your mind?"

"Probably. Jumping out of a plane without a parachute doesn't seem sane to me." Mud splotched his rugged face; clods clung in his hair. He flexed his fingers, then his wrists, testing them for sprains or breaks. "But I don't think I've lost anything else."

Assessing her own condition, Sybil saw a flash and flinched. A lightning bolt streaked a jagged path across the twilight sky. Windblown rain beat through the leafy trees and thunder rolled, echoing vibrations across the earth that jarred her to the marrow of her bones. *The briefcase.*

Panic ripped through her chest and she looked down. Mud-splashed and wet but intact, and still attached to her arm. *Thank heaven.*

Jonathan grunted, claiming her attention. "Are you hurt, Agent Westford?" When they had hit the ground, he had cushioned her with his body and taken the brunt of the impact. He'd known how to position himself and had instructed her in falling with minimal injury. She had expected their every bone would crunch or snap. Instead, she was sore and scraped and bruised but nothing felt broken.

He shielded his eyes with a cupped hand at his brow. "No, I'm fine." He reached down between them, trying to get a hand into his pocket. "You okay?"

"I think so." Between the aches from the jerk of the chute opening and the bruises from their rough landing, she couldn't be sure. Not yet. "Exactly why did you do that?"

He slid her a blank look.

She tried again. "Why did you jump out of the plane without a parachute?"

He stared at her a long second, as if her not knowing seemed incomprehensible to him, then scanned her face. "You're shaking. Are you really all right?"

"Yes," she insisted, his breath warming her face. "I'm furious with you, actually, but fine." She tried to slide off of him, but what looked like miles of twisted parachute cords held their bodies together. She couldn't move, and that infuriated her more. "Would you *please* get me out of this damn thing?"

She spoke through clenched teeth and struggled to untangle herself, but the cords wouldn't give. Westford's entire body felt hard, and, even in this situation, she had been celibate too long for a hard body to feel anything but good.

Strange, but until Gabby had started her matchmaker-from-hell routine, Sybil had never thought of him as a flesh-and-blood man, only as an agent. That felt comfortable to her. Safe. She had trusted the agent and confided in him, but then he had requested reassignment and left her. She had no idea why, and she wasn't brave enough to ask, but his leaving proved once again that when it came to men, she had lousy judgment. So this seeing-him-as-a-man business didn't feel comfortable or safe, and she resolutely avoided feeling anything she didn't want to feel. It fractured her control.

"I was trying to get you out," Westford said. "You ordered me to stop."

Angry at herself for panicking at physical contact with him, she swallowed a sharp retort. She *had* ordered him to stop. His touch had been unintentional and, like it or not, she had mixed feelings about that. Disconcerting, mixed feelings.

The mid-August heat seeped through the downpour, creating a horrendous steam bath. Drawing breath was like trying to breathe through a hot, wet washcloth. She began to sweat and clenched her jaw. "Where are we?"

"Florida." On his back in shallow water, he wriggled beneath her, creating eddies and rocking her against him, breasts to chest and thigh to thigh. Finding the sensation more pleasant than wise, she felt her face warm.

Naturally, he noticed her blush. "I'm just trying to get a knife out of my pocket, okay?"

She managed a crisp nod and hoped to heaven he hurried. It was hard for a woman to hold on to her dignity while wallowing all over a man on the wet, marshy ground. Determined to beat the odds, she lifted her chin. "I'm going to be patient, Agent Westford. I'm not going to lose control." Even as she voiced the denial her control slipped into jeopardy. "But when you get me out of this monstrosity"—she paused to glance down at the bird's nest of parachute lines, then glared back at him—"you'd better be able to give me a damn good reason for dragging me out of that airplane."

The rain pattered an unnerving staccato beat on the bent grass, spattered in ankle-deep pockets of brackish water and on the fallen leaves scattered over the swamp's earthen floor. Heavy drops tapped against the spiky-leafed palmettos and ran in rivulets down Westford's face. He sawed at the corded lines with his knife. "I have an excellent reason right now, ma'am."

She watched him hack at another nylon cord. "Well, I'd love to hear it."

The last of the cords binding her fell slack. She rolled off of him, stood up, and then primly smoothed her skirt. Her bare feet sank into the rank muck and it squished between her toes. She'd lost her shoes. Her stomach fluttered. There was a distinct, unwelcome vulnerability in standing before a man rain-drenched and barefoot in mud.

"Yes, ma'am." He sat up and stretched to cut his legs free. "The pilot asked for cream in his coffee."

"What?" She couldn't believe her ears; she had to have missed something. Maybe Westford had hit his head. She swiped at the raindrops gathering on her lashes and double-checked. Methodically slicing himself free of the ropes, he didn't look dazed or woozy, though he certainly sounded both. "The pilot wanted cream?"

"Yes, ma'am."

"I'm seeing myself passing along that rationale to the president, and the cream isn't rising to the top, Westford. You're going to have to give me more than that to take to him."

"President Lance wouldn't ask me why." Westford spared her a glance. "He'd trust my judgment."

Chastised, she conceded that David did have an enormous amount of respect for Westford, and he probably wouldn't ask. She had trusted him once. Should she again?

Wondering spawned an internal debate that seemed hell-bent on not being resolved.

Okay, Sybil, this is it. You've got one life and a choice. Define what kind of person you want to be. One who dares to trust, or one who doesn't. Courage or cowardice. It's that simple.

Simple? There was nothing simple about it. It was an obvious life-defining moment.

In the past, some life-defining moments had crept into her life through little, seemingly inconsequential incidents. Others had blown in with all the subtlety of a hurricane. This life-defining moment appeared to be a category-five hurricane spawning killer tornadoes.

Logically, everyone had times where they wondered if their judgment was up to snuff and it would make the grade or survive the cut. No one escaped self-doubt. But when a woman was the sitting Vice President of the United States and she was confronted with a situation that threatened to escalate to a global crisis, it was a bitch of a time to have to fight the battle.

Westford spared her from making a decision. He shoved the cut cords into his pockets, gathered the parachute, and then buried it in short order under a clump of sour-smelling bushes. "Let's get away from here." He clasped her arm.

"Oh, no." Sybil twisted and stepped back, out of his reach. "The last time you grabbed me like that, you took an eight-thousand-foot swan dive out of a plane and dragged me with you. I'll pass on your next adventure."

Tense and wary, he scanned the marsh and the thicket of woods to the east, then inspected the swirling gray clouds. "We've got to move, ma'am."

She had seen that look on him before. It drew down the corners of his mouth, narrowed his eyes to slits, and had never been the harbinger of good news. "Could you please call me Sybil while we're out here? At the moment, your 'ma'ams' are driving me a little crazy."

"Certainly. We've got to move, Sybil."

"I'm not going anywhere until you explain yourself."
She couldn't do it. She couldn't risk trusting him again.

Coward.

Damn right.

"I told you, the pilot asked for cream."

A clap of thunder rumbled through the swamp. At least it sounded more distant than the last one. "So, because he wanted cream in his coffee, you shoved me out of a plane and jumped out yourself—without a parachute?" She crossed her arms over her chest. "Tell me, Agent Westford. What would you have done if he had wanted sugar, too?"

Instead of answering, he caught her by the arm and started walking.

"I can walk on my own, thank you." His hand on her arm was gentle, but his grim expression left no doubt; the man was furious, and that irritated Sybil. She was a little less than pleased herself. After all, he had walked out on her, not she on him, and now he demanded her unconditional trust? Not bloody likely.

He let go and backed off a step. "You do know the plane was under siege."

Under siege? "Did you hit your head when we landed? There was no siege on that plane."

Ignoring her remark, he asked a question of his own. "Why did you bump everyone off the flight?"

"Intuition." The one thing her critics used against her at every opportunity—real or implied.

"You dumped Grace and the others on women's intuition?"

Here it came. The putdown for considering her intuition as valuable and accurate as any man's instincts. She turned and looked him in the eye, daring him to laugh at her. "Yes, I did."

"You issued a skeleton-crew-only order just because you couldn't shake a feeling? Is that how it went?"

Torn between admiring his acumen and thinking he had lost his mind, she shrugged. "That's how it went."

The rain swept down and rolled in sheets across the swamp's earthen floor. Goose bumps prickled on her arms. Annoyed, she pulled at her sopping-wet jacket, circling her arm.

He removed his suit coat, draped it over her shoulders, and turned up the collar to protect her neck. It too was wet, but it would take the bite out of the stinging rain. "I understand."

Hearing experience in his tone, she looked up into his eyes and believed he did. Because that was a known entity and far more comfortable than the shock of a siege, she focused on it. "I'll be eating dirt for a month," she predicted. "Knowing Grace, probably two."

"Maybe not." He unlaced his sneakers, removed his socks, and then put them on her feet. "That's the best I can do about the shoes." He put his sneakers back on, moved away, and then began walking.

Disconcerted by his hands having been on her feet, she blinked hard, mumbled a stilted "Thank you," and then tromped behind him, her feet making sucking sounds in the mud.

Red maples and tall, pungent cypress trees fought titi and sweetbays for space, so dense that the waning light squeaking through the clouds barely penetrated. Long, dark shadows closed around them, and a distant owl let out an ominous hoot. Sybil shuddered. She knew how to deal with concrete and political jungles, but she was totally out of her element in the swamp. Westford deserved to be canned for putting her in this position. And he would be. But she wasn't stupid. She'd fire him *after* they got out of this stormy, sweltering hellhole and back to Washington.

A solid hour of tromping through ankle-deep water passed before he uttered a word. "Stop."

She halted automatically and looked around, but saw only rain-beaten foliage, felt nothing but cold raindrops pelting against her skin and wind-whipped sawgrass slapping against her thighs. Westford cupped a hand to his ear. Clearly, Commander Conlee was transmitting a message from Home Base. And just as clearly, Westford wasn't liking what he was hearing. That had her frayed nerves threatening to snap.

Finally he looked at her. "An unknown terrorist phoned the White House and said you wouldn't be returning from Geneva. You're . . . dead."

"But they know I'm not, right?"

Jonathan shrugged. "The president is stepping on shoulders for status updates on us. Home Base knows there was trouble on the plane."

"Do they know we're trying to get back?"

"Not yet."

"Well, shouldn't we tell them?"

"My transmitter is malfunctioning. I'm not sure if it got damaged in the fall, or if the storm is messing up communications."

"What about the emergency frequency? Can't you transmit on it?"

"That's down, too. I'll check the device for damage at dawn. In the meantime, our communications are in receive-only mode.

"Terrific."

"Bitch later. Right now focus on moving. We need distance between us and our drop point." He resumed walking. "As much distance as we can manage."

He looked a little ashen and a lot worried, but he didn't look unsure of himself or his judgment. Since he was one up on her there, she followed him.

Another hour passed before a cramp in her side throbbed, the pain so severe it threatened to knock her to her knees. She grabbed the hem of his coat, wadded it, and then dabbed at the sweat and rain pouring down her face. Her eyes burned like fire and she swore her feet had died a good hour ago but were too sore and mud-caked to notice.

The twinges deepened and her leg muscles cramped. Pain stabbed through her side. She pressed a hand against the stitch, but the pressure didn't help. Finally it grew too intense to ignore. "Westford, I have to stop a second." Twenty minutes on a treadmill every morning just didn't prepare a woman for this kind of hike.

"We can't stop." He didn't slow down or even look back.

"I have to," she insisted. "I—I can't go any more." True, but admitting it still left a bitter taste on her tongue.

He turned abruptly, reached down, and scooped her up. "Rest a little."

Too stunned to speak or move, she just stared at him.

"You might want to put your arms around my neck for balance, ma'am."

Holding his gaze, she reached over his shoulder. The briefcase collided with his back. A thump vibrated through his chest into her side and he let out a grunt.

"Oh, hell, I'm sorry, Westford." Being so close to him, being held by a man for the first time in nearly two years, had her battling an attack of nerves and hormone overload. Both knocked her off-balance.

Get a grip, Sybil, and stop being stupid. Gabby is wrong. You're only of interest to him because of your job. As a woman, you're of no interest to anyone.

She listened and cringed at that cold reality.

"No problem, ma'am. I get hazardous-duty pay."

A stab of humor from the habitually serious and detached Westford? She chuckled. "That's for threats *against* me, not *from* me."

His lips didn't twitch much less curl, but a pleased twinkle lit in his eye. "Threat's a threat, ma'am."

"Sybil."

He nodded.

She had to steer the topic back to this siege business. Had he avoided bringing it up because he had gathered his wits and realized it hadn't happened? Or because he'd been giving her time to accept that it had? "I know David wouldn't ask, but I'm not him, and I'm not passing judgment on your character, I'm curious. What's significant about the cream in the captain's coffee?"

"I've known Ken Dean for fifteen years." Westford slid her a sobering glance. "He drinks his coffee black."

Determined to hold his gaze, she blinked hard three times. "I guess he could have been signaling trouble. But don't you think we should have stronger confirmation than a man asking for cream in his coffee before bailing out of a plane? I mean, maybe he was taking a stroll on the wild side, just breaking his routine. Or maybe he had an upset stomach or something."

A frown wrinkled Westford's brow. "You don't remember it, do you?"

She didn't want to presume to know what he meant. "Remember what?"

"The explosion."

The fine hairs on her neck stood on end. "What explosion?"

"Sybil." He softened his voice slightly. "The plane *was* under siege. It exploded."

"No." She couldn't believe it. She hadn't seen anything explode. How could she have missed a damn explosion? "Are you sure, Westford?"

"Oh, yeah." He nodded. "I'm sure."

"What exploded?" Had to have been minor. "Something in the galley?"

"The whole plane."

She shook against him, stunned and confused and unable to believe it. "But—but that's impossible." If an entire plane had exploded out from under her, she *would know it*.

Yet Westford seemed so sure. She stared at him and detected no trace of doubt; he clearly believed this. There had to be a reasonable, logical, plausible explanation. Maybe he had suffered a head injury. He had taken the brunt of the fall. Maybe he'd gotten a concussion and now the poor man was suffering delusions. Yes. Yes, that made sense.

Relief and guilt swam through her shaky stomach. He obviously had been injured and needed medical attention, and here she was, acting like an invalid he had to carry. She signaled him to put her down.

When her feet touched the dirt, she buried her fingertips in his wet, mud-caked hair. Coarse and thick and velvety black, its rain-slick strands glistened and clung to her fingertips.

"What are you doing?" His voice went thick, his gaze warm but wary.

Gathering evidence. She dragged her fingertips over his skull, ignoring her reaction to that warmth. "Checking for bumps or cuts."

"There aren't any." He clasped her wrists, moved her hand off his head. "I told you, I'm fine."

Reason. She had to use reason and simple logic to convince him he was injured and mistaken. "If the plane exploded, Search and Rescue would be swarming all over the place."

"It happened." He stopped dead in his tracks. "And they're not coming, Sybil. No one is coming. Not yet."

God help her. Darkness was creeping up on them, the rain was slowing them down when the need to rush was more urgent than ever, and here she stood, lost in the jungle with a man suffering from delusions. A scream of frustration threatened to escape her throat. She managed to swallow it down and summoned cold resolve. She *would* get back to D.C. before the deadline. Come hell, high water, or both, she *had* to make it back in time. So many would . . . die.

The mud smeared on her cheek itched. She brushed at it. "Why aren't they coming?"

"President Lance won't authorize it." He searched her face as if testing her, gauging her reaction. "He won't risk leading terrorists to us."

The panic within her swelled to the size of a boulder. "Terrorists?"

Jonathan let out a heavy sigh. "I can't see anyone of a friendly persuasion blowing up your plane. Can you?"

She didn't suppose so, but good grief. Maybe he was fine and *she* was delusional. "I—I guess not," she stammered. She had heard a loud pop and felt a jerk, but she had attributed that to the storm and the chute opening. Could it have been the explosion?

Wait. Wait...An image of Cramer and Harrison flashed through her mind, standing in the plane between her and the cockpit with their guns drawn. Gunshots. She'd definitely heard gunshots. Sucking in a sharp breath, she looked at Westford. "What about the others?"

He lowered his gaze, focused on the ground. "They're gone, Sybil."

"No." Shock pumped through her, robbed her of breath. "No, I would have known."

Pain flashed through his eyes. "We lost them all."

Denying the truth to the depths of her soul, she silently screamed her outrage. Cramer and Harrison, Captain Dean, Mark, and Julie—*oh...Oh, God.*

The back of her nose burned, tears stung her eyes. She couldn't cry. Not here, not now, not ever in front of anyone else. She'd fought tooth and nail not to be considered weak because of her gender. Yet the pain in Jonathan's eyes was real. As real as the pain carving a gaping hole in her chest. "I—I didn't know. How could I not know?" She trapped her weeping in her throat, clenched her teeth, and swallowed hard to keep it inside. "When?" Her throat muscles clamped, ached. "When did it explode?"

"We were already out. I was trying to position myself so the chute could open without killing us both."

He had crawled up her legs, had screamed orders at her to pull the chute cord, and she had tried, but the briefcase had made it impossible for her to reach. Fortunately, he had managed to get his hands on the ripcord. Stunned at having been dragged out of the plane, terrified by the lightning and thunder, and reeling at the reality of freefalling back to earth, she supposed the planet could have blown up and it might not have registered with her.

Dear God. Seven. Seven dead. Images of their faces ran through her mind. Regret and anger battled inside her. She should have done more. Taken a different flight. Something. But she hadn't, and now she had to live with their blood on her hands for the rest of her life. She'd never again be clean. Not after Austin, and never after this. "It's my fault."

"It's not."

"It is. I knew something was going to happen. I knew, Westford."

"You had a hunch." He gave her a steady look. "You did all you could."

Absolution? True or not, it surprised her. It warmed her, too, and she needed warmth. Inside, she felt ice cold. Westford had always treated her with respect and compassion. Even during the divorce when nearly everyone's favorite activity was ripping her to shreds. But seven lives just ...snuffed out. Fingers of pain squeezed her heart. "I should have done something different. Something more. I should have—"

"Sybil, shh." Jonathan cupped her chin in his hands. "Listen to me. Listen." He stroked her jaw with his thumb. "You did everything you could. Probably a lot more than you should have done based only on a hunch."

Blinking hard, she took his words in and drew them down deep. "Maybe." With or without trust, what Jonathan thought mattered; it always had. Raw and wounded, she met his gaze, let him see her agony. "Oh, God, I hope you're right."

"I am." He scanned the immediate vicinity for the third

time, then circled her shoulders with a steadying arm. "Come on now. We have to keep moving."

Taking solace in the comfort of his arm, she walked on.

Sometime later he stepped away and shielded his ear. "Conlee." He confirmed an incoming transmission. "They've verified the explosion. Search and Rescue and the Safety Board have convened. They're ready to dispatch, but Conlee has them on a weather hold. Severe thunderstorms."

Considering she and Westford were standing in the middle of that storm, relaying that information seemed redundant. "What does Intel anticipate they'll find?"

"Wreckage strewn three to five miles." His expression became grimmer. "A satellite isn't due to pass for another seven minutes, but with the cloud cover, they're doubtful they'll get much."

Sybil's stomach sank. "They don't know we bailed out."

"No confirmation either way, but before we left the plane, I gave the commander a heads-up, so I'm sure he considers it possible, and Intel recorded gunfire on board before the explosion."

"What about the ELT?" The emergency locator transmitter was in the tail section of the plane. In crashes, the tail typically remained intact, but even if it hadn't, odds rated high the ELT had survived the explosion. "Aren't they picking up its signal?"

He gave her a negative nod. "The weather—"

Or the bomb. "Damn it. No one knows we're alive out here, or that there could be survivors on the plane."

Jonathan rubbed at his neck, his expression a cross between dread and pity. "They know you culled the flight to skeleton crew only and delayed the return of staff and press until Monday. The CIA facilitated the order through Conlee." His eyes glossed over. "He also knows there are no other survivors, Sybil. All aboard are presumed dead."

Including them. "Is that the White House's official position?"

"It will be soon."

Great. Fabulous. Austin would love this. Her best hope was to get back to Washington and resolve the crisis before he heard that she was dead. "I see."

"The news will panic the public, but the alternative is unacceptable. If later they're informed that you're alive, then they'll rejoice."

"But what if I'm not?"

Something akin to anger flashed in his eyes. "You will be."

"But what if I'm not? What if I don't get back with the case?"

"Then the White House told the public the truth."

"This doesn't feel right." She fisted her hand and rubbed at her knuckles. "Is this one of Barber or Winston's screwy ideas?"

"President Lance's senior advisor and press secretary were not involved in making the decision, ma'am. Commander Conlee made the call. By publicly announcing your death, there's a slim chance the terrorists won't pursue you."

"But the White House has never notified the press of a death without it first being verified."

"Exactly." Westford nodded. "Conlee expects we have seven dead. He doesn't want there to be nine."

Seven dead. What could she have done differently? The security breach at top-secret Facility A-267 calling her home had demanded her actions. Already key advisors had determined that no one employed outside of the government would have all the security clearances necessary to gain access to every facet involved in this Code One crisis, which meant someone *inside* the system, occupying a high-level position, had initiated the A-267 security breach.

Sybil ran the mental gauntlet, and, at its end, her conclusions remained the same. She couldn't have changed a thing.

Westford walked in a small circle and stared into the woods. It was the third time she had noticed him doing that. "What do you keep looking for, Westford?"

"The two terrorists who integrated as crew members."

Infiltrators. Gregor Faust was notorious for infiltrating. "Who?"

"Mark was one of them." He named the relief copilot. "I didn't get a firm fix on the second one."

"But they were on the plane." He claimed there'd been no other survivors.

"They chuted out right behind us."

She darted her gaze, straining to see through the shadows. "You mean they're terrorists and they're out here, too—with us?"

"Why do you think I've been pushing you so hard to keep moving?"

Her heart banged against her ribs, throbbed at her temples. With everything else going on, they also had to contend with stalking terrorists?

Get out of here, Sybil. Now. The briefcase!

Listening to her instincts, she took off walking, pulling Westford with her. "Is this north?" She glanced back at him. The damn rain persisted, blocking out the deepening twilight haze. Without the sun, she didn't have a hint. "It seems like it should be north."

"More or less." He spun her ninety degrees left. "Maybe we'd make better time if you followed me."

No complaints from her. She was a survivalist in her world, but her world didn't exist out here. Here there was marsh and mud and only God knew what kind of wildlife. As she recalled from a piece of wetland preservation legislation a few years ago, alligators, wild boar, black bears, and snakes. Lots of poisonous snakes. Her skin crawled. She rubbed at the gooseflesh peppering her arm and chided herself because, as ridiculous as it was, she felt tempted to add dragons and the bogeyman to the swamp's resident list.

"It'll be all right," she said out loud. Whether to reassure herself or Westford, she didn't know. But they both could use the lift. "Home Base will activate my tracker and—"

"They won't do that, either." He pulled back a path-encroaching limb, waited for her to pass, and then let it loose. Rain gathered on its leaves slung in a stinging spray. "The terrorists could follow the signal as easily as Search and Rescue could."

He was right, of course. Who knew how far national security had been breached? David had a country to protect; he couldn't risk losing everything.

"My guess is they'll monitor the emergency channel and continue to transmit updates until the search team is on the ground."

"Why will they stop transmitting then?"

"If we're dead, why would they continue to transmit? They might as well phone the terrorists and tell them we're still alive."

"So we don't dare let Search and Rescue know we're okay, either?" God, they had to avoid their allies, too?

"No one. Not yet. But we have an ace. The president will flash-activate my tracker."

"You have a tracker?" Sybil was surprised. It wasn't SOP for Secret Service details. But did standard operating procedures apply? Westford had been assigned to the elite Special Detail Unit for years. Few people, including the operatives on general Secret Service assignments, knew the operational procedures for SDU.

"The president considered it prudent. We were going into a situation that could explode into war at any moment, which is why only he, the surgeon who implanted it, and Commander Conlee know I have a tracker."

Sybil digested that. "So Conlee will know you're alive and are trying to get back but he won't know my status."

"He and the president will assume that if I'm alive, then you are, too."

"Why would they make that assumption?"

"Because they know I'll protect you or die trying."

Something good warmed inside her. Wishing it hadn't,

and certain she couldn't trust it, she shunned it and stepped past a hole filled with water. "These terrorists had to infiltrate our government at a high level."

Westford agreed. "The question isn't if, but where. FBI, CIA, White House staff, Cap Marlowe's pack? Could be anywhere." He slapped at a bug on his arm. "Until we identify the enemy—in or out of our own troops—we're on our own."

The bottom fell out of her stomach. "Against Faust?"

"Or PUSH. I'm certain it's one of the two of them."

"Gregor Faust did this," she insisted, again trusting her intuition. "It fits his profile. High-level infiltration, a security breach, the Code One—but most of all, because the waiter who cut me with the knife spoke with no dialect. His English was *too* perfect. Only Faust pays that kind of attention to details."

"So you're convinced the Band-Aid incident was an attack?"

"I never doubted it," she admitted. "Faust wanted my blood. The question is: Why?"

"I wish I knew."

"We will," she insisted. "But right now we've got a more immediate problem." They were on their own. She glanced pointedly down at the briefcase and bitter panic ripped through her. "We can't *walk* all the way back to Washington, Westford. There isn't time."

"We won't. Just to the first town."

"I'm telling you, we can't. We have to get back as soon as humanly possible."

"We don't have a lot of choices." He lifted a hand. "Do you see anything closely resembling Hertz or Rent-a-Wreck in the immediate vicinity?"

Surrounded by swamp and creek and too many fragrant trees, she slipped into despair. "Oh, God." She sent him a desperate look. "We've got to hurry."

"Why?" He stopped moving.

"Think Code One calls, Westford."

"I have. Code Ones can be handled in D.C. by a number of people. Your summons home wasn't due to the Code One."

"This time it was."

He stared at her, letting her know in no uncertain terms that he felt she was holding out on him and, in this situation, he considered withholding unacceptable.

She grabbed his arm, urging him to go on, but he refused to budge. It really wasn't fair to keep him in the dark, considering the consequences. Knowing them sure as hell motivated her to keep moving, though her feet felt as if they had been through a meat grinder. "We've got to hurry because of this." She lifted the briefcase.

"I figured out that much on my own. What's in it?"

For a brief moment, she hesitated. She owed this man who had bailed out of a plane without a parachute to save her life, this man who faced annihilation along with the rest of the world. But she couldn't disclose specifics unless it became absolutely imperative to accomplishing the mission. "Just help me get home before Saturday night, Agent Westford."

"I'll do all I can." Understanding flickered in his eyes. "At least Austin won't learn about your death on the news."

"What?"

"The president is going to call him."

"Oh, hell." She walked into a spiderweb spun between two trees. Swiping at her face, she muttered. "This is not good, Westford."

He didn't ask why, but she read the question in his eyes.

"I still own fifty-two percent of Secure Environet. If I die, my stock automatically goes to Austin." Weary in spite of the gallons of adrenaline shoving through her veins, she sighed. "He really wants that stock." He wanted it, and she couldn't risk giving it to him. Not after what he'd already done. "In less than twenty-four hours, he'll drain my assets."

"President Lance won't let that happen. He'll handle Austin."

As executor of her estate, David did know about the stock struggle, and he would protect her assets as best he could. But would his best be better than Austin's? That was the question. Austin was a clever bastard—clever, cunning, and ruthless—and he would do anything to anyone to get what he wanted. Knowing David was genuinely mourning her and public focus was slivered, Austin would use every means at his disposal to bleed her dry. *Every* means.

Better than anyone else, he knew how much she loved America and the people in it. He knew how much she had sacrificed for the privilege of serving them. Just as he knew her drop in the polls proved that the Americans she loved were willing to support a man in public office who was deceiving them and his wife but were unwilling to tolerate a woman in public office who had the integrity and character to divorce her deceitful husband.

Oh, yes, Austin would exploit this opportunity. He would raid Sybil's assets, dispose of them, and hide the funds in some offshore account where no legal authority could touch them. Then he and Cap Marlowe and their reporter buddy, Sam Sayelle, would discreetly celebrate their victory.

Austin would take everything, and by the time she could act, it would be too late to do a thing to stop him. Knowing it raised the most chilling question of all.

Had Gregor Faust planned this financial devastation, too?

Chapter Six

Gregor made his way through the remote desert compound's series of well-lit tunnels that led to his command center.

Over the years, he had established three such centers, each a mirror image of the others, each twenty-two feet belowground with four-foot-thick, steel-reinforced walls, each located in a different host country he paid well to be friendly to him and to everyone in Ballast.

In his business, a man needed multiple retreats. When Interpol and the CIA got too close, going underground quickly proved to be as essential to survival as extensive armed protection and top-notch security. When a U.S. Special Detail Unit got involved, the stakes got even higher. These SDU details operated in small, stealth groups and with one goal: Accomplish the mission by any means necessary. Only a handful of Americans knew they existed. If caught, detail members were officially deemed

rogue mercenaries who happened to be Americans. Westford had been SDU for a decade. Unfortunately, President
Lance had assigned him to guard Lady Liberty, which
made him legitimate with the Secret Service and made it
imperative for Gregor to take every security precaution
possible. Host countries tended to be greedy when Ballast
waited to arrange for a safe haven after one was needed.

Gregor had been a heavyweight in the arms dealing
business for over a decade, and he had seen to it that neither he nor his organization was left vulnerable. Security
inside the compound was tight; armed guards were plentiful, motivated, and heavily armed with the best weaponry
and technology Austin Stone could design. By making the
centers identical, even his men had no idea which of the
three compounds they were occupying. Just two people in
his entire organization knew their specific, current location
and host country: the pilot who had flown his blindfolded
men to the facility and Gregor himself. Only in the case of
his death was his second-in-command, Patch, to be told.
As a rule, Gregor was rarely challenged by his men. He attributed their allegiance mostly to his reputation for exe-
cuting offenders swiftly and decisively. Yet he preferred
minimizing risks whenever eliminating them proved impossible.

In the command center, Patch sat alone at a long desk,
facing the dozen monitors receiving real-time visual data
from key locations around the world.

Gregor grabbed a yellow stress ball from his desk.
"Where are the men?"

"Resting while they can."

"Good." Squeezing the ball, he moved to Patch's side
and glanced at the monitors, halting his gaze on an old man
in a black rumpled coat, standing in front of the Vietnam
Wall in Washington, D.C. Gregor recognized him from re-
connaissance reports as Lady Liberty's contact. Unfortunately, the man remained unidentified and the nature of

their contact had not yet been determined. Her consistency in meeting the old man, however, intrigued Gregor enough that he had ordered a Ballast contact on the Hill to monitor the activity. That contact had discovered someone else already monitoring the events at the Wall: a junior reporter named Sniffer, who supposedly shared news of the encounters between the old man and Sybil Stone with his coworker and mentor, Sam Sayelle.

"Any updates from the field?" Gregor asked Patch.

"Not yet." Patch sipped a steaming cup of coffee. He hadn't slept much in the last two days, and his bleary eyes showed it. "They're on schedule for another forty minutes. The U.S. Search and Rescue team hasn't been dispatched."

That caught Gregor's full attention. "Why not?" Typically, Search and Rescue were airborne within minutes of notification of any Class-A mishap, and this one involved their vice president. By now they should be on-scene.

"I'm not sure." Patch dragged a hand through his hair. "Thunderstorms maybe—they are severe in the area—but I doubt that's all of it."

Thunderstorms could slow the team down, but they wouldn't stop it or a Safety Board from dispatching and investigating. Lance had to have ordered the delay. Gregor scanned the monitor positioned in the northern Everglades. Twilight was settling over the swamp and the storm raged. What Lance needed was a little incentive to get things moving. "Notify the local press."

"Eyewitness accounts of the plane exploding have been reported. Local news and police are moving in now."

"Good. With an advance jump, they'll contaminate the area before Search and Rescue arrives. That'll give our men additional cover." Considering the terrain—swamp, marsh, and wetlands—it would be impossible for S&R to secure more than a small perimeter. Definitely to Gregor's advantage. "Get me an update out of Washington. Let's see if Sayelle has gone public with the PUSH claim yet."

Patch keyed in a status-report request. Their Ballast-member contact had been entrenched on the Hill for over a decade and had proven extremely resourceful. Within moments Gregor watched a response appear on the computer screen. "Nothing announced. Three o'clock briefing canceled without explanation at five P.M. local. Rescheduled for nine A.M. PUSH and Ballast rumors surfacing unofficially. Ballast unsubstantiated, instinct only. PUSH responsibility claim not yet cycling."

Seeing nothing more of interest, Gregor turned away.

"Sayelle's nose *is* working," Patch said. "He's already checked in with Cap Marlowe. He'll run with the PUSH claim, and it'll have legs until after Lady Liberty's funeral."

Once it surfaced, the PUSH claim would top the news for a couple days. As long as it diverted attention from Ballast until midnight Saturday, neither Ballast nor the mission was in jeopardy.

"Give Sayelle fifteen more minutes, then call him back and threaten to take it to the *Post*," Gregor said, then asked, "Does Marlowe know what's going on?"

"Not officially, but we've cranked up the rumor mill."

Cranked up, and likely running in high gear. "What about Lance?"

"No significant action yet," Patch said. "We expected him to move quickly—he usually does." Worry deepened the creases in Patch's face, nose to mouth. "Lance dragging his heels isn't in the plan, Gregor. At least, not in my rendition of it."

But it had been in Gregor's rendition. "He's waiting for verification of Lady Liberty's death. Perhaps Westford's reputed abilities are true and he saved her." Whether she had survived was of no consequence to Faust. He had made secondary arrangements for what he needed done. If she's dead, she's dead.

"If she's not dead, Dr. Stone could get out of hand."

"Can he?" Gregor opened a file and flipped through

the pages of status reports from Ballast members around the globe. "If she survived, Austin Stone will be as disappointed as President Lance will be overjoyed. No more than that."

Gregor and Ballast would remain unaffected, provided Austin refrained from going rogue. Of course, he could do it. But surely even he would restrain himself from starting World War III. "Keep an eye on Lance and let me know when he makes his move."

"Will do."

"In the interim, activate the countdown board. Eastern standard time." Gregor glanced at his watch and then mentally converted to the First Strike Launch. It was just after 7:00 P.M. in the Florida Everglades and in Washington, D.C. "Fifty-four hours, twelve seconds." Then President Lance would unleash Armageddon.

"Saturday?" Patch asked.

"Saturday," Gregor verified. "Midnight."

Clearly receiving a radio transmission via headset, Patch lifted a fingertip, signaling Gregor to wait. "It's Alpha Team. About Lady Liberty's plane." He listened and then passed on the message. "A civilian witness just reported seeing a man piggyback down on a woman's chute. No confirmation it was Westford and Liberty, or if they survived impact."

It had to be Westford and Liberty. Only he would jump out of a plane without a parachute. "Did our men make it out?"

"Out, yes. But no reports from them since then." Patch paused to receive more information. "Bravo Team is in D.C. Moving in on Dean's family now."

If Captain Dean had miraculously survived, then Gregor wanted assurance he would continue to cooperate. The cooperation hadn't been in Patch's plan, either. But it had been in Gregor's, and he was growing impatient. His adrenaline was pumping and he was ready to move. "Warn Alpha to be diligent," he said, referring to the Ballast operatives on the ground in the Florida swamp. "Angry, Westford is bad. Provoked, he's deadly."

"And any time Sybil Stone is involved, Westford is provoked."

"Absolutely." Patch might have missed a few points in the plan, but he had nailed Agent Jonathan Westford's behavior. Patch rubbed a hand through his hair. "It's likely they're both dead. Home Base hasn't activated her tracker."

"That could mean anything." Gregor squeezed the stress ball flat. His second-in-command still had a lot to learn before he would be ready to take the number-one place in Ballast. "They could know she's dead, or they could be afraid to give us a fix on her location." Gregor thought a moment. "There's only one certainty."

"What's that, sir?"

"If there was a way to keep her alive, Westford found it."

The possibility that Westford was alive clearly curdled Patch's blood. He flipped down his headset's lip mike and transmitted. "ET Three. ET Three. Do you copy?" He paused but heard no response from Alpha. Just in case the contact was in a position where responding would comprise him, Patch relayed his message. "Widow-maker and Liberty evacuated. Survival possible. Proceed with extreme caution. Widow-maker is armed and dangerous. Do not approach without backup. Repeat. Do not approach without backup."

Patch immediately shifted attention. "Sir, we're intercepting a call between President Lance and Dr. Stone. You might want to listen in."

Gregor seated the plug in his ear, heard President Lance's voice. "Are you on a secure line?" he asked Austin.

"Your people are still requiring one."

"There's been an accident. Sybil was returning from Geneva and her plane went down."

"She's dead?"

Gregor frowned. No regret, no sadness, not even a curse—and none of Stone's usual fly-off-the-handle behavior. Lance *had* to notice it.

"The plane exploded," Lance said, his tone withdrawn, flat and unemotional. "We have to assume she's dead, but we've just begun our investigation into the cause and the status of the passengers and crew. At this point, a terrorist attack is no more probable than a mechanical malfunction."

Lance paused, but Stone said nothing. Finally Lance went on. "Let me be blunt, Austin. I'm informing you that she's presumed dead and I'm warning you not to make any slick moves on her assets."

Ah, Gregor thought, *the real reason for the call: Sybil's stock.*

"With all due respect, our personal assets are none of your business."

"Actually, they are. I'm Sybil's official next of kin, and I hold all of the legal authority that comes with that. So of course I know her Environet stock reverts to you on her death."

"We made that agreement when I founded the company."

"You made that agreement as a condition of the divorce, and *she* financed the founding of Secure Environet. I'm aware of everything, Austin, and I'm watching every move you make. False steps won't be tolerated. Be clear on that."

Gregor squeezed the yellow stress ball, finding nothing new in that declaration. On learning of her husband's deceit, Sybil had informed the president, met with her attorney, and instructed him to initiate divorce proceedings. Austin Stone had been under surveillance ever since. She also had promised Lance that she would keep her own conduct above reproach—to protect his public position on professional integrity. She'd kept that promise and had lived like a nun in the year since the divorce to protect Lance and his office. It had been foolish of Austin to attempt to deceive Lance now.

"We'll keep you informed. Don't make any long-term mistakes. Just walk the line," Lance told Stone. "Have I made myself clear?"

Apparently that was as far as Lance was willing to go to warn Stone that Sybil could be alive. Gregor rubbed his temple. "Interesting."

"Of course you're clear."

"Good. Inform those you must now. We're going to press with this. Lastly, I'll remind you not to discuss our investigation. Any mention of it will be construed as a security breach, and you will be prosecuted."

"I will be killed."

Gregor stiffened, waited, but Lance didn't deny it. The silence between them stretched. Patch glanced over to his boss, lifted a questioning brow.

Without another word, Lance hung up the phone. Gregor pulled the plug from his ear.

Patch swung around in his seat. "Dr. Stone screwed up."

He had. No one was that damn cold. In the entire conversation, he hadn't expressed one word of hope, hadn't asked once about the chances that she might be alive and just injured or taken hostage, or grasped at one straw. He hadn't asked what Lance's people were doing. In fact, he hadn't asked *any* of the questions people normally asked. Not where the plane had exploded, when it had happened—nothing.

"Yes," Gregor told Patch, fingering a letter opener. Shards of light glinted on its blade. "He screwed up."

"Twice." Patch grunted his disgust. "Lance is bound to come to the same conclusion. What kind of man lies to one who knows the truth and doesn't ask questions about an accident?"

"One who already knows the answers."

Patch's eyes gleamed. "Or one whose heart is full of hate."

Seeing where Patch was going with this, Gregor felt some of the tension melt from his neck. Was it realistic? Logical? "How would Stone react if he knew that only Sybil could save his life—and the lives of millions of others?"

"He damn sure wouldn't be calm or detached. He'd be affected."

"Yes." Gregor smiled. "Yes, he would."

Chapter Seven

"They know we're alive, Sybil." Westford joined her under a thick canopy of leaves that hung low enough to give her some shelter from the rain, then passed her what looked like a piece of bark. "Eat."

"Seriously?" She took it. It felt like bark, too, rough against her fingertips.

"Seriously." He sat down beside her, his back to the tree trunk. "It doesn't taste like much but it's better than watching you try to swallow bugs."

She did her best not to pull a sour face. "I meant, you're serious that Home Base knows we're alive."

"Yes, but they're not publicly retracting your death. Not yet, anyway."

She doubted David had retracted it privately to many, either. Shoes reversed, she wouldn't. Though somewhat relieved, the burden of being responsible for seven deaths still weighed heavily on her shoulders. "Any update on the security-breach infiltration?"

"Not yet. The engineers are going over the entire system with a fine-tooth comb, but they have to project the impact of every possible move before making any. They need time."

Time. The number-one item on everyone's list. Sybil understood the need for caution, but she also understood that someone at A-267 had committed treason, and, by God, she wanted to know who. Needing to think, she propped an elbow against a flat rock and closed her eyes.

David and Conlee would remember Westford's record. He had gotten them both through some hairy times, and he had taken a bullet for the veep—the previous veep. Lucky for her, that wound hadn't impaired his ability to perform his duties. He had been given the choice of retiring or staying with the agency, and he had stayed. If he hadn't, she would be dead now.

Humbling thought, and, yes, David would remember all of that about Westford . . . and more. "You know most of the other agents think you have some kind of psychic power."

"Ridiculous, isn't it?"

"Is it?" She'd often wondered the same thing herself.

"There's nothing psychic about it," Westford admitted. "Just honed instincts and experience."

And acquired knowledge. According to Gabby, he had developed strong skills in nearly every field imaginable. "Did your last commander really send you to survival school to make you less arrogant?" Sybil couldn't imagine Westford acting arrogant. The man never boasted, but he never pretended ineptitude either. She loved that about him.

"He did." Westford half grinned. "I ended up restructuring the course, which didn't make him a happy man."

Sybil smiled. "You didn't."

"I had to, Sybil." He straightened. "It didn't address

some significant challenges operatives routinely encounter in the field."

"The hell it didn't," Sybil said. "I went through that course, Westford."

"Three times before you passed it, as I recall." Westford looked down his nose at her. "*After* I restructured it."

She nibbled at the bark, annoyed because she liked him. Few had the brass to contradict her these days, and it appealed to her more than it should. "So it's true then," she said, studying him. "You *are* arrogant."

"When arrogance can save some operative's life, you're damn right I am."

He didn't have an arrogant bone in his body. But he thought he might. Substance over show. She liked that, too, and resented liking it as much as everything else she liked about him.

Having lousy judgment about men, and being reminded of it often, wasn't a pleasing thing to a woman. But seeing the way his playful tone transformed his face was pleasing. Westford was always attractive, but when playful, he looked downright gorgeous—and irresistible to tease. "Is it also true your hunches are impressively accurate? They say you can smell danger. Does it really have a scent?"

"Yes, it does. It's bitter." He propped his arm on his knee, obviously uncomfortable that the discussion centered on him. "But it's not an uncommon skill for covert operatives, Sybil."

"It seems unique to me." He seemed unique. Genuine. She munched down on a bite of bark. God, she positively hated liking that.

"It's not. But it comes in handy."

"I expect it does." When he shifted again, water dropped through the canopy and sprinkled them. Sensing he'd had about enough teasing and prying, she changed the subject. "So the White House has gone public with the position that all persons on board the flight are presumed dead."

Westford stiffened, silently rebelling. "Yes."

"Do you think that's our wisest course of action?" Revulsion surged up acid from deep down in Sybil's stomach.

"It gives us our best shot of getting out of this swamp alive."

"Only if the mosquitoes don't carry us off." At least she had been spared her worst fear—snakes. "What's our weather status?"

"You don't want to know."

She stared and waited.

"Remnants of a tropical system are parked over our heads," he said. Sybil groaned, and he added, "I told you, you didn't want to know."

She ignored him, again shifted topics. "I'm concerned about David. He promised to restore integrity to his office and he meant it. Lying to the public about us has to grate at him."

"I'm sure it's had him on his knees in the Oval Office. But if it can keep us alive, then he has to do it."

His meaning escaped her, but a fearful shudder rippled through her chest. "On his knees in the Oval Office?"

"Never mind."

"No way." No one had forgotten the events that previously had occurred in the Oval Office, and if David had broken his promise to the people, then she damn well needed to know. "Tell me what you meant."

Jonathan picked up on the distrust in her tone and gave her a look laced with reprimand. "He prays there often. Privately."

She felt shame for doubting David, and for the first time she understood that restoring faith to people whose trust had been broken took time *and* evidence of innocence. It shouldn't be that way but it was, even for her, and she couldn't expect more from others than she was capable of giving herself.

This incident also proved something else she wished it

hadn't. It wasn't only the men in her private life she thought she knew well but didn't, it was the men in her professional life, too. Fear twisted her stomach in knots. Did realizing that mean she now needed to doubt all her personal *and* professional judgments? Second-guess *all* her decisions? Good God, she'd be crippled. Hamstrung. Anything but effective.

"Sybil, why do you look so upset? The man was praying, not selling state secrets."

There was no way she could voice her thoughts out loud. "I wish he didn't have to lie. That's all."

"He has no choice."

Her empty stomach grumbled and ached. She rubbed it, swearing she'd trade her fortune for a cheeseburger. "Why?"

"Sam Sayelle received a call from PUSH claiming responsibility for your assassination. He confronted Barber, but our favorite senior advisor ducked him. That was a big mistake."

Barber was part of Cap Marlowe's pack, and he had a penchant for making convenient-for-Cap mistakes. "How big a mistake?" A heavy cloud moved over them. Sybil strained to see Westford through the deep shadows.

"Huge." He swallowed a bite of bark, then another. "Sayelle got ticked at being shut out of the info loop and called the commander."

Commander Conlee? "How?" Sayelle shouldn't know Home Base existed, much less about Conlee or how to reach him.

"Obviously, someone told him. Intel suspects Cap Marlowe, but Sayelle refused to confirm or deny it. Needless to say, Cap's become a mute amnesiac on the matter."

"Damn it." Sybil swallowed her exasperation. "If Cap had to do this, then why didn't he act as an intermediary?"

"Frankly, the commander doesn't know or care. He wants to establish direct contact."

"With Sayelle?" Sybil couldn't believe it. "Why?" Could this get any more complex? Austin, Cap Marlowe, Sayelle, Barber, and, she'd bet her eye teeth, David's press secretary, Winston, were all in bed together politically— and all against her.

"We're officially dead. Conlee can't transmit direct to us anymore. He needs a go-between to keep us updated."

"So he recruits a member of the press?"

"He's done it before and been successful. He just codes the messages and has the press relay them to agents in the field."

"But that was Marcus Gilbert, and Conlee trusted him. He's retired now and this is Sam Sayelle we're talking about, Westford. He isn't a patch on Marcus's ass—and he hates me." Agitated, she smoothed her dripping wet hair back, tilted her face into a gusty breeze. "David will never authorize this. Never."

"He already has." Jonathan sent her a level look. "Conlee's judgment has always been sound. Give him the benefit of the doubt."

"With my life at stake?"

"And mine."

She buried her face in her hands. Calmed herself down. "Fine," she said. "But he had damn well better be right, because if he's not, we're dead."

Tense and weary, Sybil slumped against the rock. An as-yet unidentified traitor loose inside a top-secret site, a plane exploded, seven people killed, a deadline looming that threatened mass destruction, and Conlee recruits Sam Sayelle.

David must be half out of his mind. And with everything else, he had all the condolence calls to make, including to Austin—which probably would make Sybil a pauper—and to Ken Dean's wife, Linda—which definitely would make David wish he were a pauper or *anything* other than the man making that call.

Sybil suffered a stab of guilt. Linda had made no secret of her opposition to Ken being Sybil's pilot, or of blaming her for dragging Ken to every hot spot and hellhole on the face of the planet, putting him in unnecessary danger. More than once Linda had reminded Sybil that he had a family who needed him. And more than once Sybil had called Ken into the office and offered him a lateral transfer to a less dangerous job. He had routinely refused, for which Linda also blamed Sybil. She supposed it was easier for Linda to blame her than to blame her own husband, but . . . now this.

★   ★   ★

Linda Dean had awakened from a dead sleep every single night since Ken had left for Geneva, certain she had been roused by some ominous sound. Now she was cooking dinner and she had that same wake-you-from-a-dead-sleep and raise-the-hair-on-your-neck feeling. She couldn't logically explain any of it—the sensations seemed totally unprovoked. Nothing unusual had happened in the old Victorian that had housed her family through three generations, and there had been no warnings from the security guards who patrolled the subdivision that had built up around it. Still, she glanced over to the back door and checked the alarm system. The red light was glowing; the alarm was on and being monitored.

An alarm is necessary, Linda. There are a lot of crazies out there.

We will not raise our children in an atmosphere of fear, and that's final, Ken.

So had begun their domestic war.

She had won that battle but had lost the war six months ago, when her husband announced at breakfast an alarm system would be installed that day and then promptly closed the matter to discussion. In their twelve-year marriage, that had been the first and only time anything that affected their family had been dictated and closed to discussion. Linda hadn't cared for the feeling and had no desire to repeat it, but there was something about Ken then, and ever since, that had her instincts warning her he had his reasons and she would be wise to heed them. With him working for Sybil, who knew what could happen?

Few politicians had as many natural enemies as Sybil Stone, and by making Ken her pilot, she had made Linda one of them. Sybil had no right to ask him to take on higher risks of being hurt or killed. But would Ken listen? No. Sybil Stone could do no wrong to Ken. Linda hated her for that most of all.

She pulled the cutting board out of the cabinet and placed it on the counter. They had gotten the alarm, but Ken hadn't returned to his old self. He was ... different now. Distant and closed. More often than a confident woman would like to admit, Linda had wondered if he was having an affair. Maybe with Sybil Stone.

You're being unfair, Linda. Ken has never given you a reason to doubt him.

Guilt swept through her. She rinsed her hands at the sink and then dried them on a fresh dishcloth decorated with blue irises. The kids were upstairs doing homework, and since the walls weren't vibrating from their dueling stereo systems, they obviously hadn't yet finished. In fact, nothing was moving. The only sounds in the house were those of her in the kitchen, preparing dinner.

How odd. She stilled the knife midair above the cutting board and listened.

Nothing.

Not the kids. Not the habitual whistle of wind through the shutters. Not the attic window that had rattled her entire life.

Something thudded down the hall.

She nearly jumped out of her skin. *Damn it, Linda! Stop spooking yourself over nothing.*

Something strange snagged her gaze. Ken's brown-leather journal stood spine out with her cookbooks on the shelf. Why had he put his journal there?

She'd take a look at it as soon as she checked on the kids. The only time they were this quiet was when they were doing something they shouldn't be and knew it.

She put down the knife then walked to the foot of the stairs. Staring up the stairwell, she remembered Ken's warning when he'd kissed her good-bye: *Be on your toes, honey. There are people who want us to fail, and they could stir up trouble. We've had threats . . .*

Butterflies filled her stomach. Ken had been flying dignitaries for fifteen years and never before had he so bluntly reminded her of the elevated dangers that came with his job. She'd attended the seminars. She knew the stories of politically motivated attacks against families as well as any other spouse. And she knew that some fruitcakes actually believed they could get to someone like Ken by attacking his family. It never worked, of course. But in recent years, the attacks had become more prevalent. Of course, Sybil Stone didn't have to worry about that. Now that she had divorced her husband, she had no family to attack.

Nothing moved upstairs, and, for a fleeting moment, Linda wished she hadn't vetoed the kids' vote for a Doberman, though the Udalls' dog next door, Fang, hadn't barked. He considered the entire neighborhood his territory and barked like crazy if so much as a strange car rolled down the street. A little calmer, she expelled a rushed breath. Her heartbeat slowed to a canter and her dry mouth eased a little. "Katie? Kenneth?" she called up to them.

Neither answered.

"This isn't funny." She braced a hand on her hip and stared up the carpeted stairs. "You guys answer me, okay?"

Still no response.

Pure fear unleashed inside her. She grabbed the banister, took the first six steps. The hardwood floor behind her creaked, and she paused to look back. Something hard crashed into her neck. Her knees buckled and she fell to the steps, tumbled down them to the floor at the foot of the staircase.

Pain streaked through her chest, her right ankle, her hip. She couldn't draw breath. Spots formed before her eyes; everything blurred, dimmed. Good God, was she dying?

The kids. She had to get to the kids. Steeling herself for another avalanche of pain, she rolled over, trying to get up on her knees, and strained to focus, praying she could stay conscious. Fuzzy, fluid images swam before her eyes. Three men standing over her dressed all in black, their faces hidden behind stocking-cap masks, their hands gloved. She tried to move but couldn't. Tried to scream but made no sound. She couldn't do anything to defend herself or to protect her children. Who were these people? What were they going to do to them?

A man grabbed her, pinned her arms to her sides, shoved a pungent cloth over her nose and mouth. Chemicals. She smelled chemicals. *Don't breathe. Don't breathe. Don't breathe.*

One of the men went upstairs. Linda's head throbbed, her dread doubled.

"Noooooooo, stop! Leave me alone!"

Katie's screams pierced the mental fog and stabbed straight through Linda's heart. "Please," she whispered into the cloth, staring straight into a man's brown eyes. "Don't hurt my babies. Please!"

Yet another man appeared at the top of the stairs and two of them headed down, carrying something lumped in Katie and Kenneth's bedspreads. "Got 'em. Let's go, go, go!"

Limp and unable to move, Linda felt herself being lifted.

"She's not out."

Someone shoved the pungent cloth back over her nose and mouth, pushed down hard. Terror slithered through her veins. By their accents, these men were all foreigners. This had to be about those Geneva peace talks. Ken's warning again replayed in her mind. *Oh, God, his journal. Why hadn't she immediately noticed the journal?* He'd put it with her cookbooks to make sure she found it quickly, and, being out of place, she would know to read it. *He had expected this!*

"Mom!" Katie cried. *"Mommieeeee!"*

Linda struggled against the man holding her, fought to free herself to help Katie.

The man dodged her feeble blows. "Screw drugs." He spat from between his clenched teeth, raised a beefy fist, and slammed it against her jaw.

Pain exploded in Linda's face. Certain she and her children were about to die, she slid into the dark abyss of unconsciousness.

★ ★ ★

"Sybil, you okay?"

"I'm fine, Westford." Leaning back against the rock, she lifted her gaze to the canopy of wet, dripping leaves. Her voice sounded foggy and thick and as weary as she felt. "Just fine."

He reached over and stroked her shoulder. "You don't have to be strong all the time."

"Oh?" She shot him a challenging look. "When do you recommend I be weak? When negotiating with Peris and Abdan? When a decision I make kills seven people? You jumped out of a plane without a parachute, for God's sake. You could have died, Westford." Pain exploded in her chest and tears welled in her eyes. She blinked hard and fast to keep them from falling, crushed a fistful of leaves, then tossed them to the ground. "Oh, God. You could have died."

"Every rose needs its thorn."

Confused, she snapped. "What?"

"You can let go right now," he said, his voice gruff and raw. "It's not being weak, Sybil. It's being human." He opened his arms.

Everything inside Sybil wanted to go to him, to feel the solid warmth of his chest against her face, his arms close around her. But it had been so long since she'd dared to allow herself the luxury of being comforted by a man. What if she accepted that comfort and let go, and then she couldn't stop letting go? What if she found solace in it, needed it, and she couldn't go back to burying her feelings? "I—I can't."

"It's okay. I can." Westford let her see the sadness in his eyes. "I lost two of my men. I've been a guest in Ken Dean's home. I know his wife and kids—and Cramer's wife, who *is* just a kid. And Julie's dad. Jesus, Sybil. He lived through three wars. Three of them. And now because of some damn terrorist, he's lived just long enough to see his only daughter murdered." Westford slid across the wet ground and wrapped his arms around her. "Damn it, I can." He swallowed hard. "I hurt from the bone out."

Pain flooded through her so strong and intense she couldn't tell where it began or ended, only that no part of her escaped its agony. Tears spilled down her face and burned hot against her cold skin. "Me, too, Jonathan." She lifted her arms, cradled his head in the crook of her neck, and whispered, "Me, too."

He looked up at her. The grief ravaging his face split and surprise filled the crevices. "You know my first name."

"Yes." Her voice trembled. "But I have to wish I didn't."

"Why?"

Because I like you. Because with your rose petals and thorns, you make me think and feel things I don't want to

*think or feel. Because you make me want to forget I have
lousy judgment and I shouldn't trust men. Damn you, you get
to me, and I don't want anyone to get to me ever again.*

"Sybil?" He tightened his hold on her and what had begun as a search for comfort shifted to a sensory assault.
Unable not to, she explored it, discovered a pure and simple joy and gratitude that she was alive, felt the assault
deepen and then shift again, conjuring tender feelings of
closeness, intimacy, and an intense awareness stronger
than anything she'd ever experienced.

"Why, Sybil?"

Awed and humbled and amazed by the onslaught of
emotions yawning inside her, she couldn't for the life of her
remember anything, much less why she shouldn't want to
be familiar enough to know his first name. "Because."

"Because," he said against her shoulder, his lips brushing against her skin.

*Oh, God, how was she supposed to remember when she
couldn't think?* "It—it's important."

"Not to me." His breath fanned against her neck,
warm and inviting. He lowered his hands to her waist,
lifted her onto his lap, then held her against him and caressed her back.

Too intense! Her heart skipped a beat then thudded
against her ribs, and every instinct in her body conspired,
urged her to gravitate toward him, to seek out his touch.
"Am I important to you?"

"Would I risk my life for you if you weren't important
to me?"

Cryptic. She really didn't know what she needed to
hear from him, but she knew anything cryptic wasn't it.
"You risk your life for a lot of people."

He hesitated and something in his eyes changed, hardened. "You're pushing, Sybil. But are you sure you want me
to respond to that?"

She wasn't sure of anything right now. To her, these

shifts between them seemed so evident and personal and intimate, but maybe to him they weren't. Maybe he was holding her seeking comfort from grief and nothing more. Maybe he was holding a wounded veep, not a wounded woman, and she'd crossed the proverbial line alone. "I— I'm sorry, Westford." She reverted to his last name to create distance between them and tried to scoot off his lap.

He held her firmly in place. "Jonathan, Sybil." He cupped her chin in his hands and kissed her lightly on the lips. "Jonathan," he whispered against her mouth, then kissed her again. Sweetly ... softly ... gently ... opening a door in her heart she had feared and believed would forever remain closed. His lips parted, he cruised over her face, pressed touches of kisses to her temple, her forehead, the line of her jaw, and then brushed the tips of their noses. "You're important."

She dragged in a sharp breath, and he kissed her again, this time letting her feel his hunger and heat. She reveled in the knowing, in the slumbering sensations awakened: the eager meshing of mouths and lips and tongues, exploring, straining to deepen their union; the clutching of hands, trembling with urgency, needing to be everywhere at once, to carry the heady blend of pleasure and longing to places hiding far beneath the skin touched; the clinging of wet clothes to skin that was suddenly sensitive and aware; the heat of pressed bodies seeping through rough fabric, warming them, welcoming them. Tempting them.

You're important.

In her mind, Sybil heard him again, and for the first time in a very long time, she felt important to a man. Maybe they would regret this. Maybe she was important, but to the agent and not to the man. Maybe he was attracted to the vice president, the position, and not to the woman. But whatever the truth proved to be, she would deal with it ... later. Now she just wanted to feel again. To hold and be held. To be more than her job, if only for a little while. She wanted to feel her body melt into liquid heat, to get lost in the dizzying sensual haze so long absent from her life. She wanted to know a man ached to touch her, to feel her touch. She wanted, just once, to be loved by a man knowing he didn't care what job she did, or how much power or money she had, or how big a shadow she cast. A man to whom none of that mattered. A man to whom only she mattered.

And, like it or not, she wanted to know if Jonathan was that man.

He broke their kiss, rested his chin on her shoulder, and circled his arms around her shoulders. "I probably shouldn't have done that. But I won't apologize, Sybil."

Thank God. "Me, either." Nose to his chest, she inhaled his tangy scent. Not bitter, but definitely dangerous. "I'm not sorry."

"You will be," he predicted, regret tainting his tone.

Surprised, she reared back. "Are you planning something nasty, Westford?"

"Jonathan, Sybil."

"Whatever. Are you?"

"Would I do that to you?"

"I didn't think you would, but you're giving me second thoughts."

"You'll be doing the damage," he predicted. "I'll be a passive victim."

"What are you talking about?"

"I told you. I know how your mind works."

He thought she would beat herself up over this. She opened her mouth to deny it but stopped, innately knowing he was right and she would. That truth totally soured her mood. "Your timing for sharing these insights really sucks, Jonathan."

"Yet another flaw. I'd say I'd work on it, but I won't." He released her, leaned back against the tree, and stared her right in the eye. "You're going to look at whatever happens between us and consciously decide what it means to you. You're going to consciously choose what you want. No excuses. No delusions. And no distractions." He stared up through the trees. "Personally, I'd opt for making love with you, but I know what that'll cost. Eventually you'll cool down and start thinking, though I'm guessing that could take a while." The look in his eyes warmed. "I've never seen you dazed before. I like it."

"Quit confusing me." She was dazed, damn it, and her senses were still rioting. "Are you saying lust isn't enough for you, or I'm not worth the complications?" Just how important was important?

"I'm telling you I know how your mind works." He lifted a hand. "Now, come here and let me hold you."

"I don't think I want you to," she said, but then slid into his arms and snuggled to his side anyway.

"I know you don't." He closed the circle of his arms around her and let out a sigh, rich and deep and reeking of contentment. "I don't want to hold you, either."

They didn't want the same thing: to care or matter to each other.

Somewhere in that revelation, she found solace—and she accepted that she'd become wickedly twisted.

* * *

How the hell had he gotten into this mess?

Sayelle stared across the *Herald*'s conference room table at Commander Conlee, folded his hands on the tabletop, and dropped his voice. "Let me get this straight. You want me to broadcast scripts you provide me, on the radio?"

"That's correct."

Sam's mind reeled. "Why?"

"I'd rather not say, Mr. Sayelle."

"I'm sure you would, but it's people in my position who think they're performing a service that end up doing a couple years in jail."

"This isn't like that."

Sam was losing patience. "Listen, it doesn't take a rocket scientist to figure out that you want me to pass some kind of messages. If you want me involved, then you're going to have to trust me and prove it. I want details, or you'll find yourself another reporter. It's that simple."

Conlee covered a frown by swiping a fingertip down his blunt nose. "All right, but trust works both ways. I want your word that nothing said here leaves this room, and I'm telling you now, if it does, I'll kill you. I'll also kill everyone you tell."

This wasn't a threat, just a fact. Conlee was a no-nonsense kind of man who meant exactly what he said. "I protect my sources."

"I know you spent three months in a Chicago lockup protecting a source. That's one of the reasons I'm here."

"There are others?"

"Yes. I think you're misguided, Mr. Sayelle, but basically a straight shooter. That's important to me. And you carry a personal referral I respect."

"From whom?"

A ghost of a smile curled Conlee's lip. "A mutual friend who wishes to remain anonymous."

"So what is going on here?"

Conlee hesitated. "Don't disappoint me in this, Sam. If you do, you'll have a lot of blood on your hands."

Sam wasn't sure he wanted to do this. But his curiosity was up and there was no denying it. He couldn't walk away now; not knowing the details would drive him crazy. And once he knew them, he wouldn't be able to walk away. No skirting it. This was decision time. "I understand."

"You will be broadcasting messages. No more, or less."

"To whom?"

"Vice President Stone."

"What?" Sayelle couldn't contain his shock. "But PUSH assassinated her—"

"Half the terrorist groups in the world claim they assassinated her."

"You think she's alive."

"Probably not. But we consider it prudent to deem it possible."

That sounded like an understatement if ever Sam had heard one. "Commander, I'm sure it hasn't escaped your notice—obviously you know a lot about me—but I don't happen to be one of the vice president's supporters."

"I'm aware of that."

"Then you'll understand my asking why you came to me."

"Because PUSH called you, and because a man I've respected and trusted for many years suggested you had the guts and integrity to do this job. He also said you were fair, which means you'll come to know what I've already learned."

Who would have put him in this position? And should he thank the man for it, or beat the hell out of him? "What have you learned, Commander?"

"That you're wrong about Vice President Stone."

Sam grunted. "Pardon me if I'm skeptical about that."

"Skepticism is healthy." Conlee pressed his hands flat on the table. "So, are you in?"

Stone, alive maybe? Coded messages? Changing opinions? An anonymous referral? If Sybil Stone wasn't dead, what exactly was she up to now? And if she was dead, what had she been into so deeply that it had gotten her killed and rattled Commander Conlee enough to reveal himself to a nobody like Sam Sayelle? "Hell, yes, I'm in."

"Then come with me."

Conlee led him down to the *Herald*'s basement, through a dusty storage area no one used anymore and that Sam hadn't known existed, to a small room. "What is this?"

Conlee unlocked the door and walked inside. The room was about eight by ten, and full of broadcasting equipment. Within five minutes, Conlee had shown him how to use it and handed him the key to the door. "Keep your mouth shut about this room being here. Broadcasts will be frequent for the next twenty-four to forty-eight hours. I'll personally deliver the scripts."

"Does anyone else know about this?"

"The broadcasts?"

"Yes." Uneasiness had Sam sitting on a razor's edge.

"Yes, someone does."

"Who?"

Conlee hesitated long enough to pull an unlit cigar from his shirt pocket. "Someone depending on you, Sam. Someone who trusts you not to get Vice President Stone killed, if she's still alive."

He looked earnest, and Sam reacted from the gut, realizing exactly whom the commander was talking about. "President Lance."

Conlee didn't blink much less answer him, but Sayelle knew he had been right.

"Here's the first script." Conlee passed a ten-pager over, then turned for the door.

"Wait," Sam said. "How many times do I broadcast this? When?"

"On receipt and only once. We'll take care of the rest."

The rest is what most concerned him. "Are you making tapes?"

Conlee nodded.

Sam didn't like the sound or feel of that. "Conlee, this trust bit works both ways. You'd better not be dragging me into a Watergate." Maybe he should cover his assets for insurance.

"You have my word."

"What's it worth? Remember, I haven't gotten a personal referral on you." In fact, until Conlee had walked into

Sam's office unannounced, he had heard of Commander Conlee only once, and frankly he'd thought Jean and Cap Marlowe had been sending him on a wild-goose chase.

"About as much as yours." Conlee paused, his hand on the doorknob. "You're playing a dangerous game with dangerous people, Sam. You need protection. But not from me or Vice President Stone."

"From who then?"

"Mostly, from yourself." Conlee frowned. "I appreciate your help on this. Even if things go badly, what you're doing matters. Remember that. And remember that regardless of how well you perform, she could already be dead."

He was preparing Sam, warning him of potential emotional fallout. "I understand. She could be dead. But she also could be alive."

Chapter Eight

Thursday, August 8 ★ First-Strike Launch: 51:00:27

Frustrated with her feet sucking down and sticking in the mud, Sybil struggled to keep up with Westford's grueling pace. He was a huge man, about six-four and long-legged; his stride nearly double hers. Her sore feet were raw from sharp twigs, stones that penetrated though his muddy, soggy socks, and her spirit was in even worse shape. They'd kissed. And kissed. And, God help her, she'd loved it. Now, along with everything else, she hated loving it. She was totally confused about her feelings for him, and she was totally pissed off at Gabby for making her see him as a man in the first place.

It probably hadn't meant a thing to him. He was grieving, and he knew she was grieving. Most people turn to physical affection when grieving—for affirmation that they're alive. Maybe that's all the connection had been. It had felt like more, but she had to keep her head here. Jonathan—no, Westford—Westford was more distant, less personal. Odds were Westford had kissed her not as an agent but as a man seeking affirmation of life. But had he kissed her, the woman, or his grieving veep who also had been seeking affirmation of life?

Had to be the veep. Years of interaction and not once had he ever appeared to see her as a woman. That truth felt heavy and bore down on her chest. He'd jumped out of the plane for the veep, comforted and kissed and held the grieving veep. He didn't know the woman. No one knew the woman.

And the woman mourned that truth, too.

Envy stabbed her, hard and fast and deep. It shook her, because it was envy of the veep.

Neurotic, Sybil. Ridiculous. You're envying yourself, for God's sake. You are the veep.

Sidestepping a spiky-thorn leaf, she denied it. The two were distinctly separate, different entities. But until now she thought they'd been thoroughly integrated entities. Now she knew they were not, and that scared her. The veep was confident, secure in her skin. The woman was flawed—and, apparently, frightened of her own shadow.

She hit a mud puddle. Brown water splashed up to her knee. With everything else going on, she couldn't be bothered with mustering a groan, but she did shift her thoughts to safer, external topics. "Do we have a chance of making it?"

"Honestly?" Westford squinted back at her, the rain pelting his face.

Thunder rumbled through the trees, shook the ground. She crawled over a tree branch downed by the storm and steeled herself to hear the truth. "Honestly."

"I don't know." He grasped her waist, lifted her over the trunk of the fallen, gnarled oak, then set her back to the ground. "But we'll give it all we've got."

"Damn right we will." Sybil straightened his coat on her shoulder, wishing he could be more positive, but knowing he'd have to lie to do it. What he suggested was all there was, except for hoping for the best—and praying hard that what they got proved to be good enough.

"I'm picking up a confusing transmission." He ducked down, bracing his head under a heavy limb, and cupped a hand at his ear to block out the sounds of the storm. "It's coded."

Sybil stopped beside him, waited eagerly.

He frowned up at her. "PUSH and six other terrorist groups have claimed responsibility for blowing up your plane. Intel considers the PUSH claim most credible."

Westford looked about as annoyed as she felt. "But Ballast did this, not PUSH."

"I agree, Sybil, but Home Base doesn't know everything we know."

"Can't we somehow tell them? Commander Conlee will be dividing resources to cover them both, and only God knows what Gregor Faust will do next if we don't hem him in and keep Ballast under extreme pressure."

"What do you suggest?" Westford shrugged in pure frustration. "Smoke signals?"

"Don't get cute."

"Sorry, ma'am. I was distracted."

"By the transmission?"

"More or less." He sent her a puzzled look. "You're not going to like it, but this report isn't coming in through a direct feed on the emergency channel."

"We're dead, remember?" Conlee couldn't transmit direct now. "Where is it coming from?"

"Bleed-over."

Sybil processed that. "But if the report is coded, why is Conlee using bleed-over from another channel?"

Westford grimaced. "He must really think we're dead."

"But you said they knew we were alive."

"They deduced we were because of my tracker. Evidently Intel picked up something to alter their opinion."

Gruesome deduction, but it made sense. Jonathan's tone and look scared her, and she hated being scared. "You were right. I don't like it."

"You're not going to like the rest any better." He flattened his lips. "The broadcaster is Sam Sayelle."

"Damn it." She'd known David had authorized it, so why did hearing the commander had followed through turn her insides to jelly? She had hoped Conlee would come to his senses. Why hadn't he? He knew Sayelle was in up to his neck with Cap and his rat pack. Not one of them would so much as spit on Sybil if she were on fire. But she also knew once Conlee made a decision, it took an act of Congress armed with hard evidence to change his mind.

"Definitely Sayelle. He just identified himself and gave his station's call letters. Just like Marcus Gilbert used to do."

Sybil refused to give in to despair, but this development seriously threatened her control. What did it mean? Why in the name of God had Conlee pulled in Sayelle? "What if he's altered the message?"

"He wouldn't dare. Not yet, anyway. If he intends to, he'll do the first two or three broadcasts by the book—to get Conlee complacent—and then alter them."

Westford stared down at her. "You doubt every word coming from Sayelle. Do I need to know why?"

Sybil wanted to look away but wouldn't allow herself to do it. "He's about as fond of me as Austin is trustworthy. We go downhill from there."

"So the odds of him lying to us are—"

Humiliating to admit it, but she had to be honest. "Highly probable."

★   ★   ★

Sybil could be dead.

A bubble of excitement exploded in Austin Stone's chest. He paced between the sofa and wet bar in his posh co-op. Strains of Bach's Fifth floated through the room, the tempo lifting and falling in tandem with Austin's moods. Staring at the phone receiver, he knew he shouldn't call; he was being watched. But he could use the cell phone. He had activated it after the divorce under his mother's maiden name, Madeline Kane. David Lance and his intrusive FBI henchmen weren't monitoring it.

Since the divorce, Austin had had precious little privacy. Lance and his advisors were terrified he would embarrass them or Sybil. He could embarrass some of them—he knew where the skeletons were buried—but exposing bones for others to pick clean in no way enhanced his interests. Not if he wanted the bitch to give him controlling interest in Secure Environet before her death. As he well knew, when it came to kids or anything that affected her career, Sybil Ashford Stone had no sense of humor.

She could be dead.

Maybe the challenge of getting her stock had been resolved. The battle of wills between them could be over. If the plans he had set in motion six months after the divorce—when they'd had the mother of all arguments and that jerk, Jonathan Westford, had threatened to kill him—were unfolding as advertised, she should be dead and out of Austin's way forever.

She won't be there to stop you anymore. You'll finally be free of her. Free.

Tasting power—his own power, not Sybil's—Austin paused at the oak wet bar and dared to hope. He snagged a crystal glass, poured in three fingers of scotch, and then topped it off with ice and water. Hope wasn't enough. He had to know.

Downing a long, cold draw of scotch for courage, he picked up the cell and direct-dialed a secure-line number at the White House, bypassing the switchboard and monitors. This was one call he didn't want recorded.

Richard Barber answered on the first ring, sounding irritated by the interruption. "Yes?"

Before Austin and Sybil had divorced and he had lost his direct link to inside information, he had forged this alliance with Barber. It had been productive and beneficial to them both. He let his question tumble out. "Is she really dead?"

"Not yet verified, but highly probable."

Highly probable. Austin dabbed at the sweat beading on his forehead, stared at his reflection in the mirror above the mantel, and let his hope grow. "Has our mutual friend been notified?"

"You'll need to take care of that." Barber dropped his voice. "Don't call me on this again. It's too dangerous."

So Commander Conlee was aware of the security breach, and he already suspected an infiltrator. He would be monitoring everyone from here on out. "How am I supposed to know what's going on?" Austin grimaced at a tapestry hanging on the wall. There was no way that bastard Lance would tell him anything until he positively had to do it.

"I'll call you." Barber reassured him. "Have I ever let you down?"

He hadn't, but . . . Austin put a biting edge in his tone. "Don't start now."

"I won't." The line clicked.

Silence droned in Austin's ear. Barber shouldn't let him down. Actually, he wouldn't dare. If he did, his political aspirations and career would be over and he'd be doing time in a white-collar, minimum-security prison instead of holding a key position on David Lance's staff. Yet he hadn't warned Austin about any of this before the president had called. Annoyed by that, Austin tapped the button, then dialed the phone again.

Jean Holt answered. "Senator Marlowe's office."

"Put me through, Jean."

"One moment, Dr. Stone."

Cap came on the line. "Austin, what the hell is going on? The press is all over me."

Sam Sayelle specifically, Austin speculated. "Sybil's plane exploded."

"Unfortunate," Cap said, seemingly unfazed by the news. "It's a damn shame she was tied up in peace-talk negotiations and not on it."

Austin poured himself a second scotch and water. This time only two fingers; he needed to keep his mind sharp. "Apparently she left the talks and *was* on it."

"Son of a bitch." Cap let out a low whistling breath. "What happened?"

"No idea yet. Could be mechanical or a terrorist attack," Austin hedged, deciding what he most needed was normalcy. He went into the kitchen and pulled out the fixings for a turkey sandwich, then slathered mayo on two slices of white bread. Sybil hated white bread. He pulled out two more slices. They had battled and he had won. Finally. She was not strongest or smartest, and she was not most powerful anymore. "Lance is being very closed-mouthed."

So were Cap's informers. "Did he mention PUSH or Ballast?" Just mentioning those two groups had the senator's nerves sizzling and his gaze riveting to the south wall, pinning on his office safe.

"No, but it wouldn't surprise me."

Had Austin buried a secret message in that remark? Cap let the inference slide, not certain it was wise to know. In the silence, strains of Bach came through the line. Cap hated Bach. Give him ragtime any day. "Keep me informed."

"You, too."

Cap cradled the receiver. Nervous energy coiled in his chest. He opened the wall safe, reached inside, then pulled out the white envelope that had been anonymously delivered to his office two months ago. His hand trembled, his mouth dried out, and his breathing shallowed. Shaking out a silver key, he recalled the phone message he had received the day the Ground Serve messenger had delivered the package: *When the time comes, you will know how to use it*.

Two long months of agonizing, wondering and worrying who had sent him the damn thing, and why; of waffling between whether the sender had dirt on him personally and professionally; of waiting to fall from his office in disgrace. Oh, he hadn't deliberately dealt dirty in his professional life, but no one survived on the Hill and remained lily white. Not for one year, much less thirty. Cap had done his share of stepping into the shadows. True, he had been damned cautious, but he had crossed the line now and then. Blackmail wasn't outside the realm of possibility.

The rumor mill had it down that PUSH had sabotaged Sybil Stone's plane. But for months Cap had felt that Ballast, Gregor Faust specifically, had sent the key. He was the master strategist. Yet maybe Cap was overreacting. Maybe the key he found in the package had nothing to do with the veep's plane exploding. Maybe his certainty that the incidents were connected and that Faust had created them was just the product of fear and a guilty conscience.

Christ, he hoped that was the case. Because the alternative meant that, through the key, he could be directly tied to Gregor Faust, and whether that tie had been intentional or accidental didn't matter. People on the Hill would believe it was intentional, and that would cost Cap the Republican nomination for President of the United States.

Dizzy, Cap dropped down in his seat. There was no way to explain away his reasons for not following procedure and reporting receipt of the key. He'd established the damn policy. No. No acceptable excuse whatsoever. Everyone who was anyone would be looking for someone to blame— for *anyone* to blame—and Cap had left himself wide open to be sacrificed.

He squeezed his eyes shut. Okay, he had made a huge mistake. Yet without knowing who had sent the key or what it meant, how could he have reported it? He couldn't have an independent council appointed to execute a discovery process against him. No one survived those damn things with their dignity intact. Holding on to the key had seemed right and easy to do at the time. Right. Reasonable. Rational.

Now he felt like a damn fool. Sybil's plane exploding and his receiving the key were likely related incidents. Actually, they were most likely *inter*related incidents. The gnawing in his stomach doubled him over and the truth hit him like a sledgehammer: PUSH was hyping the media. Gregor Faust had set him up.

And Cap, for all his wheeling and dealing and political savvy, had made setting him up damned easy.

How the hell was he going to get out of this?

Chapter Nine

Thursday, August 8 ★ First-Strike Launch: 49:59:01

Darkness swallowed them and the rain persisted, arrogant and bone chilling. Sybil was so tired that putting one foot in front of the other was a major challenge. She brushed against some sort of thorny vine. It snared her right leg, stabbed into her flesh and clung, and she stumbled. "Damn it!"

Westford grabbed her arm, held her upright, and then cut her loose from the tangle with his knife. "Smilax."

"Smilax, hell. It burns like fire and feels like claws."

"That's why it's nicknamed catbrier." He rubbed the blood away from the long, thick scratches on her leg and examined it. "They're not too deep."

She frowned at him. "Do you know everything?"

He frowned back at her. "No, not everything."

Remorse set in. "I'm sorry I snapped. I'm tired and cranky."

"Let's take a break."

It had been hours since they'd stopped. But if they stopped, he might kiss her again. Worse, he might not. "We shouldn't. We can't afford to lose the time."

"What we can't afford is to walk into the opposition because we're so damn tired we're bitchy and punch drunk." He stopped inside a small circle of large pines. "This is a good spot."

Sybil stepped inside the circle and didn't think twice before collapsing on the muddy ground. She couldn't get any more waterlogged or dirty, and if a snake wanted her spot, it was going to have to fight her for it. "When we get home, I'm going to double my treadmill time."

"Right." Westford stretched his jacket between two tree trunks then secured it with the parachute cord he had pocketed. Its edges created a waterfall that splattered the ground just beyond her back. Amazing, but the rhythmic splats weren't annoying. They soothed her.

"That's the best I can do without losing my pants."

Surprise rippled through her chest. "Keep your pants, Westford, and sit down."

He dropped down beside her and their arms brushed. "You're welcome to lean on me."

She searched his gaze. "I'd love to be human and let go. Actually, I've considered having a nervous breakdown—my neuroses are conquering me—but I'm just too tired to work up the steam to do it."

"I meant physically, Sybil." Braced against the tree, he bent his knees and motioned for her to come to him. "I'm softer than the ground."

"Ah, then I accept." As noncommittal as remarks come, he'd told her nothing, but grateful for the opportunity to feel anything but numb and cold and wet, she snuggled between his thighs then leaned back against his chest. He wasn't much softer than the ground, but his scent was familiar and far more comforting. Too comforting. And too reminiscent of his kisses. Recognizing that line of thought as dangerous, she veered to safer ground. "Has Intel reported further updates?"

"Not yet." Westford yawned deeply. "Try to rest for a while."

Sybil closed her eyes and relaxed against him, promising herself she'd only rest a moment. Think only of the danger and the briefcase cuff that now had abraded her wrist and made it raw, and how absurd it was that she considered their current situation to be less dangerous than merely thinking of him. Settling in, she felt his heart beat against her back. "Nice."

Jonathan agreed but held his tongue. He felt the tension drain from her body, knew the moment she fell asleep. She didn't slide into sleep peacefully; she tumbled, hard and fast. The woman was going to need some time to get used to the idea that he was a man and more time to accept what was going on between them. He shouldn't have kissed her. And he shouldn't feel guilty for not telling her everything Sayelle had transmitted. She had enough on her shoulders without worrying about things she couldn't control, too. And she would worry about them. Nothing good could come from telling her, so why did he still feel guilty?

The terrorists had given the president seventy-two hours from their initial contact to get the briefcase back to Washington. That was Sybil's phantom deadline. But what the hell was in the case? And why had the terrorists taken it to her in Geneva in the first place?

Perplexed, Jonathan glared down a curious raccoon until it backed off and took refuge under the bushes, then stroked Sybil's hair away from her face and ran through various scenarios. But he couldn't find a rationale for Geneva ... unless the package already had been there. If that proved true, then the security breach she had mentioned earlier may have occurred in the United States but the terrorists were working in Europe—in Eastern Europe, specifically. Eastern Europe wasn't PUSH territory; Ballast owned it, and this entire incident carried Gregor Faust's classic signature—including government infiltration at the highest levels, which would explain the security breach. Jonathan stiffened. All of this originated in Faust's backyard. Why hadn't Conlee or Lance put the pieces together?

According to Sayelle's transmissions, some presidential advisors considered Faust the logical candidate. Yet Intel was muddying the waters with evidence of PUSH horning in on Ballast turf, and they considered PUSH's responsibility claim credible and authentic.

Damn. Jonathan dragged a hand over his face, rustling his stubble of beard, and blinked hard to clear his tired eyes. Lance couldn't know where to apply the most pressure; not with what he had. PUSH levying the attack would make things easier for the United States. It could attack PUSH without creating an international incident. But there was no touching Faust without such an incident. Faust also had the resources and connections to disappear underground indefinitely in a number of different nations, and if he failed to reach his objective, he would kill millions without thinking twice. Faust had sold his soul a long time ago. He had no conscience, no compassion. He wasn't loyal to any man or any country. To him, anyone was expendable, and manipulating nations into war was just a profitable game. With him at the helm, Ballast was far more dangerous than PUSH, even if it had allied with China, as recently reported through Intel.

"Jonathan?" Sybil's voice sounded strained, tight.

He thought she'd been sleeping. *Jonathan, not Westford.* "Mmm?"

"Can we go on now?"

He needed to hold her. Just for a few more minutes. He'd waited years to hold her, and now that he knew what it was like, they might not survive to see where they ended up. Surely he could have a few lousy minutes. "We need to rest."

"I know." She rubbed her cheek against his chest. "But it's more important to get the briefcase back to David."

Something in her tone worried him, and she was shaking like a leaf. He looked down at her face and waited for her to explain.

"If he doesn't use the contents of this case in time, it's going to be bad."

Even rain-drenched and muddy, she was beautiful to him. "How bad?"

"By Sunday, the United States will be fighting World War III. And President Lance will have started it."

"What?" Jonathan couldn't hide his shock.

"If we don't get back and stop it, he's going to be launching the first-strike missile."

Holy Mary, Mother of God. "How strong are the odds our allies will let that happen?"

"About a hundred percent."

★ ★ ★

His bitch of an ex-wife was either dead, or she wasn't. Either way, he wanted proof so he knew whether to celebrate or exact revenge.

Downing another double scotch, this time to the sounds of Mozart, Austin stared out of his co-op window at a black sedan parked under the streetlight. Lance's men. Waiting with bated breath on the off chance Austin stepped over any of their lines. He was desperate for news, but he wasn't stupid enough to provoke them. In forty-nine hours, when the bastards got blown to hell, they would realize the mistake they had made in underestimating his power. It was a pity Lance wouldn't be killed, too, but he would be evacuated and airborne on Air Force One long before the explosion. Of course, that left him alive to suffer the guilt. Austin found that even more gratifying than seeing the president dead.

There were fates worse than death. Austin knew it, and soon Lance would know it, too. When he had to look into the eyes of survivors and try to explain to them why their parents and kids were dead . . .

Stepping back from the window, Austin again checked his Rolex: 11 P.M. No confirmation of Sybil's death from Lance, nothing from Cap, and not a word from Barber. Out of patience, Austin lifted the cell phone and dialed the number he had sworn he would never use.

Gregor Faust answered on the first ring. "Yes?"

Austin's question rolled out. "Is she dead or not?"

"We're on the ground, attempting to verify that now."

Frustration and rage mounted inside Austin. "You mean she wasn't on the plane when you hit it?" Why would Lance have called, saying she had been?

"She was on the plane. But just before the explosion, she bailed out."

"Westford." Austin spat the arrogant bastard's name. "He got her out, didn't he?"

"Actually, prelim reports say she got *him* out. He didn't have a parachute. She did."

"Son of a bitch." Austin slammed his glass down on the bar. It tipped, fell to the floor, and shattered. "Those two have caused me more trouble—"

"I know Westford once threatened you, Austin. Why?"

Austin resented the question, but he had to answer it. Faust wasn't a man to lightly refuse. "Sybil and I were arguing over the property settlement. I lost my head and said I was going to slap her. Westford overheard me." Remembering the incident outraged Austin all over again. "When I left, he followed me. He made damn sure there were no witnesses around and then made the threat: 'You ever lay a hand on her in anger and I'll kill you.'"

"Did you believe him?"

"Hell, yes, I believed him." Austin grunted. "Westford doesn't mince words or exaggerate." Faust wasn't as smart as he thought, or he would have known that.

"How did Sybil react to this?"

"I don't think she knows it. I didn't tell her, and you can bet Westford didn't. He transferred off her detail right after that, but he's still watching us both."

"What do you mean?"

"Right after he was reassigned, I woke up in the middle of the night, and he was standing beside my bed. He told me." Austin paused. "I guess he thought once he was out of the picture, I'd pick up where I'd left off, arguing with her."

"Have you?"

"We've talked about my stock, but I'm not crazy enough to push her or him."

"So you think she would kill you?"

"No, she'd just make me wish I were dead. Vice President Stone carries a lot of clout. She'd keep me globally constrained. Westford would be the one. He'd kill me."

"But he hasn't been following you or anything."

"No," Austin said quickly. Faust obviously feared the secret of his identity had been compromised. Since he killed anyone he considered careless or disloyal, Austin quickly disabused him of the idea. "Nothing like that. I've been cautious."

"Good. With or without Westford, I can't see Sybil Stone tolerating physical violence."

"She wouldn't." If Austin had slapped her that night, he probably would still have a wired jaw. Her father had taught incidental shooting and hand-to-hand combat to FBI agents as a sideline business. He had also taught his daughter those skills, and if pushed, odds were, she wouldn't hesitate to use them.

"I take it everything is ready to go on your end." Faust sounded amused. Maybe a little bored, though Austin knew the man was anything but. He was storing details on Westford and Sybil, and on Austin.

"Of course. What about you?" He removed his tie, tossed it onto a white brocade chair. "If she's alive, you won't be keeping your end of the deal."

"Do I detect a threat in your voice, Austin?"

Faust's cool and calm tone didn't fool Austin. He had pushed the terrorist too far. But, damn it, Sybil's death wasn't negotiable. "No threat whatsoever. We made an agreement. You hold up your end, and I'll hold up mine."

"We have forty-nine hours. Any deadline delay would not be healthy."

The bitch couldn't even die without causing him problems. "Veiled threats are unnecessary, Gregor. All I want is what you promised."

"Fine." Gregor hung up the phone, listened to an incoming satellite inquiry from Alpha Team's field leader, Adam, and responded to it. "Yes, ET Three. The lack of verification on the chuters does create problems. I want them resolved."

Pacing the command center, Gregor kept his gaze locked on the Florida monitor. News crews and police helicopters were braving the storm and filling the sky north of the Everglades. The ground was just as active. Professionals searched with bloodhounds; private citizens with good intentions but ignorant of investigative tactics and methods tromped through the area, destroying any evidence that would have been there. A moot point, really, since they were searching too far south of the last coordinates the relief pilot had radioed in.

Alpha Team, though in the area where Liberty and Westford had bailed out, had failed to locate them or their remains. The time lag between his men bailing out of the plane and the explosion had been sufficient. They could be alive. Yet they hadn't reported in.

"We're walking the grid now," Adam said. "Doing everything by the book."

"Don't drag your feet. You've got a mob of pros and novices on your heels—or they will be, in a couple hours."

"No problem, sir. So far, all we've found is a woman's shoe. Same color, size, and a visual match to the ones Liberty was wearing at the airport. But we can't use normal tracking methods to determine potential landing sites. The storm has done a lot of damage to the terrain."

Destroyed evidence. Gregor ran a frustrated hand over his forehead. "ET and his team are on the chopper now. They should be there within an hour. I want more than odds, I want certainty." Austin Stone was a genius, interested only in Sybil Stone's death. While Gregor personally didn't give a tinker's damn if the woman lived or died so long as she wasn't talking peace with Peris and Abdan, he didn't want Austin doing anything to surprise him. That was an unavoidable risk in forging alliances on weaponry or new technologies with scientists and designers. They knew the loopholes. Gregor had made every possible attempt to cover his assets, yet he was no fool. Austin Stone had the ability and the access necessary to create serious havoc. If Gregor missed a step, Austin would seize control of the mission. And if Sybil was alive, he would be even more dangerous and more deeply motivated to do so.

Gregor grabbed his yellow stress ball and squeezed it. That was the problem with recruiting scientists. While they were geniuses capable of great feats, they were also unreliable pains in the ass because they entered into strategic alliances with their own private agendas that often had nothing to do with his agenda. They were a lot like politicians really.

"We're doing our best, sir," ET Three said. "Conditions are slowing down the process, but we'll find them."

"You'd damn well better—before your next report. I want—"

"Excuse me, sir," ET Three interrupted. "Just a second."

Gregor paused. Maybe if the morons who hadn't been able to find their asses with both hands had found Westford's path, they could—

"Sir," ET Three transmitted. "We've located one of the chuters."

"And?" Gregor stilled.

"He got hung up in the trees. He's dead, sir. Broken neck."

"Who is he?"

"Captain Dean, sir."

So the captain was dead. Gregor grimaced. If PUSH wiggled loose from blame, the United States could tag Dean a traitor. "Leave him hanging, and have ET report as soon as he hits the ground. In the meantime, your top priority is finding out if Liberty is dead or alive."

Gregor removed his headset and poured himself a glass of milk. Dean being dead put a wrinkle in his plan. He had anticipated that the captain might lose his resolve, which was why he'd had the family abducted. But dead men can't cooperate, so now Faust didn't need Dean's family. His widow and children were useless, and they could be a liability, depending on how much Mrs. Dean knew about her husband's activities. Questioning thus far had proved that the woman had commendable stamina under torture, and she was totally ignorant of her husband's activities. Gregor supposed he should have her and her children eliminated to free up Bravo Team, which was guarding her. But Lance probably had no idea she was even missing... yet.

Watching the A-267 monitor, Gregor took a long swallow of cold milk. A group of frantic engineers were discussing possible actions they could take to halt the crisis. He felt a pang of sympathy for them. They were lost souls, too analytical to accept it, and Commander Conlee resolutely refused to bring in the system designer.

Smart man, Conlee.

On the monitor to the immediate left, locals tromped through the swamp, wearing miner's helmets with lights that cut streaks through the moonless night. A man's scream snared the others' attention and the observers stood mesmerized, watching an alligator clamp its powerful jaws around his left leg.

The man wasn't a Ballast member. He was American. Gregor harrumphed. Stupid bastard should have known it was feeding time. Their briefing had covered native wildlife.

These Americans were as weak-stomached as they were weak-willed. Gregor set his glass down on the desk. But David Lance wasn't weak-willed, and a diversion that divided his focus could prove beneficial. Gregor picked up the phone and dialed the *Washington Herald*.

When a woman answered, he affected an American, southern drawl thick enough to cut with a knife. "Evening, ma'am. I apologize for disturbing you, but is Sam Sayelle still there? I have some urgent information for him."

"He is in the building, sir, but he isn't at his desk. May I take a message?"

"Naw, I don't think Sam would appreciate hearing this in a note, but thank you kindly for the offer. If he isn't available, I'll just phone a friend of mine over at the *Post*."

"Wait," she said in a rush, clearly worried about sending someone with a hot tip to the *Herald*'s chief competitor. "Let me try to page Sam for you."

"Why, thank you so much. That would be very kind of you, ma'am." He smiled to himself and waited.

"Sam Sayelle. Line two. Urgent. Sam Sayelle. Line two. Urgent."

On his way to the parking garage, Sam heard the page and nodded at Sniffer. Fresh out of college, the kid was working double time, trying to make a name for himself. He had the nose. A little seasoning and he would be a helluva reporter. The *Herald*'s own Jimmy Olsen; only Sniffer wasn't stifled by ethical red tape or innocence. He didn't have Jimmy's innocuous appearance, either. Sniffer was built like a Mack truck: barrel-chested, well over six feet, dark coloring, and a face full of sharp angles. Not the kind of guy you want to meet in an alley late at night. "Can I use your phone, Sniffer?"

"Sure." At the desk, he turned to face his computer screen and give Sam a little privacy.

He propped the receiver with his shoulder and punched down line two. "Sayelle."

"Hey, buddy, I've got a hot one for you. You know the veep's plane went down, right?"

Who was this? The man talked as if Sam should know him, but he didn't. Yet he wasn't about to ask his name and blow a hot tip to hell and back. "I've heard." Who hadn't? It had been on the wire and plastered on every news channel around the world.

"They're saying she's dead, but who knows? Either way, that's not relevant."

Sam frowned. The second most powerful person in free-world government, and this genius claims her death isn't relevant? Sam hated the woman because she was a fraud pulling a snow job on the public, but hated or beloved, her death was noteworthy. "What is relevant?"

"It's connected. You'll have to put together how on your own. Ken Dean was piloting the plane. Word is, his wife and kids have disappeared. You might want to check that out."

"Disappeared—how?"

"Check it out, Sam. You'll be glad you did."

Now that he had been told the tip, Sam felt free to ask. "I'm sorry. I know I should recognize your voice, but I don't. Who is this?"

"What? You mean you don't even know who's talking to you?" The guy huffed, blowing static through the line. "I shoulda called my buddy at the *Post*." The line went dead.

Thoughtful, Sam bit his lower lip and hung up the phone. The PUSH caller. That's who he'd been.

Sniffer looked up at him. "You okay, Sam?"

"I'm fine." He could ignore the tip or call Conlee, but his sixth sense warned him not to mention it until he had checked it out himself. Not if he wanted to know if there was anything to it. When Sybil Stone was involved, only an idiot would take anything at face value or for granted. "Actually, I could use a little help. You busy?"

Buried neck-deep in files, Sniffer looked Sam straight in the eye. "No, sir."

"Find a home address on Ken and Linda Dean." Sam dialed police headquarters and spoke to Detective Karla Costillo. "Karla, it's me, Sam."

"I'm still pissed off at you."

He'd broken their last three dinner dates. "I'm sorry, and I'll eat all the humble pie you want to shovel my way later. Right now I need help."

Karla's reprimanding tone disappeared. "What's wrong?"

"I'm not sure," Sam admitted. "Anyone file a missing report on a family named Dean?"

"Hold on and I'll check."

"Thanks." This situation bothered Sam. Why had PUSH called him?

Karla came back on the line. "Nothing's been reported, Sam. If you want us to take a look, I need more info. Dean's a common name here."

He made the decision split second but didn't know why. "Probably just a crank call."

"Saturday night?" she asked, trying to set up their next dinner date.

"Eight o'clock."

"You'd better not break this one, Sam. Remember, I'm armed."

He smiled at her sass. He loved a little spunk and sass in a woman. "I won't."

Sam hung up the phone and looked at Sniffer. "Got that address?"

"Working on it." Scrolling through the *Herald's* accounts directory, Sniffer turned the subject. "I've picked up something interesting on Sybil Stone. You know how she used to walk to the Vietnam Wall every morning she was on the Hill?"

"Half of Washington walks by there, Sniffer. Get to the point, man."

"Half of Washington doesn't meet the same old man or

give him white, number-ten envelopes. He wears a black rumpled coat even when it's hot, Sam, and someone else is watching them and me."

Sam's stomach lurched and his curiosity slid into high gear. "Who's the old man? And what's in the envelope?"

"Working on both. I've noticed something weird that's made me more suspicious."

The entire envelope-passing affair was weird and suspicious. Was she disseminating classified information? Paying a blackmailer? "How long has she been meeting this guy?"

"About four months. I didn't give it any weight because the Secret Service had been right there with her. She's not hiding the meets or the envelopes from them."

"So what's weird that's made you more suspicious?"

Sniffer leaned closer. "When she's not on the Hill, the old man's a no-show, too."

"He knows she's going to be gone," Sam speculated. Strange. The Secret Service would have a fit at anyone having that kind of advance notice on her activities. She was setting herself up for a terrorist attack in a big way. "Who else is watching and following you?"

"A foreign guy about thirty. He's just started tagging us." Sniffer dragged a blunt fingertip down the computer screen. "Kenneth and Linda Dean, 2257 Hillside Drive."

"Let's go."

Sniffer grabbed his jacket. "I guess it doesn't really matter what the veep was doing at the Wall anymore. I mean, she's dead now, so what's the difference? The old man and the foreigner won't be back."

"*Is* she dead?" Between the PUSH caller about the Dean family and Sybil Stone's standing rendezvous with the old man in the rumpled coat, Sam had his doubts. The veep could be alive and well and up to her armpits in espionage or something equally sinister. She could have staged her death.

It wouldn't surprise Sam. Add Commander Conlee's transmissions to the equation, and she could be pulling anything.

Sam and Sniffer piled into Sniffer's van. It still had that new-car smell. Hell, Sam had no proof what he was doing for Conlee carried the weight or knowledge of the President. Conlee could be crooked, too.

Twenty minutes later they located Hillside Drive. It was a lazy winding road lined with old oaks, manicured lawns, and stately homes on wide lots. The Dean home was a three-story gray Victorian with forest-green trim. Lights from inside shone through sheer drapes on the first and second floors. The third floor was dark.

Sniffer pulled up to the curb and parked. "Should I wait here?"

"No, go watch the back door and make sure no one comes out."

"What if someone does?"

"Stop them from leaving." Sam got out of the van, walked up the bricked path to the front door, and then rang the bell.

No answer. He tried again. Still no answer.

Sayelle looked around and saw no one. Bushes rustled at the corner of the house. He stepped over and saw Sniffer's shoulder scraping against the shrubs.

"Sam, come with me to the back."

The high-pitched strain in Sniffer's voice had the hair on Sam's neck standing on edge. "What's up?"

"Something bad." Sniffer sucked in a sharp breath. "Back door's wide open."

"Did you see anyone?"

Sniffer shook his head. "But I think Mrs. Dean left in a hurry."

Sam walked inside, into the kitchen, then turned on the light. "Mrs. Dean? Anyone home?" He called out, but he didn't expect an answer. The house felt empty. A half-cooked meal stood on the stove. Pasta in a pot filled with water. Broccoli positioned on a cutting board, the knife set down beside it. A cookbook on the counter and an entire shelf packed with others under the cabinet.

"It looks like she turned the fire off on the stove and just walked out."

Sam tested the pasta pot for heat. The noodles had already been dropped into the water, but the pot felt cold. "Appears so." From all signs, she had left some time ago.

Sniffer checked the entry hall. "Uh-oh, really bad sign, Sam. Her purse is in here." He ducked back into the kitchen. "You know any woman who'd leave and not take her purse?"

Sam walked in and Sniffer pointed to a black handbag on a mahogany table. "Check the garage. See if her car is here."

He went out the back door and was back before Sam finished searching the downstairs. Nothing else seemed disturbed.

"Two cars in the garage. A Volvo and a Jeep."

Hers and Ken's, Sam figured. He walked through to the stairs. A boy's white sneaker was on the third step, and black scuff marks marred the wall. Linda Dean kept a clean house; she wouldn't tolerate scuff marks on her wall.

A bad feeling gelled in Sam's stomach. He left the stairs and moved down the hall. A doll with a frayed yellow dress that looked as if it had been wagged around a while lay facedown on the carpet. Not purposely positioned, but dropped. In a little girl's room—judging by the decor, maybe she was six or seven—the sickly feeling in his stomach melted and burned with dread. The bedspread was missing from her white canopy bed. In a room next door, obviously belonging to a boy a little older, Sam ran into the same thing—no bedspread.

He moved on to the master bedroom. Nothing disturbed there, but if this had been an abduction—it sure as hell felt like an abduction—and Linda Dean had been downstairs in the kitchen preparing dinner, there wouldn't be anything disturbed in the master bedroom. Burglary clearly wasn't the motive here. He lifted the phone. Dead. Whoever had done this had wanted the Deans, not their VCR and silver.

On a nightstand beside the bed, Sam spotted a family photo of Kenneth, Linda, and their two kids. His stomach churned. He didn't really know the man, but he had seen him around and he had briefly talked to Linda at a Christmas party once. Looking at that photo, the Deans looked like the all-American family, but Sam had an unshakable feeling they wouldn't be posing for any more photos.

His objectivity slipped and, distancing himself, he went back downstairs, avoiding looking at the doll and the tennis shoe.

Sniffer stood waiting near the kitchen door. "They were snatched."

"Yeah." The muscles in Sam's neck coiled into knots. He rubbed at them, pulled out his cell phone, and got Karla on the line. "The call wasn't bogus." The PUSH claim was credible. He had to warn Conlee—after Karla claimed jurisdiction.

The shelf of cookbooks caught his eye—one brown book in particular. He pulled it out. "Journal" was written on its front. Highly unlikely anything written in a woman's journal would give him any insight. He shoved the book back into its place on the shelf.

Sniffer looked at Sam. "This is what your hot tip was about, right?"

"Yeah." A bad taste filled Sam's mouth and a bad feeling came with it that Linda Dean and her kids were in serious trouble. If this was a typical abduction, there would be damage, signs of a struggle. There would be some evidence of serious resistance by Linda, and there wasn't. So she had either known her abductors or she had been blindsided. The alarm system was armed; the red light still glowed. So why hadn't the monitoring service called the cops? They would have...unless someone had circumvented the system.

Fear shot up his backbone. Pros staged the abduction. "Sniffer, check the box and see if the phone wires on the alarm were cut or bypassed."

"You got it."

Minutes later Sniffer was back at the door. "They were—hey, you okay, Sam? You look a little green around the gills."

Stone herself could have done this. Maybe Dean knew too much. Maybe snatching his family was Sybil's insurance. Maybe Conlee was doing her dirty work—

"Sam? What's wrong with you, man?"

He was pissed. Disillusioned, and cynical as hell. "I'm fine." Sam walked outside, toward the van. "You know, Sniffer, sometimes this job really sucks."

"Sometimes every job sucks." Sniffer stuffed his fists in his pockets, stared down the street. "Do you think somebody was bleeding the veep?"

Blackmail was a possibility. So was treason. "Maybe." Cap Marlowe needed to know about this. The caller had said there was a connection. Maybe he could shed a little light for Sam. "What have you gotten so far on the old man at the Wall?"

"Nothing." Sniffer snorted his frustration. "It's like he comes out of nowhere. I've tried shadowing him. Usually I'm good at it, but he's better."

"But you are working on it." Sam leaned against the van's front fender.

"Yeah. I hired a skateboarder to track him. I figured he wouldn't notice a kid. But the veep's gone now. When she's gone, he never goes to the Wall."

He was a pro. Being good kept him alive. "Find out who he is and what's in the envelopes, and I'll see to it Edison moves you upstairs." Sniffer wanted that promotion in the worst way.

"You got it." He looked so young Sam thought he could pose as the skateboarding teen. "This Dean abduction is wired into the veep, isn't it?"

"Yeah." How, Sayelle didn't know . . . yet.

A cop car drove down the street, heading toward them. "Let's move." Sam crawled into the van and let his mind drift. Since her divorce, Sybil Stone had appeared to be squeaky clean, but she had to be leaking critical information. When the news broke on whatever it was, Cap would feel vindicated. *Lance bypassed me for a woman, and she's a damn traitor.*

That bothered Sam. He'd made no bones about not liking the veep, but he'd watched her closely for the past year. She had lied about her medical condition, but she played straight on her job. Even a fool had to admit that she loved her country. Her committing treason just didn't fit. Her Secret Service guards knew she met the old man at the Wall; they were with her when she did it. Yet the odds of her passing inconsequential, personal correspondence were about zip. So she had either duped the Secret Service, or they were in on whatever she was doing.

If Westford were still guarding her, Sam could buy into that. He was a straight arrow, but he was also nuts about the woman. Problem was, he wasn't guarding her anymore. Yet she could still be a traitor. It was possible. Hell, in the past five years on the Hill, Sam had seen it all. *Anything* was possible. But to levy charges, he needed proof.

Maybe it was the journalist in him, the training on ethics he had learned at home and had reinforced at Marcus Gilbert's knee. Or maybe the reason had nothing to do with journalism but everything to do with that damn spark of idealism in him that wouldn't die. His inbred penchant for fairness, a commitment to truth, and Sam wasn't so sure looking in the mirror without those things would be easy for any man, much less a man who still saw reflections of that fresh-faced kid he once had been.

Whatever the reason, at this point, Sam couldn't call Sybil Stone a traitor—or deny that she could be one. Whatever she was passing the old man in those envelopes concerned Sam and, he had to admit, intrigued him. This Dean business concerned him, too. Kenneth was away from home because he was piloting Sybil Stone's plane. Now his family had been abducted by pros. The two events had to be connected.

When Sniffer turned into the *Herald*'s parking lot, Sam decided what he had to do. "Drop me off at my car, will you?"

"Sure thing."

Sam switched cars, cranked his engine, and then pulled out his phone and dialed a number he had memorized years ago. A man answered, his voice thick with sleep. "Cap, it's me, Sam." He stared through the windshield, wishing he had already unraveled this damn mess and knowing in his gut he had just scratched the surface. "We need to talk."

"Now? It's the middle of the night."

"Captain Dean's family has been abducted, it looks like your favorite politician could be involved, and she might be committing treason."

"But she's dead—"

"*Is* she dead? Do you have verification on that?"

"The White House has never gone to the press on a death without verification."

"Does that mean they didn't this time?"

Cap paused. "Give me fifteen minutes."

"I'll be waiting."

★　★　★

The next morning he'd had a bitch of a meeting.

Cap left the White House and got into his waiting limousine. "Back to the office, Dayton," he told his driver, then raised the privacy glass between them. Cap had relayed Sam's credible evidence against Sybil and the events at the

Wall, but the president hadn't reacted as Marlowe had hoped. Rather than launching an investigation, he'd scoffed. The misguided ass was bat-blind when it came to Sybil Stone, and he had been angry at Cap for merely raising the possibility of her committing treason. He hadn't believed it or even considered it possible. But this was far from over, and whatever blinded Lance to Sybil Stone's flaws didn't really matter. Sam would get hard evidence of her treason and bring it to Cap. And when he did, Cap would take it public and shove the truth down Lance's throat.

The chat with Richard Barber hadn't gone any better. What he'd said seemed distant and unimportant, and yet Cap sensed a warning in it that had him sweating bullets. Maybe Lance's questions hadn't been as innocent as they had seemed. Maybe he hadn't believed Sybil was capable of treason, but he felt *someone* close to him was capable. Combining Lance's questions and Barber's hints, it was pretty clear that someone had breached security at A-267. Cap went stone cold. Had Lance learned about the key? Could he believe Cap had committed treason?

He should have reported the damn thing. But he hadn't done it then, and it was too late to do it now. Putting the key in his safe and not investigating had been a huge mistake. He had to salvage this situation before it cost him the nomination. The question was, how?

Traffic backed up. Dayton tapped the steering wheel, watching the light and the cute brunette in a Volvo in the next lane. Cap debated, then called Austin Stone. He designed the security systems for the damn things. He would be able to tell Cap if the key was to an ICBM launch system. As soon as Barber had mentioned a terrorist attack, Cap had known the two matters—the ICBM terrorist attack and the key—were connected. Thankfully, Barber didn't know about the key, or he would have already connected the two and Cap would be sunk.

Austin answered the phone on the third ring. "Stone."

"I need your advice." Traffic was moving again. "Can you meet me at my office?"

"Sure. I'll be right over."

"Thanks." Cap disconnected the line, hoping to hell he wasn't compounding one error with another. But finding out what the key fit was critical. God help him, it really could have come from Gregor Faust or PUSH or any of the other seventeen terrorist groups now claiming responsibility for taking down Sybil Stone's plane.

Cap had considered it. He had even let fear convince him that Faust, the most dangerous of the slimy bunch, had set him up, and he'd made it easy for the man to do it. But Cap hadn't really believed it. His speculation had just been one of those worst-case scenario nightmares you weave in your mind that scares the hell out of you but is never real.

Except for this time.

Faust choosing Cap made perfect sense. He was slated to become president. Faust would let him—then use the key connection between them to blackmail Cap. A U.S. President with direct ties to Ballast? He'd be impeached before the ink on his arrest warrant dried.

Clammy all over, Cap broke into a cold sweat, feeling worse than in any diabetic sugar crash he had ever suffered. How could he ever explain not reporting a key from Gregor Faust?

This entire problem was Sybil Stone's fault. If she had demanded her security staff do its job well, then no one would have been able to plant a bomb on her plane that could explode and there wouldn't be this mess of the key to bury. Once again, her ineptitude had put him in a bad position. *Damn her. Damn her straight to hell.*

Chapter Ten

Friday, August 9 ★ First-Strike Launch: 40:00:00

Hell had to be like this.

The Florida swamp wasn't all fire and brimstone, but it was definitely a place where those condemned to being in it suffered abject misery.

Crashing down from an adrenaline high, Sybil stared at Westford's back and wrung out her jacket hem, chiding herself for not sucking it up and focusing on her mission. The truth was, she was exhausted, and like everyone else, when exhausted, she gave in to moments of weariness and feeling overwhelmed. The weather wasn't helping.

They had walked all night, and she had insisted Jonathan take back his coat, which meant she had been soaked to the skin and chilled to the bone ever since. The persistent rain had pelted her goose bumps nonstop, and every prick stung like a stab. A couple of hours ago dawn finally had broke and ushered in muggy heat, but the rain still hadn't stopped. Neither had the bugs. Mosquitoes and some kind of gnats constantly swarmed them. Her bites had bites. So did Westford's, which had her thinking godawful thoughts about wicked mosquito-borne diseases, like the West Nile virus and eastern equine encephalitis.

God, she was miserable. Tired and sore, and her poor feet would never be the same. And hungry. Good God, but she was hungry. And scared to death. Scared they wouldn't get back to Washington in time to prevent the Code One threat from causing widespread devastation and destruction. Scared her favorite warmongers, Peris and Abdan, would leave the Grand Palace without a peace agreement, go home, and start blowing each other off the map. Scared the terrorists would find her and Westford and kill them and the briefcase would be lost in the swamp forever. And scared Westford would notice she was scared and she'd be forced to admit it out loud. He had a habit of making her look at things about herself that she'd rather not see, and once she admitted the fear out loud, it would be strong *and* real, and it would sink its talons into her so deeply that she'd never again draw a breath free from it.

Don't let it win, Sybil. You've beaten insurmountable odds before and you can do it again. You have to do it again. You're responsible for their lives. You can't let them down.

She stiffened her spine and scanned the terrain, determined to find something that didn't strike her as hellish. Near a creek, cranes sat perched on low-slung limbs and dipped for minnows, and on the bank, a beautiful red hibiscus bent nearly horizontal, struggling to find sun. When she returned her gaze to Westford's back, she grudgingly admitted finding the most hellish thing of all. If she had to be miserable and scared stiff—she swatted at a bug breakfasting on her forearm—couldn't she at least be too scared to notice that she hadn't forgotten how good a well-built man looked when he was caught in the rain and his clothes were hugging his body?

Ridiculous, unacceptable, and damn neurotic thoughts, Sybil. This isn't a man; it's Westford, for God's sake.

The stupidity in that remark had her muffling a groan. What woman wouldn't notice Westford? But, by God, she had been trained from the cradle to deal with extreme circumstances, and she could deal with him. Okay, so he had earned her admiration and respect, but until she was out of public office, neither of those things made him any less off-limits than any other man. She'd given the president her word. That made any and all men off-limits. Not that she wanted a man, with or without limits. Especially a man she hated liking who made her feel and see things she didn't want to feel and see, and who got to her. After the ordeal with Austin, what woman in her right mind would want that? She wanted her career. Just her career. In it, she mattered. She made a difference. But Westford's kisses, and him holding her . . . Okay, okay, she'd liked it. Hell, she'd loved it. But he was definitely off-limits; any relationship between them had disaster written all over it.

The briefcase bumped against her thigh, a nagging reminder. She wanted her country, the people counting on her, to be safe. That's what she had to focus on accomplishing.

With renewed determination, she checked the sky. Dark clouds, heavy with rain, and no signs of a break. "Does it always rain here?"

"No, we just ran into a band from the tropical storm," Westford said without looking back. "It's stalled out until midday. Maybe a little longer."

Responding to that great news with a groan she didn't bother to muffle, she stumbled over a tree root, slipped in the slick mud, and went down on one knee.

Westford lifted her back to her feet. "Wait." He blocked the noise with his cupped hand at his ear. "Incoming."

She stopped beside him and waited, absently plucking off bits of bramble and leaves clinging to his shirt and tossing them to the ground.

Jonathan smiled at her, and the light in his eyes was

the nicest compliment she'd ever received. Swearing she wouldn't do it, she smiled back.

"Maybe you'll get this. I don't." He deciphered then relayed a portion of the radio message.

She deciphered it. "Cap Marlowe met with David this morning. He stepped on the seal on the floor in the Oval Office."

"That I got," Jonathan said. "But what does he mean about the eagle, olive branch, and arrows?"

"Normally the eagle's head points to the olive branch. By Sunday, it could be changed to one where the head points to the arrows. It's a symbol. The U.S. is at war."

"Cap feels we'll be at war by Sunday." Surprise flickered over Jonathan's face. "But how the hell could he know that?"

"Good question. Unfortunately, I don't have a good answer. Neither does David."

The wind picked up and communications shut down. "Maybe when the feeder band blows over he'll have one."

Hoping so, she started walking.

They moved on and soon picked up the rhythm they'd held most of the night. Walking in the dark hadn't been easy. Only God knew what had been out there walking with them. At least during the day, she could see what she was stumbling over and what was about to attack her. That planted second thoughts in her mind. Maybe the darkness had been a blessing.

"How are your feet holding up?"

They hurt like hell. Bruised, scraped, and cut from sharp stones and twigs and roots, and some kind of little round stickers that kept poking through Westford's socks and jabbing into her soles. "We can't stop anymore. We've got less than forty hours." She avoided mentioning her mincemeat feet. He'd insist on carrying her, and she knew by the set of his shoulder, he had been hurt more than he had admitted in his parachuteless landing. "As soon as we get the Code One resolved, I'm going to take a luscious hot shower and then soak in a bath for a sinfully long time." Until every muscle in her body stopped burning and she didn't feel bone-less any more. Maybe then she wouldn't be tempted to tie knots in her knees to stay upright. "And then I'm going to eat so much lasagna and garlic bread I'll speak Italian."

"You already speak Italian."

"Latin, French, and Spanish. No Italian," she cor-rected him. "You're welcome to join me in the feast, West-ford. We'll single-handedly stabilize the pasta economy. After we eat, we'll drink wine and celebrate our success on the mission, and maybe we'll drink enough to forget being rain-sodden and weary and—and..."

"And what?" His voice sounded softer, gentler.

She shrugged to hide the hollow ache in her chest. "I was going to say until we get past the pain of mourning our dead. But that will take longer, won't it?"

"Yeah," he said. "It will."

"Do you think they suffered?" A knot wedged in her throat, and she couldn't seem to swallow it down. She hated the vulnerability she heard in her voice, but she had been responsible for those people and now they were dead. She'd failed to protect them, and wondering if they had suf-fered was driving her insane.

He stopped and turned back to face her. "I imagine the shooting scared them, but the explosion—well, it was over fast. They didn't suffer, Sybil. Truthfully, they probably never knew what hit them."

She looked up at him, blinking hard to hold back tears that had come out of nowhere. "I thought that, and I'd hoped hearing it would make me feel better." Her chin trembled, and she clamped down, stiffened it. "Why doesn't it make me feel better?"

Empathy and understanding shone in his eyes. He cupped her jaw and dropped a chaste kiss to her forehead. "Because they're dead and we're alive."

Survivor's guilt. Just as she'd had when her parents had

died. "Yes." Westford understood. And he felt what she felt. Because that comforted her and it shouldn't, and because right now, when she needed to remain self-contained to be effective and she needed comforting, she pulled away, jerked a branch, then let it go, triggering memories of those who had died. At least they had been blessed with families and friends and people who would mourn them. She didn't have a family. Not anymore. "Westford, if we had died with the others, who would mourn you?"

"No one." He started walking.

Her chest tight, she stared at his back and followed. "Are your parents dead, too?"

"My mother is dead." He didn't look at her. "My father's in jail."

"Jail?" That surprised her. Westford was a stickler for law and order. She had assumed he'd gotten that from his parents, but apparently not. "I'm sorry."

"It's one of those things, Sybil," he said, decidedly uncomfortable. "My mother used to say my father marched to a different drummer."

Interesting choice of words. "What do you say?"

"I don't. Tobias Westford wasn't a man I could look up to and respect. He never bought what he could borrow and never borrowed what he could steal. I haven't seen him in twenty years, but I keep tabs on him."

A top-secret security clearance made that essential. "We can't choose our relatives, and mine were no better. My mother never had a clue who I was or what motivated me." No one in her life had understood her, and damn few had even tried, including Austin.

Westford grunted, definitely skeptical. "What motivated her?"

"Money." Sybil grimaced. "Hardly flattering, but true. She was a good woman, in her own way. We were just very different kinds of people."

Jonathan paused beside a tall pine to get his bearings. "So you were closer to your dad, then?"

"Actually, I wasn't. I loved them both, but Dad . . . well, I think I always disappointed him. No matter what I did, he expected better."

"You gave him better."

She pegged Jonathan with a nonplussed look. "He expected more."

"So who would mourn you?"

"Gabby." Sybil swatted at a mosquito feasting on her cheek. "The first time I met her, I knew we'd be friends forever." A flash of that meeting in the college dorm replayed in Sybil's mind. "She's a complex woman with a good heart. She would mourn."

"Yeah, Gabby would," he agreed. "David would mourn you, too, Sybil."

"That's different. He's my mentor, and as much as I care about him, he isn't family."

A squirrel jumped from one tall pine to another. It seemed crazy, especially for a woman her age, but it hurt in a thousand little ways to be orphaned. She hated not being anyone's little girl anymore.

"It would have been nice if your parents could have been there for you during the divorce."

Boy, was he off the mark. "I'm glad we were all spared that."

"Catholic?"

"No, wealthy." She kept her gaze fixed on the ground. "My family doesn't do divorce. In divorces, you divide property and assets. That's not acceptable."

"Would you have done it—gotten divorced—if they had still been alive?"

"Positively. They would have made me eat dirt the rest of my life, but *nothing* could have stopped me from divorcing Austin Stone."

Westford pursed his lips, thoughtful, and for a split

second something resembling guilt flashed in his eyes. What brought that on?

He stared off in the distance. "Maybe Gabby would mourn for me, too."

That surprised her. "Are you and Gabby close?"

"We talk," he said. "Well, she talks. I mostly listen."

"That's Gabby." Had she been playing her matchmaker-from-hell routine with him, too? God, Sybil hoped not. The thought chilled her.

They had met while Westford was guarding Sybil and occasionally had talked on the phone. Apparently they still did. Maybe she knew why he had transferred and left Sybil. "Considering what we have to do"—she glanced down at the briefcase that bumped her thigh with every step—"I'm glad we're alive. But we won't be for long if we don't pick up the pace."

"Right." His lip curled. He knew she needed to get away from old pains and strong emotions. Focusing on her job would give her that.

They walked on, and, for the first time, she found herself wondering. How many times had Westford seen his friends and coworkers die? Men like Harrison and Cramer. And how many times had he hurt from the bone out and felt unable to mourn?

His work was high risk, so probably more often than one would think. And knowing he'd taken in all that grief and held it inside created an almost overwhelming need in her to touch him, to soothe and comfort and ease the ravages left by layers of grief and pain.

"Heads up." He snagged her attention. "It's slick through here."

The ground had grown more marshy, the sand and mud softer and more slick. And the rain persisted. So did the high humidity and the damnable August heat. How could anyone stand to live here? The place had its own kind of beauty, but the weather made it hell.

"Let's stop and rest for a few minutes. We've got a long day in front of us."

"We can't," she said, fighting panic. Her defenses were too weak to risk a confrontation with the kissing-and-holding or not-kissing-and-holding dilemma. "Time is too precious."

"Look, you're so tired you're about to fall down."

"Let's just keep going, okay? If I stop, I'll sleep. If I sleep, I'll have nightmares that we need a few more minutes later and I wasted them sleeping."

"What is going to happen on the other end, Sybil? What's this phantom deadline and security breach all about? And what's in that damn case?"

It was time he knew the truth. They could die here, and if they did, he deserved to at least know why. "A key," she said. Her eyes filmed over and she blinked hard to keep the tears in her heart from falling. "Just one little key."

Westford frowned. "One little key to what?"

"An ICBM at A-267." There wasn't a doubt in her mind that Westford knew all about intercontinental ballistic missiles and A-267, an installation that housed and operated so much sensitive information and technology the site itself had been classified top secret.

"Are you telling me someone has activated an ICBM inside A-267?"

It had sounded horrible the first time she had heard it from David, and it sounded even more horrible now with seven deaths attributed to it. The terror she felt inside shone back at her in Westford's eyes. "Yes," she whispered with tragic reverence.

"And the only key to disarm it is in that case?" He pointed with his index finger.

She nodded.

"Do we know who infiltrated the site?"

"Not yet." She swallowed hard. "We're working on it."

"Without the key—"

"The ICBM launches."

"We can't shut it down?"

"Not at this time. The launch sequence has been re-configured and the stealth system that would allow us to re-capture control and deactivate has been disabled."

"Can't we just enable it again?"

"Not without blowing up A-267, Washington, and most of the surrounding states."

Westford shoved his hands deep into his pockets in frustration. "The missile. Is it a Minuteman?"

Didn't they all wish it were? "It's a Peacekeeper, West-ford." The deadliest of all missiles in the world. In thirty minutes, a Peacekeeper could take out a small country.

He blew out a long breath, raked his fingers through his dripping hair. "The eagle and arrows—the UN is blow-ing its cork."

She nodded, revealing that the transmission he had been unable to decipher had been multilayered. "Any launch will be considered a hostile attack. Some of the members have already put us on notice. You can't blame them. That position is essential to their own countries' se-curity. If the missile launches, they will retaliate."

The color leaked from his face. He understood. No world leader would jeopardize his own country's security and trust the United States' word that a launch couldn't be avoided. Our allies were about to become our enemies.

"Where's it going?"

"Before we left Geneva, to North Korea. Currently it's China. Apparently, at random intervals, the target cycles to new destinations."

Westford snatched at a thorny vine clinging to his pant leg, a deep furrow creasing the skin between his eyebrows. An armadillo scooted away, hid in the underbrush. "The bastards are deliberately trying to trigger World War III."

"I'd give up my office to be able to dispute that," Sybil said, and meant it. "But I can't."

The skin beneath Westford's left eye twitched and his expression turned even grimmer. "You said we have to get back by Saturday night. Exactly how long do we have?"

She didn't bother checking her watch. The crystal had broken during their fall. It wasn't working. The terrorists had given them seventy-two hours. She swallowed a bitter knot of fear. "Midnight Saturday."

Westford glanced at his watch then dragged his palm along his square jaw. The stubble scraped against his hand. She had been given seventy-two hours to save the world. Tough enough. But now they had just forty hours and they were still stuck in the swamp without transportation. "What happens if we don't get there?"

Sybil kept her voice steady. "The missile launches, and whoever it's targeting then, and their allies, strike back."

Jonathan absorbed that with a sharp breath. "Well, then. We'd better tend to your feet and get moving."

"My feet are fine."

"Don't waste time fighting me on this. You're going to lose."

She frowned at him and sat down on a tree stump. "You've got an attitude, Westford."

"Terrible character flaw. I'll work on it."

She lifted her hand to his face. "Don't."

He smiled, turned and soaked his shirt in the creek, and then washed and inspected her feet. "Damn, Sybil. They're raw." He grimaced. "Why didn't you tell me they were this bad?"

"I didn't know it." She settled for a half-truth. "I can't see through muddy socks, either."

Not at all amused, he crouched down, then wrapped his shirt around her left foot as a makeshift bandage. "Give me your slip."

"I'd rather not."

He held out his hand. "I know, but we're not moving until you do."

"Why?"

"Infection. There are things out here you don't want in your system."

Facing him in bare feet wasn't bad enough? Now she had to put her slip in his hands?

Crouched, he braced his arms on his knees. "The only other option we've got is my pants. You choose."

Damn him and his logic. She stood up, reached under her skirt, and then pulled down the scrap of silk and lace and passed it to him.

He didn't look at her, just focused on the task, then put his socks on over the bandages. She thought she might just love him for that small mercy.

"That's the best we can do for now." He stood up, turned, and then cut through the dense brush.

Sybil rushed to catch up, forced herself to thank him.

He ignored her. "If you can, stay in my footsteps. Two sets double the odds of us attracting enemy attention and make us easier to track."

God, but she hated the sound of that. She rolled the waistband of her skirt, shortening the length to mid-thigh. That gave her more freedom to stretch her stride, but matching his steps would still require work. Batting at the million mosquitoes swarming her did, too.

He glanced back, raised an eyebrow, and mumbled something about his transmitter. He'd tinkered with it at dawn, and, intermittently since then, he had been receiving weird, nonsensical messages that she couldn't decipher. He'd only transmitted once: a coded message about swamp buses, kids skipping school, and seniors at a rest stop.

"Why haven't you transmitted more messages from us?" she asked.

"Because I can't control who receives them."

Home Base *and* the terrorists. Considering his caution

wise, she crossed a ledge with a deep dropoff on both sides, carefully monitoring his steps. He cupped his hand to his ear. Must be getting another update. "Is it Conlee?"

"No, Sayelle. Like the others. Bleed-over and coded."

That Conlee had pulled Sayelle into this still set her teeth on edge. "What's he saying?"

"Still feeding in. Give me a second."

Something flew close, swooped low—a bird? Sybil ducked, misstepped, and landed on a sharp stone. Pain shot through her foot, her leg. Her knee gave way and she lost her balance, fell down a steep incline.

Every roll through the thorny brush clinging to the walls of the dropoff brought fresh pain to old bruises and sharp stabs that promised to leave new ones. She grabbed for a bush, curled her fingers around its leaves, but her forward momentum proved stronger than her grip. She clutched at another bush. Her arm jerked, nearly tearing loose from its socket, yet again she couldn't sustain her hold. Head over heels, she slid and tumbled farther and farther down. A large rock stabbed into her side. Searing pain streaked through her armpit, her shoulder, up her neck, across her chest, down her right side, and suddenly there was nothing underneath her. She free-fell, and fell, and finally dropped into something that splashed. The abrupt halt knocked the wind out of her.

Stunned, she struggled to grab a breath, to stay conscious, to see if the briefcase remained intact and where she had landed. Gritty brown muck, dank and thick, surrounded her. In it, nothing grew. Sludge. Slushy sludge . . . *Oh, God.* "Jonathan!"

The man-made ledge was a solid twenty feet above her. He stood on a huge, protruding rock, staring down at her, and the horror on his face confirmed her worst fears. She hadn't fallen into water.

She'd fallen into quicksand.

Chapter Eleven

Dark circles, sunken eyes; apparently everyone had had a rough night.

What had kept Cap awake? Austin Stone sat down on a visitor's chair in front of the senator's desk. Sybil being dead or alive wouldn't do it, though Cap wouldn't be sorry to learn she was dead. Certain of that, Austin found this summons even more mysterious. Cap rarely scheduled appointments before eleven. "Morning."

"Morning." Cap waited for Jean to set down their coffee cups and leave the office. When she closed the door, he went on. "This is a damned awkward situation with Sybil, Austin. I'm not sure what to say. Are you grieving or celebrating?"

"Neither, yet. I'm going insane, waiting for final word on whether or not she's dead."

"I met with President Lance this morning. It's genuine. He's grieving."

An even earlier meeting? This was serious. "For Sybil, or for the others?"

"I think for Sybil." Cap sipped from his cup. His hand trembled. "There's no sense in pussyfooting around. Is there anything in Sybil's past that would leave her open to blackmail?"

Austin didn't need to reminisce to respond, but Cap expected serious consideration, so he gave it. His life would have been easier if there had been something he could have used as leverage to wrestle controlling interest in Secure Environet from her clutches. But even the best detectives money could buy hadn't been able to find a thing on her.

Her refusal to sell him the stock baffled him and them. The divorce had been final for over a year, but she still wouldn't sell or revoke that damned blind trust. One thing everyone agreed on was that money never had motivated Sybil. She'd always had more than she could spend, and she spent judiciously—mostly funding charities that helped kids anonymously.

When Sybil was eighteen, her parents had crossed paths with a couple of lions on safari in Africa and lost. Being an only child, she had inherited their fortune. Before marrying, she had made some wise investments and had earned a second fortune. Her stock in Secure Environet wasn't essential to her financial stability, it only added to the heap. Instead of being a member of the "have" class, his bitch of an ex-wife was one of the "have mores." Austin had known she was filthy rich, but who could have predicted she'd be an ambitious, bleeding heart who wanted nothing more than to do altruistic things? Such a waste.

Austin had brought his own fortune to the marriage, though most of his assets had been on paper. Since then he had secured sufficient Department of Defense contracts for his security devices and systems to make him an extremely wealthy man. He also had done well at selling his secure-system devices to the private corporate sector, though they only accounted for about 17 percent of Environet's gross income. The rest came from contracts only Austin knew existed—contracts facilitated through Gregor Faust. Austin had been in a position to buy back Sybil's stock for years, but she had consistently refused to sell. Even his divorce attorney hadn't found out why, and the judge had refused to order her to cite her reasons. Stone couldn't force her to sell, short of murdering her. He felt certain her decision had nothing to do with spite; she wasn't built that way.

"Austin?" Cap cast him a questioning look.

"I'd have to say blackmail is extremely unlikely. There's nothing hidden in her past that could be used against her. Not that I've been able to uncover."

Cap frowned. "Then why has she been passing envelopes to an old man at the Vietnam Wall every morning? Any insight on that?"

"You suspect her of treason?" Austin chuckled.

Cap didn't appreciate the humor. Deep creases lined his face, nose to mouth. "It's possible."

"It's outrageous, Cap." Austin shifted on his seat. "Trust me. The only thing Sybil allows herself to love is this country. She's a bitch, a pain in the ass, and she might do a lot of things, but committing treason just isn't one of them."

"So you have no insight to offer, then?"

"Only that whoever told you she's crossed over is wrong." Austin's mind whirled. What exactly was going on here? The senator wasn't sharing information, he was on a fishing expedition. "She wouldn't do anything that even gave the appearance of any wrongdoing." That was a safe bet. Otherwise he wouldn't be crippled by her damn blind trust. "Think about it, Cap. Sybil? Jeopardize her precious career?"

"I agree that she wouldn't, but she is giving him something, damn it." The deep lines crept up his face and creased

Cap's forehead, and the tremor in his hand grew stronger. He set his steaming cup down. It chinked against its saucer. "Odds are slim he's blackmailing her over anything like a secret lover."

A lover? Sybil? The senator might permanently employ half the PIs in D.C. to dig up everything possible on her. He might have moles inside the White House and the inside track to her office through a source he refused to name. But for all his information, Cap Marlowe still didn't know Sybil at all. Not at all. "Zero odds on that."

Cap hiked a gray brow. "Is that your opinion, or Richard Barber's?"

"It's mine and Winston's, actually." Austin revealed a secondary White House source.

"Winston? I thought Barber was your inside contact."

"He is, and he agrees with us. She lives like a nun. No lovers, no discreet liaisons, no occasional dates. Not even an escort to professional functions."

Cap picked up a paper clip, flipped it end for end. "Is she a lesbian?"

"No evidence of that, either." Stone sighed. To maintain credibility with Cap, he had to give a balanced view, though defending Sybil irritated him. "For the past year, she's had nothing that could even loosely be termed a personal relationship."

"That's abnormal."

"It's her fulfilling a promise," Austin said, passing along White House, grapevine gossip. "When she filed for the divorce, she made Lance some promise about her personal conduct. Her only regular contact is with Gabby Kincaid. They still phone each other twice a month."

"Who the hell is Gabby Kincaid?" Cap shoved aside a stack of files, centered his cup on his desk blotter.

"Gabrielle Kincaid," Austin said. "She's a judge down in Florida, a righteous do-gooder like Sybil. They were roommates in college."

"Any evidence of a relationship between her and Sybil?"

"Oh, yes." And Austin had hated both of them for it, for making him feel like an outsider who would never be invited in. "A strong friendship—more like sisters. But nothing romantic, if that's what you're asking."

"So this Gabby could be involved in the Wall business."

"I have no reason to believe that, but if Sybil's ass is in a jam and she calls for help, Gabby is the only person she would call. And maybe Westford," he amended. "But to call anyone, she'd have to feel she had no other option." Sybil had always been maddeningly independent. That was one of her worst traits.

"Unless she's dead."

Austin agreed. "Unless she's dead."

Cap digested and seemed to have heartburn from the results. He paused a moment, as if working through something in his mind. "Before I discuss anything more, I want you to know that I'm counting on your complete discretion."

Finally they were getting to the reason Cap had summoned him. Austin had been feeding him information to use against Sybil since she had been elected and had forced him into putting their assets into that blind trust. Most of Austin's Department of Defense contracts were approved by the Armed Services Committee, which Cap chaired. Nothing in the defense budget got through appropriations without his seal of approval. Hadn't Austin continued to feed Cap inside information on Sybil through his White House associates? By this time, shouldn't his discretion be a moot point? It should be, but Cap evidently needed reassurance, so Austin gave it to him. "Discretion is a given between us."

"Almost everyone thinks Sybil is dead." From the flat line of Cap's lips, he could say more, but didn't. "I'd have to see her body to be convinced."

So would Austin.

Cap tossed the paper clip onto his desk, stood up, and then opened his combination lock wall safe. "Something else is going on here. Maybe you can help me figure it out."

Austin memorized the tumbles: *Twenty. Six. Forty.* "I'll do what I can."

"I'm counting on that." Marlowe withdrew an envelope, removed a silver key.

Austin's heart skipped a beat, then plummeted. He couldn't believe what he was seeing. "What is that?"

"I'm hoping you can tell me." Marlowe passed the key.

Austin took it, stunned and furious and doing his damnedest to keep his voice noncommittal. "I'm not sure," he lied. He knew exactly what kind of key he held in his palm.

"Can you find out what it's for, or what it opens?" Cap stood rigid, as if a sharp movement would crack his spine. "I need to know."

Stone looked up at Cap. "Where did you get this?"

"I don't know." Marlowe blinked hard. "A messenger from Ground Serve delivered it, but when Jean checked, they had no record of a delivery to my office."

"When was this?" Austin struggled to keep his tone civil.

Cap hesitated, as if debating the wisdom of telling him. "Two months ago."

"*Two months?*" Austin's stomach furled and cold rage seeped out of his every pore.

"I didn't report it." Cap smacked the heel of his fist against the back of his chair.

By regulation, the report was mandatory. "Why not?"

"Because I didn't know who sent the damn thing, what it was to, or why I'd received it."

Austin could enlighten the man. He knew the answers to Cap's questions only too well. And his knowing changed everything.

Sybil could be alive.

Faust, the double-crossing son of a bitch, was going to regret this. Everyone was going to regret this. He was sick of people putting the screws to him; as sick of it as he had been of living in Sybil's shadow. He wanted power, and, by God, he would have it. "I see."

"You really don't. Not yet." Cap sank down in his chair, swiveled to face Austin. "A couple hours after the delivery, Jean took an anonymous call. What the man said was unusual enough that she felt I should speak to him personally. I don't know who he was, but he said that when the time came, I'd know what to do with the key."

"And you think the time has come now?"

Cap nodded. "I haven't been officially notified, but I've had some people checking on why Lance pulled Sybil out of the peace talks and ordered her return."

"Media reports say the talks broke down." Including Cap's friend, Sam Sayelle.

"My ass, they broke down." Cap leaned forward over his desk. "If talks had broken down, Lance would be on his way to Geneva. No one, including the UN, wants a damn world war. Peris and Abdan both have nukes. What nation is going to sit with its thumb up its ass and wait to see if they use them?"

None. No nation could afford to be wrong. "But the diplomats haven't left Geneva. Maybe they're waiting for Lance to bury Sybil and then go over." That seemed logical—provided Sybil was dead.

"You're hearing the public version. But give it the litmus test. There haven't been any significant changes in Lance's schedule. Nothing's happened to lead anyone to believe he's going anywhere. No one else has been rushed to Geneva to take her place at the table. And no one is talking about why she left the table and was on that plane in the first place." Cap rocked forward in his chair, intense. "The reports are hype."

"So why are Peris and Abdan's premiers waiting in Geneva?"

"Chocolate chip cookies and milk." Cap looked totally disgusted. "And a daily dose of guilt."

That response Austin hadn't expected. "What?"

"Sybil's having cookies and warm milk sent to them and a message that the children are depending on them to find a peaceful solution to their challenges. Guilt is enormously powerful, and, as I hear it, she's given them solid reasons to pause and reconsider, if not enough to assure that they stay and wait for her return." Cap pursed his lips. "But she also ordered everyone possible off her flight. She even classified Grace as unessential, which had her pissed to the gills until she heard the plane crashed." Cap gave him a knowing look. "Not too wise, to piss off staffers. They'll bury you—especially dinosaurs like Grace. She's been on the Hill longer than Murphy's had a law."

"Grace works for you?" Was there anyplace on the Hill where Cap didn't have a mole?

"No. She's strictly by the book. But she and Jean talk the way people with clearances do. They can't bitch or gloat to family or friends, so they talk to others with clearances. After Sybil bumped Grace off the plane, she called Jean to vent." Cap pursed his lips. "Payback is going to be hell."

How much had Cap deduced? How much did he know about A-267? Austin shifted on his seat. "So what do you think is happening?"

Cap stared at the key in Austin's hand. "I'm not sure. But I think it's something that forced Lance to get Sybil home to help him handle it. And I think whatever that something is, it involves Gregor Faust and Ballast or PUSH, and it involves that key."

Austin clamped his jaw, clenched his teeth. So Cap didn't yet know what the incident was, but he knew there was one, and Intel had shortened its suspect list to PUSH or Faust. Okay, fine. So far, nothing he couldn't salvage. He'd known going in that Faust couldn't be trusted, and he had prepared a contingency Plan B. All he had to do was stay cool, abandon Plan A, implement Plan B, and then burn and bury them all—including Gregor Faust. PUSH would welcome him with open arms. They had approached him before, but by then he had already allied with Ballast. At the time, Ballast was stronger, more powerful, and most feared. But PUSH hadn't been idle. It was well established now. An alliance could be . . . convenient.

Austin stood up, gave Cap his most sincere look. "I'll find out what the key fits. But I need to take it with me to make an impression. I'll get it back to you in a couple of hours."

Obviously not thrilled about the key being out of his possession, Cap frowned.

"You're welcome to come to the lab with me, but opening yourself up to discovery is risky. You'd be better off trusting me to handle it discreetly. Then, should the need arise, you would have deniability." Austin shrugged, knowing the senator would never risk losing deniability or anything else that could cost him the nomination. "Your call."

Again Cap hesitated, transparently torn. "You take it, Austin—but don't keep it long. It's not that I don't trust you, it's that I don't know what whoever sent this is going to do next."

"Try not to worry." Austin feigned a concerned look. "We'll figure it out."

When Cap nodded, Austin stuffed the key in his pocket. He knew exactly what bastard had sent the key and exactly what the bastard would do next.

But Faust had no idea Austin knew he had been betrayed or what *his* next move would be, and in that truth lay Austin's strength. A strength he would use to destroy everyone who had ever crossed him. Everyone.

Including Sybil . . . dead or alive.

★ ★ ★

Was Sybil Stone dead or alive?

Sam Sayelle intended to be able to answer that question soon. With a fresh cup of steaming coffee, he locked himself in the upstairs conference room and closed the blinds on the windows leading to the hall. He didn't want to be distracted. And he didn't want anyone, including his boss, Carl Edison, who had run the paper with an iron fist for decades, to know what he was doing.

Taking a seat at the side of the table, Sam kept his back to the wall and his gaze facing the door. No surprise observers were welcome to take a look at Conlee's transcripts.

There had been six transcripts so far. That small room down in the basement fascinated Sam. The storage area had been covered in inch-thick dust and cobwebs, yet there hadn't been a speck of dust or the hint of a musty smell in the small room, and all of the equipment had looked brand-new. Sam had the feeling that broadcasts had been done there many times in the past.

Within hours of the first broadcast, he had also known that it had been genuine and on the air because he had received a healthy number of phone calls from other reporters wanting to know if he'd left the *Herald* and if his job was available. He had also received an e-mail from a listener who had heard what he'd had to say and had liked it.

After the third broadcast, Sam had put out subtle feelers in the office and, according to Sniffer, who was about as subtle as a sledgehammer, everyone—including Edison—knew about the broadcasts. Newcomers to the paper had congratulated him on the "lucky break," but none of the old-timers had said a word. Other than being baffled and relieved at not having to formulate an elaborate lie, Sam didn't know how he felt about that. Conlee had provided no cover, no suggestions, no recommendations on how he should handle inquiries. He'd only ordered Sam to handle them without mentioning him. Sam didn't know how he felt about that, either.

He spread the six scripts on the table before him and began an intense study. They were political essays, opinion pieces. He looked for patterns, repetitive key words, anything that could give him a clue what information he was passing along.

His coffee grew cold. His eyes grew blurry. And he made absolutely no progress. Which meant he left the conference room with the same question on his mind he'd had when entering: Was Sybil Stone dead or alive?

Chapter Twelve

"Stretch, Sybil." Flat on his belly, Jonathan leaned as far as he could over the ledge of the jagged rock. Dangerously close to falling, he extended his reach, but it fell far short of what he needed. The dropoff to the pit of quicksand was steeper than he had thought: fifteen, maybe twenty feet. "Come on. A little farther."

She sank deeper, until all that was above the surface was her left arm, the top and handle of the briefcase, and her head. "It's not working, Westford."

He tried—*God, how he tried*—but he just couldn't reach her with the knotted parachute cord. *Why the hell hadn't he kept more of it?* He scanned the terrain for a fallen limb, for anything long and strong enough to hold her, but he saw nothing.

"We're running out of time," she called up to him. "We both know what we have to do. Focus solely on getting the briefcase."

She moved her arm, pushed up on the submerged portion of the case. "If you could get around the rock and work from the ledge, we'd be okay, but you can't. We don't have enough cord. There isn't a way around that, so forget about me and just get the case." Sweat beaded on her brow, mixed with the rain, and dripped down her upturned face. The case surfaced, and she sank until her neck dipped beneath the sludge. "You're going to have to take it, Westford."

She was rattled, not thinking clearly. If he could reach the damn case, he could reach her. "I can't get to it." And then there was obstacle number two. "Have you forgotten the damn thing is wired? If you bust open the cuffs, it'll detonate."

Panic flitted through her eyes, then acceptance of the inevitable. "I'm going to die here, Westford. But I can't take the key with me. You've got to get it to the president."

"Sybil—"

"No. Stop and listen to me." Sybil sank more. Her chin was nearly covered. She blinked hard and fast, as if praying her courage wouldn't fail her. "The case is all that matters. Fail and a lot of people die. It's that simple."

"Just hang on, Sybil." He searched frantically. "I'm looking, okay?"

"Westford?" Sybil's voice changed, hollowed by defeat. She was supposed to lead, and leaders must have courage. But the truth was, she was afraid to die. Who would mourn her? Who would put flowers on her grave? Who would wake up in the morning and feel sad that they were living in a world she was no longer in? *Who?*

She cleared her throat, begging the thoughts to stop, and shouted up to him. "Dying is bad enough. Dying and not knowing you'll get the case to David is more than I can take. You've got to get it to David, Westford."

Jonathan didn't answer. When he got her out of this, Sybil might feel okay about having let him see her fear, but Lady Liberty would be mortified. Even if he had wanted to, he wasn't sure he could have answered her. She was steeling herself for death. Feeling that she was leaving life unloved, that she had failed to save others. Pain arced through his chest. "Be patient for a second." How could she believe only Gabby would mourn her? An entire nation would grieve. And, God forgive him, he would grieve for her the rest of his life.

She stared up at him, cold resolve and distance in her eyes. "Throw me your knife."

"What for?" he asked, pausing a scan of the area to glance at her. He didn't like that look in her eyes, or her tone. She was separate now; the woman and the vice president were two distinct entities, and one had no sympathy or compassion for the other.

"I'm going to cut off my hand at the wrist and toss you the case. I know you have the stomach for seeing me do it. You have field-surgery skills and you've been shot yourself. In your job you've seen enough blood to fill this pit."

But he had never seen *her* blood. "Are you crazy?"

"This is a direct order, Westford," she shouted. "Throw me your knife."

"I will not!" He glared at her as if she'd lost her mind. "You aren't going to die or cut off your arm, Sybil, and I'm not going to see you bleed."

"I am Vice President of the United States and I've issued you a direct order, Agent Westford. By God, you'd better follow it and throw me your knife—*now*!"

Jonathan swept a hand over his face. Hard to believe it, but the woman was dead serious—and humbling. "Shut up and listen to me." He'd hoped to avoid this, but she had given him no choice. "Do exactly what I tell you to do. Exactly."

"We're short on time."

"And you're wasting it." He glared down at her. "Roll onto your back."

"How the hell—"

"Just do it, Sybil."

She rolled, tipping her head back. "It's going to swallow my face—all at one time. I know it is. You're just trying to spare me and have me die quickly. You'd better get this case first or, so help me, I'll haunt you for the rest of your life. I might anyway. No one tells me to shut up, Westford."

He ignored her. "Spread your legs apart."

"What?"

"You're wasting time, woman. Time we don't have."

"Promise me. No matter what, this case gets to David before tomorrow night."

Damn stubborn, one-track minded— "I promise."

Finally she spread her legs.

"Now, slowly—very slowly—lift them up. Keep them spread, Sybil. Don't forget that, it's important."

She began moving. "I think you're crazy. Absolutely insane. Why the hell I'm listening to you, I have no idea. And don't you dare say it's one of your damn character flaws, or so help me, I'll—hey, I can see your socks."

"Thank God." He swiped at sweat rolling down his forehead, blurring his eyes. "Okay. Now just stay in that position. Don't move. You won't sink as long as you don't move."

"You're leaving? Good God, you can't just leave the case." Her eyes stretched wide. "You *promised* me, Westford."

"I'm not leaving."

"Then why can't I see you anymore? Where are you?"

"Just give me a minute—and don't move." Finally he spotted the limb he needed. "Just a minute."

"I can't believe you. I'm lying here spread-eagled in rank-smelling sludge, practically locked in the jaws of death, and you're leaving me to die without even trying to save the case—after you promised. You know David needs it. I'm going to fire you for this. Do you hear me, Westford?"

She couldn't see him; he hadn't returned to her field of vision. But she heard him. "Then you're going to have to live to spite me. Dead women can't fire people."

What a rotten time for him to be logical. Sometimes men could be heartless pigs. "Okay, fine. *If* I live through this, I'm going to fire you and bust your—"

He tromped through the trees and back to the rock, dragging a limb.

"You came back for it."

"You sound stunned. If I weren't a heartless pig, I'd be hurt."

"Are you reading my mind? How—"

"Gabby mentioned your fondness for the term."

From that smirk, she had mentioned a lot more. "She's a pig, too." One with a big mouth.

"Right." He spared her a glance. "Have I ever broken a promise to you?"

How could he sound so calm and unaffected? She was going to die, damn it. And he was forcing her to admit the truth when she was standing at death's door, primed to rage. "Not yet."

"Then I deserve the benefit of the doubt."

He did. "Okay."

Westford tied the limb to the rope, dropped back onto his belly on the jagged top of the rock, and then extended the limb down into the sludge pit. "Don't grab. You'll screw up your ballast. Just give me a second. I need more angle." The end of the limb hit something solid—her ribs, gauging by her grunt.

He winced; she'd have a hell of a bruise. "Sorry." He maneuvered the limb into position with the length of cord attached to it, sliding it under her right arm and across her chest. "Okay. Now squeeze with your right arm and grab the limb with your left. Get your hands around the limb as fast as you can."

She grabbed, clenched her fingers around the rough bark, and nearly wept. "I've got it." She repeated it over and again as if it were a mantra. "Are those knots going to hold?"

"Just hang on." Relief slammed through Jonathan and he softened his tone. "Don't help me, and don't hurry. Just hang on, okay?"

"Okay." Her bravado faded and her voice went with it. She sounded fragile, frightened, determined. "Okay, I can do that."

"Of course you can." He pulled the cord back to him at a steady pace. "You can do anything you put your mind to doing. I've known that about you for a long time. Gabby says it's your stubborn streak. I think it's your intense focus. You're a determined woman."

"I like your rendition better, but Gabby is probably right. My mother called it my bitch streak."

"What about your dad?" Closer and closer. Two more pulls, hand over hand, and she would be at the base of the rock. He would have her. *Oh, God, please let him have her.* Then he faced the obstacle of pulling her up without banging her against the rocky ledge.

"My dad seldom said much of anything—except for how I'd failed to meet his expectations."

"Well, at least that didn't happen often." *Steady. Steady.* He stretched and locked a grip on the limb. It was raking the rocks, scraping out chunks of wood and losing strength. It could break.

"It happened with monotonous regularity." Already thin, her voice shook. "My parents didn't like each other very much, and they liked me even less."

"I'm sorry." *Steady, damn it!* Any jerk and he could lose her. He had to keep her talking. She was calmer when talking. Her talking and calm and him pulling steady, she would survive this. *They* would survive this. "Gabby thinks you had a charmed life with your folks." One more. The jagged boulder scraped his chest. He cursed its sharp edges, but if the rock wasn't in the way, he wouldn't be struggling with this. He wouldn't have had the chance to pluck her out of the pit. No one could reach her from the ledge. If he could just keep her steady for one more pull, she'd be okay. He clasped the limb and shifted his weight, crouching on the slick rock.

"I'm sorry, too. Not about Gabby. She thought what I wanted her to think. I'm sorry about my parents." Sybil rambled, clearly trying to take her mind off what was going on around her. "They didn't know each other well. Their marriage was more of a strategic business alliance than a spiritual union. By the time they realized they had nothing in common and didn't like each other at all, they were married and I was on the way."

She was coming up. Her chest cleared the sludge. She was getting closer to the pit wall. *Too close.* He leaned back a little, using the rock for leverage, and pushed her away.

She jerked, gasped. "Hey, we're going backward down here."

"Are you in the mood to kiss a rock with your nose and knees?"

Evidently that reassured her because, without missing a beat, she picked up talking where she had left off. "You know, it's a sad thing, Westford, but I'm not sure either of my parents really loved anyone in their lives."

Something cracked. He darted his gaze to the limb and saw not just signs of fatigue from being scraped across the edge of the rock but a serious stress fracture. *What now?* He checked Sybil. Her waist was above the sludge; her waist, the top of her skirt, the tail of her jacket . . . and finally, her feet. Her feet had cleared the sludge. He couldn't leave her dangling midair and go scrounge up a replacement. This limb *had* to hold. "No one? Including you?"

"Including me." She squeezed her eyes shut, clearly struggling to keep herself together. "I have no idea why I'm telling you all this. Hell, I don't usually dare to think about it." She stretched and snared his ankle with her right hand. "You bring out the worst in me, Westford."

Jonathan dropped the limb, inched down, and grabbed

her under the arms. Realizing he had stopped breathing, he lifted her up. Tears glistened in her eyes, blurred his own. "I have that affect on some people."

"Yes, you do." She looked up at him and swallowed hard.

"I'll work on it." Her breath warmed his wet face and he smiled, backed off the rock, and then set her feet on solid ground. She clung to him, shaking hard, slumping against his chest, his stomach, his thighs, the briefcase flat against his back. There was nothing in the world that could keep him from closing his arms around her and pulling her tighter. He could have lost her. God Almighty, he had come *so* close to losing her . . .

"Don't work on it." She clasped her arms around his waist, clenching her fingers at his back, holding him in a death grip, as if only by crawling inside him would she feel safe. "You keep me honest with myself." Her heartbeat thundered against his chest as ferociously as his own pulse pounded in his temples. "I don't want to, but I think I need that."

What the woman needed was him, but she'd probably die of heart failure if he suggested it. She needed more time to get used to the idea of him being more than a guard in her life.

She shuddered, pressed her face against his chest, and clenched fistfuls of his jacket and shirt. He pressed his cheek against her gritty hair. The quicksand covering her soaked through his wet clothes and the grit grated against his skin. He welcomed every sensation, each smell and sound and tactile response. They all proved she was alive. A few more minutes of holding her and maybe he could believe it. Maybe then he could ease his hold on her. But not just yet. Not just yet.

"I almost died, Westford." She burrowed closer still.

"But you didn't." Muffled against his chest, her words arrowed into his heart. "You bury your emotions more than anyone I know, and it's not healthy. Let go, Sybil. You know it's safe to let go with me." He cupped her shoulder with his palm, rubbed soothing circles on her back.

"I don't want to let go. Not right now. Maybe not ever."

She was afraid if she did, she wouldn't be able to stop. Afraid the fear would consume her, her mask would shatter, and she would never again be in control and safe. Neither Liberty nor Sybil Stone could let that happen. After Austin, she honestly believed all that was left of her was the mask.

Realizing that, Jonathan didn't push. He just held her and kept on holding her, and what seemed like a long time later, her shaking finally eased to trembling, and then she calmed down.

Letting out a shuddering sigh, she opened her fists, splayed her spread fingers on his back, and then looked up at him. Her eyes brimmed with the tears she refused to cry, and she gave him a shaky smile that threatened to rip his heart right out of his chest. "Thank you, Westford."

No tears. No hysterics. Either of which would have been perfectly natural and acceptable. "Does that mean I'm not fired?"

"I'm still debating."

"I could quit. You're pretty dangerous company to keep these days."

"You're not quitting."

"Don't I get a say in the discussion?"

"Of course, provided you choose the option I want you to choose. You know, you're not bad looking, Westford, which is a perk since you're in my face more often than not. And I don't suppose I can be a taker and not give back."

"Excuse me?"

"You need me."

"*I* need *you*?"

"Obviously." She shrugged, and he squeezed her sides. "You're holding on pretty tight."

"The rock's slippery. I didn't want you to fall and crack your skull."

"No." She denied that possibility with pure sass and stroked his chest. "You need me to look out for you. Otherwise, you'd have made some smart-ass comment about my hard head cracking the rock."

She had him on that one. "Okay, I need you."

Sybil liked the sound of that more than she wanted to admit. But then that nag, doubt, crawled out from under its rock and raised the question she'd come to dread: *Does he need the woman or the veep?* Well, it was about time to find out. She screwed up her courage and asked, "Are you being honest, or sarcastic?"

"Are you saying you can't tell?"

Now, how should she respond to that?

While she was deciding, he asked a second question. "What option exactly are you insisting I choose?"

"Staying with me, of course," she admitted. "And don't bother trying to push off that nonsense about me being dangerous company to keep. I've always been dangerous company. That entire line of thought is a moot point."

Jonathan couldn't track that leap. "Why?"

"Because I've told you too much to let you leave me now."

"About the Code One?"

"Hell, no. About my life."

"I see. We're victims of the old I-could-tell-you-but-then-I'd-have-to-kill-you dilemma."

"It's only a dilemma if you're not where I can keep an eye on you." She let her hand slide down to his waist. "It's a huge sacrifice on my part to put up with you, but I'm willing to make it."

"For the good of your country, of course."

"Of course." She nodded, deadpan. "It's one of the many drawbacks of public service, but duty is duty." She tilted her head. "Besides, I can't repay you for saving my life by killing you. Word would get out—it always does—and that could undermine my credibility in future negotiations."

Adorable. Messy as hell, but adorable. "You could be right."

"Of course I'm right." She squeezed him to her, melding their thighs.

Jonathan would swear black was white as long as she kept touching him.

"You need to remember that you have duties, too, Westford. So which do you choose? Do you stay with me, or do I kill you?"

"I suppose if you're willing to make the sacrifice and put up with me being in your face all the time—"

"I admitted your looks were a perk."

"You did," he conceded. "I should shoulder my fair share of the sacrifices, too, so I guess I'll stay." Only God could pry him away from her now.

"Wise decision." The teasing gleam in her eyes turned serious. "Did I remember to say thank you, Westford?"

"You did."

"Well, aren't you going to acknowledge it?" She frowned. "Maybe I made the wrong choice here. Maybe I should just kill you—"

He swallowed hard and stroked her sleek chin, interrupting her midsentence. "You're welcome, Sybil."

She looked at him, beheld him, as if at that moment in time he were the only thing in the world that mattered to her. "Jonathan?"

He liked it. A lot. As much as seeing her dazed. "Mmm?"

"Would you consider it unethical or harassment or anything if I kissed you?"

His heart banged against his ribs.

"I mean, I *am* making you stay. So if kissing me would offend you in any way, then of course I wouldn't want—"

He lifted her to him, covered her mouth with his, and kissed her hard. Kissed her the way he'd wanted to kiss her since she was a junior congresswoman and he first had noticed her, with all the passion and desire and longing that he had felt for her from that day until this. *Mind?* Oh, sweet Jesus, he'd prayed for this. For her to just once—*just once*—kiss him, touch him, and want him to kiss and touch her. To just once let him show her that he loved her . . .

When their mouths parted, Sybil buried her face in the crook of his neck, swearing she hadn't felt anything she knew damn well she had felt. There was something potent in his kisses, something unearthly. If she had any sense, it would frighten her. Obviously she didn't, because she wasn't afraid, she was fascinated. She'd never felt so connected and attuned to a man. The moment he looked at her, much less touched her, it was as if a homing beacon went on inside him and she was mesmerized by it. She really hated loving that. But having felt it once, and hating loving it, she was determined to get used to it, provided he gave her the chance. There was something special about Westford. Something significantly different that she just couldn't seem to put her finger on.

I told you.

Gabby's voice, inside her mind. The reminder jerked Sybil's head right out of the clouds. *Now what?*

Try honesty.

Easy for you to say. Your judgment doesn't suck. You hated Austin at first sight. It took me fifteen years to discover he was a lying jerk. No, I don't think so, Gabby. Honesty is fine for some people, but I've tried it. It just didn't work out.

Westford is different. You said so yourself. Try honesty, Gabby repeated. *I've been right so far, haven't I?*

Okay. Okay. But if this blows up in my face, I swear I'll get Conlee to make your next assignment in Iceland—in the winter.

Fair enough.

Sybil leaned back and looked up into Jonathan's face, traced the crinkle lines beneath his eyes with the tips of her fingers. "I wasn't honest with you, Jonathan."

He stiffened and his fingers at her waist bent into her flesh. "About what?"

"You staying with me." God, this was hard. "If you wanted to go, I wouldn't kill you."

His grip gentled. "Sybil, what are you trying to tell me?"

Do it, Sybil. Do it.

Will you shut up and give me some space? This is hard, damn it. I'm scared.

Of Jonathan?

Even to Sybil it sounded ridiculous. But she was afraid of him. Of course she was afraid of him. He made her feel. He could hurt her. God, she didn't want to be hurt again.

"Sybil?" He stroked her face. "What is it?"

"I'm glad you're back with me. But I don't want you to feel stuck, Jonathan. If you don't want to be—"

"So you spilled your guts to me, kissed me, and now you're hell-bent on wrecking my career?"

"No!" How could he even think it? "I know David asked you to come with me to Geneva. It wasn't your idea, and I don't think it would have been your choice."

"So you've changed your mind already and you're trying to get rid of me."

"No, Jonathan."

"Then what are you doing?"

Irritated because he was never this damn dense when it came to his work, she glared up at him. "I'm trying to tell you that when you left me, I missed you—though, at the moment, only God knows why."

"You missed me." He sounded dazed.

She liked that. "Yes."

"So do you want me to stay with you, or not?"

Leave it to him to cut through the bone and dive right into the marrow. "I want you to do what makes you happy."

"Stay or go, Sybil?" He pinned her with an unrelenting gaze. "Choose."

"Stay." The word rushed out of her mouth, and she was furious that he'd forced her to admit it out loud. "I want you to stay."

"Why? And don't tell me because I need you. That's been established."

How could she tell him how she felt when she didn't understand it herself? She knew what he needed, but she couldn't give it to him. She didn't have it to give. She couldn't survive another mistake or take those kinds of risks again. Dear God, not again.

"I ran from you once, Sybil. I won't run again. And I won't let you run from me." He let his hand drift over her hair, down her jaw to her chin. "I understand the fears. But I have to know why you want me here. That's important to me, too."

He was as torn as she was, and just as confused. "I want you with me because... because I need you." She sniffed and inhaled a cleansing breath. "But I can't have you—not even if you were willing and wanted me. I know that, and I guess asking you to stay anyway makes me a selfish bitch." She blinked hard. "I am selfish, Jonathan. I need you in my life."

Something hard in his chest softened, and the truth settled over him like a shroud and then turned to stone. Once again he had crossed the line and fallen in love. And once again she was out of his reach. He couldn't have her because she couldn't have him. He had no idea what that meant, but apparently he didn't fit into her professional world or her plans. He'd always known that could be a point of contention, but he'd thought they could overcome it. Now, for reasons of her own, Sybil didn't even want to try. That left him with limited options. Actually, with one option: to fight against loving her with the same tenacity he had fought Austin Stone.

★ ★ ★

By the time Austin entered the sleek building traditional-ists described as the bane of Georgetown, Secure Envi-ronet was humming. The level of activity was notably higher than usual. People rushed back and forth through wide corridors leading to private offices, conference rooms, and Austin's favorite place: the lab. The air virtually crack-led with intensity, proving Plan B was unfolding as de-signed.

His adrenaline pumping, he cleared the security checkpoints, keyed and entered his private elevator, and then rode up to the seventh floor. When the door squeaked open, his personal assistant, Patrice, a very sharp black American mother of two, looked over from her computer screen. She was wearing a conservative green suit. Patrice seldom wore a suit—unless she intended to hit him up for a raise or a special perk. Which, he wondered, would it be?

"Morning, Dr. Stone." She gathered a stack of message slips from a slotted sorter on her desk.

"Good morning." Austin kept walking. "Have mainte-nance do something about that elevator door. It sounds an-cient." He entered the hallway to his private office, glanced at a portrait of Einstein on the wall, and then at his pride and joy—an original Dali. "Any notable messages?"

"Plenty of them." In his office, she poured him a cup of coffee at the oak bar and then followed him over to his desk. "It's been wild around here this morning."

Austin settled into his seat. "What's going on?"

"Several dozen condolence calls on the former Mrs. Stone, sir."

Well trained, Patrice knew better than to refer to Sybil as the vice president. At Secure Environet, he was God, and Sybil was merely his powerless former wife.

"The other messages are business related." Patrice set the cup on his blotter. "We have a security-system failure on a classified DoD site. Engineering needs you down in the lab ASAP."

Excellent. Austin nodded. Events were unfolding on cue.

"You've also got a message from the White House. Mildred. There's been no further word on the former Mrs. Stone. I'm having the media monitored in case they turn up anything." Sympathy tinged Patrice's voice. "President Lance would appreciate a personal briefing on the system failure. Evidently, the technical questions weren't answered to his satisfaction."

Nothing short of stepping in and halting the Peacekeeper launch would satisfy Lance. Austin held in a grunt. The man was in for a serious wake-up call, but he had been right to phone Austin. Raw power surged through him. His spine and the roof of his mouth tingled. In the next ten minutes, he would see to it that no one else *could* halt the launch.

Patrice opened the blinds at the window. Thin bars of light filtered into his office and streaked across his desktop, the ivory carpet, the photo of his mother on his desk. "There are a dozen other messages. Most are marked urgent. One was urgent and strange."

He sipped from his cup, wishing he'd had one less scotch last night. "Strange?"

"The caller claimed to be a friend, but she refused to leave a name. She's on sabbatical in China and would like to invite you to join her."

PUSH. Welcoming him. Inwardly, Austin smiled. "Just leave it with the others." He motioned to the desk. "I need a few minutes to get oriented."

"Yes, sir." She left the messages, then the office.

Austin locked the door, pulled out Cap's key, walked to the oak bar, and then pushed a button hidden under its top ledge. The bar wall swung open, revealing a private and compact but well-equipped minilab.

He stepped inside and removed a blue velvet-lined case from a drawer under the lab table. Two keys rested inside it, side by side. Pulling out the one on the left, he compared it to Cap's. A perfect copy. Indisputable proof that Gregor Faust had broken their agreement and double-crossed him. And, of course, it was a copy, not Faust's duplicate original. But fearing that Faust would betray him, Austin also had prepared.

He lifted the only copy of a second key. Anger surged through him, and he scratched a short, straight line on it, feeling totally justified in implementing Plan B. The chain of events it would unleash was regrettable—the impact would be significant—but now unavoidable. And once he had completely set it into motion, no one else could stop the process.

In roughly thirty-four hours, the United States would launch the first-strike missile, and the world would be at war.

Austin. Austin. His mother's voice sounded in his head. *How can you justify starting World War III?*

He squeezed his eyes shut and leaned wearily against the lab table. Even dead, she challenged him. Always probing. Always asking questions he didn't want to answer. Always robbing him of peace.

I'm not starting this war. They attacked me. Yes, I married Sybil for political advantage and money but I was fond of her, and she divorced me. Lance and his spying henchmen have constantly violated my privacy and issued me dictates. Sybil's bastard protector, Westford, had the audacity to threaten to kill me. To kill me! Agitated, Austin began to pace. *Gregor Faust attacked me, too. He's gleaned an amazing amount of Intel on me through his Ballast contacts here, and he came to me to buy my secure-system devices and then with a proposal for a mutually beneficial joint venture. He came to me and then betrayed me. And Cap is no better. Even he violated me, Mother. Year after year, I gave him inside information to use against Sybil, and yet he elected not to play straight with me.*

They were responsible for the war. No one had forced them to do what they had done. They had chosen their actions and taken them willingly. He had to defend himself. They had to know their actions against him were mistakes and that mistakes carry consequences.

But such steep consequences, Austin? Where is mercy and grace?

He stiffened against a prick of shame. *Where was their mercy and grace, Mother? What about their crimes against me? The penalty I inflict isn't revenge, it's justice. It should be substantial—and paid by them and those they have sworn to serve and protect.*

Expecting his mother to rebel, he stiffened, but she held her silence. Obviously she agreed with him. Relieved, he shoved back from the lab table and stared down at the keys. Power had the tips of his fingers and toes prickling, his chest heaving. They had forced him into taking this action. All of them. Yes, he would gain financially and also where it most mattered to him: in power. But that was secondary. They'd betrayed him. He stuffed the scratched key into his pocket. World War III was justified.

He returned the other keys to the case, placed the case in the drawer, and then removed a smaller red case from beside it. Austin smiled. Inside was a third key. When he left this lab, the security systems at top-secret site A-267 would no longer require two keys: one for access to the classified site's outer rim and inner hub and one to access the actual missile launch controls. It would require *three*. One for the outer rim, one for the inner hub, and one to halt the launch of the world's deadliest missile.

And only Dr. Austin Stone had the third key.

He moved down to a desk opposite the lab table and sat down, then booted up a computer. Unlike the sixty-odd others in the building, this terminal was not tied in to the Secure Environet network. It was his private safe system and as secure as technology and innovative thinking could make it. Only he knew it existed and that it was in the building. Only he knew the minilab existed. And only he could forward whatever he generated on this computer through a complex web of filters so that no one short of God could trace anything he disbursed back to Secure Environet.

After keying in the codes to access the system, he entered the data string that would make the White House a key player in Plan B. Scrolling down the list of Lance's most-trusted advisors, he highlighted the chosen one's name, clicked, then clicked again on his DNA report. Scrolling down, Austin stopped on line five, reversed it, and then uploaded the altered report into the system.

Upload complete appeared on the screen.

Successful, he added a second data string and then uploaded it. This command would make Gregor Faust's launch key—his entire plan—obsolete. Should he also cut off Faust's visual access to the A-267?

No, Austin decided. Let him watch events unfold there and experience the futility of being able to do nothing to stop them. He hit the "enter" key.

Again a response flashed onto the screen: Upload complete.

The wheels were now in motion, and only he could stop them.

Flushed with sheer joy at outmaneuvering Faust, Lance, and the president's entire entourage, Austin also absorbed a flicker of regret that they had conspired and pushed him to do something of this magnitude when he had spent his entire life designing security devices to protect and defend. He shut down the system and then the minilab.

A tall stack of large brown envelopes stuffed full of inflammatory evidence against Sybil rested on the far wall counter. Each had been labeled individually. All were addressed to key people in the media at virtually every major network in the nation. He collected the stack and returned to his office, placing them on the corner of his desk, then ran through a mental listing until he felt confident he hadn't left any loose ends.

Satisfied, he sat down and leaned back. He once again held the helm. This time he intended to hold onto it. It was a shame Sybil wouldn't be around to see this. But his life would be much more peaceful with her dead, and Plan B had just assured him that, if she wasn't already dead, she soon would be.

He phoned the China number. PUSH was eager. He listened briefly, laid out his terms, they agreed, and then he hung up. It was going to be a profitable association.

After adjusting his jacket lapel, he checked his tie, then left his office. He had a lot to do before leaving D.C. Lance wouldn't be the only one evacuating before the missile launched.

"Sir?" Patrice called out as he passed her desk. "Are you going to engineering now?"

"I'm on my way. Don't mail the brown envelopes on my desk. I want them delivered by Ground Serve, but not just yet. I'll call you when I'm ready."

"Yes, sir."

If Patrice saw anything strange in his instructions, her expression didn't reflect it. Grateful for that, Austin tapped the button for the elevator. He would listen to a recap of what engineering had been told through the chain of command and then get back to the president. Afterward, he would return the substituted inner hub key to Cap and tell him he had possession of a launch-code key to a Peace-keeper missile.

Lance would brief Cap on the security breach, and when he did, the senator would be compelled to reveal that he had held the key. How would he explain having it? He could pretend he never got it, but when that later proved untrue, Cap would be wide open for attack, and the man never left himself open to attack. Hadn't he always filtered leaks through Jean?

Regardless of what Cap said, the fallout against him would be immediate and incredible. Lance would insist that he resign.

Of greater interest and priority was Gregor Faust. How would he react to learning his double-cross had backfired?

Cap was blessed a bit by ignorance, but Faust would know that his decisions had set off a chain reaction that couldn't be reversed or halted or in any way be deemed a proportional response to some manufactured slight. He would know that millions were about to die, and that, for each life lost, the entire world would blame him. And he would know that every government and terrorist organization in the world—including his own—would mark him as a priority target for assassination. Ballast members would blame Gregor for making them targets. They would think that by killing him, they could diffuse heat from themselves and the organization. And Gregor would know he had as much to fear from his own men as from the authorities, competitors, and enemies.

All this and more would happen. It was inevitable now. And no one would know Austin had been involved. PUSH might wonder, but odds were against it. After all, Faust had made this entire mission appear to be PUSH instigated and executed. No, no one would know Austin had been involved.

Provided Sybil died.

Austin smiled. Very soon now Gregor Faust would no longer be indifferent. He and all of Ballast would be jumping through proverbial hoops to see to it that she did not survive.

Chapter Thirteen

"Have some nuts." Sybil passed them to Westford.

He looked down at them, then at her. "They're hickory nuts, Sybil."

"Who cares? They're not bark or roots or—what's wrong with them?"

"Nothing, if you're a duck. But they're inedible for humans."

"Damn." Sybil sat down under a roof of low-slung branches that helped block the rain and biting wind, then leaned into the oak and scraped her back against its rough bark. She popped another berry into her mouth and forced herself to chew then swallow it. "When this is over, I may never again eat another huckleberry."

"These are Navaho blackberries," Westford said from beside her. "But I know what you mean. You know you're hungry when an armadillo starts looking good."

Sybil wrinkled her nose. "I'm not *that* hungry." Wildlife

was plentiful here, but cooking presented a problem. Ballast and Search and Rescue would see the smoke from a fire. Westford had made it perfectly clear either group—or both—could be dangerous. It made her sick to hear S&R lumped with Ballast, but Westford was right. Even innocent people in the field were mixed up in this. Their infiltrator was high level and no doubt issuing orders to someone somewhere. Until they determined who the infiltrator was and the extent of that infiltration, everyone was dangerous. Right now Sybil wouldn't dare to trust even Gabby, though her friend would be devastated to know it. But even Gabby was obligated to follow the orders issued to her.

Westford cupped his ear. Sybil had picked up on his habit of blocking out the rain beating on the leaves and the muddy ground to pick up transmissions from Home Base. It still amazed her how noisy rain could be here. She'd never before been outside during the remnants of a stalled-out tropical storm, and she hoped she never would be again. She waited expectantly for him to decode and relay the message from Home Base.

"Sayelle just confirmed our suspicion. High-level infiltrator."

Inevitable, but it still infuriated her to hear it. Once she'd believed that all she had to do to raise the bar on expectations was to not be corrupt. To lead by example. She had tried, she really had. But corruption in politics was so pervasive, and its insidious promises of money or power were so seductive and tempting to those seeking personal gain, that sometimes she felt like a salmon swimming upstream. It struggles and struggles and when it finally gets there, it dies.

Stop it, Sybil. What are you doing? You can't afford to think like this. Okay, so some politicians are corrupt. And most Americans expect them to lie and to be crooked as snakes. But some people actually believe in honest politicians and they're loyal supporters. Think about them. Raise the bar for them.

You've got a job to do. You've got to keep these bastards from blowing the heart of America off the map. So knock off the philosophical pining and get your mind in gear. You and West- ford are carrying hope. Don't forget that. You're carrying hope.

Sometimes hope was sure heavy. She shoved another berry in her mouth. "Has Home Base pegged them?"

"Not yet." Westford paused again, and his expression deflated. "Damn it."

That reaction was so atypical of the unflappable West- ford that it scared her. "What?"

"Intel is convinced PUSH is responsible for all this."

"Then they must have hard evidence Ballast isn't in- volved."

He gave her a head shake and downed a berry. "Not likely. Intel says field reports indicate significant PUSH movement on known Ballast operatives. Ballast is building a strong case against PUSH."

That news upset Sybil. "Is Intel relaxing heavy Ballast observation?"

"Not yet, but they will soon. Like everyone else, they're short-staffed and, with everything pointing to PUSH, they'll have to give it priority handling."

"But without intense pressure, Faust will cut loose." Unable to swallow another bite, Sybil shoved a handful of berries into her pocket. With Gregor Faust, they had better expect the worst. "Why hasn't Intel made the Ballast con- nection?"

"Because everyone who knows what we know is dead."

"Okay, I agree. That's a major obstacle, and Faust is thorough."

"It's all that keeps him alive."

"Then why is he starting a world war?" Her stomach growled, protesting the lack of food. Resentfully she snagged a berry from her pocket. Had she really once thought their sweet scent smelled good? Right now she'd give an eye tooth for a potato chip—for anything salty.

"I don't know."

"It doesn't make sense. He wanted to stop the peace talks for obvious reasons—his arm sales to Peris and Abdan. But he's done that. I'm here, not in Geneva negotiating."

"The leaders are waiting there. Maybe he isn't convinced the talks have collapsed."

"No," she countered. "He's too sharp for that. Hell, Westford, it took me nearly six months to get those two in the same room. Without me holding their feet to the fire, they're more apt to assassinate each other than to speak a civil word. The world knows that."

"Their consciences, not their feet."

"Whatever," she said, agitated and swiping at a clod of mud clinging to her skirt. "They're not going to negotiate in good faith. You can count on it."

"So what does Faust want now?"

"That's what I can't figure out," she said. "There's just no motive where he gains anything from a world war. Not one damn thing. Not that I can see, anyway."

Westford scanned the area, then glanced back at her. "Maybe it's not him."

"We know it is."

"Do we?"

Westford wasn't blowing smoke. He was on to something. "What do you mean?"

"Ballast is tagging PUSH. What if PUSH is guilty and it set us up to tag Ballast?"

Sybil pondered the possibility, hoping this scenario had occurred to Commander Conlee and those in his think tank. "Low probability. Not impossible, but low. PUSH doesn't have the kind of connections it would need. It wouldn't just launch into Ballast-assets attack. First, it would have to build a base." That had her thinking again. "Okay, in the States, that's possible. But not in Eastern Europe."

"You're right. There's no way PUSH could muscle in on Ballast's stronghold and Ballast not know it." Westford dragged his hands through his hair. "Damn it, my mind is like sludge."

They were both exhausted, but they had to get back on their toes.

"Maybe Faust isn't the sole instigator of this mission," he said. "Maybe someone else—someone inside or outside of Ballast—that he recruited has different objectives Faust doesn't know about or want?"

"It's possible." Sybil hated this with a passion. "That gives us another unidentified enemy."

"Yes." Westford's serious expression turned to a silent rage. "One inside President Lance's administration. Nobody else would have access to everything."

Sybil swallowed a bitter knot in her throat and asked a question she wasn't at all sure she wanted answered. "What are the odds of Faust figuring this out and somehow counteracting before the launch?"

"About as good as ours of getting back to D.C. in time." Jonathan hauled himself to his feet and held out a hand.

Sybil clasped it. "I never thought I'd pray for the most feared terrorist in the world to be sharp and successful. But I'm praying exactly that for Faust."

★   ★   ★

The Ballast field team was doing its best to test his patience.

Convinced of it, Gregor Faust sat at the operations desk in the command center, scanned the monitors, and spoke into his headset lip mike. "You've been out there fourteen hours, ET." Typically, Patch needed less time to track able-bodied, noncrash victims. "Alpha's been there nearly twenty-four hours. What the hell do you mean you can't find anything?"

"I mean, there's nothing in this grid to find."

Frustrated, Gregor swept a hand over his eyes. Already

they burned from the recycled air. Search and Rescue teams were too far south, and the grid Mark had radioed in was empty. Westford or Dean must have screwed with the coordinates. "Sweep it twice and then head north." If Westford and Liberty had survived, Gregor would bet his arsenal they were on the move.

"Yes, sir. Any chance of me getting another team out here?"

The only other tactical team available was the one guarding Linda Dean and her children. Gregor had considered killing them and moving the Bravo team to the swamp but had decided to hold them in reserve. A few hostages to counter backup collateral generally proved an asset. "I'll work on it."

The phone rang—Gregor's private line. He answered with a curt "Yes?"

"You blew it. She's not dead."

Austin Stone. Terrific. "We haven't yet verified that."

"I just left a briefing. From the inferences I heard, she's alive."

"But still in the Everglades without transport, correct?"

"Purportedly."

Austin's tone hardened with a bitterness Gregor had long since associated with the man, but there was something new in it, too. Something discomfiting: authority. "Tactical has been out there since the explosion. They've swept the grid twice. We've lost two men, but—"

"She's not dead."

"I said we're on it, Austin." Gregor chilled his tone.

"Let me make this simple. Unless you want to be held accountable for starting a world war, you'd better make sure the only way she leaves that swamp is toes up in a body bag."

A cold rage snaked through Gregor. "Do not threaten—"

"Threaten?" Austin interrupted. "You can bet your arms sales to Peris and Abdan it's no threat. I'll do it, Gregor. I'll blow it all straight to hell."

The crazy bastard had convinced him. "There's a wide gap between threatening a disaster and creating one, Austin." Gregor stared at the swamp monitor. "If you actually launch the missile, World War III is inevitable. Need I remind you that what you're proposing to do will have severe long-term consequences? The responses will be immediate and proportional. The majority of life on this planet will be eradicated. In a war of this magnitude, there is no refuge, Doctor, and no one wins. I strongly recommend you harness your emotions and—"

"You're almost right. I have refuge. You, however, do not."

Damn scientists. He would never again, *never again*, team up with one of them on a campaign. "Unless you've arranged for a space-shuttle ride, you don't have refuge. Launch that missile, and you'll be killing yourself, too."

"Will I?"

Cold chills crept up Gregor's spine. "What have you done?"

Austin ignored the question. "I want her dead. Do you hear me, Gregor? I want her dead." He slammed down the phone.

What Austin had done, Gregor wasn't sure, but he felt certain of two things: He wouldn't like it, and he'd be blamed for it.

He flipped down the lip mike and radioed Patch. "ET, do you copy?"

"Yes, sir."

A few lives, or many? Gregor had no option but to choose—though really there was no choice to make. Austin's call had determined fate. ET needed a backup team in the swamp. The only team Gregor could free up and get on-scene quickly was the one holding Linda Dean and her two kids. To do that, the Deans would have to die. "A backup tactical team will be en route shortly."

In the twisted chaos only a damn scientist could create, Austin had made it clear that he had done something to place Gregor in an impossible position. Now, from a continent away, he had to stop World War III—he glanced at the countdown board—in about thirty-three hours.

And unless Senator Cap Marlowe was suddenly stricken by an attack of conscience that forced him to put his career on the line, which wasn't damned likely, Gregor had to stop it alone.

To save his own skin, he could no longer risk indifference.

Lady Liberty had to die.

First-Strike Launch: 33:10:02

Thirty-three hours, ten minutes, and two seconds until Armageddon.

Cap paced his office, barely resisting the urge to wring his hands. What should he do? President Lance had briefed him on the security-breach crisis, and he still couldn't believe it. How had PUSH or Gregor Faust managed to bypass the most advanced secure-system devices on the planet and infiltrate A-267? Less than three dozen people even knew the top-secret facility existed. Some corrupt bastard had to have aided them. That was the only logical explanation.

With the sensitive intelligence and technology housed at A-267, one leak from one person is all it takes to throw this nation into crisis.

Apparently PUSH or Faust had found the one. But had that person been recruited by agreement or by force? Better than anyone, Cap recognized that someone working on the site might have unknowingly been inducted. It had happened to him. It could happen to anyone. When Austin had returned the key and told him it was a launch key to an intercontinental ballistic missile, he had nearly had a stroke. What he hadn't had was doubt. His key was *the* key to the Peacekeeper missile at A-267.

He glared at his wall safe, secretly wishing that he could glare long and hard enough to make the key locked inside it disappear. Whatever action he took, he was personally screwed.

When Lance had briefed him on the security breach, he should have told the president about receiving the key. It would have cost him the nomination, but the nation might have been spared this monumental crisis. Lives might have been saved. Yet even if Jean took the fall for him, claiming that Cap had ordered the report be prepared and filed and she hadn't done it, he would suffer the same end result: public humiliation. With Lance's stand on integrity, he'd jerk Cap off every committee with or without teeth and launch a major campaign for his immediate impeachment. The country was sick of scandal. By the end of day one, Cap would be forced to resign. After thirty years of service, he would be forced out of office and off the Hill in disgrace.

Cap couldn't stomach that. He hadn't worked his entire life to end his political career like this. He had earned the right to better. Swiveling, he looked at the wall behind him. It was full of awards and plaques, trophies and commendations—a lifetime's worth. But if he didn't do something about this crisis, they would all be forgotten. Every good thing he had ever done would be forgotten. If recalled at all, he would be remembered as the senator who had made a deal with the worst terrorist in the world. It wouldn't matter that he hadn't. The black cloud of doubt would form over him for not reporting the key. Whoever had sent it would see to it that the cloud stayed.

Could Sybil Stone have done it?

God knew, Cap had done plenty to make her miserable. But he hadn't gone public about Austin Stone's vasectomy, which would have proven Sybil a liar on so many public stances she pretended to embrace. If he had done that, then maybe she would have retaliated with this. But without it . . . ?

Probably not, though she had to dread him disclosing it every day of her life. There was solace in that.

Lance would hear him out; he was a fair and reasonable man. But Cap would be crippled by the scandal and less than effective, if not assassinated by some zealot with a misguided sense of duty who felt compelled to protect the country from him.

"Damn it." Cap dragged his thumbs, pinching the bridge of his nose. There had to be a way out of this that wouldn't destroy him.

He sank into his desk chair. He had been labeled wily and cagey for as long as he could remember, and he considered both fair assessments. He had a flexible mind and he had always respected it. Over the years that flexibility had generated a lot of creative solutions. He *could* find a way out of this that didn't include disgrace or involve impeachment.

Certain of it, he closed his eyes, pulled himself into a deep state of relaxation, and let his thoughts flow. Fast and furious, they streamed through his mind in disjointed bits, some of which he didn't have time to grasp fully before others crowded in and overtook them. He worked his way through this static and his thoughts slowed down, became more logical and sensible. Finally a solution came to him that wasn't rooted in fear.

He was chairman of the Armed Services Committee. He had access to A-267. Because it was a classified site with an extremely limited need-to-know circle, he pulled inspections on the site himself.

So pull an inspection, Cap.

Yes. He'd pull an inspection. Thinking through the details, Cap went to the safe and removed the key. His direct line rang, and he paused to take the call. "Marlowe."

"Remember the key," a man said.

Cap's blood ran cold. "Why are you doing this to—"

The line went dead.

Cap hadn't recognized the man's voice, but his message had come across crystal clear. His suspicions about Faust and the key had to be accurate. From all Intel had provided about PUSH, its leader wasn't a strategist capable of planning an attack of this magnitude with this high a level of security. The president might be convinced PUSH was responsible for the crisis, including Sybil Stone's supposed death, but Cap wasn't convinced. This entire situation reeked of Gregor Faust and his methodology.

Blowing out a steadying breath, Cap forked his fingers, then rubbed a trembling hand over his chin. What he needed was a diversion. He dialed the phone and when Sam Sayelle came on the line, he launched into creating one. "Do you have an ID on Stone's man at the Wall yet?"

"Not yet."

"Get on the stick." Cap stared at the key, laying on his desk near the green bar light, and damned it for glinting so innocently when it controlled his future. "I really need it, Sam."

"Top priority."

"Thanks." The intercom buzzed and Cap switched lines to respond. "What is it, Jean?"

"Just a reminder, Senator. Mr. Shottley is due in thirty minutes."

Mr. Shottley was a code for Cap's insulin shot. "Thanks. I'm going to be out of the office for a while."

"But you've got—"

"Cancel everything for the rest of the day." He thought of President Lance's briefing. After Saturday midnight, there could be nothing left of D.C. Nothing but devastation, destruction, and despair. "Reschedule for next week, if possible."

"Yes, sir."

Forty minutes later, Cap nodded at the gate guard out-

side A-267, drove down the fifteen miles of deserted road
to the site, and then parked near the first of three hangars.
They looked innocuous, like a cluster of gangly metal gup-
pies tucked under a blanket of thick foliage. The cover did
help keep them out of the line of sight of prying eyes and
probing satellites. All three hangars were constructed of
concrete and steel and painted a drab army green. Each
hangar, like the site itself, had restricted access, but two of
them had little else in common with the one on the extreme left. Two housed offices. The left hangar housed
only an elevator that descended twenty feet underground
to Home Base, the command and control center for the
Special Detail Unit, and the missile.

Cap locked his car, keyed access to the command
hangar, and then walked down the empty corridor to a biometric scanner that made an iris comparison check on
both eyes to verify access approval. He rested his chin on
its soft pad and then pressed his face against its screen.
The authorization light turned from red to green, and he
recalled Jean's "Mr. Shottley" reminder.

He had forgotten to give himself an insulin injection
before leaving the office. Well, damn it, he was here now
and he wasn't driving all the way back to handle it. Mr.
Shottley could wait a couple hours.

Cap took the elevator down. He'd never liked coming
to A-267; the lack of windows bothered him. So did knowing he was so far belowground. The place looked clinical—
bare white walls, ceilings, and floors—but pleasant
enough, and it was certainly in better condition than the
Pentagon, which was threatening to fall down around
everyone's ears. Yet every time Cap entered A-267, he suffered the strongest sensation that he was entering a tomb.
No matter what mind games he played with himself or how
he directed his thoughts, he never had been able to shake
off that feeling.

A bell chimed and the door silently slid open. He

stepped out, on to the white-tile floor of an area below the hangar commonly referred to as the outer rim. Two steps off the elevator, he paused at the main security station, where a thin-faced man sat reading the regs book.

Exactly two dozen military members and unofficial government employees worked at the site. All of them were tested weekly on regulations and procedures that affected every aspect of the site. If a military member answered any question posed to him incorrectly, he was debriefed and reassigned to a less critical position elsewhere. His PCS—permanent change of station—orders were cut within twenty-four hours and he was gone. A civilian, unofficial government employee was fired on the spot, debriefed, and comfortably sequestered in a remote location somewhere for the rest of his or her natural life. That location was outside Cap's need-to-know loop, though he suspected Commander Conlee knew it. At first, Cap had considered the rigid policy stance unreasonable, but then he had learned what was at A-267. The United States could afford no mistakes. Not here.

"Senator Marlowe." The duty officer jumped to his feet. "We weren't expecting an official visit from you today, sir."

Cap let his gaze drop to the man's name badge, then to his rank. "No, you weren't, Lieutenant Gibson. I'm pulling a no-notice inspection of the site."

"Standard or extensive, sir?"

"Extensive." A standard inspection wouldn't let him get beyond the outer rim, where offices, a lounge for coffee breaks, and Home Base were located. He had to get into the inner hub, the circular core of the site. One man sat inside it at the launch-control station twenty-four seven. If ordered to strike, he would key the secure device and operate the launch controls for the Peacekeeper. Only he had the key. And only he and the president had the code, which changed every twenty-four hours. At least, that was the normal process. With Faust's infiltration, who knew the process or how it worked now?

"I'll notify the commander of your arrival, sir."

The last thing Cap wanted was to be distracted by the site commander, Donald Conlee. The man was good at his job and decent company, but what Cap needed was a little privacy. "This is a no-notice inspection, Lieutenant. Notify no one. When I'm done on the premises, I'll return here. You can inform Commander Conlee then."

"Yes, sir."

Cap turned away and began his inspection, hoping Gregor Faust hadn't done anything here that the U.S. engineers couldn't undo, but unwilling to bet on it.

★ ★ ★

Gregor Faust watched the senator move methodically through A-267 on the command center monitor.

Six months ago, on Austin Stone's last official visit to A-267, he had installed the new DNA-dependent, secure-system equipment but had delayed activating it. He also had installed his latest creation: a minute remote-viewing system he claimed was virtually undetectable by current technology. Gregor had doubted that was possible, particularly when the device had been installed in a top-secret site, but time had passed and his bird's-eye view had not once been interrupted—including during both standard and extensive security sweeps. Austin would make another fortune on this system, likely an even greater one than he had made on the DNA secure-system device.

On the wealth scale, Austin trailed Bill Gates. But he might catch him by marketing this new system. Not that the true net sales or income from it would ever appear on any IRS form or corporate quarterly report. The lion's share of sales would be on the black market.

In six months of observations, Gregor had learned a lot

about A-267 policy, procedure, regulations, and operations. But even more valuable to him, he had learned an enormous amount about American mentality. Unless Lieutenant Gibson was unconscious, he would note that Cap Marlowe looked as guilty as hell of something, and that look didn't correlate with a no-notice inspection. If Cap were anyone but a United States Senator, Gibson would note it and deduce that the man had another reason for being at A-267. But because Cap was a senator, Gregor predicted the lieutenant would ignore his instincts.

Despite all the corruption, scandals, ineptitude, and indiscretions that had permeated the U.S. government throughout its existence, Americans still believed in their politicians.

Many politicians had earned that faith. Actually, most of them had. But many had not. Cap Marlowe toed the line. He had accomplished remarkable things that had required courage and grit, and he had pulled off some things that were blatantly down and dirty, like his personal campaign against Lady Liberty.

Cap combed the building, including Home Base's command center—the one place in A-267 where Gregor did not have remote-viewing capability because Austin did not have access to the area to plant the system.

Twenty minutes later Cap stopped at the security checkpoint at the entrance to the inner hub. This station wasn't manned. Human interaction was unnecessary. Few had the access to pass the manned checkpoint in the outer rim. Anyone inside the outer rim had already been screened.

Two machines were attached to the wall. Cap inserted his ID card into the left one, rested his chin on the pad, and then pressed his face against the flatbed scanner. Its sensors would read a print of his irises and only God and Austin Stone knew what else.

Inside, Captain Mendoza, a lean man with narrow eyes and a hawklike nose, sat behind the launch desk, facing the board of controls. He and Cap exchanged a few words, then he passed the senator the log book.

"I need an activity report, too," Cap said.

On the computer, Mendoza generated an activity report. Moments later it fed through the printer. The captain retrieved it without leaving his seat—a policy breach that violated two separate regulations—then passed the report to Cap.

He backed away, stood behind Mendoza, and visually scanned the inner hub. He glanced twice and then a third time at the steel-faced mail chute embedded in the wall. Fixing his gaze on the captain, Cap opened the chute, retrieved a clear cylinder, inserted something into it, and then returned the cylinder to the chute.

Captain Mendoza hadn't noticed a thing.

Gregor grunted at the wily old senator's audacity. His intentions were crystal clear. Plant the launch key inside the inner hub for someone else to find. This way Cap keeps his crimes secret and to himself. No one would know the key had been delivered to him or that he had kept it for months and failed to file the mandatory report. No one would know Cap was involved.

Clever maneuver, but predictable. The good senator wasn't going to be able to deny his affiliation with Ballast so easily. Smiling to himself, Gregor lifted a clear plastic bubble shield on the control desk, exposing two buttons: a green one on the left and a red one on the right. He lightly rubbed the pad of a fingertip over the red button, holding a fixed gaze on the screen.

Cap stepped out of the inner hub and into the outer rim.

Gregor depressed the button.

An alarm inside A-267 emitted short, shrill bursts of sound. Red lights flashed throughout the outer rim.

The steel door between the inner hub and outer rim slid shut.

Between the outer rim and the elevator to the surface hangar, a sheet of metal slid down from the ceiling and locked into the floor, then six-inch-thick bolts slid into braces attached to the metal.

Cap stood in the middle of the outer rim, gape-jawed and spinning in a slow circle. "Gibson." He shouted to be heard over the alarm's deafening peal. "What in hell is happening?"

The young lieutenant paused running through the emergency-duties drill and tossed the senator a deer-caught-in-headlights look. "It's a lockdown, sir."

Cap let out an impatient grunt. "Well, how long is it going to last?"

Rushed and clearly irritated at the interruption, Gibson typed furiously at the computer terminal. "I don't know, sir."

"You mean this isn't a systems test?"

"No, sir." Gibson stopped cold. "It's verified and confirmed. This is not a test."

"What does it mean?"

Stark fear flooded Gibson's eyes. "It means we're under attack, sir."

"By whom?"

"We don't know."

Gregor smiled. An unknown attacker . . . and Cap was already late for his appointment with Mr. Shottley. The remote-viewing device planted in the senator's office was once again proving to be a valuable asset. Odds looked good that he would confess quickly. For his sake, Gregor hoped so. When diabetes went neglected, diabetics faced stiff, unforgiving penalties. Potentially lethal penalties. And Gregor had no intention of reversing the lockdown until Cap confessed.

Something strange on the monitor caught Gregor's eye. The inner hub was empty. Where the hell had Mendoza gone?

An uneasy feeling shimmied up Gregor's back. In six months of monitoring, he had never—not once—seen the inner hub empty. Not until now. Mendoza would have to be dead to breach protocol.

Austin.

Had all hell broken loose in Florida, too? Gregor spoke into the lip mike. "ET, status report."

"We've picked up two heat sources, sir. En route now."

Patch was going to object; he had a soft spot for Liberty. Gregor spoke into the mike. "Under no conditions is she to leave the swamp."

No response.

Gregor frowned. "Did you copy that, ET?"

"It's a little crazy here," Patch said. "Special forces are all over hell's half acre, reining in the media and locals. At most, we've got half an hour on them."

Clenching his teeth, Gregor persisted, asked again. "Did you copy, ET?"

Again, no response.

Gregor stood up, glared at the swamp monitor. "I said, under no circumstances is she to leave the swamp. Do you copy me, ET?"

"Yes, sir," he said softly. "I copy you."

Dropping back into his seat, Gregor muttered a curse. Wasn't it enough that he had Austin and Cap to worry about as well as all of the forces of the United States? Now he had to demand compliance from Ballast members, too?

Worst of all, Gregor now had doubts that his own second-in-command would obey his orders. Hearing and acknowledging the mandate didn't guarantee that Patch would execute Lady Liberty.

Chapter Fourteen

Are you being honest or sarcastic?

   Are you saying you can't tell?

   Holding up the briefcase, Sybil slid underwater in the cold creek, hoping Westford knew what he was saying when he swore the thick, matted sawgrass at the shore meant the food chain had moved on. It was the rainy season, and fresh water ran down the rivers to the coast. The wildlife would follow it.

   The water smelled more brackish than fresh to her, but she hadn't seen one of those gator slides Westford had pointed out earlier, when he had warned her to watch out for cottonmouths and rattlesnakes. Both, evidently, thrived in the area. Yet minnows darted at her legs, and where there were minnows, there were those creatures Mother Nature had feeding on them. The thought alone raised a shudder.

   The narrow creek wound to a bend and then disappeared out of sight. To the north, small clumps of cypress stood in water. There the water had to be fresh. But Westford still had insisted they drink only rainwater. Considering the deluge, that hadn't been a problem. Fish were also plentiful, but sushi wasn't on the menu, and that brought them back to the fire/smoke challenge so, with the exception of nibbling on berries and some kind of root that had all the sensory appeal of the chunks of bark, they'd fasted. That was fine with Sybil, too. She was hungry but too worried and anxious to eat without being sick.

Branches stretched over the rain-swelled rush of water like a canopy. Stones, fallen limbs, and heavy brush littered the shore. Cooled by all the rain, the water felt frigid against her bare skin, but she welcomed the feeling, and rubbed at her arms, washing away the quicksand grit.

Surfacing, she dragged her hands over her face and blew out a long-held breath. The briefcase thudded against her chest.

You need me.

Okay, I need you.

Are you being honest or sarcastic?

Are you saying you can't tell?

Why was that exchange nagging at her? Why couldn't she just forget about it? Forget about him?

Wait a second. Wait. How *could* she forget about Westford? The man had guarded her, protected her, and repeatedly risked his life for her. She was human; of course she couldn't forget him. God help her if she could ever become so cold and callous and ungrateful.

But Gabby had to be wrong. Westford had taken the risks he'd taken for his veep, not for her. Hadn't he taken a bullet for the previous veep?

He had. She rubbed at her right thigh, gently brushing the grit away from the catbrier scratches, then noticed the bruise at her ribs. Dark purple, sore to the touch, it cut a wide swathe from her side to the center of her stomach.

The jab from the limb in the quicksand pit. She had to think straight about Westford. No rationalizing or delusions or playing ostrich. Realistically, she was just another assignment, and he was only with her by David's personal request. He had always been devoted to David but not to her. He had transferred to get away from her.

And his kisses? What about those?

Trauma-induced. Affirming life. Proximity.

True. All true. An empty ache hollowed her chest and she stiffened against it, fighting a dawning truth: She didn't want to be just another assignment to Jonathan Westford. She wanted to be . . . more. And not just in her professional life, but in her private life.

In her private life? Shocked still, Sybil stood in the water, the mushy bottom curling around her toes and heels. This couldn't be true. It just couldn't . . . be true. Good God, Austin had deceived her for fifteen years, and she had let him. Hadn't she learned *anything* from that? How could she be feeling passion, desire, longing for any man? How could she even consider wanting a man in her life? Had she lost her mind?

Shaking, she splashed water onto her face, hoping it would clear her head. She was a woman on a political mission. Okay. Okay, so she was human. It was lust.

It's not lust.

Of course it's lust. And for anyone except her, lust was good. Great. Lust was acceptable. It was normal to feel physically attracted to Westford. By anyone's standards, he was incredible, and she'd been without a man for a long time. But she couldn't be attracted to him mentally or emotionally, and she sure as hell didn't want to feel lust for him personally. She had a promise to David to keep. No, no lust. She was just affirming life, too. There had been a lot of shocks. Who wouldn't seek someone strong to hold on to?

Feeling better about this, she shook off her fears about him, let go of them, and nearly smiled. How in the world had she fancied herself falling in love with any man, even Westford? After Austin, it was ridiculous. Outrageous. Not to mention impossible.

Love?

Shockwaves rocketed through her, and she locked her knees to keep them from buckling, then splashed herself more. Oh, no. No. Love wasn't logical. It wasn't an option. Not to her. Not now. Not ever again. Lust was bad enough, but love? Love was just impossible.

You're human, Sybil. Love is a human emotion. Why should it be impossible? Why should you be exempt?

She wasn't. She had tried loving a man and had failed miserably. Balancing on one foot, she rubbed the grit from her calf. She refused to be an emotional idiot twice in one lifetime.

An emotional idiot? Since when does loving someone make you an idiot?

That comment brought her up short and she stilled to consider it. Good God, had she become that twisted? That cowardly? She tilted her head back, let her jaw fall loose, and stared up beyond the tall pines and ancient oaks to the dismal gray sky. What had happened to her out here—hormonal overload? Swamp fever? Something had happened in this hellhole. That or she'd left her sense in Geneva.

Stop rationalizing, Sybil. It's cowardly. After Austin, you began hiding—from him, from men, and from yourself.

Had she really? Moving through the water, she stepped ashore and retrieved her clothes. As she dipped them in the water and scrubbed out the gritty sludge, she relived her life from the moment Cap Marlowe had confronted her with his accusations of her ethics violations on Austin's vasectomy. Relived the shame and anger that she had been lied to and betrayed and duped for so long by a man who was supposed to love her. Relived the inferiority she had felt as a woman, the humiliation of Cap Marlowe—her nemesis, for God's sake—knowing intimate things about her private life she didn't know. Her emotions had been strong then, and they were strong now. She had intentionally distanced herself from Austin.

But you distanced yourself from everyone else, too. Doesn't the fact that you refuse to call Westford by his first name prove it?

His first name, for God's sake. It was such a simple intimacy. What kind of person allows someone to put his life on the line for her time and again but keeps him at a distance by refusing to call him by his first name?

Finished rinsing her underwear, she put it on. The wet silk clung to her thighs like plaster. She had divorced Austin and had reclaimed some of her self-esteem, if not her personal confidence. At least she thought she had reclaimed her self-esteem. She eased her bra straps up on her shoulders. But in refusing to trust others and shielding herself from caring too much for anyone else ever again, had she really been protecting herself?

Or were you still hiding?

Wringing out her skirt at the water's edge, she paused and dragged her fingers over her skull, through her wet hair. The truth wasn't pretty, but she had to face it. She had shut down her personal life, and she had been grateful to feel compelled to give David her promise on her conduct. It gave her a license not to risk loving anyone again. And she honestly had convinced herself that her career would be enough—that she would feel fulfilled. But she had been wrong. Gold help her, she had been so wrong. This thing with Westford wasn't just lust.

"Sybil." Westford appeared between two fat bushes. "Hurry."

Sensing his urgency, she scrambled into her shirt and jacket, slipped to her knees in the wet sand, jerked on his socks, and then rushed to him.

He crossed his lips with a fingertip, dropped to his

knees in a thicket of mature palmettos, and whispered. "We've got company. Dig."

Dig? She fell to her knees beside him, scooped mud into a heap. Following his hand signals, they dug two trenches under the lush leaves of dense, spiny bushes. He motioned for her to lie in the first trench. Twisting, she slid inside, for once grateful for the recent downpour and thick brush.

Silently, intently, Westford shoved dirt over her. "Smear your head and face," he said, his voice a faint whisper of sound.

They worked quickly, methodically, until they both were under the bushes and buried up to their necks in mud. The birds chirped in the treetops and the squirrels leapt branch to branch, tree to tree. Sybil's heart pounded in her ears, and the reason for Westford's drastic measures appeared from around the bend.

Three men walked down the narrow shore and then fanned out into the brush. Through the leaves, she watched them move. All were dressed in black and were carrying equipment that, she assumed, included heat-seeking sensors, since they kept glancing at them. And all three men were heavily armed.

★   ★   ★

President Lance finished taping his weekly public radio chat and removed the mike from his lapel. Whether they did more harm than good was a topic of hot debate among his staff, since they aired on Friday nights and gave the weekend talk-show circuit fresh fodder that gathered steam by Monday.

Barber stepped over to him, bent low, and whispered. "They need you in the Sit, sir."

"Thank you, everyone," David said, then headed toward the Situation Room.

Sam Sayelle rounded the corner. From his rumpled look, he had been as overworked as the rest of them in the last few days. He'd also had a collision with a cup of coffee and, judging by the stain on his shirtfront, he'd lost. David whispered to Barber, "Any new word on the Dean family?"

"Not yet, sir."

"Sam." David slowed his steps. "I understand you alerted us to the Dean family situation. I appreciate your taking the initiative and checking it out."

"Any luck locating them, sir?"

"I'm hoping so. We'll keep you posted." David increased his pace, to avoid having to talk around more questions he couldn't answer, then entered the Situation Room. The two dozen men and women seated around the conference table rose to their feet. "Please, sit down." David took his chair at the head of the table.

Commander Conlee cleared his throat. "Mr. President."

David had always liked Conlee. He was in his fifties with short, spiky gray hair and a face that had seen too much misery and too little laughter. Conlee was dependable and forthright, and he never licked boots. He called things as he saw them, which was no small part of the reason he wore a chest full of medals and deserved every one of them. Conlee didn't impress easily, and he never backed down if he was right. Not such good traits on the diplomatic side of government business, but admirable traits for a commander. No one on the planet understood covert operations or operatives better than Donald Conlee. "Go ahead, Commander."

"Minutes ago an unknown party locked down A-267. So far there has been no interference with operations or any attempt to infiltrate our systems. We have nine authorized personnel locked in their individual offices in the outer rim and two locked in its reception area: Lieutenant Gibson and Senator Marlowe."

"What was Cap doing there?"

"Pulling a no-notice inspection, sir," Conlee said. "There's an added complication with the senator, sir. Dr. Richardson will brief you on that." Conlee gave Richardson the go-ahead nod.

"Without getting into medical jargon and double-talk, please."

"Of course, Mr. President," Richardson said. "Simply put, Senator Marlowe is a diabetic and he's overdue for an insulin injection. He can't get out of the outer rim, and we can't get in to give him one. Right now the senator isn't feeling well, but unless we can get some insulin into him soon, he is going to get worse. The longer the delay, the more severe his condition will become. Bluntly speaking, sir, he could crash."

Another complication David did not need. "Define crash."

"He could lapse into a diabetic coma, sir. Or he could die."

Richardson sat down, and David laced his hands on the tabletop and shifted his gaze to Conlee. "Can't we override this infiltrator's lockdown commands?"

"No sir," Conlee said. "Our controls have been rendered useless."

"So we're sitting ducks?"

"That's a fair assessment of our current position, sir."

"Someday someone is going to have to explain to me why the most powerful nation in the world is so vulnerable it loses control of its own assets."

"Forty percent budget cutbacks for three years in a row has a formidable impact, sir," Conlee said. "Vulnerability is just one of many challenges created."

Agreeing, but not inclined to debate, David returned to the matter at hand. "Is the inner hub intact?" He was almost afraid to ask.

Conlee cleared his throat, obviously not eager to respond to this one. "Intact but empty, sir."

"*What?*" The inner hub was never empty.

"Captain Mendoza was on duty," Conlee explained. "Immediately after Senator Marlowe left the hub, the site locked down. Mendoza was at his station then. But when the lockdown completed, he was gone."

"That's impossible," a puzzled Barber interjected. "There is only one way in or out. Mendoza had to have walked past the senator."

"Senator Marlowe disagrees." Conlee frowned and leaned forward against the table. "I don't claim to understand the logistics, but the statement from Lieutenant Gibson matches the senator's statement. They both say Mendoza was at the station and at no time passed the senator, which he would have had to do to exit the inner hub. They say he just vanished."

David stared at Conlee. "Mendoza could be our leak."

"We have no evidence of that at this time, sir."

"Keep looking."

"Yes, sir."

The surveillance camera in the inner hub was focused on the control desk, away from the door. If at the onset of the lockdown Mendoza had moved to the door and had stayed there, then he wouldn't be visible on camera, but the heat sensors would detect his presence. "Have we run diagnostics?"

"Simple and complex, sir."

So the heat sensors hadn't located him either. "How long will it take our engineers to run a stand-down cycle?"

"They're not sure yet. Apparently, whoever did this planted viral triggers throughout the system. To neutralize them, the engineers have to do a frame-by-frame cycle inspection. It could take days."

"We don't have days."

"I'm aware of that, sir. We're seeking alternatives."

"Alternatives? Is that it?"

"It's all we know at this time, sir."

"I want hourly updates and all crisis reports personally." David slapped his hands against the tabletop. "Anything else?"

"Yes, sir." Barber leaned forward, laced his hands atop a yellow-lined pad. Nothing had been written on the page. "I would speak to you privately about this, but privacy is a moot point, since everyone here has heard about it already."

"That includes the press, sir," Winston added, looking pensive.

"It's about Vice President Stone," Barber said.

"What about her?" Had the media somehow learned they had released news of her death without confirmation?

"What she did with Peris and Abdan has raised serious concerns about her competence."

David did his best to keep his temper in check. "Incompetent how?"

Barber's face went red. "She's having cookies and milk and a note delivered to their leaders every night to keep them in Geneva."

"Cookies and milk." Winston blew out a disgusted grunt. "In a single stroke, she's set back diplomatic relations twenty years."

David slid Winston a warning look to hold his tongue. "So I take it her strategy failed and the leaders have left Geneva."

"Actually, it's worked, sir." That came from an amused Commander Conlee.

"Then her strategy, while unusual, has proven to be both effective and successful." The president didn't blink. "Let me remind you, *we* couldn't get either of them to the negotiating table. She did." He paused, but no one disputed him, so he went on. "As it happens, I've heard from both Peris and Abdan again today. They're charmed by the vice president's gesture and they're mourning her death." He slid forward on his chair in a deliberate attempt to intimidate both Barber and Winston. "Something is wrong when our vice president gets more concern and respect from foreigners than from her own people. Think about that."

"There's more, sir." Barber glanced nervously at Winston, then back to the president. "If we want to avoid a political bloodbath, we need to address the matter quickly."

Another Watergate or Whitewater, they did not need. David's stomach soured. "What specifically is the matter?"

Barber's lips flattened to a slash. "The ethics committee has received a violations complaint against the vice president, sir."

★   ★   ★

Sam had been standing near the elevator for the past fifteen minutes, debating whether to ride up to Cap's office and tell him what had been going on. He was tempted, but Conlee had made no bones about promising to kill Sam and anyone he told about the broadcasts. Putting your own head on the chopping block was one thing, but putting someone else's there gave a man reason to pause.

He stared above the elevator at the lighted numbers, wondering what he was doing here. He had done fourteen broadcasts for Conlee now, and he'd talked with Karla about the Dean family half a dozen times, without hearing anything except "No sign of them yet. Frankly, we need a break." The kidnappers hadn't made contact, and Sniffer hadn't found a clue. With each broadcast and each call from Karla, Sam had become more convinced the FBI, or whoever was working the case on the federal level, had squelched the local police investigation. Karla hadn't said a word about input from the Deans' extended families or friends, and Sniffer had determined on first-contact attempts that no family, friends, or neighbors—none of them—had any idea anything was amiss. Sam had debated and decided to keep his mouth shut and not risk approaching Conlee or Cap Marlowe with a thing. He saw no way around that now.

So what are you doing here?

Good question. The elevator moved down to the fourth floor. He hadn't considered going to Cap's office this time. But then he had run into President Lance, who hadn't been exactly forthcoming with information about the Dean family, and it hadn't escaped Sam's notice that neither Barber, nor Winston, nor Lance had so much as hinted at the broadcasts. Not that the president would say anything outright, but typically Barber or Winston would. What really had bothered Sam was that the president had walked on as if everything were fine, and he had had the strongest feeling that Lance didn't know about the broadcasts or that he was doing them.

What if Commander Conlee was working with Sybil Stone and this treason business was valid? What if they weren't makeshift saviors but the most corrupt politicians on the Hill?

Yet treason didn't fit with the content of the broadcasts. It didn't fit her, either. Why feed her updates on the Peris and Abdan peace talks and on a terrorist-attack crisis that had happened only God knew where? Sam had watched every resource like a hawk, but he hadn't seen anything about an attack. Or any reference whatsoever to A-267. What was it? Where was it that the country was being covertly attacked?

If Sybil Stone was alive, she was putting it all on the line, including her own backside, and she was doing it knowing that PUSH or Ballast meant for her to fail. If either of those groups was gunning for him, Sam would be scared stiff. So would anyone else who had a whiff of sense. Yet she hadn't called Conlee and requested extraction. She was hanging tight and holding her silence.

In Sam's book, that meant one of two things: She was already dead, or she didn't know whom she could trust. If the latter proved true, then she had guts and grit.

Guts and grit? Sybil Stone?

A novel concept, admittedly, but one not easily dismissed. Not after partially decoding the broadcasts.

The elevator door opened.

Jean brushed his sleeve as she stepped into the lift. "Going up to see the senator, Sam?"

He couldn't do it. Not until he knew which side of the fence Sybil Stone came down on, who stood with her, and who wanted her dead. "No." Sam slid her a plastic smile and checked his watch. "No, I'm not."

"Something come up?"

"Yeah, a sexy cop I've stood up one too many times."

"Ouch." Jean smiled easily. "Crossing a woman who's armed and dangerous. You're a brave man, Sam."

"Not so brave. She's sworn to shoot me if I do it again. I don't think I'd better play the odds."

"Have you heard anything new on Liberty?"

A warning alarm went off in his head. *Think fast. Faster.* Denial was his only safety measure. "I'm sorry, Jean. I didn't hear you."

What she'd said hit her and her jaw fell slack. "It was nothing. You okay?"

Sam struggled to show no outward reaction, but for the first time in the five years he had known Jean, he looked deeply into her eyes and the look she sent back to him had his instincts humming. Jean wasn't the paragon he had believed her to be. She was something else—maybe for someone else. Could she be an infiltrator for Ballast or PUSH?

Ballast maybe, but not PUSH. Jean stuck with "the best." She'd never ally herself with anyone ranking even a close second any more than she'd fly coach on a commercial liner.

Ballast had a documented history of infiltrating, and Jean was certainly capable. It was possible. Actually, one slip of her tongue had made it probable and worth checking out.

Before the upheaval in the last election, Secret Service code names had been public information. But that policy had nearly cost the former veep his life. After his attempted assassination, the security procedure had been changed, and all code names for the brass and their families had become classified. These days those names were guarded like Fort Knox.

Have you heard anything new on Liberty?

Jean hadn't asked him for the latest on Sybil Stone; she'd asked him for the latest on Liberty.

Yet Cap Marlowe trusted Jean implicitly, filtered all of his leaks to Sam through her. So did that mean she had played Cap or that Cap worked for the terrorists, too?

Chapter Fifteen

They were going to kill her.

Buried up to her neck under a clump of thick bushes, Sybil stared out from between the leaves. The clouds overhead loomed dark and ominous, but for once she felt grateful for the long shadows obscuring the floor of the swamp. Croaking frogs, the rustling of small animals moving through the brush and in the trees, and an unseen owl's soft hoots resonated through the woods, breaking the deafening silence. She didn't dare to move, to breathe, to so much as blink for fear the three armed men after her and Westford would shoot.

"I'm picking up something here, ET," one of the men said.

A broad shadow fell over a barrel-chested man with a white spot in his hair. "I see it."

All three of them stared down at palm-size devices. Heat sensors, or some other locating device, she surmised, certain they could hear her heart banging against her ribs.

She cut her gaze left, to Westford. Swathed in mud, his head was concealed by the pungent leaves. If she hadn't known he was there, she wouldn't have seen him. That gave her hope that the three men wouldn't see them. They clearly weren't U.S. forces.

"Walk the grid," ET said, his back to her.

The other two men walked farther away from Sybil. When they moved out of earshot, he turned and stared straight through the bushes into her eyes.

Sybil clenched her jaw to keep from gasping. She didn't know what to do. Should she stay still? Move? Try to run and lead them away from Westford?

"This one is free, Lady Liberty," ET whispered, and dropped a penny inches from her nose. "For the kids and your milk and cookies." His eyes glazed. "But next time I see you, you're dead."

Before she could respond, if she could have found enough voice to respond, ET turned and walked away.

"There's no one here," he told the others. "Something has the sensors malfunctioning. Operate on visual." He led the men away from the bushes and soon they disappeared from sight.

"Don't move yet."

Sybil looked over at Westford.

"He just put his life on the line for you. Give him some space."

"Why would he do that?" Sybil couldn't imagine, but she was damn grateful for it.

"Could be anything," Westford said. "My guess is respect."

Sybil found that difficult to believe. "The man's a terrorist, for God's sake."

"That doesn't mean he's without honor. Only that he sees certain issues from a different perspective. From his view, he's justified. From ours, he's twisted. Apparently, you're not one of his twisted issues."

"He wasn't one of ours?"

"ET is Gregor Faust's number-two man."

Nothing in Westford's tone or expression told her he was being evasive, but her instincts swore that's exactly what he was doing. "Then why did he drop a U.S. penny in my face?"

"It's a U.S. penny?" Westford asked, clearly intrigued.

"Yes. What does it mean?"

"I'm not at liberty to say."

Having been in that position too often herself, where she would have to break the law to disclose some tidbit of classified information restricted to a specific need-to-know loop, she didn't push.

They stayed put until twilight gave way to darkness, moving as little as possible. The mud made her itch, and Sybil resisted scratching by craning her neck time and again to look longingly past a graceful willow to the water rushing in the creek.

Finally Westford gave her the signal. "Let's go."

They washed off in the creek. Allowing for the cumbersome briefcase, Sybil mimicked Westford, minimizing splashing, keeping all but his head under the surface of the water. Small targets, she supposed, were harder to hit.

A clopping noise sounded, echoed across the water, startling her. "Westford?"

"Helicopter. Three o'clock," he whispered, scanning the sky. "Get out of the water."

The helicopter put down in a clearing of thin grass. Sybil and Westford moved closer, staying crouched low to the ground, concealed by trees and brush and darkness. They took cover behind a line of catbrier near the edge of the clearing. The clawlike vine snagged Sybil's right arm. She gritted her teeth to keep from crying out and untangled herself. Thin streaks of blood trickled down her arm.

"You okay?"

Her arm burned like fire. "Fine," she grated out.

The chopper blades whipped the air, bending the grass. It was painted black and had no visible markings. Sybil nearly cried. "It's not one of ours."

Westford spared her a glance. "Not yet."

Should that remark elate her or scare her to death? In truth, it did both.

Before dawn, she and Westford would be at war.

★   ★   ★

Weak and clammy, Cap leaned back on a brown vinyl sofa in the outer rim's reception area, across from the security desk. Lieutenant Gibson sat behind it. He was on the phone again, this time with a flight surgeon.

"The inner doors are all sealed, sir," Gibson said into the receiver. "The only things I can get to are the reception area and the coffee bay. Nothing else."

Cap's mind felt fuzzy, as if he were hearing and seeing through layers of gauze. In a cold sweat, fumble-fingered, he worked at loosening his tie. The effort drained his strength, and he slumped down to lie on the sofa, barely resisting the urge to curl his knees to his chest.

Gibson left the desk and disappeared into an alcove. When he returned, he was carrying a coffee cup with Mickey Mouse faces on it.

He held the cup to Cap's mouth. "Doc Richardson says you need sugar, so you need to drink this. I mixed what I could find with a little water."

"Thank you." Cap clutched at the cup with both hands, drew it shakily to his mouth, depending on Gibson more than his ego would let him admit. "Is there any food here?" He swallowed the syrupy water. Refined sugar would elevate his blood-sugar level, but it wouldn't sustain it. It was midnight, and he'd missed two meals, two snacks, and two injections. "I—I need protein."

"No, sir. Nothing," Gibson said, and then grunted.

"Somebody ripped off all the sugar from the coffee bay. I found a packet shoved up under the coffeemaker to bring you what I did. How long will it last?"

"Not long." Someone had removed all the sugar and locked Cap in the outer rim. Someone had been observing him, had known he hadn't taken his shot and seized this opportunity. Someone wanted him dead. The question was, who? Only Jean had knowledge of his insulin injection . . . *Jean?* Could she be spying on him for Faust?

No. No, not Jean. She'd been his right and left hands for more than ten years. Hell, she knew more about him and his activities than his wife. "We have to get out of here, Gibson."

"We're doing everything we can do to make that happen, sir. People are locked in offices all over the building. The security scanners have been corrupted. Until we figure out what to do and how to do it, we're stuck."

"Corrupted in what way?" Cap hoped to God he was wrong, yet it seemed logical that they would need the key he had put in the inner-hub mail chute and the key Sybil Stone was carrying to reverse the lockdown. But Conlee had questioned Cap personally about Mendoza leaving the inner hub. How the man had gotten past Cap, he didn't know, but apparently he had, because now the inner hub was empty. That meant there was no one inside to retrieve Cap's key, and Sybil Stone was purportedly dead.

What if that was true? What if she was dead?

Then you'll die, too, Cap.

"We're still determining that, sir. But the corruption appears to be pervasive."

Cap drained the cup. "Thank you."

Gibson nodded, and Cap relaxed back against the sofa cushions, dabbed a trembling finger to his damp chin, and then closed his eyes. Ironic. In the whole world, the one person he most hated was the very person he now depended on to save his country and his life.

If she's not dead and she returns with the key, she could drag her feet long enough to let you die and still arrive in time to halt the launch.

Sobering thought, but true. Without an insulin injection, Cap would die long before the missile detonated. And honesty forced him to admit that, if he were in her shoes, letting him die is exactly what he would do. His nemesis would be off his back and out of his way forever. His main opposition would cease to exist, and he wouldn't have to lift a finger to make it happen.

Even as he thought it, Cap instinctively knew Sybil Stone would not drag her feet. After all he had done to make her life difficult, she would not deliberately linger and watch him die. She would find the thought of doing that morally and ethically repugnant.

He found it repugnant, but he would do it anyway.

What kind of man did that make him?

And what kind of woman did that make her?

Chapter Sixteen

Friday, August 9 ★ First-Strike Launch: 24:00:52

Surrounded by darkness, Sybil lay facedown in the dirt in a thicket of dense palmettos and strained to focus on the helicopter parked in the clearing. Its props beat at the humid, heavy air.

She and Westford hadn't moved for hours, and apparently they weren't going to move until he felt they had optimum chances for success. He had urged her repeatedly to rest, but she couldn't. Even bone-weary, she found that watching and waiting when time was short and every second was precious pumped too much adrenaline through her veins for her to calm down, much less sleep.

Westford slid closer to her, whispered at her ear. "Sayelle just reported. They're shifting all resources to PUSH."

"No." Frustration had her dropping her forehead to the soft, wet ground to fight back tears. "Faust will declare it open season."

"Not if we get back first." He slid his gaze from her to the helicopter.

Yet still they waited.

About an hour before dawn, Westford again moved close enough to whisper. "Stay here until I signal you. Then run as fast as you can to the chopper."

"I should go with you." They had watched half a dozen men armed with M-16s pour out of the helicopter. The bastards had been wearing U.S. military camouflage gear, too.

"There's only one man left on the aircraft. I can handle it, Sybil."

She nodded, but something didn't feel right. They had watched the men spread out, move in different directions at the edge of the clearing, and then disappear into the dense woods. Yet she still felt them there. If they had disbursed, why did she still feel them there? "Are you smelling death?"

"Yes, but not ours."

"I feel them here. They haven't gone far."

"I know." Westford slid on his belly, backed out from under the bushes, then crouched low and moved through the trees until the darkness swallowed him.

Because she couldn't complicate things, she didn't say anything aloud, but she whispered it in her mind. *Be careful, Jonathan. It's just swamp fever, not love, but I still need you.*

A few minutes later a shadow crossed the clearing, heading toward the chopper. Her breath locked in her lungs.

Time slowed, then stopped. A lifetime passed, and another, and then another. Finally Westford stood at the chopper door, signaling.

Sybil scrambled to her feet, circled the clearing just inside the brush. Some scraggly, thorny bush nicked her leg. Not catbrier, but the pricks still burned like hot nails. She batted at it with the briefcase, using it as a shield, and kept moving, breaking into a full-out run.

Something whizzed past her shoulder and clanged, hitting metal. A gunshot.

"Keep running!" Westford shouted.

She tucked her chin and unleashed, running as fast as she could, ignoring the stones stabbing into her feet, the tall grass slapping at her legs. Gunfire exploded in a furious barrage around her. Resisting the urge to scream, she locked her gaze on the chopper, and dug for that reserve burst of energy. Two more steps. Just two . . . more . . .

Westford jerked her into the chopper and then dove for the pilot's seat. Gunfire exploded from all sides, heavy and fast. A man's body lay on the chopper's floor.

"Keep your head down," Westford ordered, flipping controls and lifting the chopper off the ground.

Bullets streaked across the sky and hit the helicopter with resonating clangs. Cringing, Sybil covered her ears, tucked her chin and the briefcase to her chest, and stayed crouched low behind Westford's seat. Finally they were airborne.

The bullets stopped.

"Are we safe now?" Sybil stared at the back of his head.

"We're out of range. Come sit down and buckle up."

Shaking, her insides churning, she stepped over the man's body, feeling drawn to look at him. He wasn't the one called ET who had let her live. This man didn't have that white spot in his hair.

Oddly relieved by that, she stepped over a camera and other equipment, then slid into the seat and looked over at Westford. "I think I've aged twenty years since we left Geneva." She couldn't stop shaking. She laced her hands in her lap, felt them tremble against her knees.

"You look the same."

The man was out of his mind. She was scratched, scraped, bruised, bitten, and banged up, head to heel. And she was filthy dirty. "If that's true, I need serious help."

He grunted.

"Tell me you know how to fly this thing."

"I know how to fly this thing."

"Seriously?"

"Yes, ma'am."

"Fabulous." It didn't surprise her. She knew of very little Westford couldn't do. Yet that didn't calm her. Fear still lumped in her throat, had her stomach queasy and her chest tight. "Now tell me we didn't just rip off a media chopper."

"I don't think so."

"There's a ton of camera equipment in the back."

"It's a Ballast chopper. My guess is the camera is cover. Someone's posing as press."

"Are you sure it's Faust's?"

"No. But I'm sure it's not ours." He made some adjustments on his transmitter, let out a frustrated sigh, and reached for the chopper's radio. "Our media doesn't often carry weapons or pose as military members, and our own guys aren't as likely to shoot at us."

Sure of very little anymore, Sybil shrugged. "It's possible." If he thought he could get away with it, Cap Marlowe would be eager to put a bullet through her. And, of course, there was Austin. He was capable of anything.

"Agreeing makes me sick, but I'm not going to lie. It's possible." Because it was, Westford muttered a curse, put on the radio headgear, and switched to the classified, emergency channel.

"You're going to break radio silence?"

"It's okay. The channel is secure."

"Westford, there's no way to totally secure any communication. Not even in a copper-lined, underground bunker."

"It's all right, Sybil. Trust me." He flipped the lip mike into position. "Borrowed transport. Inbound."

Sybil frowned at him. "How will they know it's you?"

"They'll know."

"How?"

"Voice recognition," he clarified.

"Borrowed transport?" A man's voice came through the radio. "Whose?"

"Commander Conlee," Westford told Sybil, and then responded to the transmission. "Not ours."

"Where the hell are you?"

"Outdoors. Not at liberty to say."

Sybil frowned, perplexed. "Outdoors?"

Westford swiveled the mike away from his face. "Code for Ballast."

"PUSH is indoors?"

He nodded.

"So they won't pull resources from Faust?"

"Honestly?"

Oh, damn. Not another complication. She nodded.

"They'll verify the transmission first. If they consider it genuine, then they won't. If they don't, then they will."

"So what could be a problem? You've been SDU for years."

"The transmission is coming from a hostile aircraft, in a hostile area, with no evidence it isn't being made under duress."

Her stomach sank. Valid point. One she really hadn't wanted to hear. "Then we have to trust Conlee to figure it out." She frowned, swept her hair back from her face. "You know this trust business is really hard for me."

"Yes, ma'am, I do," he said, obviously catching her double meaning.

How could he so readily accept a lack of trust after all he'd done for her? But was he? Really? She didn't want to trust him, but she was afraid she did. God, but she hated knowing that. Hated it. "I guess I have no choice."

"Not from where I'm sitting." He spared her a glance. "Now we're going home."

Sybil just stared at him. How could he sound so calm, so unaffected? So...normal? They'd nearly died several times and people had just been shooting at them, for God's sake. This kind of stuff didn't happen to Sybil. She fought with words and ideology, not with plane explosions, swamps, or guns and bullets. "You're not worried that they'll follow us?"

"If they do, we'll handle it." He angled his head, checked his gauges. "Sybil, don't borrow trouble. Enough finds you on its own. For now you're safe. Your Mr. Tibbs would tell you to enjoy it. I say grab a little rest if you can. When we get back to Washington, you're going to be busy stopping the launch and briefing the president."

"I don't understand something. Our Search and Rescue teams are in the swamp. Why didn't we just go find them? I know about the infiltrator, but they know me, Westford. They would have to know my orders supersede their current ones."

His expression turned somber, and, in the reflection of the green and white instrument lights, she saw regret fill his eyes. "Someone on the inside has turned traitor. We don't know what position he or she holds, but we know that person carries clout. Enough clout to issue orders that carry high odds of being obeyed—regardless of what you or anyone else says. Until we identify the traitor, I won't risk compromising you."

Having no idea what to say, she said nothing, just sat there with her stomach quivering and her insides rattling. It suddenly occurred to her how many times in the last two days she nearly had died and how many times Westford had put his life in jeopardy to help her. Her voice turned froggy. "Thank you for everything you've done for me, Westford. Not just this time, but before you left me, too."

"You're welcome." His expression softened. "Sybil, do you think you could call me Jonathan? Just once in a while?"

Jonathan. A soft name that shouldn't suit him. West-ford came across hard: a bundle of lean muscle and sharp contradictions with blunt features and large, capable hands. Shoulders broad enough to carry his burdens and those of others. Spare with words, complaints, and praise. And yet the name suited him—and terrified her. She cared too much. Felt too close to him. Even if they wanted to deepen the bonds between them, there was her promise to David standing between them. She couldn't compromise on that promise, but she could grant Jonathan this one small request. She just had to remember why she had agreed. "Thank you, Jonathan."

"My pleasure."

Getting shot at, jumping out of a plane without a para-chute, nearly falling into quicksand when trying to get her out—his pleasure? Something hitched in her chest and filled her heart. Trust. She couldn't deny it or doubt it, even though she had been firmly convinced she would never be able to trust another man. Somewhere along the way, he had managed to slip under her defenses. He was inside her now, a part of her, and, God help her, she trusted him completely.

Swamp fever?

Swamp fever . . . with a kick.

Still overwhelmed, she reached over and pressed her hand against his. "You don't have to lie and say it was a pleasure, Jonathan. I know you're only with me as a per-sonal favor to David."

How did he respond to that? Unsure, Jonathan kept silent, but he carried new insight. She felt he had left her, not the job on her guard detail. *Her.* That held promise, didn't it?

She turned toward him. "May I ask you a question?"

Here it came. He refused to lie to her, and he couldn't tell her the truth. The woman would be mortified. So would he. Loving her was one thing. Letting her know it with all the obstacles between them was another. "Sure."

"Would you please stay with me until all of this is over?"

That question he hadn't expected, but he understood it. Sybil Stone had more courage in her little finger than most people had in their entire body. She was brave and fiercely protective of her country and its kids. But right now she was also vulnerable, and she knew it. She needed someone she could trust. So she was taking a leap of faith, and trusting him. "You need me."

"I said I did, and I do." She dipped her chin. "And in case you can't tell, I'm being honest, not sarcastic."

Knowing what that had cost her, Jonathan admitted the inevitable. He had tried to avoid her physically and emotionally, and he had lost. He loved her anyway. He would love her the rest of his life. "Yes, I will stay with you."

She gave him a gentle smile, squeezed his hand, and then softened her touch, lacing their fingertips and pressing their palms.

Jonathan suffered an emotional firestorm. Hesitation. Concern. Doubt. He swallowed hard, cut his gaze to look at her from the corner of his eye. She was staring straight at him. The physical intimacy wasn't an unconscious reaction to their situation; it was intentional. Lady Liberty wasn't in the seat beside him. Sybil Stone was, and this time she wasn't touching him as part of a reaction to surviving a near-fatal incident. This time she knew exactly what she was doing.

Their feelings were mutual.

A rush of pure pleasure shot through him, and Jonathan gently squeezed her fingertips. Gathering his courage, he turned his head to look at her. She quickly looked away.

This, too, he understood. They both wanted the reassurance of touching, but she feared mentioning it as much as he did. Mention it, and you risk losing it.

Apparently, neither of them was willing to take that

risk. And that was fine with him. Sometimes words just got in the way.

He stared through the windshield, the control lights casting a green and white glow through the cockpit. And when next he dared to look at her, Lady Liberty sat fast asleep.

Before Jonathan could celebrate, a transmission came through; this one directly from Conlee. "Incoming hostiles. ETA roughly three minutes."

They were being followed, and in three minutes those hostiles would be all over them. Jonathan wasn't armed. He dropped altitude, scanned the terrain, and located a thicket of woods to the east with a marginally acceptable clearing where he could land. The spot risked more exposure than he would like, but what choice did he have? He had no time and no arms.

Debating whether to alert Liberty, he hugged the trees, leaving just enough space for the props to function unhindered, decided against it, then set the chopper down and waited, his every nerve on full alert.

"ETA one minute."

The beating of props sounded, and a Ballast chopper appeared over the treetops at ten o'clock. It was armed with an M230 and Sidewinder missiles. He didn't want to think about what load it might be carrying that he couldn't see.

They'd spotted him. *Damn it!* He couldn't outrun them, couldn't hide from them even in the weak dawn light, and he didn't dare risk abandoning the chopper. There simply wasn't time for him and Liberty to hike through more rough terrain to get back to D.C.

The chopper circled, came back, and hovered on the other side of the clearing. They couldn't be lining up for a shot—at this proximity, any angle would be a gallery shoot. *What the hell were they doing?*

"Are they going to shoot us?" Fully awake, Sybil stared at the chopper.

"I don't know." Jonathan spotted a pair of binoculars near the dead man's left leg. Scrambling, he grabbed them, returned to his seat, then lifted them to his eyes. The pilot was ticked, clearly arguing with a passenger.

Conlee's voice sounded through the transmitter. "Stay put."

Fight-or-flight adrenaline gushing through his veins, Jonathan watched and waited. Was someone on the Ballast chopper conversing with Conlee?

"You don't smell death, right?"

He did. But not wanting to tell her that, he squinted against the weak dawn light slanting in through the windshield and spoke into the radio. "Visual confirmation on three. One's pulled his gun."

Sybil scurried from her seat, dug through the press equipment, but returned to her seat empty-handed. "Damn it, you'd think they'd have arms on this craft."

"Press choppers don't carry arms." But the men in this one had been armed to the gills.

"They don't dress all in black like this guy, either." She waved a hand at the dead body. "A box of bullets isn't going to do us any good without a gun."

"A gun can't compete with Sidewinders and that M230."

"*Something* would be nice."

"The M230 fires 625 rounds per minute, Sybil. It's a moot point."

"They're opening the door," she said. "What are they tossing out?"

Jonathan regretted having to answer the question. "Bodies."

First-Strike Launch: 18:30:41

The phone ringing awakened Gregor Faust from a dead sleep.

Mandatory crew rest was three hours, but from the sluggish feel of his body, he had been down thirty minutes, max, and for command to break his crew rest, the news had to be bad. Steeling himself to hear it, he rolled over in bed, shoved a pillow out of his way, and grabbed the receiver. "Yes?"

"Austin Stone is calling, sir."

Stone phoning Gregor direct didn't signal bad news, it signaled a crisis. "Put him through." He sat up and rubbed at his face. His stubble of beard grated against his hand. He glanced at the bedside clock and converted the time—5:30 A.M. in the swamp.

"She's not dead."

Austin. Never in his career had Gregor experienced more complications on a single mission. "So you've reported."

"She stole a helicopter, Gregor. One of *your* helicopters. Even as we speak, she's en route to D.C. And I suspect you have Ballast bodies in the swamp."

Why hadn't command briefed him on this before putting through the call?

"You picked the wrong man to cross."

Not a declaration, a threat. From the one man on the planet who could make it Gregor's nightmare. Fully awake, he shoved his legs into his slacks and rushed through the tunnels toward the command center. He could deny crossing Austin, but there was little use in it. They both knew the terms of their agreement. Austin aided Gregor in ending the Peris-Abdan peace talks, and Gregor facilitated the execution of Austin's sole requirement: Lady Liberty's death. "I gave the order to cancel her."

"Well, someone didn't obey it. I don't care why. All I want to know is what are you going to do about it?"

Patch and his damn Madonna complex? "What do you want me to do, Austin? Take her out in the White House?"

"How you keep your end of our agreement is irrelevant to me. Just do it. You have exactly eighteen hours and thirty minutes. Fail, and I will make good on every threat I've made." Austin slammed down the phone.

A dial tone droned in Gregor's ear. He rounded the corner into the command center. Adam, compact and feral with rock-ledge features, sat at the station, manning the monitors. "Talk to me."

"ET lost communication with Bravo Team while it was in transit. Storm-related," Adam said. "He located Bravo on the ground and reported in about three minutes ago."

Three minutes. That explained why Adam hadn't briefed Gregor before putting through Austin's call; he hadn't yet received ET's field report. That introduced a new complication. *Who had given Austin the information?*

"Bravo hit hostiles on arrival." Adam reclaimed Gregor's attention. "One man down, one missing, and one chopper lost. Confiscated, sir."

"By whom?"

"Widow-maker and Lady Liberty." Adam grimaced. "Those identities have been confirmed and ET is in pursuit."

"How much lead time does Liberty have?"

"ET reported an ETA intercept in under an hour."

So Patch hadn't refused to cancel her, or assisted in her escape, or been involved in the loss of a helicopter. Gregor weighed his choices. He could stick with the original plan, but, at this point, that boiled down to a piss-poor strategy that left him and all of Ballast hunted and blamed for starting a world war. The battle lines were clearly drawn, and the decision was Gregor's to make:

Did he throw his support to Austin Stone or to Lady Liberty?

Gregor lifted his stress ball and squeezed it flat. Admittedly, they were well-matched adversaries, yet Austin carried the odds for winning. He never issued idle threats, and he had the expertise and ability to carry his threats out. He also had the most intense personal motive: greed.

Liberty had formidable, proven assets, and a determination to succeed that would carry her places expertise and ability alone couldn't take her. She also had ethics and values she consistently had refused to violate, which made her more predictable.

Bottom line, they were selfless and selfish in approach, and that had Gregor's instincts humming a warning only a fool would ignore: Austin would protect himself and his personal interests at all costs. Liberty would take higher risks and make greater sacrifices to attain success. And if she succeeded, she would avert a war for which Gregor would be blamed.

Play the odds, Gregor.

Still, he hesitated. Austin likely had done all he could do to negate Gregor having any real choice but to support him. Still, there was an interim-measure option. He turned to Adam. "Peris and Abdan are still on-site in Geneva?"

"Yes, sir."

That settled it. "Revoke the cancellation order on Liberty and reverse the lockdown."

"Yes, sir." Adam relayed the orders to the men in the field and lifted the plastic cover on the control panel, revealing the flashing red indicator light and the green button beside it. He depressed the green one.

Nothing happened.

The system refused to release the site from the lockdown. "Try it again."

Adam again pushed the release button.

"It's still not working, sir." Panic etched his voice.

"Once more."

Adam repeated the procedure a third time, but the red indicator light continued to flash. "Someone's hacked into our system and taken control."

Austin. He would die for that, but right now Gregor had to countermand him and get someone into the inner hub to get the key and stop the launch. He stepped closer to Adam's back. "Have Systems look for a fail-safe device. Remote activation. And tell them to expect viral consequences for running diagnostics. Search and destroy."

Adam relayed the orders to Systems, and Gregor again focused on the flashing red indicator light. His most feared mission risk had now happened. He'd wanted Liberty away from the peace table. He did not want to be blamed for Austin Stone's war.

Reviewing precautionary measures taken, Gregor asked, "What's Marlowe's status?"

Adam tapped furiously at the keys, searching frantically for a back door into the system. "He's in critical condition, sir. Gibson has been on the horn with the flight surgeon, a Dr. Richardson, most of the night."

"What's the prognosis?"

"They figure he'll be lucky to last another couple hours."

With Marlowe's survival in jeopardy, Liberty's return to D.C. became vital to everyone, especially to Gregor.

"They still haven't located Mendoza," Adam said. "But when they do, they'll bust him."

Gregor frowned. "Odds are good they'll have to go to hell to do it."

Mendoza had to be working with Austin, which meant he now was dead. But why hadn't the murder been observed on the A-267 monitor? "Adam, we need to review the tapes of Marlowe inside the inner hub."

"What are we looking for?"

"I'm not sure exactly. But I doubt Mendoza left his station under his own steam or by divine intervention." There had to be something on the tape. "Did we run a chemical check after the lockdown?"

"No, sir." Adam shrugged. "It didn't seem necessary since we caused it."

"Run one now."

Adam keyed in the order, then glanced back at Gregor.

"The inner hub being empty during lockdown wasn't in the plan, was it, sir?"

"No, it wasn't." In six months of observations, the inner hub had never been unoccupied. Gregor wasn't sure which man he wanted to see dead most, Austin Stone or Cap Marlowe. Both had caused him unnecessary challenges.

"Systems is coming up empty, sir," Adam said. "They're pulling a hundred percent cross-check now. And I bombed out. There is no evidence of a back door."

"That is not what I want to hear."

"I don't much like saying it either, sir, but there it is." He looked back at Gregor. "We can't reverse the lockdown without Liberty. Dr. Stone has reconfigured A-267's security system. By the time her engineers figure out how to intervene and resume control, it'll be too late."

Rubbing the bristle on his jaw, Gregor stared at the countdown board. Fifteen hours, thirty-two minutes, seven seconds.

"What do you want me to do, sir?" Adam asked.

Gregor wished he knew. Adam expected to hear their exit strategy. Gregor always included a strong exit strategy in his mission plans. But he couldn't exit this mission. Austin had seen to that. And Adam's blind trust weighed down on Gregor. The mission logistics were a nightmare, the timing critical, and—hell, not even a strong strategist could predict exactly what Austin had done or what he intended to do next. "Have the Marlowe tape readied for review—in here, not my office. And keep looking for a way to reverse the lockdown."

Adam blinked hard three times. "Sir, if we don't pull assets and abort the mission—"

"I understand the ramifications, Adam."

"With all due respect, sir, you can't start World War III. There's no profit in it."

More important, there was no safe haven. Gregor's

stomach threatened to heave. He thought of John Kennedy during the Bay of Pigs crisis and felt a pang of sympathy. He didn't want a war on that scale any more than anyone else did, except for Austin Stone. "If World War III starts, technically it will be the esteemed President of the United States who fires the first-strike missile. Not I. I'll just be blamed for it."

"After the rest of the world bombs the hell out of the U.S."

And it retaliated. "Exactly." Gregor set the stress ball down on his desk.

"Tape's ready for review."

Gregor sat down and began watching it. Austin had gone over the edge. Even if Liberty died, he had too many other grievances with too many people to end this reasonably. Gregor had no choice now but to nail the genius doctor's ass to the proverbial wall and help Liberty stop the launch. He didn't have to like it, and he damn sure didn't have to advertise it, particularly since he wasn't convinced he could pull it off, but he had to do it. It wouldn't be easy; this was Stone's system, and no doubt he had covered himself well.

An unexpected frame shift caught Gregor's eye. He halted the tape, reversed it, and then viewed it a second time. Well, well. He rocked back in his chair. It appeared the good doctor hadn't covered himself well enough.

"Son of a bitch."

Gregor shot his gaze to Adam. "What is it?"

"The inner hub, sir. It's contaminated. Carbon monoxide level is off the charts."

Mendoza hadn't left the inner hub.

Chapter Seventeen

Saturday, August 10 ★ First-Strike Launch: 11:00:00

"What time is it?"

Jonathan checked his watch. "One P.M."

"We lost a lot of time parked in that clearing."

They had. Conlee had maintained his stay-put order for hours. Finally an Apache Longbow had shown up, carrying sixteen Hellfire missiles under its wings. Four men wearing Special Operations gear had jumped out and retrieved the two Ballast bodies. Finally the Apache and the Ballast aircrafts had departed, heading in opposite directions. Fifteen minutes later Conlee had transmitted the "all clear" and Jonathan had taken off. "We're still eleven hours out from the deadline."

A frown creased Sybil's brow. "I have a feeling this crisis won't resolve easily."

Jonathan's neck tingled, warning him that she was right. Tensing, he set the chopper down on the White House lawn.

President Lance, Winston, and Richard Barber stood waiting for them, Barber shielding his eyes from the bright afternoon sun and the wind kicked up by the whipping prop blades.

Mud-crusted and bedraggled, Sybil and Jonathan left the aircraft and walked over the cool grass, the brisk wind tugging at their hair, eyes, and clothes, at the briefcase. They'd made it. Sybil's relief weakened her knees.

David stepped forward, clasped her shoulders and squeezed. "Your socks are drooping."

Sybil looked down, saw Westford's socks scrunched at her ankles—and the welts of bug bites and deep scratches from her run-ins with the catbrier that covered her legs, ankles to thighs. "Terrible flaw. I'll work on it," she said, borrowing a bit of Jonathan's sarcasm.

He smiled, but genuine concern shone in his eyes. "Are you okay?"

"Fine."

David glanced at Jonathan, his gratitude radiating from him. "Thank you for getting back to us."

Jonathan nodded but didn't step away.

"Welcome home, Vice President Stone." Barber extended a hand.

Sybil shook it and smiled. "Thank you."

Winston didn't offer to shake. No surprise there—he had always been cool toward her—but she nodded a greeting to him anyway. He ignored it.

"I know you're eager to shower and rest, but we don't have a minute to spare. You need to get to A-267 immediately." David led her from the lawn to a waiting limo. "This opens the case." He pressed a small gold key into her hand.

A horrible feeling suffused her, and Sybil couldn't shake it. Something significant had changed. "What's happened, David?"

"New developments. Barber will brief you en route."

"Yes, sir." Sybil slid into the car.

David leaned forward, filling the crack between the car and the door. "Don't open that case now. It has a sensor. If you're not within ten feet of the hangar, it will detonate. A bomb squad is waiting at the site. They'll give you detailed instructions." David backed away, and Barber got into the car.

Barber sat facing her, Jonathan at her side. When the door closed, Barber raised the privacy glass between them and the driver. "What's your security clearance, Westford?"

"It's higher than yours."

Sybil nodded that it was, and a surprised Barber launched into the briefing. "An outside source has control of A-267. They've locked down the facility and we can't override them without risking a launch. Senator Marlowe is trapped in the outer rim."

"What was he doing there?" Sybil asked. Her nemesis was at A-267? It seemed bizarre that Cap Marlowe, the demon hunter himself, would be trapped.

"Pulling a no-notice inspection. I don't know if you're aware of it, but he's a diabetic. He's way overdue on his insulin injections. His condition is critical, ma'am. An ambulance is on-site but can't get to him. The inner hub isn't manned."

"What?" She couldn't believe her ears. From his expression, neither could Jonathan.

"Captain Mendoza was on duty when the facility locked down. But he's vanished. The inner hub is empty."

"Did we confirm that?"

"Yes, ma'am. With heat-seeking sensors."

Sybil's stomach growled again.

"Excuse me," Jonathan interrupted, looking at Sybil. "McDonald's or Burger King?"

"McDonald's. Bacon, egg, and cheese biscuit, hash browns, and a large—the largest they have—orange juice."

Barber's eyes stretched wide. "You're stopping to eat in the middle of a crisis? There are MREs in the car."

"You want us to eat emergency rations?" Sybil nearly snapped.

Before she cut loose, Jonathan intervened. "We haven't eaten a decent meal since Wednesday." He pressed the intercom button to talk with the driver. "Mickey, hit the McDonald's drive-through. Three bacon, egg, and cheese biscuits, two hash browns, and a couple gallons of OJ."

"You've got it, Agent Westford."

"You want a fast-food breakfast at one in the afternoon?" Barber looked mortified.

"He's right, Jonathan," Sybil said. "People rushing through on their lunch hours would have to wait."

"Mickey, cancel that McDonald's run. Hit Burger King. Three Whoppers. No ketchup, add mustard. A cherry pie and two gallons of iced tea."

"I'm on it." He whipped over two lanes and hung a right into Burger King's parking lot.

Sybil looked at Jonathan and felt a rush of warmth. He had remembered that she hated ketchup and liked mustard. What else had he noticed about her that she hadn't realized?

When the food was ready, Mickey passed the bags through the divider. Sybil thought she might faint from the wonderful smells. Food. *Hot food.* Her stomach twisted and churned.

"I can't believe it," Barber groused. "Vice President of the United States, and you haul a limo bearing the seal through a fast-food restaurant's drive-through window."

"Have you ever been hungry, Barber?" Sybil hardened her voice, clipped her tone. "So hungry your stomach feels like it's glued to your spine?"

"No, ma'am, I haven't."

"Then be grateful because you've been blessed and shut up about it. Starving people eat, and I happen to like fast food—even when I'm not starving." She unwrapped the Whopper. Its paper crinkled, and her mouth watered in anticipation. "I'm a little tired and testy, so I'd advise you to drop the elitist attitude and get back to the briefing."

"Yes, ma'am." He took the criticism in stride. "Referencing your plane crash. It's connected to the A-267 security breach. That's confirmed."

"Did anyone else on the plane survive?"

"Two possibles." Barber told her about the chuters. "We haven't identified either of them, but we have reason to believe one was Captain Dean."

"What reason?" Sybil pulled a long swallow of tea down her throat. She couldn't remember any meal ever tasting so good. Tomato. God, tomato exploded in your mouth and it tasted wonderful.

"His wife and two children were abducted. Sam Sayelle checked out an anonymous tip and reported it to the police. They're cooperating fully with us. When the abduction was designated a professional assault—because of Captain Dean's connection to the crisis—we took over the investigation. We don't know yet if the abduction was genuine or staged."

Sybil bit down on a crunchy pickle. Its tangy juice squirted inside her mouth. "Why would anyone consider it a staged abduction?"

"It's possible Captain Dean had an agreement with Ballast or PUSH."

"Ballast is behind this crisis. I assume the Dean case is related to this crisis, correct?"

"Correct." Barber went on. "If Dean had an agreement, then Mrs. Dean might have voluntarily taken their kids and hooked up with the captain outside of the U.S."

"Jonathan, what do you think of that scenario?" Sybil asked.

"Whoever came up with it is looking under the wrong rock."

"I think so, too." She looked back to Barber. "Linda

Dean would never put her kids in danger, and Ken is no traitor. You can take that to the bank."

"Intel analysts are investigating all possibilities." Barber avoided a direct response. "It's the responsible thing to do."

"Well, I hope they're not wasting too much time on this one. Anyone who knows the Deans will agree it's a ridiculous theory." She took a bite of tomato, rolled it around inside her mouth, and just savored it. When she swallowed, she added, "Actually, it's an asinine theory. Ken Dean routinely sheds light on America's underbelly."

"Two more developments, ma'am." Barber's expression turned sheepish, then veiled. "Both are going to be difficult for you to hear."

"After the events of the past several days, you're going to play hell shocking me, Barber. Things can't get much worse than they've been."

"I'm afraid they can, ma'am." He glanced in Jonathan's direction, looking as if he'd rather be anywhere in the world but within the agent's striking distance. "Commander Conlee has some . . . concerns."

It was like pulling teeth. "What kind of concerns?"

Barber looked her in the eye. "Your ex-husband designed the security system at A-267."

"Surely that's no surprise to anyone, especially to Commander Conlee. Austin's designed secure systems for nearly every segment of the federal government."

"Yes, ma'am. But someone *inside* A-267 corrupted this system. Commander Conlee will give you the details when we get to the site."

Her stomach clenched, and it wasn't protesting the food. "They think Austin is responsible?"

"Actually, they don't. He hasn't accessed the site in over six months. But Captain Mendoza being missing, and the system being corrupted by someone savvy on the inside, has some validity as evidence of an arrangement between them. It seems suspicious, so Intel is checking it out."

Could Austin do this? Sybil chewed a bite of burger and looked at Jonathan. They both knew the truth. Austin had the skills. He could. But *would* he?

Barber shifted on the seat. "One other thing, ma'am."

Jonathan cleared his throat. Touched his fingertip to his chin.

Picking up on the signal, Sybil dabbed at her own with her napkin. "Yes?"

Barber focused on her neck, unable to meet her gaze. "There's a strong rumor going around that you're committing treason."

Sybil choked on a long draw of tea.

"What?" Jonathan nearly came up off the seat. "Look, Barber, so far in this situation, the vice president has nearly lost her life three times. She's exhausted and still up to her ass in alligators. This is no time for you to be joking around."

"I'm not joking, Agent Westford."

Treason. Her? Sybil couldn't swallow. She had a mouthful of tea, but there was no way she could get it down. Absorbing the shock, she slotted her disbelief, her outrage. How dare the bastards even consider her capable of committing treason?

"It's related to what Intel believes is an unconnected matter, ma'am," Barber said. "Some reporter leaked word that you're passing envelopes to an old man at the Vietnam Wall."

"Oh, for Christ sake. We know all—"

Sybil silenced Westford with a look.

Barber waited for one of them to clarify and disclose the nature of the association, but Sybil couldn't talk. And even if she could, she wouldn't defend herself against something so stupid. A reporter. No doubt, Sam Sayelle. So much for him having a change of heart about her because he had done the broadcasts. Indignant as hell, she lifted her chin. "Word is wrong."

"The president and Commander Conlee agree," Barber said. "At least for now. But there are others, so if you'd care to elaborate..."

Sybil looked over at Jonathan, automatically checking his shoes. He was still wearing his sneakers, of course; there hadn't been time to change them. Unable to gauge the seriousness of this—hell, wasn't treason *always* serious—she looked to his face. His jaw was locked down as tight as A-267, but no doubt glinted in his eyes, only fury, and she was grateful to see it.

Until that moment, if asked who in the world would believe her unconditionally, she would have named only Gabby. Now Sybil could add Jonathan to the short list. She felt good about that. Scared stiff, but good.

"Ma'am?" Barber prodded. "Would you care to elaborate?"

She stared him right in the eye. "No, I wouldn't."

The limo stopped in front of the three hangars. An ambulance sat parked near the one on the left and a dozen armed men stood on point, surrounding the building. Commander Conlee moved toward them, his stride long and eager, a stubby cigar clenched between his teeth. Jonathan got out of the car. Barber and Sybil followed.

"Commander," she said to Conlee.

"Ma'am. Westford. Good to have you back."

"Thank you. I appreciate the broadcasts, but Sam Sayelle, Commander?"

A sly-fox quirk twisted his lips. "Of all the media, who would you consider the least apt to help you?"

"Valid point. But can we trust him?"

"He got a solid, personal referral from a man who held my life, and the lives of my men, in his hands for years."

That worked for her. She nodded. "What was the holdup in the clearing?"

"That'll have to wait, ma'am." He nodded toward a

safe-zone area where five men stood waiting for them. "Bomb squad is this way."

Bomb squad. Sybil's stomach flipped. "What are the odds of the briefcase blowing up when we unlock it?"

Conlee answered without shifting his gaze. "Fifty-fifty."

Her breath caught, and she swallowed a gasp, wheeled her gaze to Jonathan.

"Seventy-five, twenty-five," he said, then turned to Conlee. "It's not a simple system."

"Two known sensors. One is building proximity."

"What's the other?" Jonathan asked.

Conlee's frustration surfaced. The creases in his face deepened to grooves. "We don't know."

★   ★   ★

Sybil followed the commander over the asphalt.

She was filthy, caked with dry mud and vegetation from the swamp. Her clothes had been reduced to rags. She wore no makeup, and her hair was wind-tossed and wild. All of that conspired, yet none of it succeeded, at making her feel the least bit uncomfortable. But she hated—hated and resented—what walking toward the left hangar's drab green entrance in Westford's socks was doing to her insides. That bothered her nearly as much as the seventy-five, twenty-five odds of the briefcase blowing up.

Wearing a man's socks was such a personal, intimate— *and sincerely insignificant*—thing. Why did it bother her so much? Why did bare feet bother her so much?

Five men stood waiting just outside the entrance door. Suited out in black bomb gear, they reminded her of the three men in the swamp. Their expressions were equally serious.

"This way, ma'am," Conlee said. "We have a dilemma and you need to make a choice. It'll take another forty minutes to get bomb gear that'll fit you here. We can wait. But by then Senator Marlowe will be dead."

Terrific. Sybil gave Conlee a negative nod. "That's unacceptable."

"Ma'am, I strongly recommend you wait," Jonathan said.

"I'm not going to let him die out of fear of what could happen, Jonathan."

"Take my gear, ma'am," the squad leader said. "It's not a great fit, but it will give you some protection. It's better than nothing."

Touched, Sybil smiled. "I can't do that, either, but thank you for offering." Terrified, and doing her best to hide it, she looked back to Conlee. "Let's do it."

Conlee hesitated, shot Jonathan a worried look, but finding nothing in his expression to convince him they could change her mind, nodded. "This way, then."

In the distance, Sybil saw a Plexiglas-shielded desk and, another twenty yards beyond it, a circular concrete pad. "Wouldn't it be safer over there, in the testing zone?"

"Proximity to the building," Jonathan reminded her of the Ballast sensor.

She stepped up to a makeshift table within twenty feet of the hangar. Jonathan moved to her side. The commander stopped across the table from her. Both looked as peaceful as if they were meeting at a casual social function. "You two need to get behind the shield."

"I trust my men," Conlee said, clenching his jaw.

"So do I, but I don't trust Ballast," she said. "I know they're responsible, and if the need should arise, I'm expecting you two to prove it and help President Lance get us out of this."

The squad leader set the case on the table and slid the commander a telling look.

"It'll be fine, ma'am."

She shifted her gaze to Jonathan.

"I'm not leaving you again." He spoke softly, but steel etched his tone and he was looking at Conlee, not at her.

How could they be so calm? She should issue them a direct order, but it would do about as much good as their objections to her not waiting for the gear, so she saved her breath.

"Has our current situation been explained to you, ma'am?"

A member of the bomb squad took the key.

"Not completely, Commander," she said, doing her damnedest to focus on what the man was saying. Her heart was racing, thundering in her head, drowning out his voice.

"Command doesn't have control of the facility, and the source perpetrator is unknown."

"It's Ballast, not PUSH. Didn't you get our message?"

"We got it, but we haven't been able to substantiate or verify it. Our resources are stretched pretty thin."

Jonathan reiterated their certainty that the Band-Aid incident in Geneva had been a deliberate attack.

"That, too, is going to have to wait. Our number-one priority is to regain control of this facility. Secure Environet and our engineers are working on it. The entire security system has been overridden—they're working on that, too."

"So Austin is here?"

"No, ma'am. His engineers are working out of their own offices. Only Dr. Stone has A-267 clearance, and he needs team support to get what we need before midnight."

The cuff jiggled at her raw wrist, and Sybil's heart nearly banged through her ribs. "How many are locked in there?" She knew she'd been told at some point, but for the life of her, she couldn't recall just then.

"Eleven in the outer rim, including the senator. Barber explained the senator's medical challenge, right?"

"Yes, he did." So had Conlee. He, too, was rattled. That was comforting.

The squad member ran some tests on the case, including some kind of scan. Sybil forced herself to look away, to not think about what he was doing. "How long has he been critical?"

"Too long. Dr. Richardson is amazed he's still alive." The commander's gaze drifted to the case. He flinched, then stiffened. "The doc's done what he can by phone, but the senator doesn't need advice, he needs insulin, and that we haven't been able to get to him."

"Everything's testing clear," the squad leader said. "I'm going to insert the key now."

"Wait." Jonathan, who had been intently studying the cuff, looked at the squad leader. "You can't remove the cuff until the case is opened."

"I see no evidence or reason—"

"Take my word for it."

The squad leader looked to the commander. "Sir, we can remove the cuff and get Vice President Stone out of harm's way."

Sybil looked at Jonathan's face and knew the only way anyone would open the cuff without first opening the case would be over his dead body. "Open the case, please."

"But ma'am."

"Open the case, Lieutenant."

"Yes, ma'am." The leader's glare warned Jonathan he had better not be wrong.

Another jiggle at her wrist, then a loud click, and the locks on the case snapped open.

Tensed, Sybil waited for the explosion. Ten seconds lapsed. Ten more.

Jonathan's eyes glinted. "Now key the cuff."

The metal shifted against her wrist bone, and she drew in a sharp breath. "Westford?"

"They're done, ma'am."

The metal shackle fell away, and she swallowed a sigh of relief. At least in this, they had won. "What was the second sensor?"

The bomb squad member shrugged. "Nothing showed up in the case, ma'am."

"Ballast never does anything without a purpose. See if we can find it."

"It's in the cuff," Jonathan said. "It activates only if you remove the cuff before you disarm the case."

"How did you know that, Agent Westford?"

"The building proximity warning," he said cryptically, leaving it to the squad leader to decipher it beyond that.

Sybil looked at the squad members, circling the table, and met each gaze, one by one. "Thank you."

The squad leader smiled. "You're welcome, ma'am." He took several steps back, joined the circle, then all five of them turned their backs.

Sybil considered that odd for a second and then realized that knowledge of what was inside the case could exceed their security clearances and they had positioned themselves to block the view of the others present. She allowed herself to relax and breathe again, then grasped the popped clasps on the briefcase and opened it wide. Inside, nestled on a solid bed of foam, was a small silver key.

"Make sure nothing is connected to it," Jonathan said. "No triggers."

Sybil pulled a visual and saw nothing, then lifted the edge and let her fingertip slide under the key. "It's clear."

He nodded, and she lifted the key out of the foam, eager to shut down the launch. "Where is the checkpoint?" she asked Conlee.

"This way."

The three of them moved into the hangar, down a white-tiled hall unmarred by doors or windows, to an elevator. Outside it, two machines hugged the wall.

"You know they've reconfigured the system, ma'am," Commander Conlee said. "It now requires more than just the key. The device has a new, and unfortunately unfamiliar, DNA-recognition security code."

"What exactly is that?" An uneasy feeling pitted her stomach.

"I've just been briefed on it myself, but I'll share as best I can. It's a new device, both in technology and in design. Biometric secure systems, as you know, use unique, individual traits—such as the iris of the eye, fingerprints, bone structure—to positively identify specific, authorized people. This DNA device works in a manner similar to biometric devices and photocopying machines. An authorized user pricks their left thumb and then presses it to this plate." He pointed to what looked like a small, absorbent pad.

"The chin pad?"

"It used to be a chin pad. Now you bleed on it. The pressed-thumb blood smear then contains the user's thumbprint. The system converts the print and the user's DNA to digital data and then compares both to stored, authorized user's digital data. It's a more complex system and, according to our experts, impossible to beat."

"What happens if you use the key without the DNA blood match?"

"Ordinarily, we think an alarm notifies security. On this system, it activates a trigger that results in an immediate Peacekeeper launch."

That deeply disturbed Sybil. What if she had been killed in the explosion? In the quicksand? By ET, the Ballast man with the white spot in his hair who had given her the penny and let her live because of the cookies and milk for Peris and Abdan, or by the snipers from the helicopter? "How do we know it's configured for my blood?"

"We don't—not for fact. The terrorists, who are still identifying themselves as PUSH, claim it is, but we haven't been able to verify that yet. At this point, any attempt we make to verify could escalate a launch. They also reported that the blood must be fresh. No keeping stock in a fridge and pulling it out when it's convenient."

"For the last time, it's Ballast, Commander. They're just ducking responsibility."

"Why?"

"I'm not sure." Sybil's feet throbbed from walking on concrete and tile. She shifted her weight, hoping the pain would ease up.

"Until we know that, we can't risk not covering both."

"Fine." She shifted her weight again. "So we have to take Ballast's word on it that it's my blood?" Sybil hated this. "Why would Faust make it so difficult and then so easy for us to resolve a crisis he created?"

"Second thoughts?" the commander suggested.

"Maybe." She looked to Jonathan.

He shrugged. "Maybe he doesn't want the missile to detonate and strike China."

"Ballast has no interests in China," Sybil reminded him.

"PUSH does," Conlee interjected.

"Could be why Ballast chose it to blame." Sybil cocked her head. "Maybe Faust only wanted to stop the peace talks and continue his arms sales to Peris and Abdan. Maybe he never wanted to launch the missile."

"Possible." Conlee nodded. "But wouldn't President Lance pick up negotiations where you left off?"

"Yes."

"I have to disagree."

Sybil and Conlee shifted their gazes to Jonathan, and she asked, "Why?"

"Because without you, Peris and Abdan's premiers wouldn't be in Geneva. They didn't agree to the peace talks because they feared refusing the United States. They agreed to meet because of you. The president couldn't *get* the warmongers talking, so how could he *keep* them talking?"

"Jonathan, I asked you not to call them that."

"Yes, ma'am," he said, without swinging his gaze from the commander.

"Lance could," Conlee said, "if Peris and Abdan thought she was dead."

"You're in the ball park but not on base," Jonathan countered. "Faust needed a fail-safe to keep us preoccupied long enough for the seeds of doubt between Peris and Abdan to take root and grow. Even the UN doubted anyone other than Vice President Stone could pull off any kind of success."

Conlee crossed his arms over his chest and mulled that over. "I have to admit, your deduction seems logical. But is it accurate?"

It felt accurate. Yet this whole situation felt like... more. What more, Sybil didn't know, and that irritated her immensely. "I'm not sure. Is China still the target?"

"No, ma'am. Pakistan. But it's still cycling. So far, this is the fourth country targeted."

Faust had made arms deals with Pakistan. Major money. She'd had a hell of a time getting them to the negotiating table a year ago, and Faust still had ties there. Bombing them didn't seem to be in line with Faust's goals. "Have the cycles been verified?" Something in this target business just didn't fit.

"That's in progress, ma'am."

She didn't like having to rely on Faust's information, but he couldn't want a world war any more than anyone else. "Let's go then."

Clearly as concerned about them acting on Intel provided by Ballast or PUSH as she was, Commander Conlee passed her a blue lancelet and then nodded to one of his men. "Get the medical team on point."

Sybil didn't look at Jonathan, but she felt the heat of his gaze. It felt comforting. She didn't like liking that, but she no longer hated it. Twisting off the rounded top of the lancelet, she exposed its sharp point. "Does it matter which thumb?"

"Instructions call for the left thumbprint, ma'am."

"Sorry. I remember you mentioning that now. There's just been a lot to absorb quickly."

"Amen, ma'am."

She pricked her left thumb, pumped it against her bent fingertip, and then pressed it against the absorbent pad and inserted the key.

"Wait for the green light," Conlee said.

Sybil watched the device pad. A green light flashed on and stayed lit. Her heart in her throat, she offered up a prayer. *Please, God. Please, let this work*—and then she turned the key.

The elevator door slid open.

Sybil started to go inside, but Jonathan stopped her. "Security sweeps first."

Within five minutes, the clear sign had been given, and the medical team had gone in to retrieve Cap, armed with huge syringes of MD-50—massive doses of sugar—and insulin.

They returned with him laid out on a white-sheeted stretcher. He was still alive, but not conscious. His skin pasty-white, his lips blue-tinged, he barely resembled the vibrant man who had been her most fierce opponent on the Hill.

Sybil spoke briefly to the medics, then watched them load Cap into the ambulance and drive away.

Jonathan joined her, sent her a questioning look. "They're hopeful?"

"Yes."

"Well, it's a cleanup operation now," Conlee said, then stopped a major walking past him. "Staff in the conference room. Five minutes. Priority shift."

They had survived the crisis. "We did it, Jonathan." An almost overwhelming urge to weep washed through her.

Jonathan's eyes held that secret smile he saved for her. "Yes, ma'am, we did."

"Ready to celebrate with that pasta dinner I owe you?" She smiled at him.

LADY LIBERTY 257

"Yeah. I've always wanted to learn to speak Italian. Eating pasta sounds a lot better than hitting the books."

Teasing her. Emboldened, she did a little teasing of her own. "It could take more than one dinner to grasp the entire language." Her heart threatened to stop. Any second it would just stop beating and that would be it.

"I'm willing to go for it." He slid a hand into his pocket. "Are you?"

Boy, that was a tough one to answer. Just once, couldn't her heart and head agree? "Yeah, I am." She pressed her fingertips to her lips, stunned that she'd spoken.

"Commander!" The squad leader came running from the hangar. "We've got a major problem, sir."

Conlee joined Sybil and Jonathan, turned to the soldier. "What now?"

"The inner hub won't open, sir. It's on a separate secure-device system."

Oh, God. Sybil's elation vanished.

"Is it the same kind of system?" Conlee asked.

"Yes, sir. But the gurus say Vice President Stone's DNA won't open it, and neither will Ballast's key."

"Whose DNA will open it?" Sybil looked at Conlee. "Has anyone else reported receiving a key?"

"No key reports, and we haven't yet identified whose DNA they used."

"We have to get that hub open to stop the launch, Commander." Sybil stated the obvious. "Have you checked Agent Westford's DNA? He's been with me since Geneva. Ballast could have used his."

"They didn't," the squad leader said. "We ran everyone in the A-267 need-to-know loop, and none of them matches."

Sybil caught the time on Conlee's watch. "We've got ten hours, Commander."

"I know, ma'am."

The last remnants of joy at their success faded and the pressure returned to Sybil tenfold. "What can I do to help?"

"Give me blanket authorization to breach the Privacy Act and to skate around normal procedures. I need to extend the search, and I don't have time—"

"I need a phone."

Conlee unclipped his cellular from its case attached to his belt. "Ma'am, you do know Austin Stone designed this system."

"Yes." She had to be careful here. Every word out of her mouth would be received and reviewed under heavy scrutiny. Too harsh, and she would be perceived as a bitter ex; sour grapes. Too soft, and they would think she was protecting him. Sybil wasn't harsh or soft, and this wasn't personal. Yes, she knew Austin, and she knew too damn well that he had no loyalty and he was capable of the worst kind of betrayal. But she wasn't weighing in on this based on a personal perspective. "Have you done a thorough check to see if he was deliberately involved in the corruption?"

"Yes, ma'am. He looks clean. He hasn't been to the site in over six months, and he allowed us full access to his personal and professional records. We went through everything with a fine-tooth comb and found no evidence that he had your DNA." Conlee's expression clouded. "I'm not sure how to put this, considering the circumstances, ma'am."

"Commander, you're talking to your vice president, not to Austin Stone's ex-wife. Say what you have to say."

"My gut tells me he has to be involved. I don't know to what degree, but it's his design. Yet he doesn't have your DNA—no one does except Home Base—so that tells me he can't be involved, and yet . . ." Conlee wanted to say more but hesitated.

"Your gut still insists he is?" Sybil finished for him.

"Up to his eyeballs." He nodded. "I'll be first to apologize if I'm wrong, but there it is, ma'am."

"I understand, and if it's any consolation, I feel it in my gut, too." Something niggled at Sybil's memory but stayed just out of her reach. Something from a long, long time ago. "If he isn't involved, we can use his expertise. If he is involved, then we need him where we can keep an eye on him."

"Neutralize him," Jonathan suggested.

Conlee nodded his agreement.

"All right. Pull him in under the umbrella of helping us," she told Conlee. "If he does help, fine. If not, we know where he is and what he's doing."

"It also keeps him from bugging out," Jonathan added. "If he is involved and the missile launches, then he'll go down with everyone else. Equal risks."

"Levels the field," Conlee said, "but it leaves us wide open to further corruption. Hell, when he starts pounding on that computer keyboard, only he and God know what he's doing."

"Which is why the computer you put him on will simulate the network but not be connected to it," Jonathan said. "Then our engineers can test his every move before it's made or implemented in the actual system."

"Okay." Appreciation warmed Conlee's eyes. "Okay. We'll need to upgrade his surveillance rating. Monitor all his calls, his every move."

"In these circumstances," Sybil said, "I'd consider that prudent."

"We'll need authorizations for that, too."

"Fine." Sybil held out a hand for his phone, and Conlee passed it to her. She dialed a number and then put the receiver to her ear. "This is Vice President Stone. Get me the attorney general . . ."

★   ★   ★

"Austin set up two DNA secure systems."

"Inside A-267?" Gregor set down his glass of milk. It splashed over the rim and soaked his desktop. Rounding the desk, he joined Patch at the monitors.

Patch glanced at his boss. "Liberty is the first one, but who is the second?"

Damn scientists. Gregor let out a sigh ripe with frustration. "Circumvent and find out. The crazy bastard might have programmed it with mine."

Horror streaked through Patch's eyes. "Then how are we going to stop this? We can't send them your DNA."

"No, but we can send it to Marlowe."

"He might not live. He's still critical, Gregor."

"Jean will live."

Patch's jaw dropped. "You're trusting Marlowe's secretary with this?"

"She's a staffer, not a secretary, and she knows more about the senator's business than he does." She also had been working with Gregor for over a decade, keeping him informed on matters of interest occurring on the Hill and, through Grace, in Lady Liberty's office. Patch, however, had no need to know that.

Gregor stretched forward, adjusted the contrast on the A-267 monitor. Images of engineers and armed soldiers rushing around in the outer rim filled the screen.

"I don't understand why Dr. Stone did this." Patch sipped coffee from a steaming mug. "Why the second key and DNA?"

"Marlowe must have connected with him on the key." Without revealing it as a Jean-relayed fact, that was the only thing that made sense.

"But the DNA?"

"Think about it, Patch. Austin Stone designed the system and he holds the patents. Of course he would be pegged as the initiator in this attack. If all eyes turned from Ballast to him, to protect himself he would have to have someone in position to take the fall. You know Americans. They always have to have someone to blame. Austin is giving them someone other than himself. That person is blamed, and he is free to leave the country—and to launch the missile."

"His plan has developed a glitch." Patch spared Gregor a glance. "They've called him in to help them. No one has called it a house arrest, but once he's at A-267, there's no way Conlee's going to let him leave."

Gregor agreed. "He has the Widow-maker and Lady Liberty to thank for that, not Conlee, though I'm sure the commander agrees. Liberty is sharp. Which is one of the reasons—aside from his Secure Environet stock—Austin so adamantly wants her dead." Gregor lifted a hand. "It's a solid strategy. Once the second DNA person is identified, Conlee will believe he or she is guilty."

"Liberty won't buy it."

"But she's handicapped. As Stone's ex-wife, any position she takes invites skepticism."

"The second person could be the Widow-maker." Patch swiped at a coffee ring on his station desk.

"Too obvious and not enough venom. Westford threatened to kill Austin. He'll want more in the way of revenge."

"Who then?"

"My guess is Barber or Winston. In differing degrees, Austin recruited them both. Or maybe Marlowe." Gregor tested a deduction and it withstood feasibility. Stone was systematically attacking everyone he believed had crossed him.

"I'll call the lab and have them run comparison checks." Patch reached for the phone.

"Put a rush on them." To protect himself, Gregor was going to have to intercede yet again and help Liberty keep the vindictive Austin Stone from killing them all.

Chapter Eighteen

Saturday, August 10 ★ First-Strike Launch: 9:45:21

Bunches of flowers lined the fence of the Embassy Row mansion. Seeing them stunned Sybil, tugged at her heart, and a lump homesteaded in her throat. They were for her. Because people thought she had died. Would they be as pleased to learn she had lived?

Treason.

Jonathan clapped a hand to the back of her neck and pushed.

She doubled over. Her cheek hit her knees. "What in hell are you doing, Westford?"

"You're dead, remember?"

"Still?"

"Unless you want to cause heart attacks on your front lawn. People are lined up on both sides of the street."

Mickey drove through the gate and stopped right outside the front door. "All clear, Agent Westford." He passed his cap back through the privacy window.

"Okay." Jonathan looked over at her. "Move fast, straight inside." He shoved Mickey's black cap down on her head. "Do not look back toward the street."

Definitely Westford. She missed Jonathan's tender touch.

He opened the door, motioned, and they ran into the house.

Though eager to shower, change clothes, and get back to the office, Sybil paused inside the front door and inhaled deeply. Vanilla and eucalyptus scented the air. Her official residence was the people's house, lovely and brimming with special touches left by former families, but the rotten plumbing and other touching flaws made it just imperfect enough to be a home.

Strange, but since the divorce, she hadn't thought of anywhere as home. When this crisis was over, she was going to change that. She was going to change a lot of things. Looking down death's throat changed a person. What had been important simply wasn't, and what was important she had been ignoring out of fear. Well, no more. Her priorities had shifted and she intended to reclaim her life, and if she was at all lucky—she turned to Jonathan—more.

Certain he would recall her housekeeper's name, she said, "Emily is visiting her daughter, but she keeps the guest quarters just off this hall prepared all the time."

"She does." Jonathan closed the front door. "I know my way around. I'll be fine. Go on, get to your shower."

"I need to make a couple of calls, but I'll hurry." She smiled. "We just ate an hour ago but I'm starving. Are you?"

Guards were stationed all over outside, but Jonathan pulled a security check in the rooms off the hallway anyway. He paused to answer her. "We'll grab something on the way back."

"What are you looking for?" She paused midhall. "Is something wrong?"

"Everything's fine, ma'am."

She frowned at the formality. "Are we back to 'ma'am' again?"

"We're not in the swamp anymore."

That hurt, and it shouldn't. "I see." They were home now, and for reasons she couldn't fathom, he wanted distance. She didn't like it. She could respect it, but it hurt. She had hoped they had come to mean more to each other. "Do you want a robe so you can shower?" He had to itch as much as she did, and a robe was the only thing she owned that could possibly fit.

"I had clothes and a new transmitter sent over. They're in the guest room."

"I thought you fixed your transmitter."

"I don't trust it." He toed off a sneaker. "I've told Conlee not to assign a new guard detail just yet. I'm on twenty-four seven until this is resolved. We need mobility and a little more stealth than we can get with a detail of agents tagging along, so they're stationary here until further notice."

Honoring his promise not to leave her. But that was professional, not personal. She wanted him with her because he wanted to be there, not out of a sense of duty. "I should have thought of it. Thanks, Jonathan." Feeling somber, she turned to walk away.

"Sybil?"

She stopped near the staircase, secretly thrilled that he had called her by name. Not that it meant anything. But it could mean something, couldn't it?

Good God, you're neurotic. Clutching at straws.

She looked back over the slope of her shoulder at him.

"When you can, give Gabby a call. I'm sure word that you're alive will be all over the news soon, if it isn't already—the president might even have called her—but she probably needs to hear your voice." Longing lit in his eyes. "I would."

If their positions were reversed, so would she. "I will."

Gabby would be obsessing, but how did Jonathan know it? "Jonathan, how often do you and Gabby chat?"

"Every couple weeks." He leaned against the door frame. "Being a judge is hard on her."

"It is," Sybil agreed. "She's used to a far more active life."

"She's hooked on danger," he amended, putting it more bluntly. "So we talk, she gets it out of her system, and then she goes back to her courtroom, grateful for her quiet life."

Jealousy and envy streaked through Sybil. It stunned her—that she felt it at all, much less so intensely, and—of all people—toward Gabby. "You two are close then?" He clearly knew she was assigned to covert ops.

"We're friends." Jonathan grunted. "Frankly, the woman's a pain in the ass."

"She's my best friend, Westford." Sybil gave him a warning glare. "The closest thing to family I have."

"True, but she's still a pain in the ass." He didn't seem fazed by her tone or her glare. Actually, he seemed to find both amusing.

"Excuse me?" Was he teasing her? Unable to tell for sure, she followed a hunch. "You like her."

"About as much as an aching tooth."

An aching tooth? Totally lost, Sybil searched for an explanation, and hoped his next remark wouldn't be as confusing as his last one. "She annoys the hell out of you, asking questions you don't want to answer?"

"Oh, yeah."

Ah, now she had it. "But when she stops nagging you, you miss her."

He nodded. "Yourself aside, have you ever met anyone else as opinionated or bossy? Or as full of spit and vinegar?"

Since he'd put Sybil in the same category, she resented that remark. Or she would, if she understood it. Yet coming on the heels of an aching tooth, it didn't sound like the

words of a man toward any woman he considered a romantic interest. That lifted her spirits. "Spit and vinegar?"

"Sorry. Parental influence," he said. "She's sassy."

Gabby was sassy. "And sloppy." Sybil smiled. "I used to
hate wading through her clutter. Wherever she took something off, that's where it fell and stayed until I read her the
riot act." Now Sybil lived alone, and nothing was ever out
of place. She hated that, too.

"She's not happy."

"She hasn't mentioned being unhappy. I'd understand
her hating Florida's humidity. Honestly, Jonathan, the
weather there is miserable. But I thought she loved being a
judge." Sybil stuck to Gabby's cover.

"She does. She's damn good at it, too." He said it too
quickly for it to be anything except an innate reaction.

"You sound shocked."

"I was," he admitted. "She's as opinionated as a bullet,
Sybil."

She was, and always had been. So had Sybil.

"But, to tell you the truth, I've been a little worried
about her." He leaned a shoulder against the wall. "She really is unhappy."

He definitely knew Gabby was a covert operative under Conlee's command. But they hadn't ever worked together. Sybil knew that as fact. Gabby was kept separate
from everyone in and outside the system and only worked
special projects. How had Jonathan found...? Ah, of
course, Conlee would have shared her bio. Jonathan was
ready to step in for Conlee, should the need arise, and
Gabby had spent time with Sybil and Austin while
Jonathan had been assigned to her detail. "When I call her,
would you like to say hi?"

"No, I'm not in the mood for an inquisition. You tell
her we've been in the swamp for a couple days, and she's
going to nag you to death with questions."

Did Gabby pull her matchmaker-from-hell routine on

him, too? Wishing she knew exactly what he meant, she wrinkled her nose at him. "I don't get nagged. I'm the veep. Too many secrets."

"Right."

Sybil smiled at his sarcasm. Nothing so mundane as her position would keep Gabby from nagging or plying her with questions. "Can I give her a message from you?"

He thought a moment. "Tell her I'm breathing and she owes me fifty."

"You made a fifty-dollar bet with her?"

"I won." He smiled. "That'll drive her nuts."

"I'm going to have to work on you to be nice to my friend."

"I started being nice to her *because* she was your friend," he countered. "But Gabby grows on you."

"So does bacteria, but that doesn't mean you like it."

"I like her." He looked from the doorway back to Sybil. "She loves you."

"It's mutual. She's been an important person in my life. My best friend." She crossed her arms over her chest. "So who should I remind you to call so they can hear your voice and know you're okay?"

"No one." He looked away, studied the ceiling. "With the job, I don't have much time to develop friendships."

No one? He had no one? "Crazy hours, huh?"

"Bitchy bosses."

He *was* teasing her. "Those, too." And he was trying to change the subject. Jonathan did that a lot, whenever she got too close to the bone of something he didn't want to look at up close. "I'm sorry you haven't had a Gabby in your life."

"Me, too." He looked vulnerable, hurt, and he trusted her enough to risk letting her see it.

Taking a leap of faith, she walked back to him, lifted a hand to his forearm. "I'll be your friend, Jonathan."

He stared at her a long moment, looking torn between

opening up and totally shutting down, and then he sighed. "I'd be the luckiest man alive if it were that easy, Sybil."

The hallway light shone on his face. He dipped his chin to look at her, casting shadows on the wall, on her, and she had the strangest feeling that he had loved long and hard and the woman had never known it. Could anyone really be loved like that and not know it?

Maybe, but it wasn't going to be her. She was going to risk the fall and settle this woman versus the veep debate inside her head. "But it's not that easy between us, is it?"

He hesitated, closed his eyes, then opened them and looked down at her with regret. "No, it's not. It never has been, and it never will be."

Was that why he had left her detail? Because he cared for her and felt he shouldn't? It was possible; she had been his married boss. She wanted to know but couldn't ask him. Not now, not yet. She needed a better grip on their relationship, and he needed to overcome some of the pain in his eyes. "I'd want to know you were okay." She moved closer, lifted her arms, and then hugged him hard. His arms wrapped around her and he sighed against her neck. A long moment later, she screwed up her courage and admitted the truth. "Actually, I'd need to hear your voice, Jonathan."

He lifted her chin and met her gaze, trailed a fingertip along the line of her jaw, then dropped a kiss to her forehead. "Me, too."

Swallowing hard, he backed away, shutting her out as clearly as if he had stepped behind a wall. "You'd better get moving. We need to get back. Your feet need medical attention."

"Later. For God's sake, Westford. You don't say, wait, hold the crisis while I tend to my feet." *We're not in the swamp anymore.* "Give me twenty minutes," she said, then wound through the house to her bedroom.

Two minutes later she stood in the shower, swallowing

rapidly again and again. He couldn't see them being friends and he'd kissed on the forehead, not the mouth, so he didn't want more than friendship, either. She was important to him, but what exactly did that mean? They weren't in the swamp anymore. So he wanted to back off from her now? So the near-death trauma had worn off and he'd gotten his needed dose of affirmation of life?

Whatever his reasons, she should be grateful. Relationships were messy. One between them would make their lives even more complicated. He was being wiser about this; thinking with his head, not his heart. But she didn't feel grateful or relieved. She felt . . . hollow.

She lifted her face to the stream of water and tried to imagine what it would be like to be loved by him, but even with her hormones running amuck, she couldn't imagine it. That was just as well, considering. He'd been pretty clear that he didn't want to imagine it.

But she did. And she knew she would.

Resentment burned in her stomach. Fear joined it. The last time she dared to love a man she ended up lied to, married to him, lied to again, deceived and betrayed and humiliated, and it still wasn't over.

You ended up called on the carpet and blessed out by the likes of Cap Marlowe, for God's sake. He called you a corrupt fraud, and you had no idea what he was even talking about. Wouldn't he be pleased to know he had actually caused your divorce? Wouldn't he just love it?

She snagged a bar of soap and scrubbed her arms, wishing she could wash away those memories and that the water would stop stinging her cuts and scratches. That confrontation with Cap Marlowe wasn't one she would ever forget. But living through it once was bad enough. She didn't want to relive it again and again.

After rinsing, she soaped again and wondered how long it would take to get the smells of the swamp out of her pores. Jonathan had been right to apply the brakes. He'd go on to

another detail, and she'd go on with her work. It didn't feel
great, but it was for the best. She had a promise to keep.

Rinsing off the last of the soap, she watched the water
swirl clear at what was left of her feet. The only parts of
them that weren't bruised were cut and now bleeding.

Damn it, she missed him already.

Her heart wrenched, and, for the first time, she admitted without fear or regret that her work wasn't enough. She
wanted more. She wanted to care for and to feel cared for
by someone special who shared her life. She wanted to
know that if she died, one man—*just one man*—would
mourn. Was that asking too much?

*Oh, God. You're in serious trouble here. This doesn't
sound like swamp fever.*

Wrapping a thick, fluffy towel around her, she walked
through to her bedroom. But even its soft peach and green
decor failed to soothe her. Flustered, she picked up the
phone and then flung herself across the bed and called
Gabby.

Some things never change.

Gabby answered, sounding so sad that a lump slid into
Sybil's throat. "Hi," she said. "It's me."

"Oh, God, it's true!" Gabby said in a shaky rush. "I
knew you couldn't be dead. I would have felt it, and I
didn't. I told Lisa it wasn't possible, but she thought I was
nuts."

Gabby had mourned, and her clerk, Lisa, had tried to
help her through it. "Has she been threatening to lace your
coffee with Prozac again?"

"Prozac, Xanax, you name it. If she doesn't straighten
out, one of these days I'm really going to fire her."

Maybe when hell froze over. Gabby and Lisa were
close, not that it stopped either of them from making
threats. "Uh-huh. Then you'll be bitchy for six months because you won't be able to find anything." Lisa had her own
rendition of job security. Even the FBI had failed to break

the code on her bizarre retrieval system. "Remember last year when she had emergency surgery? You were nagging her for the location of files in the damn recovery room."

"True." Gabby's sigh crackled static through the phone. "You should have stayed dead until this challenge is over. What's Westford thinking?"

"He hasn't mentioned it."

"Why the White House? Someone caught your chopper landing on film. The word is you're okay, but you don't sound okay, so are you? Before you answer that, remember who you're talking to here."

"I really am fine—bruised and scraped from head to toe, and in a helluva hurry at the moment—but fine."

"Tough. Let whatever it is wait. Indulge me for a few minutes. Your death was devastating, Sybil. God, I was pissed at you for dying on me—and, for the record, you're a lousy liar. You're not fine."

"Go easy on me, okay?" Sybil checked the clock. She had ten minutes, but after Gabby's comments, Sybil couldn't not linger a minute or two. Gabby needed the idea of Sybil being alive to really soak in and become real to her. "It's been a wicked week and I'm in denial."

"Oh, hell. This is serious. You've only been in denial once since we got drunk and went skinny-dipping in old man Morris's pond, and then you ended up marrying Mr. Snip It." Gabby groaned. "Spill it. I want details."

"The short version is Jonathan went with me on this trip, I fell in love with him, and I don't want to love him or anyone else. I can't ride that emotional roller coaster again, Gabby."

"Are you afraid you'll be riding it alone?"

"That's only part of it." Sybil stared at the bottles of colognes on her dresser. "This past year—since the divorce—has been the best year of my life."

"It's been the safest year of your life, not the best one. You haven't had to take any personal, emotional risks."

"Whatever," Sybil shot back. "I liked it. I want to feel that way again. I have enough trouble here without—" Laughter crackled in her ear and she paused to regroup. "Gabby. What is so damn funny?"

"You. Sybil, you've been on the Hill too long. You're trying to legislate your heart."

Sybil let out a sigh deep enough to rattle windows. "I'm scared spitless, you heartless bitch. Show me a little empathy, even if you have to fake it."

"I know you're scared." All traces of humor left Gabby's voice. "Mr. Snip It did a real number on you. But Jonathan isn't like that lowlife weasel, and you can handle whatever you have to handle. You used to know that. Frankly, this promise you made David about men is turning you into one weird woman, Sybil."

Feeling weird, and not at all sure she could handle this love business, she glanced at the clock. "I'm out of time. Jonathan said to say hi and that you owe him fifty dollars."

"Damn." Gabby's sigh crackled static through the phone. "Tell him the check's in the mail."

"What's this bet about?" Sybil rifled through her closet, looking for shoes, though the thought of putting them on her tender feet made her sick to her stomach.

"You on a secure phone?"

"Yes."

"He bet there'd be a terrorist attack in Switzerland. I bet it would happen after you got back to the States."

It appeared they both had been right. "Hold that check." None of her shoes fit. Her feet were too swollen. She snagged her sneakers as a last option before slippers.

"One last bit of advice." Gabby's voice went serious. "You've never been a coward. Don't start now. Tell Jonathan the truth. Trust him." Gabby cleared her throat to signal the matter was officially closed. "And tell me one more time you're really okay. You being in denial makes it hard to believe."

Trust. The one thing hardest for her to give. "I'm fine.

Honest. My feet took a serious hit—just with bruises and cuts—and my ribs ache like hell, but otherwise, I really am all right."

"One more question. Have you slept with him?"

"Gabby. That's none of your business."

"Have you?"

Sybil glared at the ceiling. "No."

"Are you going to?"

Frowning at the receiver, she let out a huff she meant for Gabby to hear. "That's your second question, and I'm not answering it, either."

"God, you're a prude. I'm not pleading Westford's case, but consider it, Sybil. He's gorgeous, and he has a body to die for. If he's as good at sex as he is at everything else—"

"I'm hanging up now," Sybil said in a singsong voice. She cradled the receiver to the sounds of Gabby's laughter.

Westford as a lover. That was enough to conjure a batch of raw nerves. She hadn't been with a man since Austin. What if she'd forgotten how to—no, no. This was definitely not the time to think about this.

Thanks to Mr. Snip It, there might not be a later time . . .

Sybil shot the clock a pleading look. Nearly two-thirty. Nine and a half hours until impact. She sent up a quick prayer that she would be all right one minute after midnight, too.

And once again her thoughts zeroed in on the crisis. *Austin, what have you done? What have you done?*

First-Strike Launch: 09:31:03

Austin Stone couldn't get over it.

Faust had routinely masterminded the most devastating terrorist attacks on the planet and yet he had failed to kill one unarmed woman—even after he had eliminated

her plane and her people, and had isolated her with no resources.

Sitting behind a computer desk in a spartan A-267 office, Austin glared at the white walls and floors. Not only
was Sybil alive, she had ordered Commander Conlee to
make Austin part of the crisis-intervention team. How the
hell was he supposed to leave D.C. before the launch when
he was restricted to the building?

Oh, Conlee hadn't told Austin he couldn't leave, but
he had no illusions. If he tried, Conlee would stop him.
Would he place him under formal arrest?

*Don't panic, Austin. Without a resolution to the DNA mys-
tery, they have no evidence. Without Sybil, they have no resolution. So she's not dead. So what? Just discredit her. A whacked
hornet's nest creates a swarm, and swarming hornets sting.*

"We appreciate your helping us with this, Dr. Stone."
Conlee stood near the door and sipped from a can of cola,
holding an unlit stub of a smelly cigar between his fingers.

"Certainly." Austin peeled his lips from his teeth and
forced himself to smile. "I'm glad you asked. I resent anyone corrupting my designs."

"I'm sure you do." Conlee nodded, then returned to
the outer rim.

Dozens of engineers in offices all along the corridor
were hacking through the complex computer system, looking for a way to stop the countdown. But they wouldn't find
one, and neither would Austin. What he would find was a
way to get out of this hangar. His plane left at eight, and he
intended to be on it.

A swarm would scatter their focus. He could let them
find Mendoza's body, he supposed. The man had had to
die, of course. Recruited to assist Austin, he had known too
much to not be a threat. But verifying his death wouldn't
create a diversion substantial enough to allow Austin to get
out of A-267. It was the right time, he supposed, to whack

the hornet's nest. While everyone was dodging the swarm and being stung, he could escape.

He reached for the phone, carefully debating his words. Home Base would be listening to his every word.

Patrice answered on the second ring. "Dr. Stone's office."

"I'm going to be tied up a while. There's a stack of correspondence on my desk that needs to go out today." It wasn't necessary to get specific. The brown envelopes were the only things he had left on his desk. Everything else had already been shipped to what would become his new home and country. PUSH had been extremely accommodating. Patrice would know to contact Ground Serve and have the envelopes delivered.

"I'll take care of it now, sir."

"Thank you. And you might as well take the rest of the weekend off. Looks as if I'm going to be busy here for at least that long."

"Thank you, Dr. Stone. I'll see you on Monday."

On Monday she would be dead. "Be prepared to stay late. We'll have a lot of catching up to do."

"I will, sir."

Austin hung up the phone. Sam Sayelle would get a jump on the others. Austin's instructions to Ground Serve had been explicit on that. Sayelle would break the story of Sybil's treason, and, in a matter of minutes, it would be a hot topic on every network. With her credibility shot, her orders would fail, and Austin would be free to move at will.

He hoped it happened before the bitch realized that only she held the key to the DNA mystery.

*   *   *

Sybil couldn't believe it. Mere minutes, and already Westford was rushing her.

She grabbed the ringing phone from the bathroom vanity, returned to her perch on the side of the tub, then crooked the receiver between her shoulder and ear and returned to doctoring her feet. "I'm hurrying, Jonathan. I can't get the damn Band-Aids to stick. I put Neosporin on the cuts, and now the bandages just won't stay put. How did you make them work?"

"Put the sticky part where there is no salve."

It wasn't Jonathan.

Oh, damn. Heat rushed up her neck, flooded her face. "David?"

He let out a little chuckle. "Hi. Sorry to interrupt your first-aid session, but we need to touch base, and I've only got a second. I'm still in teleconferences, soothing tempers at the UN, but I wanted to make sure Barber had briefed you on this treason rumor."

"Yes, he did." She sat up and rubbed at her forehead with her fingertips. A dull pain throbbed in her temples. "I guess I should explain."

"I know you haven't committed treason."

"No, I haven't." It took a pretty paranoid bastard to perceive Gil or what went on at the Wall as a threat, and Sayelle should know she wasn't stupid enough to commit treason right under the Secret Service's collective noses. The notion was ridiculous.

"You can explain later. Right now, Pakistan is on the line. Hang with this domestically, Sybil. Every leader in the world is outraged and gnawing on my ass. I'm counting on you to make things right at home."

"I'll do my best." She rubbed at her forehead. "Are Peris and Abdan's premiers still in Geneva?"

"Oh, yes. A courtesy call might keep them there until this is resolved and you can get back to them. Ingenious touch—the cookies and milk."

"It was a long shot. What about Linda Dean? I'm worried about her and the kids, David." She soaked a cotton ball in peroxide and dabbed at her foot.

"No update, but be prepared for the worst. Ballast has targeted families in the past."

"I know." And executed some of them. Both she and David hated negative thinking, but they had to be realistic.

"Sybil, why would Faust target Ken Dean's family?"

"Good question." She stretched and dropped the cotton ball into the trash. "I wish I had a good answer." Faust certainly had a reason. He always had a reason. "Jonathan and I are looking into it."

"I've got to go. Russia this time." He let out a sigh that created static in the phone line. "Keep me posted—and keep a sharp eye on Sam Sayelle. I know Conlee swears he's okay and he did the broadcasts for us, but he could cause problems for you on the treason issue."

Three things about that warning worried her. In David's mind, she had a treason *issue*. She believed to the depths of her soul that if Sam Sayelle could hurt her, he would. And right now, she didn't have a spare eye to keep on him.

First-Strike Launch: 08:41:22

"I found Marlowe."

Sam Sayelle swiveled his chair away from the computer terminal to look at Sniffer. Light from the window sliced across his desktop, where someone had placed a thick roast beef sandwich on white butcher paper. Had to be Annie. She was the only staff assistant who bothered with things like this. A paper cup of something hot and steaming sat next to the sandwich. "Where is he?"

"St. Elizabeth's. He went into a diabetic coma earlier today. He's still critical, but they think he'll survive. He's definitely out of commission for a while." Sniffer eyed the sandwich. "Can I have half? I missed lunch."

Probably out of commission for the presidential nomination, too. "Help yourself." Sam motioned for Sniffer to take the sandwich. Why had Cap been taken to St. Elizabeth's? Why not Bethesda? Strange. "Did he suffer any brain damage?"

"It's too soon to tell." Sniffer took a bite and chewed, his expression noncommittal. "I talked to his nurse. He nearly died, Sam."

She *talked* to you?"

He grinned. "I told her I was his godson."

"You better hope he dies. He'll take serious exception to your pretending to have a family tie to him."

"But I do. I *am* his godson."

"Why didn't you tell me?" Had Cap placed Sniffer here to watch Sam?

"I didn't tell anyone. I like doing things on my own." Sniffer shrugged.

Admiring that, Sam turned the conversation back to the topic most pressing. "So what did the nurse say?"

"After such serious episodes, patients are often mentally scrambled. It takes a few days to determine the long-term impact. He could suffer wicked synapse misfires, lose some gray cells. Or he could zip through it like it was nothing." Sniffer cocked his head and captured a bit of shredded lettuce clinging to his lip with his tongue. "Until he comes around, they just don't know. It's a tossup."

Sam thought about that. Where had Cap been when this had happened? He hadn't been at the office; Jean had cleared his calendar. She could be covering for him, of course. She would do that. But ordinarily she wouldn't think she needed to lie to Sam to protect the senator. That could mean she was covering for Conlee. To keep Sam from telling Cap he had decoded the broadcast messages and knew more of what was going on than Cap knew.

"Sam?"

Sniffer's tone snagged Sam's attention, warned him he was repeating something he had already said. "You've got a package." He pointed to a slender man wearing a blue and white uniform, holding a large brown envelope.

"Sorry."

"No problem." The man extended an electronic tracker. "You have to sign for it."

Sam scrawled his name, then took the envelope. Hand-delivered by Ground Serve on a Saturday and marked "Urgent" in huge, red letters? Someone considered it important, and it wasn't Conlee. "Thanks."

The messenger left, and Sam pulled out the contents. He scanned them and felt betrayed to the bone. In decoding the broadcasts, he had come to admire Sybil Stone. But this exposé proved his initial instincts about her had been right after all. Conlee had to be running interference for her. Sam let out a long, low whistle.

"Hot stuff?" Sniffer asked, clearly curious.

"Lethal." Sam grabbed the phone and called his boss, Carl Edison.

Carl answered, sounding annoyed. "What?"

"It's Sam, boss."

"This better be good. I'm on the seventh hole for the first time in two weeks, and you just made me bitch up the best game I've had going all year."

The boss was highly annoyed, but Sam was used to his fits of temper and blew it off. "You need to come in. I just got a package from Austin Stone on our illustrious vice president that's so hot it's blistering my fingers."

"The treason thing?"

"Yeah." Sam's instincts slipped into high gear. Austin Stone could be setting her up. Sam would have to independently verify everything remotely questionable. Cap liked Austin so Sam tolerated him, but he didn't like him, and he certainly didn't trust him. Conversely, he had hated Sybil. But through this crisis he had reluctantly, even begrudgingly, come to admire her. With each new broadcast, she had fed that spark of hope in him of seeing a genuine patriot in office. Yet he still hadn't trusted her. That conflict had been driving him crazy. At least, it had been until he'd gotten the envelope. Now he held damaging evidence that, not only was she not the real thing, she was as corrupt as politicians come.

"I'm on my way," Carl said. "I think I'll bring Marcus in on this, too. Any objections?"

Marcus Gilbert. If anyone had insight into this, he would. The man had retired, but he was still an icon and hot-wired to the Hill. Frankly, Sam would feel better about this if Marcus did offer an opinion. "None whatsoever."

On an otherwise blank page, someone had handwritten a message. "Flip five."

What the hell did that mean?

Chapter Nineteen

"I'm having to resist a powerful urge here, Westford." Sybil stared at the mountain of reports spread across her desk-top. She had been studying them intently since finishing the calls David had asked her to make, but all she seemed to be gaining was blurred vision.

"What urge is that?" He sounded wary.

She glanced up, wondering if he was hoping the urge was personal, or praying it wasn't.

Damn it, Gabby, did you have to plant thoughts of making love with him in my mind?

Her imagination was working overtime. Aloud, she said, "The urge to toss up my hands, cry 'uncle,' and down a bottle of scotch." They had been through the heap twice and they hadn't found anything significant not already doc-umented. Commander Conlee had assured them that everything doable was being done and everything check-able had been triple-checked, and yet—

"Does it help to know I'm feeling it, too?"

That comment could be personal or professional. She rotated her left ankle, wishing her feet would stop throbbing, got her breathing back under control, and risked a look at him. "Define *it*."

"That niggling feeling that we have the whole puzzle." Jonathan straightened up and rubbed at the small of his back, rustling his crisp, white-cotton shirt. "We just haven't recognized all the pieces and slotted them."

"That's the one." It was, professionally. She sloughed off a wave of disappointment and focused on business. Her mind raced, unwilling to slow down, unwilling to accept that the clock was ticking on the launch and they couldn't stop it.

"Okay, look," Jonathan said. "We're bone-tired and our minds are mired in surface clutter. We've been through this a million times. We know how it works. Back off a few minutes, clear our heads, and let things find their proper place."

"We don't have time to back off." She shuffled reports, working through a maze of tidbits that seemed random and jumbled and disjointed.

"Take five, gain ten." He rubbed his palms together. "I'm going to go get us some fresh coffee. Let it rest. When I get back, we'll tackle it again."

"If you insist." Sybil slumped back in her chair, let her head rock back, and stared at the ceiling, certain he was right. They had been in tight, tense situations a lot of times and had made it through them. Would they make it through this one?

He stepped toward the door, stopped, then turned back and walked over to her, his mouth lined with grim determination. He kissed her breathless and muttered, "Maybe now I can think," then walked out the door.

Smiling like an idiot, she closed her eyes and ordered herself to ditch the static in her mind and let her thoughts drift. Jonathan was right. Surface and sensual clutter clogged the brain. And she had tons of both to ditch.

Mentally she tossed the clutter into a huge, rusty Dumpster. Almost immediately her thoughts quieted. Images from the last few days drifted in and out. Images of Jonathan, tending to her feet, holding her at the edge of the quicksand pit, clasping her hand in the helicopter and smiling that special smile he saved only for her, and telling her he would need to hear her voice. Whether she liked it or not, wanted to or not, she cared about him. A lot.

I told you it wasn't swamp fever.

Go away. Now isn't the time to settle that battle. *The crisis . . .*

Determined, she focused on images of Harrison and Cramer, of Julie, Mark, and Captain Ken Dean, letting them flow freely through her mind. And then unexpectedly older images replaced them: her mom and dad's last anniversary party, her sixteenth birthday, rooming with Gabby at college. The night she had met Austin. He had been irresistibly charming back then—except when he was around Gabby.

From the moment they'd met, it had been instant hatred, and nothing she had been able to say had swayed either of them. The two had kept Sybil caught between a rock and a hard place, but unwilling to lose either of them, she had played the peacemaker, run interference, and, at times, barely managed to keep them from killing each other. She should have paid more attention to that instant hatred. Instead, she had loved them both, and in goodwill gestures to her, her best friend and her husband had tolerated each other with unspoken hostility.

Mr. Snip It is up to his nasty nostrils in this crisis, Sybil. Think about it.

Not surprised to hear that declaration in Gabby's sassy voice, Sybil let her thoughts drift where they would and memories of the early years with Austin came back to her.

He had been so young and alive and full of ambition then. So charming and mysterious.

Get real. The man was secretive. Secretive, Sybil.

He was. Especially about his work. In all their years together, only once had he confided in her, and then only because he needed something from her.

That need and the current crisis collided, slammed into her, and she sat straight up in her chair. "Oh, God."

Jonathan. She had to tell Jonathan. She scrambled from her desk, her office, and into the hall, pain shooting from her feet up to her knees. Hurrying toward the kitchen, she saw him come out, carrying two cups of coffee.

He took one look at her and rushed his steps. "What's wrong? Did you find something?"

"Not exactly." Her stomach lurched. She put a hand over it to calm it down.

"This is no time to be cryptic. You look like you've seen a ghost."

"In a way, I did." How could she have forgotten this? How?

Press Secretary Winston walked by. Jonathan stared him down, led Sybil back into her office, and then closed the door. "Talk to me, Sybil."

She licked at her lips, uncertain where to begin. "I remembered something that happened a long time ago. Something with Austin."

"Okay." Jonathan set the coffee cups down on a table near a sofa.

"He could have my DNA. It's possible, Jonathan."

"Intel didn't find any evidence of it."

"Just hear me out." Chilled, she rubbed at her blue silk sleeve. The smooth fabric felt good, calming against her palm and fingertips. "When Conlee told me about the DNA secure system, I got that intuitive feeling. You know the one I mean."

Jonathan nodded, reached for his coffee cup, and downed a steaming sip.

"I couldn't peg it then, but a minute ago I remembered."

"Remembered what, exactly?"

"What it was he needed." That comment earned her a vacant look, so she went on to explain. "Sorry. I'm not a hundred percent," she said, stating the obvious. "This happened a long time ago. We weren't married yet."

"Ah." Jonathan settled on the sofa with his coffee and motioned her to join him.

"Austin came over one night really excited." She slid onto the sofa beside him, absently tucked her feet up under her. "He had this new device—I'm nearly positive it's the same one, though he didn't describe it in detail. He never told anyone specifics on his designs." She nodded toward her coffee cup. When Jonathan reached for it, she resumed talking. "At any rate, both systems work essentially the same way."

"Austin designing the system isn't in dispute." Jonathan passed her the cup.

She clasped it, relishing its warmth against her hands. Her insides felt like they'd been squeezed inside a block of ice. She was freezing. "No, but his not having a record of my DNA is a significant part of the reason so few feel he's behind this missile launch."

"I'm missing the significance in this."

"That's because I haven't gotten to it yet." She swallowed a sip of coffee. It tasted fresh and strong. "He was ready to do trial studies on an experimental system he had designed. But he didn't want to bring in anyone from the outside to be a subject—Austin didn't just get paranoid about corporate espionage, he's always been that way—and he couldn't use his own DNA without sacrificing credibility in his test results. But requesting a subject would have created a major challenge."

"Why?"

"He was employed by Divetal then. It would hold the patent on any design he created."

"Austin wanted to keep the patent on this device himself." Jonathan set down his cup.

Sybil nodded. "He worked on the design at home and held it privately until after we founded Secure Environet."

"You were the subject in his trial studies?" Jonathan asked, clearly getting the picture.

She nodded. "He needed my blood. That's what I remembered."

Understanding brought dread to Jonathan's eyes. Then confusion. "So why didn't Intel find your DNA in his records?"

"I don't know. But doesn't the fact that it's not showing up tell you something? Only two people in the world knew I was the subject in that study: Austin and me."

Jonathan snagged his jacket, which was draped over a wingback chair, pulled it on, and then smoothed down an upturned lapel. "If you had died in the swamp, then there wouldn't be anything or anyone left to link the A-267 corruption back to him."

"Exactly."

Worry clouded Jonathan's eyes. "Are you going to tell Conlee?"

"Of course." She forced a strength she didn't feel into her voice.

Jonathan's lips flattened to a slash. "You know he could consider this proof you've been working with Austin all along. He could name you as a co-conspirator."

Especially since she hadn't reported the blood incident until now. "I understand the risks. Some will think I'm a bitter ex-wife, others will think I'm protecting him. But regardless of what anyone thinks, I can't *not* tell Conlee this, Jonathan." She smoothed a hand over her hair. "Austin is supposedly neutralized, but I'm not comfortable banking on it. Actually, I'd like to confront him myself but, considering the circumstances, that would be less than wise."

"I have to agree."

She hated revisiting his betrayal even in the abstract, but she had to be specific and honest. The stakes were too high to hide behind pride. "Austin is brilliant. He's a genius, Jonathan. And I've had the unfortunate experience of learning firsthand that, when it comes to getting what he wants, he has a diabolical mind and no conscience."

Jonathan mulled over her comments, worrying at his lip with his teeth. "I guess there's no point in delaying, then. We'd better go talk with Conlee."

She clasped Jonathan's arm and looked him right in the eye. "I won't be as blunt with the others, but I want you to know where I stand."

"All right."

"Inside, I know Austin hooked up with Faust. I wouldn't be surprised if he's also hooked up with PUSH and a half-dozen other groups. The man covers his assets. Regardless of what we find, I know he's responsible for this crisis, Jonathan, and I know he'll carry it through to the bitter end. He hates me, and he resents everyone in D.C. because they didn't force me to resign over the divorce. Not even when I dropped into the gutter in the polls."

"There's no love lost between him and me, either," Jonathan admitted.

Sybil had to choose. Did she address the question that had kept her tossing and turning nights, or did she seal it away forever and always wonder? "Why did you threaten to kill him?"

"How did you know I had?"

"David mentioned it recently. He assumed I already knew."

Her hand on his arm was shaking. Jonathan rubbed the back of it, warming her fingertips on his palm. "Remember the night you argued in the Blue Room and you told him to leave?"

"Not specifically." There had been many arguments.

"It doesn't matter. He threatened to slap you, so I

followed him out to make sure he left the premises. He stopped to talk with Barber, and I overheard him say he was going to hire a couple of thugs to beat the hell out of you." The memory clearly renewed his outrage, but Jonathan kept his voice level and even managed to shrug. "I took exception to it."

"I see." Her heart thudded in her ears. She screwed up her courage to ask the question that had bothered her more than she cared to admit for longer than she cared to admit. "Is that why you asked to be reassigned, or did I do something wrong?"

He dropped his lids, veiling his eyes. "I lost my temper. Me getting emotionally involved was a luxury neither of us could afford."

What exactly did that mean? Had he gotten angry with Austin for what he'd said, or had he been angry with himself for losing control? Or maybe anger had nothing to do with it. Maybe he was just afraid that losing control, even for a moment, could cost him his life. She could ask him, she supposed, but his face looked brittle enough to crack, and he had done so much for her already. She couldn't justify putting him on the proverbial hot seat. "Thank you for clearing that up."

"You're welcome, ma'am."

Well, hell. They were back to that "ma'am" business again. She knew why she should run from him emotionally, but why was he running from her? She stood up and gave in to the urge to sigh. "Jonathan, could you knock off the ma'am stuff and just be like you were in the swamp? Please. That's the you I need."

Wishing he would hold her as he had at the quicksand pit, she dropped her gaze to the floor and saw black sneakers. He expected trouble. Probably not trouble with her, but with Conlee. He was probably right.

"All right." He stood up, and their hands brushed.

Turning, she clasped his arm and nudged him to face

her, but he didn't move to take her into his arms. Disappointed, she looked up and met his gaze. "There's one other thing you need to know that I won't state bluntly with the others, Jonathan. It could make you hate me. I don't want that, but not telling you would make me hate myself."

He lifted his brows, making no promises, and then waited for her response.

"Austin might have had help, but I know he dreamed up this nightmare at A-267, and no amount of evidence will convince me he didn't. He's good at manufacturing proof to back up his lies. If we manage to stop the launch, I'm going to devote the rest of my life to proving he murdered Harrison and Cramer and the others and to finding Linda Dean and her children." Sybil's voice thickened with steely resolve. "But if Austin launches this missile, legally or illegally, I'm going to see to it that he blows up with it." It went without saying that she would be left behind in the evacuation and be blown up, too.

Austin Stone's days of leaving victims in his wake and just moving on were over.

He had taken her blood.

Now she would take his.

Chapter Twenty

Eight hours, fifteen minutes, and twenty-seven seconds left. The Home Base briefing room at A-267 was frigid and about as interesting as an unpainted canvas. Stripped to essentials, the walls were bare but copper-lined to deter the intrusion of listening devices. Furnishings were limited to twelve straight-back chairs and an oblong wooden table that stood scuffed and scarred by years of use and too many crises.

Commander Conlee objected to making anyone comfortable during briefings. Comfortable people relax their guard—and tend to be long-winded. In the commander's opinion, briefings at A-267 had no business being either.

Sybil and Conlee sat at opposite ends of the table. While he looked tense and formidable, she felt as if someone had kicked her hard in the stomach. He *could* name her as a co-conspirator. She *could* lose everything, including her job and her freedom. Suspicion *does* breed contempt. If

Jonathan hadn't been standing near the door, she probably wouldn't have been able to get the words out. With his back to the wall, his arms folded across his chest, and his expression neutral, he appeared totally passive. But she knew. Deep down, in those secret places she had sworn after Austin to forget she had, she knew she had Jonathan's full support. He was there with her every step of the way.

"Commander," Sybil said. "In our very first briefing, you taught me the three necessary ingredients to solving crimes. I've never forgotten them: means, opportunity, and motive."

"I remember, ma'am."

"In this crisis, we've got all three on Austin Stone as a suspect. We know A-267 is a classified site and access to it is severely restricted. We know Austin designed the system and his corporation maintains it. So his means and opportunity to reconfigure the system are established facts." Now came the risky part. "What you might not know is that he has motive."

"Which is?"

"To set me up, Commander."

"Possible. But only if he has your DNA." Conlee rolled his stubby cigar between his forefinger and thumb. "We've gone through his records with a fine-tooth comb. Your DNA just isn't in his possession."

"There is no way all of his records could have been checked this quickly."

"His last extensive inspection was three weeks ago. We just had to pull everything from then forward and scan it in."

"Scan it in?"

"Because of the sensitive nature of his work with us, all of his records are subject to full review. We scan a copy of everything."

Well, hell. She wished she'd known that before now. "For how long?"

"In his case, since Secure Environet was founded."

Too late. "But nothing from before then?"

"There is nothing from before then."

"In this case, there is. I'm going to have to digress, but, please, just hear me out," she said. "This is embarrassing, Commander, but you need to know it to understand the significance of what I'm about to tell you."

"I'll treat whatever you say with discretion, ma'am."

Grateful, she nodded. "If I had died in the plane explosion, my fifty-two percent of Secure Environet stock would automatically have reverted to Austin. He has repeatedly asked me to sell him my interest, but I've elected not to do that." Please, God. Don't let Conlee ask her why. "Fortunately, a judge supported my decision. That infuriated Austin. Greed and the desire to hurt me—because he couldn't force me to relinquish the stock—could have motivated him to concoct this crisis and get involved with Faust and maybe with PUSH."

Jonathan felt sick. Greed and a desire to inflict pain on one person was a hell of a reason for committing treason. Yet he felt confident that Austin Stone would consider it logical and reasonable. More likely than not, he'd consider this crisis a proportional response to the wrongs committed against him.

"Reasonable deduction," Commander Conlee said. "But the fact remains that he hasn't accessed this site and, unless he's memorized it, he doesn't have your DNA. We've checked and double-checked everything else."

"He could have it, Commander," Sybil said. "I realize my credibility could take a nosedive because I didn't report this immediately, but the simple truth is I only just remembered it."

How would she react to that remark if she were in Conlee's shoes? She'd be skeptical as hell, but she hoped she would be open-minded, too. "Years ago I was an unnamed subject in one of Austin's experimental trials on a security device. He could have my DNA from then. I think it should be double-checked."

"This was from before the two of you founded Secure Environet?"

She nodded. "It was a private project he was working on at home while he was employed at Divetal."

Conlee rolled his tongue inside his cheek. "We wouldn't have picked up on it then. Divetal owned his patents. We picked up their records."

"These trial studies weren't incorporated then." A question came to mind. "But why wouldn't they be part of the new system's records? Didn't he bring in this new design through Secure Environet?"

"They should have been included. He would have had to substitute the trials from another incarnation of this system for those of this incarnation. Otherwise, he never would have gotten authorization to proceed in the project and we would have picked up on the DNA match."

Too nervous to sit any longer, Sybil stood up and clenched the back of her chair. Her knuckles knobbed, whitened. "Look, the bottom line is Austin is *not* innocent in all of this, Commander. I strongly believe he and Faust are working together. I can't prove it—not yet—but I know it."

Pensive, Conlee tugged at his lower lip. "You realize how this looks?"

At least he wasn't summoning security—though he looked as if he were considering it. "Unfortunately, I do."

Conlee glanced at Jonathan, who gave him a nod so slight that if she hadn't been watching for it, she would have missed it. "We'll do what we can," Conlee finally assured her. "But due to the extenuating circumstances, I think it would be best if you leave the investigation to us."

"But—" Sybil started to interrupt.

"We need to move, ma'am." Jonathan cut her off. "We've all got a lot to do and"—he paused and looked pointedly at his watch—"only eight hours to do it."

Conlee sent Jonathan a look of pure relief. While he would do what he had to do to get his job done, Conlee clearly wasn't enthusiastic about going toe to toe with Lady Liberty. She had a reputation for sticking to her guns until her competition folded, and both men knew that reputation had not been given, it had been earned.

Jonathan and Sybil exited the facility and returned to his Volvo. Heat rippled through the leather interior.

She snapped her seat belt into place and then shoved her sunglasses up on her nose. "So what exactly do we need to do? Or were you just getting me off the commander's back?"

Tired, scared, and admittedly embarrassed by her former husband's lack of ethics, she was itching for a place to dump her frustration, but it wasn't going to be on his head. "First, you've earned your credibility, so the commander believes you. You hover, and you create doubt. He starts to wonder if you think you need to be there to do damage control—to protect Austin or yourself. Others, aside from Conlee, are going to have those same suspicions. So he's protecting you by taking you out of the line of fire."

Jonathan cranked the engine, then adjusted the air vent to blow in his face and cool him down. "For what it's worth, I believe you. And I believe you're right and Austin is up to his crooked neck in this crisis. If he's convinced he's going to blow himself to hell and back, he might just abort the launch—provided you're not in his face, reminding him why he started the damn crisis in the first place."

"I'm sorry." Sybil glanced over at him. Tired and stressed out enough to forget her inhibitions and fears, she revealed the truth. "I don't like what this is doing to me inside. I married him, Jonathan. I can't believe I married a man like him."

"You also had the wisdom and good judgment to divorce his lousy ass. You can't look at one without the other." Jonathan put the car in drive and headed down the dusty road, back toward town.

"You know, I love that about you." She hadn't meant to say it out loud, but now that she had, she couldn't take it back. There was nothing left to do but brazen it out.

The hint of a smile curved his lip. "What?"

He didn't seem upset. He did seem interested. She stretched an arm over the seat back. "You look at both sides of things and make me be fair to myself."

"You have a hard time with that. Everyone gets a fair shake except you." He glanced her way. "Everything isn't your responsibility or your fault."

Being frank with him wasn't so bad. Actually, it felt pretty good. "Thank you."

"For believing in you when you're telling the truth?"

He seemed just outraged enough by that circumstance to be endearing. Touched, she covered his hand. "For being you."

"I'm good for you, Sybil." He gently squeezed her fingers.

He sounded almost militant, as if he were trying to convince her, and maybe even himself. "Yes, you are."

A motorcycle whizzed past. The rider didn't have on a helmet. She swallowed a sigh, refused to worry about him, and looked at Jonathan. He kept his gaze fixed straight ahead, beyond the windshield. "Jonathan?" Her throat felt thick. "I want to be good for you, too."

Jonathan braked for a red light, let the words soak in and become real. For years he had wanted to hear some remark, see some sign that she thought of him as more than an agent, and finally, when he had convinced himself that it just wasn't going to happen, she had. How long, he wondered, would it take him to really understand how her mind worked? Every time he thought he had it nailed, she did a one-eighty on him. And since Geneva, the woman had sent out more mixed signals than a pay-per-view channel scrambler.

"I love that about you, too. That I can feel that way and tell you."

"You're making me crazy, Sybil."

"Is that good or bad?"

"I'm not sure yet." He wished to hell he knew. "Maybe both."

She tapped her sunglasses up on her nose, adjusted her safety belt. "All I meant was that if you think or feel it, you say it—straight out. I admire that."

"I don't." He also wished she'd take off those damn dark glasses so he could see her eyes. "In fact, I rarely say what I feel with you."

"Now you're making *me* crazy." She smiled. "Whether or not you realize it, you're blunt, Jonathan, and opinionated. It's nice."

Along with everything else standing between them, they didn't need to add false impressions. Already they had a healthy list. "Opinionated, yes. But you're mistaken on the other. I feel a lot of things I don't say." That had to be the understatement of the millennium, particularly where she was concerned.

"For example . . ."

"You confuse the hell out of me." He looked over, then right back at the road. A rusty Ford swerved into his lane, and he slowed down to give it space. "One minute I think what's happening between us is personal. The next I don't fit into your plans. I can't keep up."

"Me, either."

That remark earned her a look she'd been feeling for a while.

"You might as well stop glaring. I'm not at all afraid of you. All I meant was that you confuse me, too. Actually, it's not you but me who confuses me. I mean, I confuse myself. No, what I really mean is, the way you make me feel confuses me."

"I'm getting dizzy, Sybil."

"Sorry. It's the way you make me feel. That's what's confusing." At the moment, she looked baffled and unnerved. "You see, I like you."

"We've known each other for years and you just realized that?"

"No, I've always liked you, but not like this. This is . . .

different." She blew out a sigh. "Frankly, I'm having a hell of a time with this, Jonathan."

"That I understand."

Relief washed through her. "Thank God. I was afraid you wouldn't. This isn't a comfortable place to be alone."

"Oh, no. I do. Trust me on this one."

She grunted, then ate a streak in her lipstick, pondering her thoughts. "You make me feel special and important to you."

"You are important to me."

"I know you told me I was, Jonathan, but you make me *feel* it. There's a difference. I don't like it. The difference, I mean." She pointed at a blue Taurus. "Watch that guy. His brake lights are out." Without missing a beat, she turned back to her topic. "And I love the way I see myself through your eyes. I hate loving that." A dreamy smile touched her lips. "But I think every woman needs that sense of feminine prowess, Jonathan. Most don't know they need it, and some probably never get it, but it really changes the way a woman feels about herself. I've never had it until now."

"You've always been feminine." He sounded surprised.

"I haven't always felt feminine or attractive."

"You're kidding." His voice was dead-level flat. "But you're beautiful."

Her face warmed. "It's been a long time since anyone has thought so."

"Sybil, thinking has nothing to do with it. Look in the mirror, for Christ's sake."

"You're missing the point, Jonathan. That's just surface clutter. The important stuff isn't reflected in glass, it's reflected in a man's eyes when he looks at you. You feel it in his hands. He touches you as if you're some priceless treasure. He talks to you, not at you, and he hears and listens and respects what you have to say. Those are the things of real beauty, Jonathan."

He swallowed hard. "We need to change the subject."

Surprised by the harshness in his tone, she stared at him. "Did I offend you?"

"No."

If his voice got any sharper, it would cut stone. "I did. I'm sorry—"

"You didn't offend me, okay?"

"Jonathan, I might have trouble verbalizing my intimate feelings, but I'm not stupid. You're clearly upset. I didn't mean to make you uncomfortable, and I'm trying to apologize, damn it, so let me and let's—"

"I am not upset," he said, enunciating each word distinctly. "I am, however, fighting an intense urge to park this car and make love to you, so unless you're in the mood, you need to change the damned subject."

Stunned, she gaped. "Oh." Her voice came out as a breath of sound.

"Quit looking at me as if I've sprouted a spare head. I didn't mean to make you uncomfortable, either." He rolled his gaze. "I'm only human, Sybil."

Her heart beat hard and fast. He had to be teasing. He did that a lot—teased her. Of course that's what he was doing. But he didn't look like he was teasing, and he certainly didn't sound as if he were. If his words had been any stiffer they could have walked to her ears without sound waves. "Do you really want to make love with me, or are you teasing?"

"I'm not teasing."

"Really?" She bit a goofy grin from her mouth.

"Oh, yeah."

"Do you hate it?"

"I did, but the idea's growing on me."

Jonathan Westford vulnerable? She never would have believed it. Even seeing it, she had trouble believing it.

He made a sharp left turn. "Regardless, now isn't the time."

Time. The crisis. Good God, she'd forgotten about the crisis. "Of course it isn't."

He braked for a stop sign and watched a group of teens cross the street, carrying skateboards and Roller Blades. "I've had about enough of this back and forth from personal to professional business."

"Me, too."

"First chance, we need to talk through some things. Figure out how we want to handle this and where we're going with it." He tapped the accelerator and moved through the intersection. "I'll warn you right now, I'm going to be asking you how I fit into your plans."

That seemed to be a touchy point with him. Why? "Jonathan—"

"Not now." He clasped her hand and held it on his thigh. "After."

He didn't seem angry, but something had pricked his pride. She'd rather discuss it now, clear the air, and put him at ease if she could, but he obviously needed a little breathing room. Heart-to-heart chats about feelings were probably about as alien to him as they had become to her. "All right." She lifted her purse from the floorboard. "So where are we going?"

"To do a little sleuthing." He grabbed the neutral topic with both hands and a grateful heart. "Cap Marlowe's alive. He's taking his time at coming around, but he could be cognizant in a couple hours."

"Do you think Cap is in with Austin?"

"I think it's possible. They've been discreetly associating since you took office, and you were experiencing negative info leaks during the marriage."

"But Austin's been gone for over a year and the leaks haven't stopped. Cap still knows things that have to come from staffers." She dug through her purse, pulled out a roll of cherry Life-Savers, and offered them to Jonathan.

He took one, then passed back the roll. "That's where Barber must come in. The night I threatened Austin—"

"He was talking to Barber."

Jonathan nodded. "What if during the marriage, Austin passed Cap the leaks? After you gave Austin the boot, then Barber stepped in and fed the information to Austin and/or Cap."

"It's possible. Easy enough to verify with phone records," she said. "But why would Barber get involved with them?"

"Sybil, the man spends half his day every day jockeying for his next job." Jonathan draped an arm over the steering wheel. "He's the brunt of dozens of staffers' jokes about it."

"He wants a key position in Cap's administration."

"That would be my guess."

Sybil popped a Life-Saver into her mouth, tilted her head, and stared out of the windshield. "And Cap shows up at A-267 to pull a no-notice inspection right in the middle of this crisis."

"That's what we need to check out. It strikes me as too coincidental." Jonathan tapped the vent, directing the air away from his face. "I know we're jammed for time, and these are tough questions, but we need to answer them."

"The Senate is bound to call for a complete investigation. If we don't find the answers now, we probably won't find them at all. They'll be buried long before the official inquiry."

Jonathan nicked the turn signal. "Which is why we're on our way to Cap Marlowe's office now."

★ ★ ★

Foot traffic in the building was heavy. If Security found that odd for four on a Saturday afternoon when Congress wasn't racing against the clock to wind up or down, the staff didn't show it. Sybil and Jonathan were admitted with courteous nods and bored expressions.

They took the elevator up to Cap's office.

Jean sat at her desk, twisting a gold earring dangling from her lobe. Obviously, she was waiting for them. "May I help you?" Her voice was terse, deliberately distant.

Sybil wasn't welcome here. Being as circumspect as possible, and about as warm as a butcher's meat locker, Jean made that evident.

Jonathan went to Cap's office door. "We need the key."

"The senator doesn't allow anyone in his office when he isn't present."

Sybil had little patience and no time for this. "Open the door or I'll get a warrant."

Beaming resistance, her lips thinned to a fine line, but Jean reached inside the top drawer of her desk, withdrew the key, and then unlocked the door. "I will have to report this, Mrs. Stone."

Refusing to address her by her title was an intentional slur, but Sybil let it slide. She actually admired Jean's loyalty to Cap. Loyalty was a relatively rare treasure on the Hill. "Certainly."

Jonathan looked around the office, then began a methodical search, ceiling to floor.

Sybil checked the obvious: Cap's calendar, the last number dialing in to his office, his desk drawers. Nothing had been scheduled on his calendar for Friday afternoon, which came as no surprise. A-267 itself was classified. He wouldn't note an inspection on it. "When the senator left the office," she asked without looking over her shoulder, "did he mention where he could be reached?"

Leaning against the door frame, Jean bristled. "No. He usually does, but this time he didn't. That's necessary at times, as I'm sure you know. Right before he left, I reminded him to take his injection. He gets busy and forgets, so I track them on my scheduler and remind him. I—I don't know where he was when he became ill. Actually, I wouldn't have known he had become ill if Mrs. Marlowe hadn't called me from St. Elizabeth's."

Jean was afraid, carrying the burden of guilt, and she was obviously seeking absolution. Understanding all about that need, Sybil gave it to her. "It isn't your fault, Jean."

"That's what Grace said." She shrugged, knocking her shoulder against the hard wood.

Sybil's assistant, Grace, had never hidden the fact that she and Jean were friends, and that never had concerned Sybil. Both were longtime staffers and professionals and, while there had been a steady flow of leaks from Sybil's office and/or home to Cap, Sybil felt confident none of them flowed from Grace. "She's seldom wrong about anything."

That comment seemed to surprise Jean. As if trying to hold in a sudden swell of emotion that felt too big to contain, she crossed her chest with her arms. "But I didn't see to it that he took the shot. I just used the intercom. If I'd gone in..."

"Why didn't you go in?" Jonathan closed a desk drawer, opened another.

"I—I don't recall now."

Sybil frowned. The woman clearly did recall, but for reasons of her own, she elected to be evasive. "Have you spoken with Mrs. Marlowe in the last hour?"

"Yes." Worry haunted Jean's eyes. "He still isn't coming around."

"I hope he does, Jean."

She looked confused, torn. "Mrs. Marlowe phoned the medics to raise hell because they didn't take him to Bethesda. They told her you ordered them to go to St. E's. Why did you do that? Bethesda would have been more private."

"Because I was afraid he would die. St. E's was closer."

Jean looked surprised. "Mrs. Marlowe was right. She said you saved his life."

"That's not important." What else had Mrs. Marlowe said? "He's getting the care he needs. That's all that matters."

"Ground Serve." A man in the outer office elevated his voice. "I need a signature."

Startled, Jean jumped and then went out to him.

"We're not going to find anything here," Jonathan said. "Or learn anything from her."

Agreeing with him, Sybil nodded. They walked out of the office and, when she passed Jean, she glanced at the messenger. He held his head down, keying something into his tracker. Something about him seemed familiar, but the Ground Serve uniform didn't feel right.

She looked at Jonathan out of the corner of her eye but couldn't tell if he had noticed the messenger. Unreadable expressions were an asset to Jonathan, and he had honed the skill to an art form. Unfortunately, guessing what he was thinking when he didn't want anyone to know was impossible.

"Thanks, Jean," he said, then walked on at Sybil's side to the elevator.

On the elevator, he kept his thoughts to himself. When they got outside, she tilted her head. A sharp gust of wind plastered her gray slacks against her legs. "Where to?"

He opened the car door for her. "We wait."

She slid inside. When he got in on the other side, she asked, "What are we waiting for?"

"To see what Jean does." He slid the key into the ignition.

"You think she'll report to Cap?"

"I'd say the odds are good as soon as he's conscious." He spared her a loaded glance. "And they're even better that he wasn't at A-267 for an inspection."

There was something in Jonathan's tone, a certainty that hadn't been there earlier. "Did you recognize that Ground Serve messenger?"

"Not specifically, but I have seen him before, somewhere."

Maybe it wasn't just her intuition, pounding out warnings. "You're suspicious of him."

Jonathan nodded.

"Why?"

"I smelled death."

First-Strike Launch: 07:47:47

The smell of antiseptic burned his nose.

Flat on his back with his eyes closed, Cap Marlowe assimilated familiar sensations. A blood pressure cuff circling
his upper arm tightened and slackened at regular intervals.
A clip attached to his right index finger gauged his blood-
oxygen levels. An IV dripped fluid into his left arm, and a
heart monitor emitted a steady beep that assured him his
ticker was fine and he was still in the physical world. Definitely in a hospital.

He hadn't yet opened his eyes or let anyone know he
was awake. In the past, bedside remarks made over the unconscious had proven most honest. But how had he gotten
here?

He had been locked in the outer rim at A-267, and
that young lieutenant—Gibson, his name was Gibson—
had poured sugar water down his throat. After that . . . nothing. Nothing, until now. Had he told them about the key in
the mail chute?

"You go on to the cafeteria and get a bite to eat, Mitzy.
I'll stay with him."

Jean, talking with his wife. Cap opened his eye to a slit
and saw Mitzy leaving the room. Her eyes were red-
rimmed. Damn, she'd been crying.

Jean pulled a brown envelope out of her purse and
then moved to Cap's beside, her heels clicking on the tile
floor. "Senator, I know you're awake. Open your eyes and
look at me."

Cap opened his eyes.

"Good." Jean scanned his face. "Do you understand me?"

"Yes." His tongue felt thick, too big for his mouth.
"How did I get here?"

She briefed him succinctly, then dropped her voice to a
whisper. Worry clouded her eyes. "I think that same messenger was at the office today—the one who brought the key."

Cap's heart rate spiked. "What did he want?"

"He brought this." She held up the envelope.

"Open it," he whispered, feeling as if he were talking and seeing through a veil of fog. "Tell me what it is."

Jean ripped open the end of the envelope, slid out two documents and a small Ziploc bag. She scanned them, then cast Cap a puzzled look. "One is a DNA report. No name on it."

"What's that?"

She held the plastic bag where he could see it. "It looks like a used Band-Aid. There's blood on it."

Still, Cap had no grasp on this. "Anything else?"

"A handwritten note." Her puzzled tone turned bewildered. "This is odd."

Chilled, he tugged the twisted sheet up over his chest. "What does it say?"

"Flip Five." She looked over at him. "Do you understand any of this?"

Unfortunately, he did. "Not really." Whose DNA was it? Why had Faust sent it to him? "It could be a constituent's profile," he said. That had happened a couple of times before, when someone was embroiled in a parental custody suit or a paternity dispute. Jean would buy it.

"Maybe, but this man fit the description of the key messenger, Cap."

What was Cap supposed to do with these things? He had no idea, and he damn sure couldn't ask. "Are you certain it's the same man?"

"No, I'm not. Peggy signed for the key, remember? I didn't see him then. But he matches the description she gave us and he was wearing the Ground Serve uniform. It looked new." Peggy, Jean's assistant, had noted the newness of the uniform during the original delivery.

Matches the description. Did Cap throw away everything he had worked for in the past thirty years based on a "matches the description" ID and a nameless DNA report?

Guilt stabbed at him. Sybil Stone had risked detonating the briefcase bomb to save his life. There was no way around that. Situations reversed, he wouldn't have saved hers, and there was no way around that, either. He appreciated her taking the high road, but he didn't want to needlessly throw away the presidential nomination.

If this diabetic episode had happened anywhere except at A-267, squelching word of it would have been impossible. But luck had been with him on that. Now he had to move forward in a business-as-usual manner. That did not include being saddled with Sybil Stone on his ticket in the next election, and it damn sure didn't include running against her. Not with her being a media hot commodity as a woman on a mission for her country who had just survived a plane crash.

She was destined to rebound in the polls now, and he fully expected she would end up with higher ratings than she'd had before her divorce. Americans love scrappers and survivors.

And they hate traitors.

Cap looked over at Jean. "Get in touch with Sam Sayelle. Tell him I need to see him as soon as possible."

* * *

Marcus Gilbert had been retired for over five years, but he was still the best strategist on the Hill. Even more important to Sam at the moment, Marcus still had more connections in town than Ma Bell had phone lines.

Sam left the *Herald*'s parking garage and stopped by Sniffer's basement office. The young man sat at his desk, his tie hanging loose, his hair ruffled from finger-forking it, buried to his armpits in reports. "Any word on the Wall man?"

"Nothing." Sniffer expelled a sigh that could power a windmill. "I'm trying, Sam, but I'm a new kid on the block. I don't have your connections. It's just like I thought, though.

While the veep was gone, he dropped off the face of the earth. Now that she's back, well, maybe he'll surface again."

Not likely, Sam thought. Once he broke the story of what was in the envelope, there was no way Sybil Stone would dare show her face anywhere in the city. "Keep checking."

Sniffer nodded and Sam walked on, heading upstairs for the meeting.

"Hey, Sam?"

He paused and looked back. "Yeah?"

A hopeful gleam lit in Sniffer's eyes. "Any word on the Deans?"

"Not yet." Sam had the feeling there wouldn't be any word on Linda or the kids. Not publicly. If what was in the envelope panned out as an accurate gauge, not for a long time.

He went upstairs, then down the hall to the conference room. Carl Edison sat talking with...Marcus Gilbert? It was. Sam hardly recognized the man. Marcus and Carl were about the same age, same basic weight and height, but where Carl was meticulous about his appearance, Marcus had become a slob. His shirt and slacks had more wrinkles than fabric, and he didn't just need a haircut and a shave, he could use a good shearing. And when had he grown a beard?

"Thanks for coming in." Sam sat down at the conference table and dumped the contents of the envelope onto the table. "Ground Serve hand-delivered the envelope. A note inside said the carrier had twenty more to deliver to different major media resources, but not until I authorize delivery."

"Why you?"

"I don't know, Carl. The source probably believes I have no respect for the veep."

Marcus arched an eyebrow and thrust out his lips. "Is that still the case?"

How could Sam explain? His feelings about her were

chaotic. Growing admiration, no trust, grudging respect. Reveal that, and he'd sound like an idiot. "Not exactly," he hedged.

"Who is the source?" Carl asked.

"Austin Stone."

"Inflammatory material against his ex-wife. Raises serious credibility questions." Carl lifted a photo of Sybil Stone talking with an unidentified man. "Who's the guy?"

"According to Austin Stone, Gregor Faust. But no one's verified a positive ID on him."

Marcus examined the photo carefully and then tossed it down on the table. Whatever his opinions were, he kept them to himself.

"I agree on the credibility," Sam said. "Austin would love to see her spit-roasted." His nose itched. He swiped it with a fingertip. "Cap Marlowe introduced us, but I don't really know Austin, and, truthfully, I didn't like him."

Marcus tapped at his lips. "Why not?"

Sam wished he could be specific and exact. He couldn't. "Gut reaction." He hadn't put it under a microscope, he'd just gone with his gut and stayed away from the man.

"Your midwestern values maybe?" Marcus asked. "He was still married to the veep and talking her down."

Surprised, Sam nodded. That had annoyed the hell out of him.

"He has a rep for it," Marcus explained the insight.

Carl reviewed the last of the evidence. "His lack of loyalty might be an issue, but he's done an excellent job of making it look as if she violated their blind trust. What's that about?"

"Austin's company," Sam said. "Secure Environet works mostly with the federal government. Sybil owns fifty-one percent of the stock. When she got elected, she insisted all their holdings—hers and Austin's—be placed in a blind trust to avoid even the appearance of a conflict of interest. He took exception but finally agreed."

"Fifty-*two* percent, Sam," Marcus corrected him. "And he agreed under her threat of divorce. The blind trust was a deal-breaker."

"Okay," Carl said. "So she insists on this blind trust and then breaks it. She tells the public she can't have kids, but here's proof Austin was sterile before she married him. So she doesn't discriminate, she lies across the board."

"Compelling case," Marcus said to Sam.

Excitement bubbled in Sam's stomach. "How should I use it?"

"Don't." Marcus grimaced. "It's bogus."

"It can't be bogus. It all fits. The kids, the stock—the woman's being blackmailed for something, damn it, and it sure isn't her love life."

Marcus shoved the papers away. "Who's blackmailing her?"

"We don't have an ID on him yet." Sam shifted on his seat. "But he's been observed by our guys and the Secret Service. We think he's a go-between for another source. Looking at this, I think that source might be Gregor Faust."

"I imagine that's exactly what Austin Stone wants you to think," Carl said. "What's this?" He held up a page with only two words written on it. "Flip Five."

"No idea," Sam said.

"It's bogus, Sam." Marcus stood up, grabbed his raincoat, and shrugged into it. "You do what you want, but you asked for my opinion. Now you've got it." He lumbered over to the door. "If you do use it, you might want to ID your go-between first and find out what that 'flip five' means. It's significant or it wouldn't have been included." He slid his gaze to Carl. "If you print anything using this as source support, you might want to check with legal first and make sure the liability premiums are paid."

"Damn, Marcus," Carl sputtered, clearly flustered.

Marcus ignored him, glanced back to Sam. "Did you tell Marlowe about Conlee?"

Stunned, Sam stared at him. Marcus knew about Commander Conlee. He had to have given Conlee the referral. The broadcast room downstairs, the senior staff ignoring Sam's broadcasts—at one time, Marcus must have done broadcasts like Sam's for Conlee . . . or for his predecessor. "No."

"Why not?"

"Hell, I don't know, Marcus. Maybe she's not who I thought she was, and maybe everyone involved in this isn't who or what they seem. I don't know why not. I just couldn't make myself do it."

"I wouldn't." Marcus moved toward the door. "The real thing is easy to spot, Sam, but you've got to have your eyes open to see it."

"Will someone tell me what in hell you two are talking about?" Carl cut in, clearly clueless and ticked off about it.

"You don't want to know." At the moment, Sam wished he didn't know. He held up the envelope and shouted at Marcus's retreating back. "Why do you think it's bogus?"

"You're the reporter," he said without looking back. His hands stuffed in his pockets, he lifted them, and the tail of his coat fanned out. "Figure it out."

Had Marcus been saying she was or she wasn't the real thing? "I'd forgotten how much I hate his riddles." Sam slumped in his chair, still holding the envelope. "I am going to use this, Carl." And he would. If only to call down Conlee and get some straight answers.

"Your call." Carl took off his glasses and shoved them into his shirt pocket. "I'll back you, but know what you're doing. Caution was never one of Marcus Gilbert's trademarks. If he says what you've got is bogus, you better make damn sure it isn't. Check it all out, verify it, then check it all again. Double source everything. Marcus got to be an icon because he's sharp and seldom wrong. That's worth remembering. Now who's this Conlee he mentioned?"

Sam debated. Carl Edison was his boss, but Conlee had meant what he had said about killing Sam and anyone he told. His threat proved stronger, and Sam couldn't shake the feeling Carl asking the question was a test he had better not fail. "Just a mutual acquaintance. No one of consequence."

Carl's eyes gleamed with approval. Sam had been right about the test, and he had made the right choice. If he had told Carl, the man probably would have burned up the phone lines calling Conlee to tell him.

The broadcast room had been used before. Apparently by Carl *and* Marcus.

"Don't make me sorry I'm backing you, Sam," Carl said, then left the conference room.

Sam gathered up the contents of the envelope. His phone vibrated against his hip. "Sayelle," he answered, frustrated because he hadn't gotten the overwhelming support he had hoped to get from either of them, and because he couldn't yet answer all the questions pouring through his mind.

"Sam, it's Jean. Senator Marlowe wants to see you right away. He's at St. Elizabeth's. Can you get over here?"

Sam scooped up the last of the papers and checked his watch. "Give me fifteen minutes."

"I'll tell him you're coming." Jean hung up.

Sam put his phone back in its case. Actually, this worked well for him. Cap Marlowe knew more about Sybil Stone than anyone else in the world, except maybe for Westford. But Westford was out of reach.

That spark of hope, dimmer than ever, demanded the truth. Was she Sam's long-awaited patriot, or the most corrupt politician to turn traitor in the history of the nation?

First-Strike Launch: 07:20:47

"Marcus Gilbert says it's bogus."

Propped up with fluffy pillows in his hospital bed, Cap

Marlowe reviewed Sam's evidence against Sybil Stone. For Marcus to come out of retirement long enough to look at this collection meant that he knew the truth and he was saving the *Herald*'s proverbial ass. If Sam knew Marcus as well as did Cap and the old-timers on the Hill, he would realize that. But of course he didn't.

Cap shifted his gaze to Sam. "Did Marcus mention insurance premiums?"

"Yes, he did."

That was it, then. "Don't authorize delivery to the rest of the media."

"I have no intention of sharing my scoop with my rivals."

Not at all surprised, Cap resisted the urge to spit on the photo of the man tentatively identified as Gregor Faust and positively identified as a member of Ballast. He slid the contents back into the envelope and then passed it back. "Don't you think Austin Stone knew that?"

"I'm sure he considered it."

"You can bet your ass on it." Cap gripped the bedrail and squeezed until his knuckles went white. "So why did he leave authorization up to you?"

"I don't know. My disdain for Sybil Stone hasn't exactly been a secret, and he obviously wants to smear her to kingdom come. But something doesn't fit. There has to be more to this."

There was more. Too much more. Cap tugged the sheet up on his chest. Austin had known Sam would bring the package to him, and it carried two messages. The same "Flip Five" note Cap had received from Faust and another one that terrified him: that Austin wasn't in a position to fix what was broken at A-267. "Give me some time, Sam. I have a bad feeling about this. I want to check it out."

"But we can finally nail her." Sam lifted a hand, protesting. "How the hell can she explain her affiliation to Ballast?"

Odds were, she couldn't. But then, neither could Cap Marlowe. "You're forgetting this so-called evidence came from her ex-husband." He lifted a questioning brow. "You want to put your credibility on the line for that?"

"No." Sam's jaw slackened, then resignation burned in his eyes. He checked his watch. "We both work on verifications until two A.M. That's the best I can do and still make the deadline for the late edition."

Two hours after the missile at A-267 was set to detonate. Cap felt torn. He had the opportunity to fry Sybil Stone for treason here. She would cease to be an obstacle the moment this hit the airwaves. Guilty or innocent, her career would be over. But President Lance had his hands full, trying to stop the missile launch. Now wasn't the best time to divide his focus. More worrisome was a deep sense of knowing that settled like stones in Cap's stomach. If the launch was successfully aborted, it would be as a direct result of Sybil Stone playing a critical role in aborting it—a role that, he hoped, would allow him to avoid disclosing the location of the key and admitting that he had received the DNA report and soiled Band-Aid. "That sounds reasonable."

"Keep me posted." Sam set his foam cup on Cap's tray, then left the hospital room.

Cap lifted the phone receiver and dialed a direct line to the White House, wishing he were at the office rather than at St. E's. But the hospital stay was essential.

She could have let you die. If she had waited for that bomb gear, you would have died. If she hadn't ordered them to take you to St. E's, and they'd followed A-267 protocol and taken you to Bethesda, you would have died. You're going to repay that by leveling charges of treason against her? If she were guilty, why not let you die? You're a thorn in her side, a wound that constantly seeps and never heals. Why do everything she can, including endangering her own life, to help you live?

Why, why, why? Cap didn't have a clue.

"Yes?" Winston answered the phone.

"Is the issue resolved?" Winston would know Cap meant the missile crisis.

"Not yet, Senator. We're still cross-checking staff for matches, and so far a new instrument hasn't surfaced."

Cap felt the blood drain from his face. He had both: the bloody Band-Aid and the key.

She could have let you die. She risked her life for you.

He shunned his nagging conscience and looked at the clock. Seven hours and twenty minutes until the launch. Sweat beaded on his forehead, on his upper lip. Disclosure would kill his chances for being nominated much less elected, if they weren't dead already, but he couldn't keep silent and silence the world. His mouth went dust dry. "You might want to cross-check me, too."

"You?" Winston failed to hide his surprise. "Why?"

Staring down at the DNA report Faust had sent him, Cap tried and failed to admit the truth. "Call it a prudent measure."

"I'll pass the word along. I suppose it's not outside the realm of possibility, considering your position on the Armed Services Committee."

Cap hung up, suddenly clammy and sick to his stomach. He hauled himself out of bed and dragged his IV pole to the bathroom. At the sink, he splashed his face with cold water. Faust could have used Cap's DNA. With his Ground Serve deliveries, he was systematically building a case against Cap as a co-conspirator.

Snagging a towel from the rack, he dabbed at his face and met his eyes in the mirror.

Damn it, Cap, first you underestimate Austin Stone, the son of a bitch, and now you're hearing but you're not listening to me. She could have let you die.

Guilt flooded through him. He should have played this straight from the start. He should have...but he hadn't. He studied his face, the line of his jaw, the weariness in his eyes, and a sadness that yawned soul-deep smothered him. Thirty years of service, layers and layers of bureaucratic red tape and bullshit, and he'd survived it, flourished in it, only to come to this. This time he hadn't tiptoed over the line; he'd obliterated it.

His enemy had saved his life, and he was going to return her kindness by destroying what was left of her life. She didn't need the DNA to stop the launch; Conlee would find it in the cross-check. But she did need the key Cap had put in the inner hub's mail chute. Yet to give it to her, Cap had to expose himself. At this point, Intel's antennas were on full alert. No anonymous caller could phone and remain undetected. Cap *would* be exposed. The vultures on the Hill would peck his bones clean. His life would have been lived for nothing. For . . . nothing.

She could have let you die.

His conscience pulled hard. He stiffened against it, leaned against the sink for support, and closed his eyes, ashamed that even now, with so many lives at stake, he was still looking for a way to hide.

For the first time in his life, Cap Marlowe looked at himself in the mirror and hated what he saw.

What if you're wrong about her? What if Faust set her up just as he did you? What if Marcus Gilbert is right and the evidence is bogus? Have you ever known him to be wrong?

Cap wanted to run from these questions and couldn't. But it was yet another question that worried him most.

What if everything Austin Stone and Barber and Winston had ever told him about Sybil Stone had been fabricated or distorted?

He stared himself in the eyes. If that proved true, then even the grace of God and His most infinite mercy wouldn't be merciful enough to help him.

Chapter Twenty-one

As with some other U.S. intelligence-gathering agencies, only a handful of high-ranking officials could pinpoint Home Base physically, and it didn't exist at all on paper.

The intricate covert system worked only because the "Special Projects" handled by its staff didn't formally exist. Nor, for that matter, did its staff. On paper, all were assigned to other, overt positions. Military members were officially buried in Personnel and civilians in various human resource agencies. The reasoning for isolation was similar to that of other agencies, including Area 51: sensitive, potentially explosive political consequences at home and/or abroad.

Where the agencies differed was in the one area of ultimate importance, diplomatically and domestically. Area 51 had received media attention. People could drive near but not enter it, and they knew it existed. Home Base existed within A-267 without public knowledge, access was extremely restricted, few people had seen it, and no one ever had spoken of it in any public forum. Its nonexistent status provided those in the need-to-know loop with the two things they most wanted: a lack of vulnerability and deniability.

Leaders hated being asked questions they didn't want to answer. Secrecy and deniability protected them from both.

At least Home Base hadn't been exposed or become public knowledge yet. That was vitally important, since Home Base operatives also handled special projects where they acted as a check-and-balance system on other operatives. On occasion, it was essential to have Home Base operatives spy on spies. Sybil couldn't help but hope that none of the Home Base program would be exposed.

Inside the Home Base facility, Sybil sat in a soundproof booth in the back of a viewing room at a long, carved desk that faced the wall of screens. A technician sat out front, handled the films, and communicated with the booth via intercom. The vice president lifted a forkful of sesame chicken from a carton and took a bite, keeping her gaze fixed on the largest screen, centered on the wall. For the last hour, she and Jonathan Westford had been seated in the darkened booth, reviewing footage collected by covert operatives worldwide that could help them identify Gregor Faust. "We have a little over seven hours left, Jonathan."

"I know." He bit down on an egg roll, chewed, then swallowed. "We've checked out everything accumulated in the last month, and we're still coming up dry." He depressed a button to give the film technician instructions. "Go back to March, Max, and run the time line back from there."

Sybil bit down on a crab rangoon—cream cheese and crab stuffed in a wonton and fried crisp. Her arteries would hate her, but the things tasted wonderful. Since returning from the swamp, she couldn't seem to get enough to eat. A sobering thought crossed her mind. Here she sat worrying about her arteries, and this could be her last meal.

Sprawled back with his feet propped on the corner of a desk, Jonathan suddenly sprang forward and slammed a palm down on the intercom button. "Stop, Max. Back it up a few frames. There. Bring that up on the big screen."

Sybil set down her carton. The familiar face of her relief co-pilot appeared. "My God, that's Mark," she said. And he was standing next to a known member of Ballast.

"There's one of our chuters." Jonathan again pressed the button. "Print that and pinpoint the location."

A minute passed, then Max answered. "It's in North Africa, sir. But nothing of significance noted in the immediate vicinity. Just a grass airstrip and half a dozen bungalows. Really isolated terrain. Nearest town is thirty miles away."

"Perfect for clandestine meetings," Sybil said. "Do we have an ID on the second man?"

"It's possible he's Gregor Faust," Max said. "But that's not verified, and we're currently sitting on seventeen additional Faust reports—all on different men. None carries conclusive proof of his identity."

"Press on, Max," Sybil said. They kept scanning, searching for a connection to Austin Stone or an identity on the second chuter. One month, then two. Before Conlee had brought Austin Stone in under the guise of assisting, he had last accessed A-267 six months ago. He had to have struck a deal with Faust before then and avoided recent access to divert blame.

"Sybil?" Jonathan sounded troubled. "You know we might not unravel this in time."

"I know." She hated it, wanted to deny it, but facts were facts, and they had to face them.

"Something's sitting heavy on my shoulders." He dabbed at his mouth with a paper napkin. "If I die tonight, I want to do it knowing the truth."

"What truth?" Where was he going with this?

"It's none of my business, but I need to ask you something. Is that okay?"

She didn't feel comfortable agreeing, but she felt even more uncomfortable disagreeing, considering their circumstances. Whatever this was, it weighed on Jonathan. "Okay."

"Did I cause your divorce?"

"What?" That she hadn't expected. How could she expect it? It was absurd.

"Did I cause your divorce?" he repeated.

The question didn't sound a bit more logical than the first time she'd heard it. "Jonathan, what in the world would make you think that?"

"Austin had a problem with walking in your shadow. I knew it. Hell, everyone knew it. I threatened to kill the man, Sybil."

"You had nothing to do with my divorce." She shoved the food across the desk, farther away from her. "I swear it."

Silence fell between them. Jonathan didn't ask, but the question of what *had* caused it hung over them like a rain-swelled cloud. Sybil would rather not think about the past, much less talk about it. Surviving that kind of humiliation once was a hell of a blow to a woman's dignity. But she didn't want to lie to Jonathan to avoid the indignity of humiliation, either. He deserved better from her. He deserved the truth. And she would tell it to him. But she wasn't strong or brave enough to look at him while she did it.

Fixing a blank stare on the screen, she confessed. "Austin wasn't content with me. He hadn't been for a long time. I tried to make him happy, but he...just wasn't. He never mentioned being unhappy enough to want a divorce, and I couldn't see any advantage in getting one, so I accepted the way things were between us and just went on living."

"You were afraid of what a divorce would do to your career?"

"Indirectly." God, but that sounded cold and ugly. "We know what impact it had now. But then I really wasn't thinking about that specifically. I was thinking that my career was all I had left. I didn't want to lose it, too." The stark truth didn't sound much better, but she'd take a fragile esteem over cold and ugly any day. Her mouth felt like cotton, so she sipped some iced tea and then went on. "Since grade school, all I've wanted is a family and a political career." She shrugged. "We never had kids."

"So you divorced Austin because of the vasectomy."

Austin's vasectomy. Few things in the world had the power to hurt her as much as Austin's vasectomy. "Actually, I didn't." God, but this was hard to admit, especially to Jonathan. What he thought mattered, and she would sound like an idiotic fool. The worst kind of idiotic fool.

"Before and after we married, Austin and I often discussed having children. When I didn't conceive, I went in for testing and found out I was fine." Her throat threatened to close. She swallowed hard to clear it, then pushed on. "Austin resisted but finally underwent testing, too. By then we had been married for several years. It turned out that he was sterile." The lie she'd been fed and had believed for years burned in her throat, her chest, her heart.

"Why didn't you adopt?"

"Austin refused." Memories of their many arguments about that raced through her mind in shattered images. She stiffened against them. "Finally I just quit raising the subject. It wasn't worth the hell it caused. He'd give me the silent treatment for days. Sometimes longer. I hate to admit it, but the truth is, right before we actually separated, I'd bring up adoption so he would give me the silent treatment. I needed the respite." Her face went hot. "That's not the kind of thing that belongs in a marriage, you know?"

Jonathan nodded, sifted through what she'd said. "So if he was already sterile, why did he have a vasectomy?"

"Austin had the vasectomy a year after we married—

right after I financed the founding of Secure Environet."
Bitter, Sybil looked away, studied the images cycling onto
the screen. "I suppose he would have had it done sooner,
but he wanted to make sure he didn't have to give me a
child to get his company founded." She took a cleansing
breath, trying to let go of the anger, the bitterness of his betrayal, the sense of failure she felt as a woman, the disillusionment she discovered in a relationship that had been
founded in trust. "He's told some people he had it done before we married—he even altered the date on a doctor's report to prove it—but he didn't have it then. He waited until
he was sure he had the money for his company."

"I'm sorry."

The tenderness in Jonathan's tone had her fighting
back tears. "Me, too." She had gone into marriage with
such high hopes and dreams, with such determination to
have that closeness and intimacy absent in her parents'
marriage. Instead, she'd gotten Austin and had worse.

"Yet you stayed with him."

She nodded. "This isn't very flattering, but the truth is I
didn't know about the vasectomy until many, many years
later." She wanted to hide, to run away from the ugliness, the
humiliation, the betrayal. Good God, how she had staggered
under the weight of that betrayal. Even now she couldn't escape it. And, though tempted, she wouldn't hide it from
Jonathan. "Not long after David and I were elected, Cap
Marlowe came to my office. We had a horrible confrontation, Jonathan. Horrible." She shivered at the memory. "He
accused me of fraud—because I publicly favor children's issues. He swore he was going public with the truth."

She shrugged and risked glancing at Jonathan. "I didn't
know what truth he meant, so I asked. That infuriated
him." The veins on his neck had bulged out like thumbs
and his face and neck had turned wine red. "He told me he
had proof that Austin's sterility was self-inflicted."

"He had the altered doctor's report."

"Yes!" The shock and anguish she had felt then returned now, and all her muscles contracted at once. Pain and betrayal. Stunned disbelief. "I guess Cap saw from my reaction that I hadn't known. He never went public, though I've expected him to every day since then. It's the first thing I think of when I wake up in the morning: that today might be the day he destroys me politically." The day he takes the one thing in her life she had left to take.

"So then you confronted Austin?" Jonathan sat forward in his chair now. His feet flat on the floor, elbows bent and resting on his knees, he stared down at his sneakers.

"Yes." She pulled in a breath, praying to draw courage in with it. "He confessed. He hadn't told me because he feared losing me—and he might have," she admitted. "I can't say I would have stayed married to him, Jonathan. I wanted children so badly. I just don't know what I would have done."

"Some questions we can't answer, but we damn well deserve to be asked." Jonathan hurt for her. The betrayal, the lies, and disillusionment at having a partner you couldn't trust. One of the worst parts had to have been her learning about something so important and private from Cap Marlowe. Of all people in the world, why him? That had to have knocked her to her knees. "So that's why you divorced him."

"Not really."

That surprised Jonathan into looking at her. He had assumed the vasectomy had sealed her rocky marriage's fate.

"I won't say it was easy because it wasn't. But I forgave Austin for that. Some men just aren't meant to be fathers." She leaned back in her chair. "Do you remember when we stopped in Columbus, I think—at that elementary school?"

"How could I forget?" Jonathan chuckled. "Every kid in first grade had to have a turn hanging on my arm."

"They loved you." Sybil smiled at the memory. "Austin was with us that day."

Jonathan thought back but, for the life of him, he couldn't recall Austin being with them at the school. "Was he?"

She nodded. "He wouldn't come in to the classroom with us to talk with the kids. He wouldn't even leave the car."

"That's right." He'd sulked most of the afternoon, too. "I'd forgotten."

"That wasn't an isolated incident, Jonathan. Some men just don't relate to children. Austin not only doesn't relate, he doesn't like them. So he avoids them. His not having children was a blessing."

"But you would have been a wonderful mother."

"Yes, damn it, I would have," she said frankly. "But I chose to marry him. I loved the man I believed him to be, and when I married him, I believed he loved me. It isn't right to ask someone for more than you know they're capable of giving. Austin never knew his father. His mother hated the man, and Austin learned to hate him through her. I think he believed all fathers were hated, so he chose not to become one."

Too tense to sit any longer, she stood up. "I don't know that, it's just a supposition. I do know he would hate being a father. Anyway, I forgave him and we went on. It was hard, but I accepted I'd never have kids of my own."

And she'd publicly declared that they hadn't had children due to a medical challenge, letting everyone assume it was hers and not Austin's to spare him any discomfort. After all, she was the public figure by choice. He'd married into it.

She clasped her hands. "Then Cap dropped his second little bomb."

Jonathan watched her closely, instinctively knowing what he heard next would be the real reason she had divorced Austin.

"You know Secure Environet deals mostly with government contracts. And when I was elected, to avoid conflicts of interest, we put all our financial assets in a blind trust."

"Yes." All things considered, she really hadn't had much choice on that.

"Austin resisted. Actually, he resisted and resented. I had to threaten to divorce him to get him to agree. Frankly, that made me suspicious. I wondered if he and Cap had made a side agreement for preferential treatment. So I investigated, but I never found any evidence of Cap favoring Austin. The day of our second confrontation, Cap brought proof that I had violated the blind trust. I hadn't, but Austin had. How isn't significant, but it created huge credibility problems for me."

Jonathan imagined her learning about the vasectomy and then about this trust business. Austin Stone had gone for her jugular and succeeded. "So you forgave him for lying to you about kids, but you divorced him for lying about money?"

"No," she protested. "Lying to me was one thing. But when Austin broke the blind trust, he violated the American people I swore to serve and protect. The combination of lies was too much. I couldn't forgive him. Inside, I just wasn't strong enough to fight for him any more. I didn't want to fight for him any more. By then I hated him more than I loved him."

Another sacrifice, and yet she had refused to play the martyr. Kids and her career, all she'd ever wanted. The damn fool had to have been deliberately trying to destroy her.

Sybil walked a short path along the desk to him. "I ordered Austin out of the house, met with the president and told him the truth, and then I hired a divorce attorney."

"And Austin fought you every step of the way."

"Yes, he did." She grunted and grabbed another crab rangoon. "But don't delude yourself into thinking it was because he loved me. He didn't. Austin Stone only loves power. He wanted my stock and I wouldn't give it to him. He tried to force me into a buy-back. Fortunately, the judge agreed with me. After months of Austin dragging things out, I finally agreed that the stock would revert to him on my death. That's when he signed the divorce papers."

"And when he began planning your death." Jonathan wished he'd killed the bastard when he'd had the chance. No wonder she had asked about the thorns in the plane. From the sounds of her marriage, there hadn't been many rose petals but, man, had she had thorns.

She stared at him, her eyes stretched wide. "I didn't consider him capable of murdering me then."

"What about now?"

"Now I have to believe it. It's happened, Jonathan." She blinked hard. "Austin's tried to murder me."

The pain in her voice ripped at his soul, and Jonathan swore he'd give everything he owned to be able to disagree with her. But he couldn't do it without lying, and both Lady Liberty and Sybil Stone had heard too damn many lies. Instead, he drew her into a hug. "I'm so sorry, Sybil."

"Knowing a man you once loved wants you dead really sucks." She closed her arms around Jonathan's ribs, squeezed, and held tight.

"Yeah." He dropped a kiss to her temple. "But we're not all bastards, though I wouldn't blame you if you doubted it." Austin Stone, Cap, Sayelle, Barber, and Winston. She had little reason not to doubt it.

"I know." She reared back to see his face. "You're nothing like Austin, Jonathan."

So serious, those eyes. So clouded by pain, and memories of promises broken, and dreams denied. "Sybil." He cupped her face in his hands, seeing more than feeling his own slight tremble. "You deserve so much good. I wish—"

"What?" She waited but he didn't answer, just beheld her, and the warmth and tender care shining in his eyes touched her far deeper than any words could reach. "What do you wish?"

He pecked a kiss to her chin, then shook his head and backed away. "You don't want to know. Not now. The timing is all wrong."

She opened her mouth to protest, then fell silent.

Jonathan stepped away. Later would be soon enough. After the crisis. Providing they found a resolution and there was a later, after the crisis. Because he wanted that more than he ever had dared to want anything, he closed his eyes and forced himself to focus on the business at hand. Austin Stone had taken enough. He wasn't getting any more. Not from Jonathan, and if he could stop it, not from Sybil.

Weighing in the divorce and stock factors, Austin had been ripe for a Faust proposal. Jonathan let his thoughts flow, testing, measuring, and slotting possibilities into place. Austin agreed to give Faust the inside track to halt the peace talks, and Faust agreed to kill Sybil. Faust continues to sell arms to Peris and Abdan, and Austin gets back his Secure Environet stock. Everyone wins.

Except Sybil.

"Jonathan." Sybil's tone turned brittle, wooden. "It—it's Austin."

He looked up at her. She stood completely still, staring through the Plexiglas at the screen. "Is that a photo of Faust?" she asked. "It looks exactly like the sketches. Exactly."

Jonathan turned and locked his gaze on the large center screen, pressed the intercom button. "Freeze it, Max."

Five men stood, their glasses lifted in a toast: Faust, Mark, Austin Stone, ET—and Ken Dean.

Jonathan's stomach soured and the taste in his mouth turned bitter. Dean. A man he had known fifteen years. He'd had dinner in Dean's home, had gotten to know his wife, Linda, and their kids. And now the reason for their disappearance seemed all too clear.

"The second man from the right," Sybil said. "What is he holding in his left hand?"

"A penny."

Sybil sucked in a sharp breath. "He's the guy from the swamp. ET."

"I know."

"Why the penny, Jonathan? What does it mean?"

"He's signaling that the man to his immediate left is Gregor Faust."

Sybil didn't ask why. Intel operatives had many signals. The placement of a finger on a glass, the positioning of a pair of glasses on the nose, or a penny held in a specific hand. "I'm confused," she said. "Faust religiously refuses to be photographed. How did we get this?"

"Intel satellite would be my guess."

"Oh, sweet Jesus, no." Sybil tugged at Jonathan's sleeve. "The man on the far right. That—that's Captain Dean."

"Yes, it is." A world's weight of disappointment bore down on Jonathan. "He's our second chuter."

Chapter Twenty-two

Saturday, August 10 ★ First-Strike Launch: 07:00:00

Sybil had been angry many times, but never had she been angry enough to kill. She was now. Her jaw clenched so tight her teeth ached. Shaking all over, she depressed the intercom button. "Max, who signed off on this frame?"

"Winston, ma'am."

"Trail it." She waited, her gaze locked with Jonathan's.

"He forwarded copies to Commander Conlee, Senator Marlowe, and Richard Barber, ma'am."

Jonathan frowned. "This doesn't make sense. Barber or Cap might protect Austin, though I can't see it. Not in a case like this. But Conlee?"

"They never saw it," Sybil speculated. If the commander hadn't been included on the list, she would have considered it possible, but not Conlee. So who stopped them from—she stilled. "Max, who was the courier on the delivery?"

"Captain Mendoza, ma'am."

Understanding flickered in Jonathan's eyes. "Austin got to Mendoza."

Nodding, Sybil reached for the phone. Before she could lift the receiver, Jonathan's hand came down on hers, and she glared up at him.

"Who are you calling?" he asked.

"Conlee. Austin is going to jail."

"We need more evidence."

"We have evidence."

"Sybil, I know you're trying really hard to be calm and reasonable, and I'll tell you the truth. In your shoes, I'm not sure I'd do nearly as well as you're doing. But we need answers more than we need justice. In about seven hours, a missile we've launched is going to blow a lot of people straight to hell. We've got to focus on the bottom line and get what we need to stop it."

"Which is what I am doing," she said, seething. "Listen, there's nothing I'd like more than to beat the hell out of Austin Stone right now. But if we can nail him—and this frame of film does that, Jonathan—then maybe, just maybe, I can force him into telling me how to stop this damn missile from detonating."

"Austin folds under pressure?"

"No. But considering whoever we target will launch a proportional response that's going to blow him straight to hell with the rest of us, he might just change his habit this time."

Jonathan dragged a hand through his hair. "He's going to say you're out of your mind. That he has as much at risk as the rest of us—his life. Conlee and the others are going to believe him because it's true. They're going to assume he's rational and sane and, if he could stop the launch, he would. That's why we need strong evidence. We need proof he was leaving D.C."

That made her think twice, then a third time. "You're right." Sybil grabbed a phone book, looked up a number, and then dialed.

"Who are you calling now?"

"Mary," Sybil said. "Austin always uses her travel agency, and he—" Someone answered the phone, and Sybil shifted to talk to her. "Mary? Oh, good. This is Sybil Stone. I need to double-check Austin's flight with you." A pause, then: "That's right. M. Kane." Another pause, then: "Could you fax me a copy of that ticket and his itinerary?"

She hesitated, listening, then her jaw went tight. "I don't care if Dr. Stone told you it was confidential. This is a matter of national security, Mary. That supercedes Dr. Stone's wishes, but if you feel sending the fax violates your ethics, I'll be happy to send over a couple of officers with warrants and IRS agents to take care of it." A pause, then: "I'd appreciate that." She motioned to Jonathan to get her a fax number. "No, I'm not at the office. Just a second."

Jonathan gave her the number and she passed it along. "Thanks, Mary."

Sybil hung up the phone, her eyes gleaming. "The bastard was going to Beijing."

"About as far from here as you can get without renting a rocket." Jonathan rubbed at his temple. "Who's M. Kane?"

"Madeline Kane Stone was Austin's mother. He always travels under her name to get out from under my shadow. He has a real thing about my shadow."

Sybil cocked her head. "If he was going to Beijing to get away from the missile, doesn't it seem ridiculous that he'd target China in the first place? The latest target is Libya. Before then it was Pakistan. But the first target was China."

"He's snowing us." Jonathan grabbed the phone, dialed Conlee. He filled the commander in on developments and then offered a suggestion. "We need to check for time-delay implementation codes on the system reconfiguration and have the techs search for runners on the target. Austin Stone wouldn't target China. He planned to live there."

Commander Conlee was still swearing when Jonathan hung up the phone. "If you weigh in Faust's asylum countries and add in Austin's, he isn't left with many target options."

Sybil sat down, braced her hands in her lap, and thought through the matter. "He's targeting us." The moment she said it, she knew it was true. "He wouldn't start a world war, and targeting *anyone* else would do that, Jonathan. He wants us humiliated and embarrassed. He hates me, and he hates David for having the Secret Service watch him and for not demanding my resignation. Don't you see? He hates *us* most. He hates *me* most."

"He bombs us, and he hurts you." Could anyone be that full of hate? "It feels right."

"I'm certain of it. If he's going to blow up anything, it will be us."

"Call Conlee." Jonathan passed her the phone.

Sybil translated their deductions to Conlee, who brought the president on the line.

She listened, then shared her views. "It's possible, David. If he thinks he's a cornered rat, he will attack. Maybe your way, he'll think he's gotten away with all this. We blame Faust, and Austin thinks he will walk away. If he believes that, he might stop the launch. Maybe. But I honestly think he hates us more than he loves his freedom."

"You could be right," David said. "We need to bring the staff in and compare notes. Full briefing in the Situation Room in thirty minutes."

"I'll be there." At least Cap Marlowe wouldn't be sitting in, tossing cutting remarks in her direction. He'd make up for it later, though, and thanks to Austin, he would have plenty of fodder. Cap would no doubt use it lavishly, both privately and publicly.

"Sybil." David sounded grave. "I hate to be the bearer of more bad news, but we just received a CIA report from the Caribbean."

She knew what was coming. The president had used that same tone when a terrorist attack had killed fourteen soldiers on a peacekeeping mission in the Middle East. "Linda Dean?"

"She's dead, Sybil. She and her children."

Chapter Twenty-three

Saturday, August 10 ★ *First-Strike Launch:* 06:30:22

Sybil turned off the car radio and looked out through the windshield. "It doesn't have to make sense, Jonathan. We're discussing my feelings here, not something you dictate or legislate." Gabby would be proud of that remark. "Logically, I know I'm not responsible for what Austin has done, but I *feel* responsible." Seven dead on the plane. Linda, Kenneth, and Katie Dean. And only God knew how many under the current threat of death. Of course she felt responsible. "That's why I have to offer to resign. Maybe David won't accept it—I hope he doesn't—but I have to make the offer."

Her feet and ribs hurt like hell, her bug bites itched—how long the swelling would take to go down, she had no idea—and she was as sore as she was scratched and bruised, head to heel. And tired. Never in her life had she been this tired.

Jonathan signaled with his blinker, then changed lanes. "Think about the kids, Sybil."

That remark didn't make a bit of sense. "I don't understand."

"American adults are too cynical about politics. We've survived scandals, corruption, indictments for lying under oath, pardons that never should have been granted, dirty elections. We've been put in the position of having to explain oral sex to our kids, not because of Hollywood releases, but because they've heard all about it on the six o'clock news. Hell, you name it, we've endured it. We expect politicians to lie, cheat, and steal. We've lowered the bar so damn far on what we expect and what we'll tolerate from them that it's sickening."

Her jaw tightened, and it infuriated her that she couldn't say he was wrong. Infuriated, and embarrassed. "I realize politicians have a sordid reputation, Jonathan, but I'm doing my best to change that."

"Yes, you are." He gave her hand a gentle squeeze. "That's exactly my point. You and David are changing that, and others are following you. That's why you can't resign. Other politicians are following, Sybil. Americans look at you and see someone worth emulating. Parents can look up to you and teach their kids to look up to you. You revere and respect them all. With you the kids aren't condemned to cynicism. They get a shot at the dream."

Her heart swelled in her chest. He admired her. He appreciated what she was trying to do. She stared at him, so moved she was unable to utter a word.

Jonathan saw her stunned expression and grimaced. He had said too much. But, damn it, the woman had to know these things. "Tell me one person who fights harder for kids than you do. Just one. You can't just walk away and leave them."

"Jonathan, I—I'm so touched. But I'm just one person. I don't really make a difference in American society. Not like you're suggesting. I wish I did, but I . . . I don't."

"The hell you don't. Every day, Sybil. Every day." He

braked for a red light and looked over at her. "Good God, you're serious."

She nodded.

"You're wrong." Maybe he was blunt, but he was honest, too. "Listen, you said you always wanted to be a mother. Well, you've done that. You don't change diapers or wipe snotty noses, but you make sure America's kids have medical care, that they're safe in child care centers and in their homes. Now you're making sure they get the support money recovered from deadbeat parents. With you they get a shot at the American dream. If you're not here, who's going to watch out for them like you do? Marlowe? Do you think he really gives a damn about them?"

Moved nearly to tears, Sybil stroked his face. "It's okay, Jonathan. I understand now. Calm down."

"No, not as long as you're talking about resigning. You can't walk out on them, too, Sybil." Despair edged into his voice. "Not you, too."

His mother dead. His father in jail. Jonathan had no one. He had been walked out on, and he didn't want other children to go through that. "I understand what you're saying, and every word is going straight into my heart. I swear it. But I have to make the offer. I've cost David a lot, and he's trying so hard to restore integrity to the office. For all the reasons you've just given me, I can't cost him more."

Jonathan expelled a frustrated sigh. "You'll take heat, but it won't last. You know it, and I know it. It's pride."

"It's not pride or even the humiliation. I swear it's not. I hope David won't accept my resignation but, at the end of the day, I have to look into my own soul, and I have to be comfortable with what I see there. I have to offer." She smiled up at Jonathan. "If David accepts it, maybe I'll send you over for a chat."

"Don't patronize me."

"I wasn't," she insisted. "I was dead serious." When he

cast her a doubtful look, she leaned over and kissed him deeply, with tenderness and heat.

Separating their mouths, she looked into his eyes, her own soft and warm and welcoming. "In my whole life, no one has taken up for me like you just did, Jonathan. I love many things about you, but, well . . . This is the nicest rose petal I've ever been given."

If there had been one remark holding him on the edge of loving her, that one would have pushed him over the top. Considering he'd fallen long ago, it was the remark that carried acceptance instead. He loved her. He might as well just resign himself to saying to hell with the odds, take his hits about not fitting into her plans, forget liking or not liking it, and accept it, because either way, love was here to stay. "Obviously, I love a lot of things about you, too."

"Do you hate it?"

"No, not anymore."

"I'm glad." She stroked his face. "You matter to me, Jonathan. You always have."

Mattered wasn't love, but it wasn't indifference, either. Mattered had possibilities and potential. Mattered could modify plans. Maybe.

She loved him. She might not want to love him. Loving him might screw up her plans, but she did. She loved him. His heart played Ping Pong with his ribs and the words he'd wanted to say since he had first held her by the quicksand pit nearly tumbled out of his mouth. But good sense prevailed. She wasn't ready to hear them. Not yet. It was going to take a while for these concepts and emotions to sit easily on her shoulders. And that was fine. For her, he could be a patient man. She loved him but hated loving him. Eventually she'd come around. Maybe by the time their first kid was born, or when he graduated from high school. Surely by then. Or maybe by the time they had a second one. He could wait. Images of her face when he finally told her he loved her flashed through his mind, lingered, and the thought of them making love, building a family and a life together had him hard and hot and kissing her again.

A horn sounded from behind them.

The light was green. Begrudgingly, Jonathan stepped on the gas and headed to the briefing. But it was the memory of that kiss, and not the crisis, that lingered in his mind.

Finally he mattered.

*   *   *

A dozen men sat around the conference table. Sybil knew most of them, though there were some strangers in the group.

The president briefed them on where they were globally, which sounded grim. In short, if the missile launched and targeted any other country, then that country *and* its allies would retaliate. The best of the news was that a majority of the world leaders believed this crisis was a terrorist attack and empathized. After all, if the proverbial shoes were reversed, they'd be walking down this same path. Their bottom line was that they couldn't put their own countries at risk. Since Sybil would follow the same line of thinking, she could hardly fault them for their positions.

"Commander Conlee?" David nodded for Conlee to report.

"Agent Westford suggested we check for time-delay implementation codes, and we found them programmed into the system the same day Austin Stone last accessed A-267. That was *two* months ago, not six. He also deleted evidence and the record of his access but, now knowing what to look for, our experts have recovered both. Agent Westford also recommended we check for bogus cycling on random targets. He was right about that, too. Regardless of what the loop tells us, the target is A-267. The missile will detonate in position. It will take out all of A-267, D.C., and most of the surrounding states. If we hadn't discovered that information, it also would have destroyed all evidence of Austin Stone's involvement in this crisis."

Crushed by betrayal that ran so deep she couldn't tell where it began or ended, Sybil passed Commander Conlee the fax from Austin's travel agent, Mary. "A copy of Austin's ticket." She looked at the president. "He booked a flight for Beijing tonight. Apparently he's established an alliance with PUSH as well as Ballast."

"I have to say," David commented, "I couldn't see Faust strategizing a world war."

"I believe his objective was limited to stopping the peace talks with Peris and Abdan, sir," Sybil said. "So he could continue selling arms to both sides."

Barber interceded. "Do we know whether Dr. Stone has shared his technology and designs with the Chinese?"

"We do not," Conlee said. "Our engineers have to project the potential cause and effect of every action before taking any, Mr. President. We've got all qualified personnel on every facet of this situation, but we could run out of time before completing the investigation. It's going to be close. If Dr. Stone believes he's caught, he has no incentive to stop the launch. As it is, we have positioned him to where he can walk out a hero—short term—by finding a miracle solution to the crisis."

David heaved a sigh. "He's playing cat-and-mouse games with Faust to bring the U.S. to its knees."

"And to humiliate me." Sybil hesitated and then added, "As long as I didn't return from the swamp, he was above suspicion. But in letting me live, Faust compromised Austin."

"Faust *let* you live?" Barber asked. "You mean that figuratively, right?"

"No. One of his men looked me in the eye and said he was letting me live because of a negotiation tactic I implemented with Peris and Abdan, but the next time we met, he'd kill me."

"That proves Faust didn't want a world war, either," David said. "I'm sorry about Austin, Sybil."

"Me, too." She forced strength she didn't feel into her voice.

A silver-haired man with laugh lines in his face and gnarled hands gained David's attention. "May I say something, Mr. President?"

"Senator Jamison is filling in for Cap Marlowe," David told the group. "Go ahead, Senator."

"It's about Captain Dean, sir. Now, I know it looks bad for him, since he was the second chuter and all, but his family being murdered gives one pause, and him aligning with that Ballast bunch doesn't fit his psychological profile."

Barber cleared his throat. "Intel reports they thought Linda had been on the island waiting for Ken Dean, sir, which is why they've suppressed information on him. He has been confirmed as the second chuter. That makes him a traitor."

"He wasn't, Richard." Sybil refused to believe it. "Ken Dean was a good, honorable man. There's no way he would have put his family in jeopardy, not willingly. I've thought about this a lot and I've spoken with Agent Westford about it. He's known Ken Dean for fifteen years. We believe Captain Dean was acting as a rogue agent. He exceeded orders and put himself in the position of appearing to be a traitor, but he acted in our best interests."

"A pilot acting as a rogue double agent?" Barber grunted. "That's hardly credible, ma'am."

"The captain broke protocol, Barber. He dropped altitude, depressurized the cabin, and warned Agent Westford to get me off the plane. He facilitated our safe exit before the explosion. That's credible—and fact."

"And his family?" David asked, his expression noncommittal.

"They were killed," Winston said. "Maybe Faust abducted them to force Dean to do what Faust wanted done."

"And once Dean was dead, there was no need to continue to hold them," Barber said. "At least that part of this scenario sounds reasonable."

It was reasonable; grim and grisly, but reasonable. "Look, I know I can't prove all of this," Sybil said. "I may never be able to prove Captain Dean's innocence. But without his intercession, I am sure I would have died and Austin would have gotten away with treason and murder. Ken Dean did *not* commit treason, David. He was a hero."

David lifted a VCR tape. "Your suppositions might not sound credible, but they are right. I received this copy of a tape from Grace about an hour ago by special messenger. She said Captain Dean gave her the original just before she was kicked off the flight. Captain Dean told Grace that if there was any trouble with the flight to put this tape in my hands."

David set the tape down on the conference table. "Austin Stone and Faust had agreed to act long before they decided when to act, or on what specific situation they would act. Ken Dean put himself in the line of fire without authorization or orders to try to stop Faust. Our resources, as well as those of our allies, have repeatedly tried and failed to capture and convict him. Ken thought, working from the inside out, he could succeed."

"Do we have supporting evidence backing up Dean's tape?" Barber asked.

"Not yet," Conlee answered.

David looked at Barber. "How is the DNA cross-check coming?"

"Slowly, sir. We've got everyone possible working on it."

David nodded. They were about out of time and everyone knew it. In less than six hours, the missile would detonate and millions would die.

It was a small satisfaction that Austin Stone would die with them.

Winston asked about public disclosure, and David responded that there would be none. Principal parties had considered a seventy-two-hour evacuation impossible. "This isn't New Year's Eve, Winston," Sybil said. "The cruelest thing we can do is to tell people so they can spend every minute between now and then watching the clock and dreading midnight."

"Keep working, folks." David stood up, ending the meeting.

"I need a moment," Sybil told him.

"Sure." He led her to a private room just down the hallway, sat down, and motioned for Sybil to join him. "I really am sorry about Austin, Sybil."

"Thank you. It goes without saying how sorry I am that he's done this."

"No need. He has nothing to do with you."

"David, you know that's not true. Which is why, if we live through this—" Oh, God, just thinking the words had her chest in a vise "—I'm going to resign."

She had been afraid Austin would pull something underhanded, which is why she had refused to sell him the stock. But never in her wildest dreams did she believe he would jeopardize an entire country. Her ex was a murderer and a terrorist. If she didn't resign, the public and the Senate would demand it. Only a coward would put David Lance in that position, and she couldn't just follow her mantra—*Say what you mean, and mean what you say*—when it was easy or convenient. She had to live it all the time—including now.

"We'll discuss it later, if we successfully resolve the crisis." David dismissed her offer. "Peris and Abdan's premiers are still in Geneva. I doubt anyone else could have managed to keep the warmongers there." He wiggled a finger in her general direction. "They were both extremely upset by the news of your death, and they're elated to hear you're still alive."

"They're good men."

"They're ruthless men."

"Being ruthless has its value, David." She hiked her chin. "Sometimes it's the only thing that keeps a nation's people alive and safe."

"That kind of insight is why you're vital to my administration." David slid toward the edge of his seat. "I know we're in serious trouble, Sybil, and that Austin played a huge part in causing it. I can imagine how much knowing that upsets you, but the bottom line is Austin is responsible for Austin, not you." He stood up. "I'm lifting your ban. Commander Conlee made the recommendation for your protection, but you don't need it. I have complete faith in your integrity. Our hands are tied here until we get a match on the DNA, or until it occurs to Austin that he's going to die with us. But I have an urgent project for you to handle."

"Of course."

"Phone Peris and Abdan. The timing can't get any better. They're both receptive and ready for peace. A call from you will get them moving."

He wanted her to resume negotiations *now*? "All right."

"I haven't lost my mind," he assured her. "Unless I miss my guess, very soon now we're going to need excellent relations with Peris and/or Abdan."

"What do you mean?"

"You're going to have to convince them that the Peacekeeper missile they believe is targeting them really isn't. You're the only person on the planet they might believe enough not to launch a preemptive strike."

"But the missile *isn't* targeting them."

"You're right. But humor me, and prepare them anyway."

"Is there something going on I don't know about?"

He shook his head. "Just a hunch."

Sybil walked to the door, paused, and looked back at him, her heart in her eyes. "Thank you, David." He'd know she meant about the resignation.

"My privilege." He nodded to lend weight to his words, then motioned to her feet. "Why the sneakers?"

She grunted. "I'm not picking up Jonathan's habits. My feet are swollen. These are the only shoes that fit."

David slowly studied her face and the bruises. "Are you really all right?"

She had to be honest; he had that look, signaling he was getting one of his infamous hunches. "Physically, yes."

He held her gaze, and empathy filled his eyes. "Ah, I get it now."

"Get what?" What had he seen or imagined?

"I think you've picked a lousy time to realize you're in love."

Boy, had she. "Is there ever a good time?"

"Probably not," he conceded. "It always knocks you on your ass."

It did. Hard. "I need to modify my promise," she said, her apology in her voice. "I don't stand a prayer of a chance at keeping it, David. I tried denial, but it didn't work. Nothing worked."

"Didn't for me, either," he confessed. "Consider it modified."

Agitated, she swept a hand across her forehead. "Can we save this conversation for later? I'm anxious enough right now."

He swallowed a chuckle. "It's love, not an execution squad, Sybil."

"You have your frame of reference, and I have mine." She cracked the door open, then paused again and squeezed the knob until her knuckles ached. "If we don't find a way out of this, you evacuate no later than eleven."

"We're going to find a way out."

"Eleven, David."

Their gazes locked, and all her fears on what that evacuation meant reflected back at her in his eyes.

David stuffed his fists in his slacks' pockets, and nodded. "Eleven."

First-Strike Launch: 04:55:12

In an isolated A-267 office, Austin Stone backed away from the computer terminal. His chair squeaked, and he tilted his wrist to see his watch through the overhead light's glare. The bastards thought they were clever, and they were, but he was brilliant and nobody's fool.

He stood up and then paced the narrow room, desk to door, door to desk, again and again, silently cursing Commander Conlee, Lance, and Sybil.

Always Sybil. Interfering. Overpowering. Emasculating.

He curled his fingers into fists at his sides. But not this time. This time he was going to overpower her. This time she would fail *and* feel the loss. He still had time to make a flight—any flight, anywhere.

Sam Sayelle had failed him just as magnificently as all the others, but that, too, Austin could repair. He lifted the phone receiver and dialed.

"Ground Serve. How may I direct your call?"

"Clayton Rendel, please." Austin stared at the computer screen. He'd bypassed the engineers' filters and firewalls. They had meant to block his access to the system. Fortunately, he had also considered that they might try to do this, and he had programmed in a back-door access. They had discovered he was online with them relatively quickly and had locked him out. But in the interim, he had implemented the program that provided an escape. The launch could be aborted—if they found Cap Marlowe's key.

You should tell them where it is, Austin.

His mother's voice, nagging at him. Tugging at a conscience he no longer heeded. They knew he was involved in creating the crisis and had assumed a covert posture. The program now could abort the launch, but only with the key, and only if he wanted the launch aborted. If the evidence against him proved sufficient to result in his being sequestered in Leavenworth, he would rather be dead. And if he had to die, he would rather not die alone. He would take as many others as possible with him—including, of course, Sybil.

"Rendel." He finally came on the line.

Austin turned his attention back to the phone, again choosing his words carefully to avoid Home Base complications. "Sam Sayelle."

"Yes, sir," Rendel said. "Within the hour."

"Excellent." Satisfied that Rendel had accepted this call as the one from Sam Sayelle authorizing delivery of the media packets, Austin glanced at his watch. The press would have four hours to crucify Sybil before the launch. Personally, Austin would have appreciated more time for momentum to build, but four hours were better than none. And under such conditions, minutes could seem like lifetimes. "Thank you."

Before Rendel could respond, Austin hung up the phone. Sam would be blamed for sharing the manufactured information on Sybil. And every major network would air it as fact, naming Sam as their source. He would lose his credibility, his job with the *Herald*, and then, along with the rest of them, his life.

And until the moment she drew her last breath, Sybil would feel the burden of guilt and responsibility. She would know she had caused the crisis—it was her fault and she was to blame. She would know that Austin held true power. That she had battled him, and he had beaten her.

She would know he had won.

Chapter Twenty-four

Jonathan met Sybil in the hall outside the room where she had offered President Lance her resignation. She looked pale and weary, and maybe a little dazed.

"You okay?" he asked.

She looked up at him. "No."

Jonathan's heart sank and the tension coiled inside him ratcheted up. Had the president accepted her resignation, then? Jonathan refused to believe that. David protected, and he never ran from a fight. Jonathan could ask her, but she looked as fragile as the china his mother had "saved for good" in the dining room they never used, and making Lady Liberty crack wasn't on his list of preferred duties.

They walked out the door. The moon slipped behind a cloud and its light all but vanished. Near the limo, he motioned to Mickey to stay put in the driver's seat, then opened the door. Its hinges creaked. Sybil got in, and Jonathan followed. "Where to?"

"My house." Her voice thinned. "It's empty of potential traitors."

"To the residence, Mickey," Jonathan said, transmitting simultaneously to Home Base through his headset. "And when you get a minute, the door hinges back here need a couple shots of WD-40."

They were halfway to Embassy Row before she said another word. "David refused to accept my resignation, Jonathan."

Thank God. The limo paused at a red light. A Toyota packed with teens stopped beside them, their radio blaring and beating a drum solo in Jonathan's head. "Of course."

She glanced over at him, her eyes shining overly bright. "I hate him," she said softly. "I know I shouldn't hate anyone but, God forgive me, I hate him."

Austin, not Lance. "The man's made your life a living a hell—personally and professionally—and he's tried to kill you. You're human, Sybil." This was one time when words didn't get in the way. She needed them. "I know you feel guilty, but you're not responsible for what he's done at A-267, or to the staff on the plane, or to Dean's family. Feeling guilty is pretty human, too. Yeah, I'd say hating him is normal."

She laced her fingers in her lap and tucked her chin to her chest. "I've hated him a long time. Since before I found out about the vasectomy."

Before then? Jonathan thought he knew her well. He thought he had learned all there was to know about her, and he was certain he understood her better than anyone else. But he hadn't known about the reason for the divorce, Cap's confrontations, or this. She still held her secrets.

"I tried to love him. I really did. But I couldn't do it. I respected him as a scientist but not as a man, and I worried about him being so bitter he would do something like this. Austin never has been the paragon of support he publicly professed to be. He has a deep-seated bias against women—especially self-reliant women."

"He's a power vampire. He feeds off of others. Draining them makes him feel stronger."

"He's a thorn." She leaned her head back against the rest, propped an arm against the door, and sighed. "Remember that old saying, if you want to know how a man will treat his wife, look at the way he treats his mother?"

"I've heard it."

"I should have paid attention to it. Austin hated his mother. I don't mean he didn't like her. I mean he hated her. If I'd paid attention to that saying, I could have spared myself a lot of years of hell."

"There's no sense in beating yourself up over things in the past. You can't change them."

"I know." She sounded devastated. "Some men put their wives down publicly. So far as I know, he never did. But he made up for it privately. He had a cruel, vicious tongue, Jonathan. And he loved nothing better than humiliating me with it."

"Sounds twisted."

"It was." She swiped at the vent, directed the air flow away from her face. "He used to beg me to ask him for help or to ask him to do things. I rarely did. I thought maybe my asking would make him feel needed and significant."

"I take it, it didn't."

"No." She let out a little laugh, but there was no humor in it. "I'd ask, and he'd refuse to help. It didn't matter what the request happened to be—it could be something as simple as getting me a cup of tea—but he took great pleasure in refusing. Then he'd badger me into asking him for something else. I hated him for that. He was cruel, Jonathan. I know what he did wasn't abuse in the horrific sense of what some spouses live with on a daily basis, but I lived in fear of him publicly humiliating me. For as long as I can remember, he threatened to before every social function we attended."

"Hell, I'd hate him, too." Jonathan retrieved a bottle of

water from the minibar. "It rates as abuse in my book." He pressed his hand atop hers, stroked the backs of her fingertips. "I'm sorry you had to go through that."

"I'm not. I guess I should be, but I'm not. It made me stronger and wiser." She turned on the seat to face him. "Strong and wise enough to know that the minute he realizes he can't fly to Beijing tonight, he's going to kill himself and everyone else with him."

"We thought he would save himself."

"We were wrong. When all the pieces came together in my mind, I saw this through his eyes. The truth is, he hates me more than he loves himself."

Jonathan thought back to the swamp, back to her fear of dying without ever having been loved, and that context made what Austin had done and was doing to her malicious. It was also untrue. She wouldn't die unloved. Jonathan might wish he didn't love her—that would be easier on her—but he did. He'd known it in his heart since he had threatened to kill Austin and asked for the reassignment off her detail. But in his head, he had only accepted it. When he thought he had lost her in the swamp, he felt love sneak up on him and knock him to his knees. Sooner or later, he supposed, loving each other would sit well on both their shoulders—provided they survived the night.

"If we don't find a way to stop the launch, David is evacuating at eleven. That should be long enough for him to get to safety, don't you think?"

"Yeah." Had she heard something in the briefing that left her no choice but to abandon hope? "Are you giving up on the rest of us?"

"No. It's a precautionary plan. But I'd be lying if I said I wasn't afraid."

He lifted their laced hands to his mouth and kissed her knuckles. "There you go, acting human again."

"Jonathan."

"I know, Sybil." He held her hand against his jaw.

"No, you don't."

Mickey pulled into her circular driveway and parked the car, and Jonathan looked over at her. She looked a breath from tears but serene, too. He didn't understand the serenity.

"I have something to say to you." She swept her hair back from her face. "Odds are I'll screw this up. It's been a long time since I've allowed myself to think about things like this." She clasped his hand in both of hers. "You've been good to me, Jonathan. Better than good. Your support's never wavered—not even during the divorce, when I was the brunt of as many tasteless jokes as Clinton's intern." She paused, aligned her thoughts. "I don't think I've ever told you how much that meant to me. And I know I've never told you how much you mean to me."

She's talking to you as her guard, not as a man, Jonathan. You caught her at a vulnerable time earlier. She doesn't love you. How could a woman like her love you? She has everything. What could you give her that she doesn't already have without you? Just keep your mouth shut, or you'll make an ass of yourself—if you haven't already.

Certain his conscience had a better grip on the truth than his heart had, he nodded.

Sybil blinked hard, let her gaze rove over his face. "It's really hard for me to say this. The selfish part of me is afraid of being here without you, but I have to face it."

Without him? What the hell was she talking about? "Face what?"

Her eyes glossed over, sober and serious. "When David evacuates on Air Force One, I want you to go with him."

And leave her to face whatever came alone? No way. No damn way. "No."

"Jonathan, listen to me—"

"No, Sybil."

"But David is going to need you. When he comes back

here, facing what he'll find ... You have to be here to help him through it."

"No." Jonathan clenched her shoulders. "I promised I wouldn't leave you until this is over. I'm sticking to it."

"I'm asking you to go." Tears slid down her face. "Please, Jonathan, for me."

He couldn't help himself. He leaned forward, pressed his forehead to hers, and got a grip on his emotions. His heart was racing, his blood pounding through his veins. "I left you once. I can't leave you again." He leaned back, looked into her eyes. "Even for you, I can't leave you again."

He didn't love her. Sybil's breath caught in her throat. He respected and admired her, but he didn't love her. He never said he loved her. If he loved her, he would go.

Jonathan opened the limo door, closing the subject, and Sybil stepped out, worn but not defeated. She'd have to bring the matter up again later, after she got David to intercede, and after the Peris/Abdan phone conference. Grimacing, she again cursed Austin and Gregor Faust for putting them in this position and keyed the front-door lock.

One way or another, she wanted Jonathan on that plane.

First-Strike Launch: 03:51:01

Gregor Faust stared at the A-267 monitor. "Do we have verification of the DNA delivery to Marlowe?"

Patch nodded. "Jean brought the package to the hospital. She also planted the taps. We have audio in his room and a wire on the phone."

Gregor looked at the countdown board. Three hours, fifty-one minutes, and one second until the launch. "Apparently the senator has decided to die rather than suffer the humiliation of exposure."

"Some leader." Patch grunted. "He'll let the damn missile detonate to protect his stupid reputation, knowing it's going to kill him. What kind of leader wouldn't abort the launch?"

"One who will never lead." Gregor sipped from his glass of milk. Cap was either demented or damned clever—he couldn't be certain which, but either way, the man had exceeded his patience.

Patch cleared his throat. "You better take a look at this." He motioned to the A-267 monitor.

Austin stood directly in front of the remote-viewing device. Tilting his head back, he looked straight into the eye of the camera. Gregor stepped closer. "Increase the volume."

Patch hit the control.

"You ruined everything, Gregor. My flight left without me. Now I'm going to die in this cave. But that's all right, really, because I'm taking Sybil with me. I'll be here one minute and gone the next. I'll never know what hit me. You're going to be around for the real fireworks. Everyone in Ballast will be scurrying around like rats, looking for someplace safe to hide. But there won't be any safe place, Gregor. I've seen to that. You will suffer, and I hope they take a long, long time to kill you. PUSH is eager to help them, of course. Shifting blame is convenient, but it carries consequences." Austin backed away from the monitor.

Gregor glared at the image of Stone, now pounding on the office door. "Let me out of here! Conlee! You can't lock me in this tomb. I'm leaving!"

"When a genius breaks down, he really breaks down," Gregor said, fascinated by the process. And when it was complete, knowing he was taking all those he felt had crossed him with him, or leaving them to misery, Austin really would be ready to die.

"Lady Liberty wouldn't sit on the DNA report," Patch said. "She'd do anything to stop the launch. Anything."

She would, Gregor agreed. Even if doing so would

cripple her professionally and/or personally. "But she's neither corrupt nor suffering a mental breakdown."

The phone rang. Patch answered it, listened for a moment, then hung up and looked back over his shoulder at Gregor. "You're not going to believe this."

"What?" Gregor chugged down a swig of milk.

"Every major network in the U.S. just received packages of evidence that Liberty's committed treason. Complete with photographs."

"Impossible." Gregor knew the treasonous types—hell, he'd targeted and exploited them all around the world—but Sybil Stone wasn't one of them.

"You're with her in the photograph."

The heat drained from Gregor's body. For fifteen years he had avoided photographers or avoided being identified in those photos he couldn't evade. Outside the tight group of his senior staff, he remained anonymous. Even general Ballast members believed he was just another member and had no idea he was Gregor Faust. The CIA and perhaps even Interpol had his picture on film, of course, but they had no way of identifying the man photographed as he. Not until now. Now, when Westford and the SDU were involved. Now, when Gregor was about to be blamed for starting a world war. "Austin?"

"Not according to our D.C. source. She says that they were released by Sam Sayelle."

"Impossible. Sayelle gains nothing and loses everything by releasing that information to his competitors." Jean had to be wrong about this. Austin must have foisted himself off as Sayelle, the son of a bitch.

Patch turned his back to the monitors. "Gregor, which command center are we in?"

"You know that unless I die that information is confidential."

"I know that if we're in Peris or Abdan and that missile

launches, we're screwed. They like Lady Liberty, Gregor. We'll be dead inside an hour."

Gregor snagged his yellow stress ball and squeezed it flat. Patch was right, of course. "Which is why we're not in either."

Relief washed color into Patch's tense face. "Maybe she can still stop it."

"That remains to be seen." How ironic life was at times. The second-in-command of all of Ballast put his unswerving faith in the actions of the female vice president of his sworn enemy.

Even more ironic was that his first-in-command happened to agree.

Chapter Twenty-five

Sybil sat in her office at home. She would have preferred to make this call from the office, but with a traitor loose in the White House, her office there couldn't be deemed safe. Faust would probably know what she said to the premiers before they themselves knew. She couldn't risk that.

Jonathan had been in and out of the room, talking constantly between a digital phone and his Home Base transmitter—at times, on both. She liked watching him move, his resolute stride, his sure-footed step. He had to be as afraid as she was, and yet he didn't appear panicked.

For once, even the soothing peach and cream decor in her office didn't soothe her. Neither did the sweet vanilla-scented potpourri that Emily kept fresh, in strategically located bowls. Actually, considering the circumstances, Sybil supposed it was idiotic to expect anything would calm her down. No one in her right mind would be calm now.

Cap would claim her uneasiness was because she was

a woman cast in a traditionally male role, but it was rooted in common sense and logic. And fear.

The conference call with Peris and Abdan had started with greetings. Once comments on her death and the successive reclaiming of her life had been dispensed with, peace between the two of them became the topic of hot debate. While both leaders had remained in Geneva, neither seemed inclined to give much ground on their mineral-rich land-dispute issue. And she was just weary enough, and scared enough about what would happen in a little over three hours, to say screw diplomacy and get blunt.

The ceiling-fan paddles whirled above her head in the middle of the room, casting striped shadows over her desk, over the thick rug in front of her desk. "Gentlemen, please," she interrupted their heated exchange. When both fell quiet, she went on. "I know President Lance has been in touch with you and explained our current challenge."

"He has."

"Of course."

"Then I hope you will walk in my shoes for a moment and be circumspect in sharing with anyone what I am about to say."

"You have my word, Vice President Stone."

"Mine, as well."

"In about two hours President Lance is going to evacuate and I'm going to be at the site where the explosion will occur. At midnight, I'm going to die, and frankly, I'd like to die knowing that the two of you will be at peace."

Sybil's eyes stung. She blinked hard. "Don't you see that Faust wants war between the two of you? He's manipulating you for money and power. If you're at war, you need his weapons—either of you. Both of you. So long as you two are fighting, Ballast can't lose."

"On what do you base this judgment?"

Sybil frowned at the receiver, picturing the Abdan

leader in her mind. "Based on the fact that both of you are buying arms from Ballast."

Silence.

More silence.

At least they spared her from refuting hollow denials. "Listen to me, please. Faust doesn't lose, but your countries do. And your people lose, too. Alone, both of you are vulnerable—economically and strategically." She paused to let that remark claim its rightful weight. "I've gotten to know you both, and I believe you're honorable men and strong leaders. Your countries are full of loyal people. If you order them to fight, then they will. But what good will come of it? War is destructive. It prohibits growth, and nothing good and lasting can come from it. Instead, I beg you to use your honor and their loyalty more wisely. Revere the blessing of your people, and each other's people. You each have strengths the other needs."

Too emotional. Far too emotional. She reined in her passion. "Because what happens to you is so important to me, the terrorist might well cycle the target yet again. He could target one of you. I don't know that this is going to happen, but it would cause me pain, and he seems to gain great pleasure in that."

"If that occurs, I have no choice but to protect my country."

"Indeed."

"No, you don't understand. It's a simulation. If the missile detonates, it's going to detonate here. It isn't going anywhere else, it just appears to be launching."

"What guarantee do we have of this?"

"My word." She paused a moment, let the declaration settle between them. "I'm asking you not to launch a preemptive strike. I'm asking you to wait until the simulation shows the missile's impact. Then you'll know the truth."

"Then we will have sustained the strike. We won't be able to respond."

"You'll be able to respond, but you'll have no reason to. Please, trust me."

"I will take this request under advisement."

"As will I," the Peris premier said. "But this I cannot vow to you, Mrs. Stone. I must give the matter due thought."

She didn't dare press further. "I appreciate your willingness to consider my request." A hard knot formed in her throat. "I have to focus on my country's needs now. I must do all I can in the time I have left. But I'm asking the two of you to please keep working toward peace." She debated, deduced she had nothing to lose, and added, "And I'm asking you to make a promise I can take with me."

"If I can, I will."

"She wouldn't ask if it were unreasonable."

The Peris leader's comment made her smile. "Promise me you will approach your negotiations, pledging to yourselves, your people, and to me that you will act in good faith." She swallowed hard. "I know you both have the courage to die for your countries. I want your promise that you have the courage to live for them."

Jonathan leaned against the wall just outside her office, watching her and listening intently. Somewhere between the request not to launch a preemptive strike and the promise to negotiate in good faith, she had toed off both shoes. That always upped her odds to 100 percent in Jonathan's book, and he wondered how long it would take for the premiers to know they were goners.

She had faced so many challenges and trials in such a short time, Jonathan wouldn't be surprised to see her knocked flat on the floor, or huddled in a fetal position, screaming "uncle." Instead, Lady Liberty absorbed the hits and kept fighting passionately for peace between others—and not just to protect U.S. interests. Sybil fought passionately for them, for their people. For all of them.

Her respect for human beings, all human beings, came

first, Jonathan realized. David sensed it. The Peris and Abdan leaders sensed it. And it was for exactly that reason
they all had trusted her to handle these negotiations. She
had earned their respect and, undoubtedly, their admiration. She had earned his trust, but had she earned theirs?
Enough for them to risk eating a Peacekeeper missile?

Trust.

That's what Austin destroyed in her. That's what she
didn't have that Jonathan could give her.

*It didn't matter what the request happened to be—it
could be as simple as getting me a cup of tea—but he took
great pleasure in refusing.*

Austin. Sybil knew Jonathan was different, but reminding her couldn't hurt. He mattered. When a man mattered,
plans could be modified. He went to the kitchen, filled a kettle with water, then put it on the stove to heat. Just as the
burner coils glowed red, Sybil's second phone line rang.

He lifted the receiver. "Westford."

"Westford, what the hell is going on up there?"

Recognizing the woman's voice, he frowned. "Not now,
Gabby."

"I see you left your sweet disposition in the swamp."

"I don't have a sweet disposition." He leaned a hip
against the cabinet, stared at the hot coil. "You want anything in particular, or did you just call to annoy me?"

"I live to annoy you." She laughed. "I'm checking on
Sybil. Is she really okay?"

How did he answer that? "She's tied up at the moment."

"Jonathan." The teasing lilt left her voice. "Is she still
in denial?"

Man, how he wished he didn't know what she was talking about. "Most of the time, we both are. But now and
then, the shields slip." He pulled out a tray and a box of Earl
Grey tea. It was Sybil's favorite. "I don't fit into her plans."

"What plans?"

"She didn't say." He unwrapped the teabags and tossed the papers into the trashcan under the sink.

"And you didn't ask?"

"No, Gabby, I didn't ask." He listened for the kettle to whistle, hoping it would rescue him soon as a legitimate reason to end the call.

"Uh-huh. And you're giving her time to get used to you. Kind of letting it sneak up on her that she loves you— covert-cupid style."

From her tone, Gabby didn't care much for his tactical approach. Hell, if she had a better one, he'd welcome it. "Well, yeah."

"Jeez, Westford. Years of carefully orchestrated phone calls, and you blow it. Did I teach you nothing about her?"

Torn between being ticked and seeking advice, he gave the phone receiver a glare hard enough to draw static. "You orchestrated your phone calls to us?"

"Sybil didn't tell you she calls me the matchmaker from hell? Never mind. It's true, I am—but I only get involved when I know I'm totally on target."

"Well, you picked a hell of a time to miss." He stuffed a hand in his pocket. "She doesn't trust me, Gabby."

"Of course she doesn't trust you. She was married to a man who lied to her for fifteen years, Westford. The only way she'll ever move off the dime and trust is if you blast her off."

"I'm not blasting her anywhere. You, of all people, should understand why." Sybil had been blasted more than enough for one lifetime. "She doesn't want to love me."

Gabby sighed. "For a smart guy, you're being really stupid. She doesn't want to love anyone again ever. But she does love you. Think about it. Why would she say she doesn't want to love unless she does love?"

"No, she doesn't love me. For a little while, I deluded myself into thinking she did, but she doesn't. I matter, but I'm not loved. I don't know if she could love me and won't let herself, or if she just doesn't love me because I don't push the right buttons for her. Either way, she doesn't love me."

"Dirt dumb."

"Gabby, you're ticking me off."

"Good. Maybe then you'll have enough sense to take a risk. She loves you, okay? If you can screw up the guts to go for it, you'll both be glad you did."

"Glad, or banned from her life forever. Damn high risk."

"Damn high potential. How much is love worth to you, Westford? How much is she worth to you?"

Everything. He dropped the teabags into the pot. Poured in the hot water. "I've got a plan."

"Make it a good one. I'd like to live long enough to see her really happy just once in her life. At least once in her life. And you, too."

So would he. "I'll try."

"I'm pulling for both of you."

"Thanks." He hung up the phone, not sure how to feel about Gabby's orchestrating their phone calls. Though tempted to be angry, he couldn't do it with a clean conscience. Gabby loved Sybil, and she wanted them both happy. How could he fault Gabby for that when he wanted the same thing?

He set up the tea tray and then returned to Sybil's office. Wondering if she would even notice, he filled a cup for her and then set it near her elbow.

Austin had pushed her into asking and then had refused to give.

Jonathan would give before she thought to ask.

*   *   *

Sybil hung up the phone, ending the conference call, stared at the teacup a long moment, and then walked around her desk to Jonathan.

He set his cup down on the edge of her desk. "Were you successful?"

She stopped in front of him, tilted her head back, and looked up, into his eyes. "No promises, but they're talking, and if David's right and the target cycles to one of them, they're considering not launching a preemptive strike."

"That's good."

"Maybe."

"It's good." He glanced down, and the hint of a smile touched the corner of his mouth. For better or worse, his plan was working. She noticed. "You forgot your shoes."

She looked down at her bare feet, cut and bruised and swollen. "So I did." Lifting her gaze to his, she gave him a lazy smile. "Thanks for the tea."

"You're welcome."

She stepped closer. "It meant what I think it meant, right?"

"Depends." Arms hanging limp at his sides, he didn't move. "What do you think it meant?"

Doubt slithered through Sybil. Maybe she had misunderstood. Maybe him bringing her tea had been a kind gesture and nothing more. She blinked hard and fast. "I—I'm sorry, Jonathan. I—I thought—" She stepped away.

He blocked her retreat. "I promised I'd stay."

"Until the crisis is over." For the veep, not for her.

He lifted a hand, dragged his knuckles along the line of her jaw, and the look in his eyes softened. "I promised I'd never leave you again."

He had. At the A-267 hangar, when they'd been about to open the briefcase. But . . . no. No, he had been talking to her, not to Conlee. Her heart beat hard and fast and she trembled. "We'd have to be crazy to even think about—"

"We'd be insane. But we're going to do it anyway."

"We are?"

He nodded.

"Why?"

"Because it's right. Because the idea of not doing it is more painful than anything that could happen by taking the plunge." He wrapped her in his arms and kissed her, long and hard and deep, then reared back and looked down into her eyes. "Resignation is a wonderful thing, Sybil. Defeat has its upside, too."

One of her hands at his chest and the other at his waist, she felt as dazed as he looked. This was insane. He could hurt her. She didn't think she could take being hurt again. The pain cut too deep, the suffering lasted too long. She had barely recovered the first time, and she had sworn to never again put her heart on the line. "I don't think—"

"Don't bother, honey." He stroked her hair, her cheek. "You can't say anything I haven't already thought a thousand times."

"But it's not simple between us." Her face mirrored her confusion, layers of fear and longing and doubt and desire and hope.

"It never has been." He smiled to soften the blow. "But none of it matters. Trust me on this one. I've been at this a lot longer than you."

He loved her. Not the veep, not the image, but her. "You don't look a damn bit worried about walking in my shadow."

"What's to fear? I've walked in your shadow for years."

The truth hit her like a sledgehammer. He never had been worried about endangering his own life on her detail. He'd transferred because he loved her and he was afraid that endangered her. "It doesn't matter what we think or say or what we had planned, does it? This . . . thing between us. It's just there." She couldn't bring herself to say "love." He hadn't and, coward or worse, neither could she.

"It's there."

She stared at him a long moment and a furrow formed between her brows. "How do you feel about it?"

"I don't like it worth a damn."

Never had more sincere words been spoken, or reciprocated. She smiled. "Me, either."

"But it isn't going anywhere," he said. "I know that for fact. Whether I'm with you or away from you, or I fit into your plans or not, or what I do and don't want—none of it makes a damn bit of difference. For a while, thinking you'd be ashamed of me, that I wouldn't fit in your world, knocked me off balance."

"What?" Shock widened her eyes. "But you're a great fit."

"Yeah?"

She nodded. "Perfect."

"Good, because even that doesn't matter."

"Nothing seems to, I have to agree."

"So it is that way for you, too."

She nodded, slipped her arms around his neck. "Yeah, it is."

He lifted his hands, let them slide along her waist to her back. "Since it's going to hang around anyway, what you think about us riding along? Willingly, I mean?"

"We don't seem to have much choice, so we might as well." She stood on her toes and kissed him again, letting her thoughts tumble joyfully into what her heart already knew. Planned or not, wanted or not, feared or not, a special bond connected them. A bond that ignored denials and pleas and fears, and plans and intentions and promises. A bond that wouldn't fray or ravel or fade. A bond that would endure.

The phone rang.

Grumbling curses on the caller's head, Sybil stepped out of his embrace and answered. Five more minutes, and they would have been making love. For a woman who had abstained for nearly two years and had only just discovered she was loved by the man she loved—even if neither of them had worked up the courage to utter the "L" word yet—this was *not* an easy-to-swallow interruption. "Stone."

"Commander Conlee here, ma'am."

"Yes, Commander." Looking as disappointed as she felt, Jonathan gathered their cups and put them back on the tray. He still wore black sneakers. She hated seeing that but could hardly object to his silent prediction of trouble.

"The president is on with us, ma'am," Conlee said. "I wanted to let both of you know that our situation here has changed. Dr. Stone has forced our hand. He demanded we let him leave or arrest him, so we arrested him. We haven't yet interrogated him or made any accusations, and he hasn't said anything. We're in a Mexican standoff, more or less, waiting for someone to break. Frankly, I don't think it's going to be he."

"It won't," Sybil predicted. Arresting Austin assured it. He had nothing left to lose. "He'd rather be dead than in jail. He's accepted the inevitable."

"Sybil," David cut in. "I know you're not talking about death."

"That's exactly what I'm talking about," she said. "He's going to do it, David. He's going to let the missile launch."

"Do you think Cap Marlowe might be able to influence him?" David asked.

"No," Sybil said. "Austin and Cap used each other. There's no bond between them."

Jonathan stilled and Sybil knew from his posture that some piece of the puzzle had slid into place. "How are we coming on the DNA cross-checks, Commander?"

"Still working on them, ma'am." Conlee hesitated, then added, "This might sound a little out of left field, Mr. President, but your boy Barber made a special request that we run Senator Marlowe's DNA. We asked for a basis but all Barber would say about it was that he considered it prudent."

"No insight on that, I'm afraid," David said. "Sybil, what's Peris and Abdan's status?"

"If the target cycles to them, they're *considering* not

launching a preemptive strike. No promises, except to negotiate with each other in good faith. We'll hear back from
them before midnight." Barber had to be Austin's in-house
connection. This was one coincidence too many, forming a
triad among him, Cap, and Austin. If at the end of the day,
Barber could have gotten them out of this quagmire and
hadn't done it, Sybil swore she would strangle him herself.

"Stay in touch." David hung up.

"Anything else, Commander?"

"When will you be on site, ma'am?"

Jonathan looked at her, eagerly waiting for her to get
off the phone. "How long before we'll get to A-267?" she
asked him.

"Maybe an hour. We have to make a trip to St.
Elizabeth's first."

She cupped her hand over the mouthpiece. "St.
Elizabeth's?"

He nodded. "I remember where I saw the messenger."

"An hour, Commander." She hung up the phone, then
asked Jonathan, "What messenger?"

"The one in Cap's office. When we were leaving, Jean
was signing for a package from Ground Serve. When we
were going over the film on Faust, I saw this guy in a photo
who looked familiar but I couldn't place him. Now I have."

"He was the messenger." Sybil assimilated that. "A direct link between Faust and Cap."

"It appears so."

"Let's go." Sybil shoved on her sneakers, cringed
against the tenderness and the pain, and snagged her purse
off a chair. "Senator Marlowe has some explaining to do."

"To hell with explanations. They can wait," Jonathan
said. "Let's hope he's got the key to the inner hub."

Chapter Twenty-six

"I think we'll get farther if I go in alone."

Jonathan checked Cap's room, took the at-ease stance outside the door, and then gave Sybil a go-ahead nod. Sybil walked in. Cap was sitting up in his hospital bed, his glasses resting on the end of his nose.

"Sybil." He turned down the volume on the television. A baseball game was in-progress.

"Hello, Cap. You're looking a lot better than the last time I saw you."

His cheeks and neck flushed. "Did I thank you for getting me out of there?"

"Yes." She lifted her chin. "You lived."

"Is this a social visit?"

"No." She stepped over to his bedside. "I know you received a package from an associate of Gregor Faust's." He opened his mouth to deny it, but she held up a staying hand. "Don't lie to me, Cap. We're in critical trouble, and

I'm not here to debate. In two hours a lot of people are going to die."

No response.

"Cap." She sat down on the side of his bed. "If we get lucky and find a way to survive this, very soon you're going to run for President of the United States. You're going to meet Americans face to face and tell them how you're going to make their lives better. You're going to ask them to support you, and when you win their confidence and that election, you're going to take an oath to serve and protect them. Don't you think they should be alive and aboveground, not buried below it to hear all this?"

"I don't trust you, Sybil." He dipped his chin, glared at her. "I wish I did, but I don't. Hell, I don't even trust myself anymore."

"If you let these people die . . ."

"I didn't start this, and I can't stop it. I would if I could, but I can't." The truth burned in his eyes. "Regardless of what you think of me, I do love this country. I'm not perfect, but I have tried to serve it well. I can't tell you what I don't know."

"I understand." Wishing she didn't, Sybil stood up and opened a virtual door that allowed him to save face. "And I know you're the most connected man on the Hill. I need your help, Cap. If you can find out anything about this—anything at all—now is the time."

"I'll do what I can."

"Thank you." She turned and walked to the door.

"Sybil?"

She paused and looked back at him.

"That day we, um, talked about Austin. You didn't know until I told you, did you?"

The vasectomy. Even now he demanded his pound of flesh. "No, Cap, I didn't."

"I'm sorry." A thick furrow formed between his brows

and sincere regret filled his eyes. "I believed...Then I wasn't sure..." He sighed and stopped himself. "I'm sorry."

"I know," she said, forcing herself to hold his gaze. "I knew when you didn't release the report to the media."

"You didn't know about the blind-trust violations, either."

A statement, not a question. Still, she gave him a head shake.

He looked as if he wanted to say more about both but couldn't make himself do it. "I'll let you know if I hear anything."

"I appreciate it." Sybil walked out of the hospital room.

Jonathan fell into step beside her. When they got on the elevator and the door closed, he asked, "Anything?"

"He denied knowing anything."

"I sense a *but* in that." He pushed the button for the first floor.

"*But* he knows plenty," she said. "I gave him a graceful way out—to find out what he can from his connections. Now we just have to wait to see if he has the courage to take it."

"What does your intuition say?"

Jonathan trusted her instincts, her woman's intuition. Loving him for that, too, Sybil clasped his arm and leaned against him, appreciating his solid warmth at her side. "I think he somehow got snared into a part of this, and he couldn't find a way out. I also think he's a better man than I believed him to be. But I honestly don't know what'll he do. I wish I did."

"Ground Serve was delivering something to his office, Sybil. We only need the DNA and the key. His part—and he did have a part or he wouldn't have pulled that no-notice inspection—had to be in it."

The elevator jarred to a halt. The bell rang then the door slid open. Sybil stepped out. "The answer is there."

"Where?"

"In those deliveries." Leaving the hospital, she looked up at the night sky. So many stars. Pretty. "It has to be in those deliveries."

Midway through the parking lot, she suddenly stopped and clutched at Jonathan's sleeve. "Do we have security cameras inside the inner hub?"

"Yes."

"Can we access them from outside it?"

"Of course." Understanding dawned in his eyes.

Sybil nodded. "We can see what he did there that day."

"The tapes have been reviewed, Sybil." Jonathan ran a security sweep on the car, then opened the door for Sybil to get inside. "There was nothing on them."

He walked around, settled in behind the wheel, and then cranked the engine.

"What if the 'nothing on them' was like the nothing on the Intel tapes we reviewed?" Sybil kicked the air-conditioning up a notch. "The one where we found the photo of Faust?"

"Good point, ma'am. We're on our way."

First-Strike Launch: 01:45:00

Austin Stone sat in Commander Conlee's office. A mural of eagles in flight covered the far wall, giving the illusion of open space and blue sky. Misleading but welcome when stuck underground and robbed of fresh air, natural light, and any sounds of nature.

Conlee sat behind his desk, his frustration with Austin apparent in his voice's sharp edge. "You called this meeting, Stone. Start talking."

A green bar lamp on the desk spilled amber light over the chair's leather arms, giving them a rich brown patina Austin appreciated even now. "I'm in a gregarious mood, so I'm willing to negotiate."

Conlee crossed his arms over his chest. "Can you stop the launch?"

"Yes, I can. Your experts were good, but the delay on implementing the loop and disconnecting me from the network gave me all the time I needed to alter my previous programs. Your original key will open the inner hub."

"What about the DNA?"

"That and the launch key, you don't have."

Originally Austin had configured the secure system to the inner hub using Gregor Faust's DNA. Poetic justice. Yet after Gregor had double-crossed him, Austin had been left with no choice but to incorporate a cover for himself in Plan B, so he had changed DNA codes. He'd also found changes at A-267. Worrisome changes, because they meant Faust had an in at A-267 aside from the one Austin had provided. The Ballast contact had proven to be Austin's contact, Captain Mendoza, which of course made killing him necessary.

"What do you want?" Conlee pushed.

Resenting the handcuffs circling his wrists, Austin slid him a reproving glare. "A face-to-face meeting with Sybil and the media. Sam Sayelle from the *Herald* and one representative from the major networks, Fox News, CNN, and MSNBC."

"For what purpose?"

"That will be disclosed in the meeting."

"You're not giving me much to take to the vice president."

"I'm giving you the only possible means of stopping the Peacekeeper from launching. I'd say I'm offering you a lot, Commander. She will agree with me."

"I'll take the matter under consideration."

Austin stood up. "Remember, Conlee. I'm not a patient man."

"Guard!" Conlee shouted a summons.

The door opened before he'd finished calling. Two armed guards escorted Stone out, then back to detention.

Conlee hated that sorry-ass scum sucker. Just talking to the man made him feel as if he needed a long, hot shower. Shaking off the feeling, he put in a conference call to the president and Lady Liberty. When he had them on the line, he passed along Austin's proposal.

"Why does he want the media?" David asked.

"He wants to cast a shadow I'll have to walk in."

"Sybil, I know you're in an impossible position on this," David said. "So am I. I either risk the meeting and compromise you, or I refuse the meeting and watch the missile detonate."

"It's a simple decision," she said. "A-267's security has already been compromised. We have nothing to lose by bringing in the media. I'm on my way, Commander."

"Sybil, you don't have to—"

"Yes, David, I do. This is our only chance. To live with myself, I can't *not* do this."

"Ma'am," the commander cut in. "I didn't like the looks of him. He's got something nasty in mind. I don't know what, but I'd bet my retirement on it."

"You'd be right." She paused, and then added, "He means to humiliate me."

What Austin didn't understand and, Conlee suspected, never had was that Lady Liberty would gladly forfeit her pride to save lives. That made it difficult to relay what he must tell her next. "I'm afraid there's more bad news. About three minutes ago we experienced a cycle shift. We have a new target."

Sybil didn't have to wait to know where Austin had targeted. Deep down, she had known he wouldn't be able to resist stabbing her with one more thorn. "Peris or Abdan?"

"Actually, both."

"I'm sorry, Sybil," David said. "I'll talk with the premiers immediately."

"David, how did you know he was going to do this?"

"You wanted them to have peace. Targeting them would hurt you most."

"Because Austin is Austin." She reached for Jonathan's hand.

"Because Austin is Austin."

Chapter Twenty-seven

Saturday, August 10 ★ First-Strike Launch: 01:32:00

On the A-267 elevator, Jonathan smelled that smell. Dark. Dank. Evil. "Sybil." His tone carried a warning. "This isn't a good idea."

She placed a hand against the sleeve of his black jacket. "It's all we have."

Resigned to that truth, Jonathan pushed the button. The elevator began to descend and he leaned back against the wall. "The president should have started the cross-check on key staff sooner."

"You're right. He talked with everyone, but he should have taken the investigation farther. We knew we had a traitor on staff soon after the crisis started—long before we got out of the swamp. But I understand David's reluctance. He backs up his team. If he didn't, he would have asked for my resignation before the divorce."

Instead, he was refusing to accept it now. "I'm glad

about that, but this isn't a political game of strategy. We're facing the threat of annihilation."

She rubbed his sleeve. "You and I know that, but part of David's genius is that he sees them as the same. There are times when that's advantageous and times when it's not. That's why he needs us. We see the difference."

The death stench grew stronger. "I don't want you going in there alone."

"I won't be. The media will be there, and Commander Conlee."

"And me."

Sybil hated what she was about to say, but she had to do it. "I don't want you in there, Jonathan."

"Why the hell not? I'm in your life now. We're riding this relationship together willingly, remember? That means all the way, Sybil. Marriage, kids—a whole life."

The bottom dropped out of her stomach. "You want to marry me? And have kids?"

"Well, yeah." He seemed confused. "I mean, we don't have to have kids literally. There are a lot of kids out there already who need parents."

"What about older ones?" she asked, unable to digest all of this.

"Hell, they need us most. Everyone wants to adopt babies. The older ones just keep getting shuffled around until they outgrow the system. Yeah, older kids works for me."

A burst of joy erupted inside her, spread warmth from her head to her heels. "Well then, I guess we'll have to get married. It'll make adopting easier."

"That was my thought on the matter." He'd grab whatever straw he could to get her used to the idea of marrying him and building a life together.

"Right." She sounded sarcastic, but she was happy. Jonathan loved her and he wanted to marry her. She wanted kids, and he wanted her to have them. God, what a special man, and how lucky she was to have him. She'd been so

fearful she'd nearly let their chance slip away. Just how close
she'd come to doing that had her queasy.

"So, considering I'm going to be the father of your children—mmm, how many children are we talking about here?
Just a rough estimate is fine with me."

"Four or five, I thought," she suggested, half serious,
half trying to shock him. "Or is that—"

Clearly picking up on what she was doing, he didn't
miss a beat. "That works." The playfulness left his voice,
warning her he might sound as if he were teasing but in
truth he was dead serious. "But it's not just for you, Sybil.
The kids, I mean. I love kids."

"I know." She remembered him that day in Columbus,
playing with the children.

"So, considering I'm going to be your husband and the
father of your children, why are you banning me from this
confrontation with Austin?"

She shifted on her feet. "Because Austin's goal is to humiliate me. I can handle that, Jonathan. Really I can. But I
can't handle you watching him do it."

Jonathan gripped the handrail and squeezed. Better
than any other living soul, he knew what that admission had
cost her. "It wouldn't change the way I see you, honey. You
have to know that."

"I do." She also knew it would take an army to keep
Jonathan from going for Austin's throat. "But it would change
what I see in your eyes when you look at me. I—I don't want
to sacrifice that, too." Her face flushed and earnest fear
flooded her eyes. "Please. Don't ask me to sacrifice that, too."

Jonathan thumbed a joint in the handrail with his nail.
"He's going to humiliate you and then refuse to tell you what
you need to know to stop the launch, isn't he?"

"Probably," she hedged, then caught his reprimanding
expression and confessed. "I'd say the odds are ninety-nine
percent that he'll refuse."

"Then why do it?"

"Because there's a one percent chance he won't refuse. I have to try." She smiled. "Besides, being humiliated by him isn't anything new. I can take it."

"You shouldn't have to take it."

Never had truer words been spoken. "No, damn it, I shouldn't. But sometimes we don't get to choose."

The elevator stopped.

"Please, Jonathan."

He nodded once, hard, clearly under protest.

"Thank you." Sybil glanced down at his feet. Seeing his black sneakers put her in the right frame of mind to deal with whatever lay ahead.

Lieutenant Gibson stood at the security station. Sybil nodded and walked in his direction. "Didn't the commander offer Gibson some down time?" she whispered to Jonathan.

"He refused it."

Sybil understood. So far as he knew, the crisis had started on his watch with the lockdown. He needed to see the challenge through. "Remind me to recommend him for a commendation. He was wonderful with Cap."

"I'll remind you to tell Grace. She'll see to it."

Commander Conlee intercepted her, looking annoyed as hell and about as amiable. "The media is here. I'm having Dr. Stone brought out now."

"Where are we meeting?" Sybil nodded to a guard at the mouth of the corridor leading to Home Base.

"Conference room." Conlee looked at his watch. "We've got less than two hours, ma'am."

Walking in that direction, Sybil grew more and more tense. Austin would degrade her in every possible way. She knew to expect the worst from him. And she turned inward, depending on her unfailing source of strength to get her through this. *Please, God. Give me the courage to do whatever I have to do*.

She walked into the conference room. Seven familiar reporters, including Sam Sayelle, and their six cameramen

stood lined up against the wall. "Thank you all for coming."
She walked to the head of the table and sat down.

Conlee sat down on her right. "Would you like a glass of
water or something, ma'am?"

Her insides were shaking so hard that anything she put
down her throat would just come right back up. "No, thank
you."

Two armed guards led Austin Stone into the room. He
was wearing handcuffs, leg shackles, and a smile. "Good
evening, everyone."

No one responded.

Not seeming at all slighted, he walked over and sat
down at the foot of the table. "Let's not waste time, since we
have so little of it left." He turned to look at the press. "As
you may know, I am prepared to launch a Peacekeeper missile at midnight in retaliation for undue interference in my
life by the federal government.

"A Peacekeeper is the most destructive missile in the
U.S. arsenal. Its kill zone is extensive. Washington, D.C.
will cease to exist. And, of course, everyone in it will also
cease to exist. Several surrounding states will be heavily
damaged, and more people will die." Austin paused, allowing the gravity of the situation to settle in. "I am giving the
United States one last chance to atone for its crimes against
me. And I want the truth to be perfectly clear to everyone. I
am not an evil man. I am a victim who has been manipulated
by the government and this administration. The only way to
stop them from committing more wrongs against more people is to force them to admit what they've done. That brings
us to why you and Vice President Stone are here."

He looked back at Sybil. "I believe you have a favor to
ask of me."

Still. No fidgeting. No unnecessary body language.
Austin was sharp; he would pick up on it. And God help her
if he once smelled her fear. He would own her, and he would
know it.

It's just a thorn, Sybil. That's all. You can handle thorns. Appreciate those, too.

Her confidence grew. Austin knew they had him, and he had reconciled himself to dying and taking them with him. "Yes, I do have a favor to ask," she said. "I want you to give me the DNA identity to open the inner hub and the key needed to abort the missile launch."

Totally unprepared for this, the media members let out a collective gasp.

That pleased her former husband immensely. "You have constantly interfered in my life and my business, Sybil." He spared her a quizzing look. "Why should I grant you any favor?"

He couldn't be serious. He was playing with her and, God, she resented it. "Because if you don't, millions of people will die. Mothers, fathers, grandparents, and children. Regardless of what has or hasn't been done to you, you have no right to murder innocent people and cripple the government of this country." She paused and considered strategy, then dropped it and spoke from her heart. "Austin, your war is with me. Your hatred is hatred for me. No one except me should bear responsibility."

He rubbed at his chin. "Are you saying you're willing to accept full responsibility for everyone?"

She didn't like this. Not at all. Her flesh crawled, and she had to physically restrain herself to keep from squirming. "If you will abort the launch, yes, I am."

"Because you're such a good person," he said with a mocking lilt in his voice. "Such a patriot and a devoted leader."

"Because it's my job," she said, her own voice deadpan flat. "I love this country, and that means loving the people in it. When I took the oath, I made them promises, Austin. I have to keep them. But my willingness doesn't have anything to do with how much I love this country, or whether or not I'm a leader. It has to do with being a human being. One life for many. It's not a hard choice."

"I'm not going to kill you, Sybil."

"Aren't you?" She visually challenged him, wondering if she knew him better than he knew himself.

He shrugged. "Okay, I am. But only symbolically now. Later you can die with everyone else—unless you do exactly what I want you to do."

Then she'd live with shame. How damned predictable he had become. "Look, will you just say what you have to say and get this over and done?"

"Ah, the clock is ticking. We mustn't forget that." He rocked back in his chair. "I'm certain you've contacted the board at Secure Environet and I've been replaced as its chair. Am I going to be forced to sell my stock?"

Caught between a rock and a hard place. Did she dare lie?

No. No, he expects that. He wants that. He knows the truth. This is one of his attempts to push your back against the wall. Lie, and you become exactly what the public believes about far too many in public service: a corrupt politician. You'll be just another political thug.

"A forced sale has been ordered by the board due to your conduct."

"Have you sold your stock?"

"No."

"What happens to my money?"

"Your assets have already been frozen. When the sale is permitted by the court, the proceeds will be held in an escrow account until you're tried and convicted. If a judge finds you guilty of treason, he'll probably order your assets be delivered to the United States government as partial restitution to compensate the country for debts incurred by your acts of murder and treason."

"Murder?" He grunted. "But I haven't yet killed anyone."

"Linda Dean and her two children would disagree. And I'm sure Captain Mendoza would, too."

Anger that she knew about Mendoza seized Austin. His

hands fisted, he glared at her. "Do you want to stop this launch or not?"

Had she done the wrong thing by giving him the truth? His eyes had that feral glint. With Austin, that glint was far more dangerous than even intense anger. Sybil hadn't seen it often, but when she had—oh, God—hell had come to call. "I do."

"Fine." He leaned forward, folded his hands atop the table. "Get on your knees and beg me, Sybil."

The camera lights were bright. Sybil stood up, heard the media members' surprised murmurs. She glimpsed Sam Sayelle out of the corner of her eye. His face looked as if it had been carved out of granite.

Commander Conlee let loose his outrage. "Now see here, Stone."

She held up a hand to silence him. "It's okay, Commander."

"The hell it is, ma'am."

She looked over at Conlee. His neck veins protruding, his face turning dark red, he shoved an unlit stubby cigar between his teeth and clamped down on it. Simply put, he was ready to kick ass. She had to calm him down. Digging deep, she summoned a semblance of a smile and deliberately softened her voice. "Commander, it's only pride."

Their gazes locked, and she saw the moment he recalled their earlier conversation. *He's going to humiliate me.* "To save lives, I'll gladly give him my pride." She walked around the table toward Austin.

He scooted back his chair, distancing himself from the table. "Since you value your pride so little, forfeiting it is inadequate compensation. I want more." He draped his chained wrists over a chair arm. "I want you to strip, Sybil."

She stopped midstep. He couldn't mean—oh, but he did. She could see it in his eyes.

"You hide the truth under your conservative suits, but I see you for what you are, and so will others." He lifted lazy lids and his hatred for her emanated from him. "Your choice. If you want what I have to give, then do it. If not, I'll see you in hell."

Sybil cursed him in her mind. Cursed everything about him. What kind of man forced a woman he knew felt uncomfortable and vulnerable at being barefoot in front of others to strip naked? "You son of a bitch. You'd never pull this stunt on a man."

"There would be no need. A man wouldn't hide behind his clothes as you do. What? Are you afraid to let the world see you as you really are? Are you terrified that John and Jane Q. Public will learn all your words about loyalty and caring and integrity—well, that they're just words? It's crunch time, Sybil. Do you really mean what you say and say what you mean? You love America, right? You want to save lives, right?"

Her convictions were on the line. But more so, lives were on the line. *One percent.* No matter how uncomfortable, how degrading, she had to take that one percent chance. It was all they had.

It's just a thorn, Sybil. No more, or less. You can deal with thorns.

Jonathan's voice, him reassuring her in her mind. Ironic, since he would be with her, if she hadn't specifically asked him not to be in the room. Of course, even an army wouldn't have kept him from killing Austin by now.

"Well?" Austin speared her with an open challenge.

Just a thorn.

"All right, Austin." Sybil swallowed her pride and removed her clothes. Battered and bruised from head to foot, marred by whelps from bug bites, scratched and scraped raw from her collisions with the handcuffs, the catbrier and the rock and limb, nicked and cut—she was a mess, and that was fine. Honest. As imperfect outside as she was inside. She draped her clothes across the back of a chair.

"Your shoes, too, Sybil." Evil gleamed in his eyes.

He knew. The pathetic bastard knew it was the shoes

that mattered most. Never in her life had she hated anyone more.

Thorns. Think thorns, Sybil. Think about the things Jonathan said about the kids needing you. Someone to look up to, to emulate. Think about them. Not Austin. Them.

"Of course." She toed off her sneakers. The leather rubbed over a cut on her right foot, and it began to bleed. She stepped away from her shoes, held her head high, her back ramrod straight.

The whirring cameras stopped.

Commander Conlee turned and faced the wall.

The journalists and cameramen followed his lead, until all Sybil could see of any of them, including Sam Sayelle, was their backs. Gratitude swelled in her chest, and that too fed her confidence. Who would have expected it here? Of all places, here, and now? *A rose petal.*

"No!" Austin shouted. "I want them to look at you. I want them to film this and release it all over the world. Everyone must see you for what you really are. The high and mighty Vice President Stone, the second most powerful person in the free world, on her knees to me. Begging *me* for *my* mercy."

No one moved to face them.

"Damn it, turn around!" Exasperated, Austin sputtered. "I won't tell her. So help me God, I won't tell her!"

It's only pride. It's only pride. It's only pride. Just a thorn. No more, or less. Just a thorn.

Sybil forced strength into her reed-thin voice. "Commander, Sam, all of you, please, just do what he says."

One by one they turned to face her.

Austin wagged a finger at the cameraman standing beside Sam. "Get the cameras going."

When Sybil heard the whir, she risked a glance at the media, certain her face was bloodred. But none of them was doing a microexam on her body. None of them looked away from her eyes.

Deeply moved by the show of respect, she blinked hard, and with renewed strength, she faced Austin. "All right. We've done everything you asked. You've taken my pride and you're welcome to it. You've humiliated and degraded me, and that's fine, too. I concede defeat to your superiority. You've won, Austin. You're strongest and most powerful. Now give me what I need to stop the killing. *Please*."

He glared at her for a long moment. "No."

She'd expected it, but hearing it . . . *Oh, God, please*. She couldn't fail now. Not now. Not on this. "You gave your word, Austin. Do you want the world to see you this way? As a man with no honor?"

He smiled, obviously not giving a damn what anyone thought anymore. "I lied."

"Austin, think about it, please. You can't let all these people die. You've accomplished so many wonderful things, but if you do this, people will never remember them. This is all they'll remember." She paused to swallow hard, to mentally regroup. "This is your life-defining moment, Austin. It's your chance to make right your wrongs. Don't throw it away. Please, don't throw it away and condemn people you don't even know to death. Please."

"Eloquent but useless, Sybil. I'll never tell you. If you weren't so damn stupid, you would have known it before you walked into the room."

"I did know it," she said softly. Genuine regret washed through her. "But I had to try—for all of the people you're going to murder, and for you."

"For me?" He guffawed. "That's absurd."

"I had to give you the opportunity to do the right thing, Austin. I've done that. You're choosing not to take it, and that's your decision to make. My conscience is clear. You *can* still clear yours. You *can* stop this and turn it all around. No one has to die tonight."

"Everyone here has to die tonight. Otherwise I'll spend the rest of my life in Leavenworth, and I will *not* do that. The most I can do to redeem my jaded soul is to remind you, before you die, that some good will come out of this."

She damn sure couldn't see it.

He hardened his voice, slid her a cold smile. "Our financial ties will finally be severed."

"Millions of people are going to die, and you're talking about money?" Her temper threatened to explode. "Good God, Austin. Tell me it's not true. Tell me you're not the coldest, sickest bastard I've ever had the misfortune to know."

"I love you, too, darling." He gave her a cocky smile.

Love? Love? And smiling? "How dare you?" The rage in her burst loose. She lunged at him, connecting with his jaw. Sharp pain shot up to her elbow.

Austin's chair toppled over. He hit the floor with a dull thud. The cameramen and reporters scrambled out of the way.

The hallway door flew open. Jonathan rushed in, saw her standing nude and Austin sprawled on the floor. "Are you all right, ma'am?"

"I'm fine, Agent Westford." She was shaking like a leaf. "As we expected, he refused to disclose anything." Her back rigid, she gathered her clothes and walked out of the conference room, then into the rest room across the hall.

No one in the room made a sound. The chains on Austin's ankles twisted and he struggled to get upright, but no one moved to help him. Jonathan nodded his way. "What's he doing on the floor?"

"She belted him with a decent right cross," Conlee said. "He deserved worse."

"Did he put a hand on her?"

Conlee chomped down on his stubby cigar. "Only his face against her knuckles."

Sam walked over to Jonathan and cleared his throat. "We recorded this on a closed loop. Tell her we're having a little bonfire outside. No one leaves here with a copy."

Something was different about Sayelle. Jonathan

wasn't sure how to read him. "Why was the vice president in her birthday suit?"

"Was she?" Sam looked Jonathan straight in the eye. "I didn't notice." He turned and called back over his shoulder to the other reporters. "Anyone pick up on the veep being in her birthday suit?"

"No."

"Not me."

"The veep? No way, man."

"Get real."

A guy with a camera on his shoulder yelled out, "What you smokin' over there, Sayelle?"

Sam pursed his lips. "Are you sure that's what you saw, Agent Westford?"

They were protecting her. All of them. His chest went tight, and he rubbed at his neck. "Maybe I was mistaken."

"I'd bet on it." Sam started toward the door, paused, and then turned back to Jonathan. "I know you think I'm a bastard for the way I've written about her, but I want you to know I really thought . . . well, let me put it this way. I walked in this room a cynic with one spark of hope left at ever finding an honest politician. And then I saw what she did." He shook his head, swallowed hard. "She's the real thing."

Understanding exactly what he meant, Jonathan nodded.

Conlee called for the guards and motioned to Austin. "Get him out of my sight."

"You'd better be nice to me, Commander. Regardless of Sybil's little temper tantrum, she wants what only I can give her. That's her weakness, you see. She doesn't realize it, but I do. She loves others more than she loves herself."

"Get that scum sucker out of here before I kill him myself."

The guards led Austin out. The bruiser on his left elbowed him in the ribs. "You're gonna be sorry for what you did to my veep, asshole."

Jonathan imagined Austin would regret it, provided any of them were alive to regret anything. "What the hell happened in here?" he asked Conlee.

"Lady Liberty just took care of a little business." Conlee grunted, gave his head a little shake. "Even naked and on her knees she had more dignity than that sorry bastard."

"And more compassion," Jonathan said.

"Yeah." Conlee looked surprised that Jonathan knew it when he hadn't even been in the room.

"I've seen it before—in other ways," he explained.

"You'd better go see about her," Conlee whispered. "She was taking it on the chin, but I know she's embarrassed, and she needs to know she shouldn't be. With what's at stake, anyone would have done the same thing."

For her it went deeper than embarrassment, and into how she had handled it. But Jonathan kept that to himself and nodded. "I'll give her a minute and then go in." Unless Jonathan missed his guess, she was going to be angry, not embarrassed. Austin hadn't given her what she needed. For Lady Liberty, that was the bottom line.

Conlee stepped toward the door. "I've been around many years, and most veeps just kind of fade into the woodwork. But not Liberty. People with power usually have the devil's own time being humble. What she did here tonight took grit and guts, but it took more humility than I thought one body could hold. I'm proud of her, Jonathan." Conlee's voice deepened and turned gruff. "It's been a long time since I could say that about a honcho on the Hill. It feels damn good."

First-Strike Launch: 01:15:00

The Peris and Abdan premiers sat in a salon at the Grand Palace Hotel in Geneva, watching a monitor that had been delivered earlier that evening with a message for them to view it together. Though the messenger had declared himself an envoy of the United States, both leaders had recognized the high-ranking member of Ballast, who was known both as ET and as Patch.

Liberty had just left the conference room at A-267.

"Even under these conditions, she gave him an opportunity to redeem his spiritual self," the premier of Peris said. "She has a most compassionate nature."

"And a formidable right cross."

"That, too." The Peris leader reached for his glass, twirled it by flexing his wrist. Ice clinked against its sides. "I didn't think Americans were capable of humility."

"Or of holding such a deep respect for life."

"He meant to humiliate her."

"She let him and, in doing so, exalted herself." Abdan's premier stretched an arm across the back of the sofa. "I find her courage humbling."

"Enough to do what she asked from us?"

"Yes. Her concern for us and our people is genuine," Abdan's premier said. "I would wish that she would live. But if she is to die, I would have her die knowing we fulfilled our promise to her."

"We negotiate in good faith?"

"In good faith."

The premier looked his counterpart right in the eye and admitted what they both knew but never had confessed. "We also raze Ballast's command centers in our countries. No sanctuary. And we do this after we call Gregor Faust and tell him to stop this missile attack, if he can."

"Agreed." The Peris leader lifted his glass.

Both premiers drank deeply and then picked up phones.

★ ★ ★

Patch stared at the monitor, misty-eyed. "I knew she would make any sacrifice to save her people."

Gregor had known it, too. But knowing it and watching it happen incited vastly different emotional responses in him. He had always respected her as a strong adversary. She'd earned it. But he still had been willing to kill her. Business was, after all, business.

Until now.

Now that he had seen with his own eyes the depth of her commitment, the nature of her heart, and her willingness to sacrifice for others, he not only couldn't kill her, he couldn't stand by and watch her die. There was no honor in it. And honesty forced him to admit that, though it played only a small part in his decision, he wanted the opportunity to kill the disloyal, degrading, humiliating Austin Stone personally. "Get her on the phone."

Patch turned and stared at Gregor, gape-jawed. "You're going to help her?"

"Yes, I am."

"It'll cost you millions."

"Yes, it will." Peris and Abdan would destroy two of his three command centers. "But a world war would damage Ballast more." Gregor supplied a rational cover, though his thoughts traveled a far different path.

In Lady Liberty, he saw the goodness that could be in people. He hadn't seen it often. He had cut his teeth on war, the threat of war, and the ravages of war. This goodness intrigued him. And while he had the reputation for having a black soul, even he had his Achilles' heel, and Lady Liberty had stomped on it.

She wasn't corrupt.

She wasn't a taker who sucked society dry and gave it nothing. She wasn't insulting life by using and abusing it.

She was, as Sam Sayelle had said, the real thing.

Many leaders were respected and beloved and could be worthy of the honor, but in Gregor's experience, there were far too few of them to squander even one. The world was a better place because she was in it—even if her presence complicated his life.

Gregor had no illusions. His soul was stained black and he did lack loyalty to any country. Men bowed to him in fear. They respected his ability to destroy them—and he could and would destroy them. But they bowed to her in honor and respect. Lady Liberty would lift them up, build them, help them become stronger.

He had no family, few friends, and no life outside his work—all things they had in common. Yet unlike the lady, if he died, no one would leave flowers at the fence outside his home, and no one would weep over his grave. No one.

Gregor turned toward Patch. "Pull in the field teams and put the men on alert. We'll be underground for the foreseeable future." Why did he care if anyone would grieve for him? What did it matter? Dead was dead.

The contrast is humbling, Gregor. Humbling. What manner of legacy do you wish to leave? One of striking fear in the hearts of people like Liberty, or one embracing the traits of character you have seen her embrace? You are not condemned to your current path. Every moment of every day for all of your life, you make choices. You are free to choose whatever you wish. You choose your legacy, Gregor.

"Gregor, I'm not sure ..."

Hearing a mumbled drone, he turned to Patch. "I'm sorry, what was your question?"

"If the missile launches, the United States will be sitting with its jugular exposed. It's only going to hit the U.S." Patch lifted his hands, palms up. "No world war. So why are you giving up millions to help her?"

For the same reason I will never harm her. Gregor poured himself a glass of milk and then reached for the phone. "Because I can."

Chapter Twenty-eight

Saturday, August 10 ★ First-Strike Launch: 00:59:00

"This is Sybil Stone." She held the receiver, cradled between her shoulder and ear, and stared at the clock in the A-267 office she'd commandeered. Less than an hour. *Less than an hour!*

"On the DNA," a man said. "Cross-check White House senior staff. Flip Five."

Sybil went rigid in her seat. She'd heard that phrase before, seen it before, and then, too, it had felt familiar. But from where? Her instincts warned it was a literal instruction, but could that be true? Could it be that simple? "What about the key?" she asked, unable to peg the identity of the man on the other end of the line.

"If I had it, you would hold it in your hand," he said. "But I do have some insight. I'm not responsible for this."

Oh, God. Faust or PUSH. It was Faust or PUSH calling her. "Austin Stone is responsible."

"Yes, he is. I'm prepared to feed you a security clip

from your inner hub. Your copy contains a dubbed feed loop that hides what's really going on. Mine doesn't. I nearly missed seeing it myself. Will you accept it?"

Sybil's heart thudded hard. "Do I have your word it won't corrupt our system?"

"Will you trust my word if I give it?"

She recalled Jonathan's remarks on honor. Different perspectives, different goals, different viewpoints. ET and the penny. He'd let her live. "Yes, I will." God, but she hoped she wasn't making the biggest mistake of her life.

"Then you have it."

Sybil had reviewed their copy of the tape, along with several of their best analysts. On it Cap hadn't gone into the inner hub, yet he *had* been there. The analysts had found the loop, but there was no backup system in place to give them the truth on what had happened during that time lapse.

Only one person could be on the other end of the phone line, and he had just compromised himself to help her. "Thank you, Mr. Faust."

"You're welcome, Lady Liberty."

The line went dead. Sybil hung up, her heart thumping hard against her ribs. "Jonathan, that was Faust! Where's a copy of the DNA report on me—the one that opened the outer rim?"

"Faust is *helping* us?" Jonathan rifled through a stack of papers, scanning. He thrust over a stapled segment of papers. "Here's the original report."

She compared them, scanned down to the fifth line. It didn't match, but—she reversed the fifth line—it matched perfectly. It was literal. "We've got the DNA secret!"

She grabbed the phone, called Conlee. When he came on the line, she issued her orders on a rushed breath. "Cross-check White House senior staff members' DNA for the match, but only after you reverse the fifth line in each of the reports."

Jonathan interrupted. "Tell him to run Richard Barber and Winston first."

She passed along the message. "Let me know as soon as you can."

"We still need the launch key." Jonathan looked at the clock and frowned. "It's five after eleven and the president hasn't evacuated. You'd better call him, or he'll drag his feet too long." Sadness filled his eyes, and he moved to the door. "I'll give you some privacy."

The phone rang. Sybil answered it. "Stone."

"Congratulations," David said. "Peris and Abdan have agreed to exercise restraint and not launch a preemptive strike. They want you to know that they're keeping their promise. What's that all about?"

The spot in her heart reserved for her favorite war-mongers warmed. "They're negotiating in good faith." She hated to be abrupt but time was short. "Gregor Faust gave us the code to break the DNA challenge. He didn't do this, Austin did. Faust doesn't have the launch key."

"How do you know that?"

"He told me."

"That's a surprise. And you believe him?"

"Yes, I do. He has total access to A-267, David. I imagine Austin saw to that, too. He's feeding me the missing minutes from the inner-hub security tape, which means he has a remote viewer inside. Jonathan and I are going to view it as soon as the transmission is complete."

She looked up at the clock and her throat went dry. Eleven had come and gone. She licked at her lips, and her tone deepened. "David, it's time." He had to leave.

"Yes." His voice went husky. "Sybil . . ." His voice faded.

What did you say in a situation like this? Nothing was enough. Everything wasn't enough. You lived, you loved, you shared the joys and troubles of each other's lives, but there wasn't anything you could say to express all your feelings in mere words. It couldn't be done. "I understand,

David. And me, too. Just stay safe, okay?" She swallowed back tears. "And do me a favor."

"You don't ask for favors—ever."

"I'm asking now." She curled the edge of a piece of paper, her hand shaking. "Order Jonathan to go with you." Tears fell freely to her face.

"I already did." David's voice turned tender. "However this turns out, I'm going to need him, and I knew you'd want him here to keep me in line—"

"I do." The president was astute. One of his many admirable qualities.

David expelled a regretful breath. "He refused, Sybil."

"A direct order from you?"

"He said he'd left you once and he'd never do it again." Her chest went tight. "Damn misguided maniac."

"That maniac loves you, Sybil. He's loved you for as long as I can remember."

That shocked her, and yet it didn't, even though Jonathan had never given her the words. "Since before the divorce?"

"Try from when you first came to the Hill."

Knowing that made this harder. "Damn it, David. Make him go."

"I would if I could. But short of abducting him, I can't. Jonathan made his decision with his eyes wide open. Simply put, he'd rather be dead than alive without you, Sybil."

"I don't want him to die." She swiped at her tears. "I don't want anyone to die."

"Me, either." David sniffed. "I'm praying for you. For all of us."

"Don't stop—and get out of here, David. Do the responsible thing. Now."

"I'll be in touch as soon as we're airborne." He blew out a sharp breath. "Good luck, Lady Liberty."

She hung up the phone, slapped at her cheeks, and

ordered herself to bury her emotions deep. Now just wasn't the time.

The phone rang again, and again she answered. "Stone."

"Barber's a match."

Conlee. She stared at the clock. Thirty minutes. *Thirty damn minutes.* "Get him down here, Commander. Fast."

"He's on his way, ma'am."

"What progress have we made on the launch key?"

"With Barber's DNA, we'll have access to the inner hub. But the gurus say the old key to the launch station no longer fits. We don't have the launch key."

Jonathan talked with Lieutenant Gibson at the door then came over to her, holding an earpiece transmitter. "The president is airborne. Communications are up."

She nodded. "Commander, switch to Home Base emergency transmissions."

"Yes, ma'am."

Sybil hung up the phone, put the transmitter on, and then spoke into the lip mike. "Mr. President, we're up and running."

"Good," David said. "I understand Barber is a DNA match."

"Yes, sir," Conlee said.

"Is he our leak?"

"I'm afraid so, sir," Sybil said, seesawing a pencil on the desktop.

Conlee jumped in. "Nothing classified, only insights, from what we've discovered thus far, but he's the leak, sir. He's on his way to the site now. He was a little . . . resistant."

Sybil couldn't blame him for that. She'd rather be a lot of other places herself. Near the door, Jonathan motioned to the viewer and mouthed that Gregor Faust's film was in and waiting down the hall.

"Westford, are you copying?"

Jonathan stilled, propped his hands on his hips. "Yes, Mr. President."

"Have you interrogated Austin Stone?"

"No, sir."

"Do what you have to do, but find that key."

"Frankly, sir, I could beat him to death and he wouldn't tell me."

"What do you recommend we do, then?"

"The only thing left to do, sir." Jonathan met Sybil's gaze. "Hope the engineers are wrong, that Austin somehow tricked the launch system, and try the key that's configured to open the inner hub. It's all we've got."

"Keep the line open."

"Yes, sir."

In the viewing room, Sybil and Jonathan sat down in the soundproof booth. Max's voice fed in through the intercom. "Ready?"

Jonathan pressed the button on the desktop. "Go, Max."

The clip played. Mendoza sat at the launch control desk. Cap stood in the hub, requested the reports, walked to the mail chute, inspected it, returned to the desk, and then walked out. The lockdown alarms sounded, the door slammed shut, and Mendoza breached protocol, left his seat and searched frantically for the launch key—and didn't find it. "Air vent. Something...oh, God!" He beat against the door, slamming his fist against the panel again and again, trying to force it open. Then, in seemingly slow motion, he slumped against the wall, slid down to the floor, and died.

Sybil did her damnedest to snuff out emotion and observe with analytical objectivity, but failed. *God rest his soul.*

Jonathan was on the phone with Conlee. "Run a chemical check on the inner hub."

"It's not a nerve agent," Sybil said. She'd seen the

impact of nerve agents on Iraq footage. Mendoza had died an easier death.

"It's been done. Carbon monoxide was off the scale. We've flushed it," Jonathan relayed to Sybil, then hung up the phone.

"We have proof now that Mendoza was murdered."

"But we don't have the key." Jonathan stood up. "So do we go with what we've got?"

She nodded. "We have no choice."

They walked down the hallway and into the outer rim. A small cluster of people had gathered at the door to the inner hub. The secure-device machines taunted her, and Sybil looked over at Conlee. "Get Austin plugged in for me, Commander. I have to try just one more time." Twenty minutes. *Twenty minutes.*

A moment later Austin's voice came through the transmitter. "I'm not going to tell you, Sybil."

"The willingness to die and dying are two different things," she reminded him, memories of Mendoza fresh in her mind. "Who in hell are you trying to impress?"

"Don't be absurd. I'm not trying to impress anyone."

"Where is the key, Austin?"

"I don't know."

"Liar."

"Sybil, I'm sincere. I don't know."

"Maybe I can assist your memory." She clenched her fist, glared at the door to the inner hub. "We are going to survive this. You will be tried and convicted. That leaves you staring into the eyes of a lethal injection. If we have to change the law to make that happen, I'll do it. And, so help me God, Austin, I'm going to be the person holding the damn needle. Do you hear me? The last thing you'll see in this world is me holding the needle."

He hung up on her.

"Oh, God, no. No." Shaking, she looked up at Jonathan. "He really doesn't know."

"Then who does?"

An airman ran over with a little Ziploc bag and handed it to Jonathan. "Senator Marlowe said to put this into your hands, Agent Westford."

"What is it?" Sybil asked.

Jonathan took a look. "The Band-Aid that came off your finger in Geneva."

"But we ran it through our lab," Conlee said.

They had. Sybil looked at Conlee. "I take it this means ET is one of ours."

Conlee didn't confirm the suspicion, but he didn't deny it, either.

ET had let her live. That night in the swamp, hidden beneath the bushes near the helicopter. The pennies. Of course. And he'd let them know that Ballast had managed to intercept matter being transferred from one field operative to another. They needed to alter their current methods.

Evidently Gregor Faust wasn't the only one infiltrating high ranks. ET was Faust's second-in-command. He was also an SDU or CIA agent. And with the pennies, he had finally gotten them a positive ID on Gregor Faust. Sybil hoped Ken and Linda Dean somehow knew that.

Richard Barber arrived, looking pale and sweaty and scared stiff. Hell, they were all scared stiff. No one, with the exception of Austin, wanted to die. "Over here, Barber," Sybil called out to him.

"I don't understand this. Why do you need me here?"

"Austin used your DNA. His personal way of thanking you for all your insights on me. Did you share anything classified?"

"I'd never do that!"

"I'm glad you have some principles, even if loyalty to the current administration isn't one of them."

"I don't like you."

"I'm irrelevant, Richard. You promised to protect the office, and you didn't do it."

That remark hit him like a cold slap of water, and his indignant expression crumbled. "No. No, I guess I didn't."

"Well, you're lucky. You get a chance to atone and ease the burden on your conscience."

He clearly hated the sound of that. And feared it. "How?"

"You get to open the inner hub," Sybil said to him, and then spoke to the president. "David, we have three minutes. We're out of options, so we're going with the key we have. Austin could have used it for both the inner hub and the launch key."

"What if he didn't?"

"We don't have anything else to try."

"Barber, get over here," Conlee called him to the secure device at the wall.

Sybil paused and faced Jonathan. She couldn't let him die not knowing he was loved. "Jonathan, I—"

"I know," he interrupted, touched her cheek. "So do you."

Looking into his eyes, how could she not know? She nodded.

"Madam Vice President?" The Commander said.

"Right here." She moved to Barber's side.

"Here's the key," Conlee said, then shouted back over his shoulder. "Lieutenant Gibson, run a countdown for us, please."

"One minute, fifty-five seconds."

"Go ahead and bleed, Barber," Sybil said.

He pricked his thumb with the lancelet, pressed its bleeding tip against the absorbent pad.

Sybil held her breath and inserted the key. Sweat trickled down between her breasts. *Please, God.*

"One minute, twenty seconds."

The red light went out.

The green light came on, and she turned the key.

The thick bolts slid free, back into the wall, the sheet of metal lifted, and the door opened.

"Let's go." Sybil rushed inside and stumbled over Captain Mendoza's body. Packets of sugar littered the floor around him.

"One minute."

Sybil swallowed hard, prayed harder, and raised the key to the control centered on the launch station desk.

"A thorn!" Jonathan screamed, lunged at Sybil, and knocked her arm away from the launch system. The key clanged on the tile floor.

She jerked around, back toward him. "What?"

"Faust insisted you view the film right away. Mendoza's murder wasn't urgent. What else did we see on that clip? What else did we see?"

Sybil mentally reviewed the clip, then thrust a finger toward the wall. "Cap inspected the mail chute."

Jonathan scrambled to the mail chute, withdrew the tube, and then opened it. A second key tumbled out into his hand. He passed it to Sybil. "Compare them. Do it fast, Sybil."

"Fifty seconds."

"They're different." Mortified, she held one in each hand. "Damn it, David, they're different." *Think, Sybil. You've got to think.*

"Forty seconds."

"David." Sweat rolled in sheets down her body. "I'm going to choose. I realize this should be your decision, but it's not. I'm here, and I'm making the call." She gave him absolution, freedom from the horror of living with having made the wrong choice. "I need the code."

He reeled off the daily code.

"Thirty seconds."

Sybil punched in the code, looked over at Jonathan, then at the two silver keys in her palm. One had a scratch. Sybil's heart soared. Austin always had done that with his keys. The one that was newest—*the right one*—he scratched. The mark was fresh. *A rose petal? Or a deliberate trap?*

"Twenty-nine seconds, ma'am."

She swung her gaze to Jonathan and warned him. "It's a Hail Mary pass."

He nodded. "Do it."

Sybil moved back into position, inserted the key, turned it, and sucked in a sharp breath.

The flashing red countdown stopped. *Twenty-seven seconds.*

She stared at it, unable to trust her eyes, to believe it was over, but the glaring digits didn't flicker. Slowly she exhaled.

"Sybil? Sybil, are you there?"

David's voice filled the room, breaking the silence and the dam of collective fear.

Relief flooded through her. Her eyes blurred, and she smiled at Jonathan. "Yes, David. We're here." A tear rolled down her cheek. "We're all here."

"Air Force One is coming home!"

Pandemonium erupted. On all sides of her, people laughed, whooped, hugged, shared shoulder slaps, atta-boys, and high fives. Tears streaming down her face, she dipped her chin and headed straight for Jonathan. He opened his arms wide, and she stepped into them. "We made it, Jonathan." She circled his waist and buried her face in his chest. "We really made it."

His cheek against her hair, he hugged her hard. "We really did."

"Nice work!" Conlee's clap to Jonathan's shoulder vibrated through Sybil's chest.

"Damn nice work. You two make a helluva team." Conlee looked down, noticed Jonathan's bloody knuckles. His joy in the moment vanished abruptly, and he narrowed his eyes. "What happened to your hand, Westford?"

He pulled back from Sybil. "I hit a wall."

Austin was being led out of the facility by two armed guards. Sybil saw the bruise on his jaw, knew she hadn't inflicted it, and frowned at Jonathan. "You hit a wall with Austin's face?"

"More or less." Jonathan shrugged.

Conlee smiled. "Thanks for not killing him."

Sybil frowned. "Commander, since when do we thank someone for not killing someone else—even if we think they deserve it?"

"Since that someone else homesteaded in the proverbial ditch and tried to drag someone who didn't belong there into the ditch with him." Conlee grunted and shoved his cigar stub between his teeth. "Besides, a damn lot of paperwork comes with a corpse."

"Sybil?" David's voice sounded through the transmitter.

"Yes, sir?" She strained to hear him over the roar of the celebration, cupping her hand over her ear as she had so often seen Jonathan do.

"Press conference in forty-five minutes. I can't get back that fast. You'll have to handle it. Word is out that we've had a terrorist attack."

Damn it. "Some of the media was already here?"

"One of Richard Barber's contacts. Tell him he's fired. On second thought, don't. I'll handle that as soon as I get back." David's tone proved Barber wouldn't find the experience pleasant. "Commander, are you still with us?"

"Yes, sir."

"Could you have Barber escorted to my office and have him wait for me? Tell Mildred to watch him like a hawk, and see if the attorney general would be interested in joining us. Tell him he'll be issuing a couple of warrants in the near future."

"Yes, sir."

"Oh, and, Sybil?"

Nearly giddy with relief, she smiled at Jonathan and resigned herself to reality. They'd managed to pull off a hell of a victory, but celebrating it would have to wait. David was celebrating the way he always celebrated big victories and close calls: by diving into work. It was his personal rendition of affirming life. Personally, she let her gaze drift down Jonathan; she'd opt for the lovemaking rendition, but David was the boss. "Yes, sir?"

"I know that after all you've been through this is going to be hard to stomach, but you need to be ready to answer questions on that treason nonsense. Winston will brief you at the office in a half hour."

"All right." Resentment warred in her. No matter how much she gave, they wanted more.

"Don't take any guff."

She wouldn't have to take anything from the media. She'd walk through the door. They'd go for her jugular. She'd hit the floor. And that would be that. "I won't."

"I'll be there as soon as I can. After all you've done, for you to have to do this—" He muttered a curse. "It's insulting, Sybil."

"It's all right, David." She wasn't crazy about the idea herself. It was insulting, and it stung. She dragged her hair back from her face. Hell, call a spade a spade. It hurt.

And as weary as she had been from the events of the last seventy-two hours, this treason business snatched her joy at their success and wore her down in a way the crisis couldn't because it attacked the one thing she had left: her character.

Chapter Twenty-nine

The White House Press Room was buzzing.

News had broken that the United States had averted a terrorist attack less than an hour ago and members of the media had poured in, quickly overflowing the room. It was the middle of the night, and yet the turnout wasn't really surprising. Friday's canceled briefing had the media edgy. Everyone had known something significant was about to break; they just hadn't pinpointed what. Sybil Stone's plane exploding had everyone hanging close.

Sam took his usual seat in the third row and was surprised to find Sniffer sitting on his left, holding a brown envelope that looked too familiar. Scanning the other media members, Sam felt his stomach pump acid and sour. Many of them held the brown envelopes. He hadn't authorized Ground Serve to distribute them—after what he'd witnessed at A-267, he never would—so why had it?

Austin. Sam looked at Sniffer. "What are you doing here?"

"The veep is going to brief us on the terrorist attack."

He held up the envelope. "But I want to ask her some questions about this."

"Where did you get that?"

"The source isn't disclosed, but the material seems authentic enough."

Definitely Austin. Sam's blood boiled. The jerk was attempting to use the media to humiliate Vice President Stone again. "It's more dirt on Sybil Stone, right?"

Sniffer nodded, looking perplexed. "Yeah. Did you get one, too?"

"Don't use it." A man spoke from the right side of Sam, his voice distinct and familiar.

Silence overtook the room, and Sam turned toward the voice: Marcus Gilbert. "What are you doing here?" And why was he holding Linda Dean's journal?

Sniffer tuned out, kept his head buried in the envelope's contents, eager to be intimately familiar with the facts before he slammed Sybil Stone with them.

"Moral support," Marcus said.

"For whom?" Sam tried lowering his voice, but a pin drop would have sounded like an explosion in the suddenly still room. Sniffer withstanding, all gazes had locked onto them.

Marcus stuffed a hand into the pocket of his rumpled black coat. "I understand the veep had a challenging weekend. She's survived a plane explosion, several near-death experiences—including being shot at and nearly blown up while stopping a terrorist attack on American soil. She also risked her life to save Cap Marlowe's." He paused and listened to the shocked reactions of the other media members. "I'm here to say thanks—and to tell her she can count on me for whatever, whenever."

That declaration caused more than a few surprised gasps, including one from Sam. It was a well-known fact that Marcus had a strict bias against female politicians. He had made ignoring them an art form long before Sybil

Stone had appeared on the Hill. Most women knew Marcus only by reputation, and in the form of heartfelt advice from others who warned them to stay away from him. "Are you two friends?"

"No."

Images of her naked and on her knees, begging Austin for all their lives, shot through Sam's mind. In her position, would he have as much courage? His voice faded to a whisper. "I was wrong about her, Marcus."

"A lot of people were." He passed Ken Dean's journal to Sam. "Don't look at it. Just give it to her."

"Why?"

"Because while some people thought Captain Ken Dean was a traitor, she didn't. This proves she was right."

"His wife's journal?" Sam had seen it, stacked among her cookbooks.

"It's not hers, it's his. Ken Dean was frustrated by failed attempts to stop Gregor Faust and Ballast, so he went rogue to try to stop them himself."

"Which is why Linda and the kids were abducted."

Marcus nodded. "Vice President Stone defended Dean blind. No proof, no evidence. She judged him by his character, and she trusted him. She didn't have a lot of company, but that didn't matter. She did what was right. Give her the book so she can prove it."

"I will." Sam took it. "I can't believe I was so damn wrong about her. I thought I had good instincts."

"You do. It's like I said, a lot of people were wrong about her."

"But not you?"

"No, I was wrong, too. I just discovered it before the rest of you." Marcus dropped his voice to keep this part of their conversation private. "That's why I warned you again a few months ago to keep an eye on Cap Marlowe."

"Warned?" Sam felt sick inside. "I thought you were telling me he was a good man."

"He *is* a good man, but he's a politician first." Marcus cocked his head. "That's what he most envies about Vice President Stone."

In Sam's mind, more and more pieces of the puzzle slid into place. "I understand now, Marcus." A knot formed in his throat. "She's the real thing."

"Real?" Their conversation caught Sniffer's ear. "She's as corrupt as they come. I have the proof right here."

Marcus spared the junior reporter a warning look and raised his voice several decibels, clearly wanting everyone in the room to hear him. "If I were you, I wouldn't use that proof."

"Why not?" Sniffer still didn't look over at Marcus's face. He rifled through pages of documents and supporting photographs. "There's all kinds of—"

"It's manufactured bullshit."

"How do you know that? You haven't even looked at it." Sniffer swiveled his gaze, giving Marcus a hard look for the first time. Recognition lit in his eyes and his jaw dropped loose. "You're the man from the Wall."

"Oh, shit." Sam dragged a hand over his forehead, feeling a wall-banger of a headache forming behind his eyes, thumping in his skull. "It's you?"

He nodded.

Sam glared at Sniffer, who looked embarrassed enough to start a forest fire. "You didn't know Marcus Gilbert?"

"I'd never seen him." Sniffer shrugged. "He looks different in his pictures."

Sam gritted his teeth and reminded himself that Marcus had retired before Sniffer had even graduated from college, much less had come to work for the *Herald*.

"Let me tell all of you a story," Marcus said loudly enough to easily be heard. "Four months ago I started taking a morning walk to the Vietnam Wall. The vice president saw me there and said hello. The next morning, when she walked past, she passed me an envelope. Twenty dollars was inside it."

"She's bribing you with twenty bucks?" Sniffer snorted.

"I didn't know why she had given me the money. I was intrigued, so I went back." Marcus elevated the pitch of his voice. "Every day I saw her at the Wall, and every day she passed me an envelope. If she planned a trip, she would put a twenty in for each day she would be gone."

This intrigued Sam, but it puzzled him, too. "Did she ever explain why she was giving you money?"

"No, she didn't. Once she asked my name. I told her it was Gil. The only other words the woman ever spoke to me were 'Good morning, Gil. Isn't it a gorgeous day?' He blinked and let his gaze travel reporter to reporter. "One rainy morning she passed me the envelope and an umbrella. There was a hundred-dollar bill inside and a note that read 'Stay dry, Gil.'" He grunted and a smile lifted the corner of his mouth. "Finally, the humbling truth dawned on me. She had no idea who I was."

Marcus paused, clearly remembering the incident, and then went on. "I approached a member of her guard detail on the matter. Naturally, he had been concerned about the contents of the envelope early on, and so he had asked her what was inside. She said that, while she preferred to help people anonymously, she didn't want her actions to raise any concerns. Essentially, she thought I was a homeless vet. The money was for food."

Sam grunted and smiled. "So much for the allegation of treason."

"Yeah." Marcus's eyes shone brightly.

Sniffer looked as if he wished the floor would open up and swallow him down. "But you're Marcus Gilbert. You're a millionaire."

"I know that, kid." Marcus's eyes twinkled. "But she didn't know it, and she didn't know me. I looked homeless and hungry, so she fed me and gave me money to get out of the rain." Marcus let his gaze slide from person to person throughout the room of familiar, respected faces. "Which is one of many reasons I'm going to offer her my services, if she chooses to run for president."

Sam's mind reeled. The great Marcus Gilbert putting his muscle behind a woman? Who could have ever expected it? But after what Sam had seen at that missile site, he felt as Marcus did about her. A woman president would be a hard sell to the general public, but what the hell? Sam would put his stock in her. When he thought about how close he had come to publicly levying accusations against her, he got a little nauseous. Not only would he have lost his professional credibility, he would have screwed her up professionally and personally. Factoring in what he now knew about her firsthand, he would have regretted that the rest of his life. "Don't attack her, Sniffer."

"What?"

"Don't do it," Sam warned.

"I *am* going to do it. You're just pissed because you didn't get the evidence."

Marcus stood up. "Let me make myself perfectly clear on this, kid. I respect and admire Vice President Stone. She loves this country more than anyone I've ever known, and I've known plenty of good people, including a fair number who've occupied the Oval Office. I don't give a damn whose godson you are, you hurt her, and your career will be over before it starts. I'll see to it."

With thirty years of connections to draw on, Marcus could see to a damn lot. Sniffer would play hell snagging a job for a third-rate rag. Sam again offered the kid some healthy advice. "He's saving your ass, Sniffer. Be grateful, not stupid."

Sniffer glared at Marcus, at Sam, and then at the others in the room, many of whom held brown envelopes, and finally the fire in his eyes died. "She's real?"

Sam nodded.

Sniffer gave Marcus a sharp nod as a thank-you for saving his backside, then walked up to the podium and set down the brown envelope.

The Fox News correspondent followed and left his envelope on top of Sniffer's. Reporters for CNN, MSNBC, and others followed, all depositing their envelopes of evidence against Sybil Stone on the podium.

Marcus Gilbert's word still carried a ton of clout.

★   ★   ★

Sybil entered the press room with Jonathan.

Near the door, she stopped next to Winston, who relayed what had happened with Marcus Gilbert. Jonathan's expression turned tense, strained. He dreaded this confrontation as much as Sybil. Now the cat was out of the proverbial bag on Gil being Marcus Gilbert, and she'd have to confess on that, too.

Sheer exhaustion conspired with dread and her courage faltered, threatened to dissipate. Jonathan knew it, and gave her a smile meant to reassure her. But it was plastic and forced, and so was her smile back at him. To see how he really felt, she looked down at his shoes.

Black loafers.

Loafers, not sneakers. Sybil's smile turned genuine. This wasn't going to be that bad. Jonathan had taken off his sneakers. Okay, it would be bad, but she could handle it. He knew it, and so did she.

Stiffening her spine, she walked through a sea of cameras and reporters—and stopped next to Sam Sayelle. "Gil, I'm glad to see you've come out of retirement." He had a press pass clipped to his coat's lapel.

"You knew who I was?" He was stunned and not at all certain he liked what he was hearing.

"Not at first," she admitted. "A member of my staff told me."

He frowned. "Then why did you keep giving me money?"

"You were donating it to a soup kitchen and matching the funds." She shrugged. "Together, we fed a lot of people."

He laughed out loud. "Clever."

Smiling, she lifted a hand. "Why are you here, Gil?"

His eyes gleamed, but the lingering traces of laughter faded from his voice. "I wanted to tell you I'm glad you're alive."

Sybil smiled and pressed a hand to his forearm. "Thank you. That means a lot to me."

"More than you realize," Sam mumbled.

Sybil switched her gaze to Sam. "Excuse me?"

"He said," Marcus interrupted, "he's glad you're alive, too."

That surprised her. Broadcasts aside, she would have ranked Sam Sayelle as one of the front-runners on her executioner's squad, though he had seen to it all the A-267 tapes of her had been burned on the premises. "Is that right, Sam?"

"Yes, ma'am." He lifted his chin, squared his shoulders. "That's right."

She studied him carefully. He seemed sincere. But then a lot of people on the Hill seemed sincere. Still, tonight she would take anything positive she could get. "Thank you. For everything, Sam."

He understood the reference and passed Dean's journal to her. "This is for you." Dropping his voice, he whispered, "The commander might want to take a look at Jean. It's possible she isn't only working for Cap. And watch what you say around Winston. He isn't dangerous, but he isn't a fan."

"I appreciate it." Puzzled, she accepted the journal and then walked on to the front of the room. When she stepped behind the podium, she looked down. *Dozens of brown envelopes?*

She opened one, shuffled through the damning photographs, and couldn't absorb the shock. They looked real.

Authentic. But none of them—*not one of them*—depicted anything she remembered ever happening. Would any of the reporters believe her?

Of course they wouldn't. They would believe what they saw with their own eyes—in the pictures. Seeing visions of a Senate investigation, she clutched at her churning stomach. Her knees went weak, and she broke into a cold sweat. They had played her for a sucker. Lulled her into complacency in preparation for the kill.

Lifting her gaze, she slowly scanned the room, not sure what to do or say. Was this another of Austin's cruel visions of justice? Or had someone else done this to her? And what in heaven's name did she do now?

"Madam Vice President." Sam rescued her. "We received those envelopes from Austin Stone. The information in them is bogus. We're just returning them to you—so you'll have them as evidence, if you want to file charges against him."

Sybil slid her gaze to Jonathan. He was smiling, and this time it was genuine. Things really were going to be okay. They had given her the benefit of the doubt.

She tucked the envelopes under the podium on a shelf. "I, um, appreciate your checking this information for authenticity prior to releasing it. People with less professional integrity would have damaged me first and asked questions later. I—I'm grateful."

Marcus and Sam rose to their feet and clapped their hands. A sea of media members joined them. Their applause echoed through the room and through the chambers of her heart. The back of Sybil's nose stung and her eyes burned.

She'd expected them to go for her jugular.

Instead they welcomed her home.

Chapter Thirty

"It went well."

"I'm still in shock." Sybil smiled at Jonathan, walking beside her back to her residence. Light cast from neon signs on storefronts spilled on the sidewalk and stretched into the street. They'd have to get back in the car soon, but for the moment, she was riding an adrenaline high and needed to walk, to feel the fresh air and savor the quiet of the night. After the intense pressure of the past seventy-two hours and the press conference, it seemed perfect to be walking with Jonathan, feeling calm and peaceful and joyful at just being alive.

"The president showing up to laud you is normal, but Cap Marlowe, busting out of the hospital to get there to sing your praises?" Jonathan grunted. "I'll be in shock over that for a long time to come."

A tossed cola can sat on the sidewalk between a trash receptacle and a green recycling bin. Sybil scooped it up then dropped it in to be recycled. "Don't be too amazed by Cap's support." Chilled, she rubbed at her arms, her left wrist still tender and scraped raw from the metal briefcase cuff. "Faust set him up and he doesn't want that exposed. But by the time I need him to endorse my next proposal, he'll hate me again."

Jonathan laughed, draped his jacket over her shoulders, and then clasped her hand. "He envies you because you've got what he wants, and you're good at it."

"That, too." She smiled up at him.

"Some things never change."

Sybil went quiet, studied the cracks in the sidewalk, the banner flapping in the wind outside the bakery, the lights of the black limo creeping down the street, following them. "I suppose some things never change," she said, sharing her thoughts. "But other things do. And then those changes create new changes." She linked her arm with his, leaned against him so their shoulders touched with each step. "I guess change is like momentum, Jonathan."

He placed a hand atop hers on his arm. "How's that, honey?"

"Well, a whole group of people step up to the line to race, but no one moves. Then one person does, and some of the others follow. Then someone sprints, and more people sprint. Then someone runs. And before you know it, you've got people running, sprinting, and walking, and fewer and fewer are content, standing at the line."

He stopped and turned toward her. "What the hell are you talking about?"

She shrugged. "Corruption in politics."

"What?" He didn't even pretend to understand.

So much for his knowing how her mind worked. Oddly pleased by that, she kept her voice level, matter-of-fact. "Things are changing, Jonathan. Soon corruption won't be expected or considered normal—it isn't in vogue any more because David moved off the line."

Mickey stopped the limo at the curb, and Sybil skipped a beat. This was a big leap for her. Actually, it was a Grand Canyon kind of leap. "I'm not content standing at the line anymore, Jonathan."

He frowned down at her. "You hit the Hill running, and you've never been corrupt."

Steeling herself, she fingered his jacket. It carried his scent. She liked that. A lot. "I meant I'm not content personally."

"Oh." He slipped a hand into his pants pocket. "I'm going to spare myself some mental anguish here and just ask. *Exactly* what do you mean?"

"I mean I ran the race with Austin, hit a wall, and got knocked back to the line." She stared at the knot in Jonathan's tie. She could do this, she could take the leap, and now she could look him in the eye while doing it. "I mean I want to run again . . . with you. Not because it's inevitable, or my hormones are forcing me to, but because I really, really want you." Her heart knocked against her ribs, thundered in her temples. She lifted her lids, met his gaze, and held it. "I hope you were serious about us, because I was very serious. I love you, Jonathan."

He pressed his lips flat. "What about your plans? I don't fit into them any more now than I ever did."

"You sound bitter. Why?"

"Because I want to fit, damn it. I'm not perfect, but I'm not bad. Actually, I come in handy now and then—like when you bail out of planes or fall into quicksand pits."

"Jonathan, are you thinking I'm ashamed to love you or something idiotic like that?"

"It's crossed my mind."

If his grimace was any gauge, it had done more than cross his mind. It had nagged at him. "I'm not. I think you're a wonderful man." She patted his chest, apologizing. "I meant I didn't plan to ever love any man again. Austin should have cured me for life. But then you came back and everything changed. You scared the hell out of me, Jonathan. I didn't want to care for you—and I tried not to—but it was there, and before I knew it, it was love. Do you know how neurotic loving you has made me?"

The look in his eyes softened and warmed, and he smoothed back a strand of hair the wind had blown over her face. "Yeah, I think I do."

"Do you really?" He was back in mask mode. She couldn't tell a thing by his expression or his body language.

"You scared the hell out of me, too. You still do." He nodded, again stuffed a hand into his pocket. "You weren't the only one to promise yourself not to fall in love."

What was she supposed to make of that? Of all of this? He hadn't responded to her asking if he had been serious about them, he hadn't responded to her telling him she loved him, and now he talked of promising himself not to fall in love, and he hadn't said whether he'd kept that promise, either. When they'd been at A-267 and all but certain they were going to die, he'd almost said he loved her. He definitely left that impression, but he hadn't given her the words. She wanted a home and a family, but she wanted him to want her, to love her, not to be with her willingly because his hormones forced him to come along for the ride.

If she had even an ounce of sense, she would keep her mouth shut and let this go. But she couldn't do it. She couldn't hit a wall while standing on the line. "I know you came back to me only as a favor to David."

"That was true. But it's not why I'm here now. I promised you I'd stay."

She recalled it. On the helicopter, leaving the swamp. "Until the crisis was over. It's over."

"Yeah, it is."

He didn't have to look so damn cheerful about it. "So I guess you're saying you'll be returning to Home Base for your next SDU assignment, then." Her chest went tight. She couldn't look at him. It took all she had left to find enough of her voice to say what she needed to say. Since he hadn't disabused her of the idea, this is what he wanted to hear. "I'm going to miss you, Jonathan."

He tipped up her chin with a finger and searched her face, her eyes, as if he were doing his damnedest to see straight into her soul. "I told you, I'm not leaving you again."

What precisely did he mean? Unsure, she slipped off her pump, touched the cool concrete with her toes, grounding her. "You're not leaving the veep, or you're not leaving me?"

"It's a moot point, Sybil. You're one and the same."

"It's not a moot point." She swallowed her pride and leaped. "When we're together, I need to know you're with me. I've fallen in love with you, Jonathan, and I won't always have this job. What happens then? Do you leave me then?"

"I'm going to say this one more time: I'm not leaving you again." His eyes widened. "Did you just say you love me *and* you're *in love* with me?"

Of course the two were different, but his startled reaction proved that to him, those differences were monumental. Her nerves stretched tight. "Well, yes."

He looked dumbstruck, and skeptical. "Are you sure?"

"Unfortunately." She lifted her chin. Gabby had been right. No matter how hard you try, you just can't legislate the heart.

"Since when?"

Amazing, but he really was surprised. "I think when I was in the quicksand." She fingered his shirt placket, rubbing the smooth fabric between the second and third buttons. His heart thumped against the backs of her fingers, beating as hard and fast as her own. "You knew you could get me out, and you didn't laugh at me for wanting to cut off my hand." She blinked hard. "It meant a lot to me that you didn't laugh, Jonathan."

"There wasn't a damn thing funny about that."

"But I convinced myself it wasn't love."

"Lust?" he speculated, as if he too had been in denial.

The truth, though honest, wouldn't do much to make him feel better. But that she could share it anyway, made her feel great. "Not love, not lust."

"What then?"

She wrinkled her nose at him to soften the blow. "Swamp fever."

The edge of his lip curled. "Well, isn't that flattering?"

She chuckled. "It worked until you brought me the cup of tea. When you set that cup on my desk..." Feeling tender, choking up, she gave herself a second, then went on. "It was like a door opened inside me and all the meaningful things you've done for me over the years flooded through"—her voice cracked—"and they just kind of added up until my heart felt full." She paused to take in a steadying breath, to relive and again appreciate the joy of that moment. "That was the first time I dared to believe that maybe you could love me, too."

"I've always loved you, Sybil." He gave her shoulders a gentle squeeze. "But then I fell in love with you, and you were already married. No matter how you look at it, that's a bad combination. I had to walk away."

So he had requested reassignment to get away from her, but because he loved her. She moved closer, held him to her, and stared deeply into his eyes. "But you still love me, and now we're a good combination, right?"

"Oh, yeah." He smiled from the heart out and dipped his head to kiss her.

"Thank God." Sybil met him halfway, opened her heart, and welcomed him.

In the years ahead there would be challenges and trials and probably some healthy disagreements, but there would be joyful times, celebrations, and healthy agreements, too. And whatever came, good or bad, they would face it together.

Stepping off the line hadn't been easy for either of them, but considering the prize, it had definitely been worth the risks. They'd won. And they'd never again be alone.

Standing there on the cracked sidewalk, with the wind teasing them and their mouths joined, the truth hit her. All her life she had wanted two things: a career in politics and a family to love who loved her. She, who had been carrying hope of ending the crisis before it devastated, had not done the same for herself. Long ago she had given up hope on her dreams for her personal life. And she'd been wrong.

It takes a lot of heat to temper steel.

It did. And it took a lot of heat to temper people, too. To temper Sybil. It took time and trials to get not what she thought she wanted but what she most wanted and needed to the depths of her soul. Now she understood the difference and the value of both.

She wasn't the woman she had been when she'd created those dreams for her life. She was the woman she had become. And that woman wanted to share her life with Jonathan Westford, to share their dreams. That woman had discovered the lasting treasure of having a man continue to believe in her when she had given up on herself. That woman understood the marriage of souls and the power of hope.

"All right." Jonathan tapped at the transmitter in his ear.

At a loss, Sybil reared back, stroked his ear. "All right? That's it? Actually, I thought that kiss was pretty wonderful."

"It was fantastic." He nodded toward the limo. "I meant them. Standing out in the open is making them nervous. Easy targets."

Dreamy, she gazed up at him. "Fantastic, huh?"

"Oh, yeah." Pure male appreciation crossed with ego.

"I give you fantastic, you give me swamp fever. Now there's a thorn."

"You're going to be lording that over me for the next fifty years. I just know it."

"Longer," he promised. But he was smiling when he said it.

Finally she had the love she always had longed for in her life, and they were alive. Alive, and together. "Let's go home, Jonathan." She dropped her voice, soft and seductive. "I have a rose petal with your name on it."

Smiling her special smile, he led her across the sidewalk to the waiting limo, and radioed Home Base. "Lady Liberty is on the move."

About the Author

VICKI HINZE has published fourteen books and lives with her husband in Florida, where she is working on her next novel, *Lady Justice*. Readers can visit her website at www.vickihinze.com.

The most valuable agricultural
crops in the U.S. are dying—and this
is no natural disaster.

Senior Special Agent Gabrielle Kincaid,
best friend to Vice President Sybil Stone
of *Lady Liberty*, must stop the death
and destruction that threaten to
destabilize the U.S. food supply, economy,
government and its people—
provided she can convince her partner,
agent Maxwell Grayson, not to carry
out his orders to kill her.

Vicki Hinze's thrillingly realistic portrayal
of espionage, corporate terrorism,
and covert government operatives will shock
and keep you on the edge of your seat.

Read on for a preview of *Lady Justice*,
on sale in the summer of 2004.

Hundreds of U.S. flags flew on the docked cruise ship.

Tonight there would be a fireworks display that would set the American passengers' spirits soaring, but Jaris Adahan would no longer be aboard to see it. He would, however, enjoy the irony in the Americans celebrating Independence Day on the very day he had helped to make them dependent.

After checking the brim of his white baseball cap to make sure the U.S. flag pin was secure, he tugged it on and then gave himself the injection that would protect him from exposure to the contaminate. He ran a length of thin, clear hose down his sleeve, holstered the canister under his arm at his side, and mentally reviewed his checklist. He had already contaminated the ballast tanks, and the handrails and decks at the ship's exit points he would not be using to depart the ship. He had bleached his quarters, destroyed all evidence of his ever having been aboard, exchanged his passport and visa for new ones, claiming yet another false identity, and, while still at sea, he had disposed of the empty contaminate canister.

He had three more canisters: one in the holster and two in his backpack. All were full.

After a last look to make sure he hadn't missed anything, he left his cabin, went down two floors to the largest common area on the ship. On the far side, just down from a boutique, he ducked into an obscure alcove and then soaked the soles of his shoes, hoping Cardel Boudreaux hadn't used all of the Warriors' luck on his leg of the mission.

Just the idea of explaining to the honchos that they'd royally screwed up on a seventy-million-dollar contract made Jaris nauseous. He could only imagine how the honchos had reacted to the possibility of having to inform the Consortium. The anxiety probably had them all chugging down Xanax and stress-tabs, and drinking Mylanta by the gallon. Jaris sure as hell would be.

Luckily, the kid on Cardel's plane had lived.

A woman walked by, holding the hands of her twin girls. Remorse pricked at Jaris. They weren't as young as Cardel's toddler—thse girls were five, or maybe six—but they were laughing.

Jaris liked the sound, and resented liking it.

Do not notice them. Do not.

Noticing brought nightmares. Nightmares, regret. He'd learned that the hard way.

Irritated by his breach of discipline, he shut out the sights and sounds and smells of all the people in the busy lobby, and then left the alcove. It was time to get off of the ship.

Dispensing a thin film of clear, odorless contaminate through the tubing in his sleeve, he saturated every handrail in his path. And because it happened to be on his way, and because he needed to make restitution for his discipline breach, he sprayed a tempting-looking luncheon buffet set out on deck.

No one stopped him, or slowed his progress. He walked off the ship, then the dock, and made it to the U.S. border without incident.

There, foot traffic was heavy, and people waiting to enter the country stood in long lines. The noon sun beat down on them, raising sweat and tempers. Jaris ignored them and moved line to line, scanning the customs officials' uniforms, looking for his Consortium contact. Finally, he spotted him. Middle-aged and nondescript, he was wearing a U.S. flag pin on his lapel.

Jaris stepped into the man's line, shutting out the sounds of a young boy whining for a drink of anything to quench his thirst. When his turn arrived, he handed over his new passport. "Blistering sun today."

"Blistering." Recognition shone in the man's eyes. "They say tomorrow will be hotter."

Certain now he had made the appropriate contact, Jaris passed over the canister from his backpack. A canister the official had been well paid to use to contaminate an imported shipment of fruit. What kind of fruit, Jaris was not told, which meant, in the foreseeable future, he would avoid eating any.

The official waved him through, and he walked onto U.S. soil.

The canister in his holster was now empty, and he had made delivery on another. *Two down, and one to go*.

One that required only an afternoon walk through a few maize and cotton fields. . .

U.S./Canadian Border * Thursday, July 4th

Sebastian Cabot sat in his car at the Canadian border, too consumed by thoughts of his family and memories of his youth to spare any concern on getting caught.

The trunk of his Chevrolet Impala was filled with contraband cans of pâté. Simply put, he was smuggling. He had made no declarations to the customs official but, if what the Consortium had told him proved true, he wouldn't be challenged.

After September 11th, that alone was enough to scare the hell out of John Q. Public. But because there was more, it made Sebastian sick.

He slung an arm over the steering wheel to cool the sweat from his armpit, and inched the car forward in line. Who would have thought that having a few celebratory drinks after winning the biggest case of his twenty-seven-year-legal career would have led him to this? To Sebastian Cabot, attorney extraordinaire, friend of the court and champion of underdogs, smuggling pâté?

And soon, to worse.

His stomach slid into knots under his ribs. It was a damn tragic end to a life lived with purpose. He knew it, but he was powerless to change it. The Consortium had made that clear—and they'd hired an entire damn cell of Global Warriors to deliver the message proving it.

Sebastian had understood only too well. The Consortium and its Warriors left no unturned stones. He was not safe. His wife and their three children were not safe. Even his secretary, his second cousin Oscar, whom he hadn't seen in twenty years, and his damned dog were not safe.

And there was only one way any of them would ever be safe again.

"You're clear to proceed, sir." The official nodded.

"Thanks." Sebastian nodded back. The U.S. flag pin on his white golfing hat bobbed. Driving on, he headed south.

By early afternoon, he was in California's Napa Valley: the heart of wine country in the United States. He thought about pulling into a truck stop for an artery-clogging meal of the cholesterol-packed, fried foods he had avoided for the last three years under doctor's orders—today he could eat anything guilt-free—but his stomach churned, and he decided against it. The work he was about to do had his system riled up enough without throwing it a grease-fest. So he drove on, to a vineyard, and then pulled off onto the shoulder of the road.

The tires turning on the loose, dry dirt raised a little dust cloud. He waited a moment for it to settle, looked up and then down the asphalt road. Heat rippled in waves off it. The entire area seemed desolate. No people. No cars, or trucks. Nothing in sight except row upon row of lush grapevines basking in the hot, summer sun.

Sweating profusely, Sebastian gave in to his foul mood. Arrogant bastard, the sun. It should be storming.

Don't even think about it, Sebe. Do this, and every angel in heaven will weep.

His mother's voice. She had been dead for ten years, but he still missed her and loved her to distraction. And she still issued him the kind of warnings she had imbedded in his head and heart his whole life. The conscience tugs that had worked to keep him in church on Sundays; in the band in high school, when he wanted nothing more than to quit; off drugs in college, when everyone short of God was experimenting with them; and in law school long after he wanted to drop out. Hands down, she had been the most influential person in his life.

But even she couldn't help him now.

He got out of the car, opened the trunk, and then the first can of pâté. He didn't give himself an antidote injection. There wasn't one. Not that it mattered.

Stooping low, he used his pocketknife to empty the tin onto the ground, amongst the grapevines.

Sebe, think. Think! How many years of sweat and dreams—how many lives are you destroying?

I know, Mom. Don't you think I know? His throat went thick and a tear leaked out, rolled down to his chin. *I'm sorry. I hate what I'm doing. Damn it, I love my country and the people in it. You know I do.*

Then why? Why become a smuggler and a saboteur? Why become a traitor?

He blinked hard, his chin trembling. *Because as much as I love my country, I love my family more.*

But, Sebe. Sebe, this is wrong. This is unforgivable. You can't—

His chest tight, he closed his mind, shut out her voice, and moved on to the next vineyard. And then to the next, contaminating them one by one with the tainted pâté.

When he had emptied the last tin, he tossed it back into the trunk. It clanged against the others, bled dry and hollow. Sebastian slammed the lid shut, got back into the car, and then drove north, into the Sierra-Nevada Mountains.

His conscience nagged at him. Merciless. Unrelenting. Each tin contained millions of biologically engineered grape louse, which would destroy the grapevines from the roots out. By the time the poor growers realized they had a problem, they'd have lost seventy percent of their plants—and the grape louse would have spread to even more vineyards.

The California wine industry would be crippled, if not destroyed.

And European vineyard and wine stocks would soar, generating significant profits for the Consortium.

Sebastian didn't personally know any of the Consortium members, but he hated them all. They considered themselves a profit-seeking, strategic alliance of international businessmen, but they were a self-serving group of terrorists who would manipulate anyone by any means necessary to achieve their financial goals. What they were forcing him to do proved there was no limit to the amount of damage, or to the number of lives they were willing to destroy. The bastards had no consciences, no morals or ethics, and no mercy.

And most terrifying of all, they had forced him to be just like them.

Sebastian swiped at his throbbing forehead with a shaky hand. If only he could go back to that night . . .

How many times had he wished it? Hundreds? Millions? What did it matter? There was no going back.

Resentment and regret burned deep in his gut. He hadn't had a single drink since that night, yet his abstinence changed nothing. *Nothing.* He had tried everything; there was no way out.

The Consortium had him by the short hairs and they had offered him only one option that kept his family alive. Only one. And though it went against everything he had believed in and had worked for all his life, he had taken it.

God forgive him, he had taken it.

And in his mind's eye, the angels had wept.

Near Lake Tahoe, the temperature plunged. He cranked down the air-conditioner to warm up, pulled out his digital phone, and then dialed the number he'd been instructed to call.

"Yes?" A man with a thick European accent answered in a clipped tone that grated on Sebastian's raw nerves.

He clamped down on the steering wheel, glared into the taillights of an eighteen-wheeler on the road in front of him. "It's done."

"Very well."

"My family—"

"Will be safe, Mr. Cabot. In our line of work, keeping one's word is essential. Your debt is paid—provided you stick to the terms of the agreement."

Sebastian broke into a cold sweat. "Done." He disconnected, drove on for twenty minutes, and then dialed a second number.

A Cayman woman answered in a crisp voice. "First Island Bank."

"I need to verify a deposit, please." He waited until she put him through to a second woman, and then made his request, adding the account number.

"And the account owner's name, sir?"

"G. D. Cabot." Sebastian revealed his wife, Glenna's

name and then added the additional personal information that would be requested to prove he had authority on this account.

"Yes, Mr. Cabot," the woman said. "A five million dollar deposit was credited to your account today. Certified funds."

That was it, then. "Thank you." Sebastian hit the end button on the phone, considered calling his wife and kids, but then thought better of it. A call home wasn't on the list, and who knew what dangers the Consortium or their Global Warriors would attribute to an unscheduled call. They could feel Glenna or the kids were a threat.

No, as much as he craved hearing Glenna's voice, Sebastian couldn't risk it.

But he wished he could. She had the most soothing voice he had ever heard. He had married her for that voice. When nothing else could, it relaxed him. They'd had a good marriage. A good marriage, good kids, good everything. And he'd lost it all because of one night. One damn night, and one too many martinis . . .

Remorse gnawed at him. Sebastian stiffened in his seat, drove on down the winding roadway. Steep cliffs lined the road. Twice, so far, he had seen pretty waterfalls. The next one he saw—

Bridal falls. Off to his right. At least a hundred-foot drop. Perfect.

He pulled an image of Glenna and the kids on the sailboat last summer from his memory. Holding it fast in his mine's eye, he stomped down on the accelerator.

The car lurched, ripped through the guardrail. Metal crunched, glass shattered, and the car sailed out, over the gorge.

Sebe! Oh, God, no! No! Sebe . . . !

Moments stretched into lifetimes and a strange noise filled his ears. Weeping. The angels really were weeping. For him. Humbled, awed, he cried out, "I'm coming, Mama."

The Impala plunged and tumbled, crashed into tree branches and trunks and sharp rocks. It burst into flames.

The Consortium had issued an ultimatum.

Sebastian Cabot had followed his orders explicitly.

Including the order to die on impact.

Washington, D.C., * Friday, July 5th

"You're busted, Lieutenant Gibson."

Senior Special Agent Gabrielle Kincaid stalked around the conference table, as rigid and tense as only the infuriated queen bitch of the highly skilled Special Detail Unit of the Secret Service could stalk. She stopped behind him, just off his left shoulder, and then bent low and whispered in his ear. "How does it feel to know you killed seventeen civilians, three seasoned SDU operatives, and two FBI agents?"

Gibson bowed his head, looked down from the copper-lined wall in the top secret Home Base headquarters' conference room to the scarred table that had seen too many crises and even more ass-chewing debriefings. He didn't dare to answer. Agent Kincaid would only get more steamed, and she was already close to boiling.

In his days as a security monitor at Home Base, Gibson once had seen her boil. It wasn't an experience he was eager to repeat, much less instigate.

Agent Kincaid did not suffer in silence.

"You know we're America's last line of defense," she said from behind him in a tone that raised the hair on his neck. "Our missions are critical to the nation's safety. They require total and complete anonymity—absolute secrecy. There aren't a hundred people in the entire country who know SDU exists, for God's sake. That's essential to our effectiveness." She paused, lowered her voice a decibel, and then went on. "This was training, Gibson, but if you're going to survive the transition from active duty military to SDU operative, then you'd better get one thing clear in your head right now. SDU is a stealth operation. You never, *never*, sacrifice its secrecy. Good agents who have devoted their lives to this unit have popped cyanide or been killed by other good agents in this unit to protect it. That's a fact of life here. Burn it into your brain if you have to, but don't ever forget it again."

"I won't, ma'am. I know the drill." He risked a glance at her. "It was just a momentary lapse."

Dressed appropriately in sleek black, she tossed her sun-bronzed hair back from her face and glared at him. "Then you also know that if you had one of these momentary lapses on an actual mission, everyone in the unit—including Commander Conlee and every single operative currently on missions worldwide—would be killed. Inside of twenty-four hours, all evidence that SDU existed would be eradicated. *All* evidence, including us." Her green eyes burned nearly black with disdain and fury. "I'm not ready to die because you're sloppy or incompetent and having momentary lapses, Gibson."

Gibson's stomach heaved and stuck somewhere in his ribs. "It won't happen again, ma'am."

"It had better not." She walked around the table, leaned across it, and planted her spread hands on its scarred surface. "Understand this, too. My first obligation is to the security of the United States. You screw up again and I'll kill you myself."

How could anyone so beautiful be such a vicious, merciless bitch?

Her partner, Maxwell Grayson, would say it was God's sense of compensation and balance, but Gibson considered it more likely God's twisted sense of humor, reserved to make men crazy—or His secret weapon, used to scare them spitless. Either way, Gibson believed her every word from his toenails up. It was common knowledge in the unit that if Gabby Kincaid said something, you could take it to the bank and cash it. Or, in his case, to the graveyard and bury it. "Yes, ma'am."

She folded her arms across her chest. "I'll be back in two weeks to either bust you out of SDU or to certify your final training mission. I have no mercy, Gibson. Remember that," she warned him. "Now, get the hell out of my face."

Gibson wasted no time leaving the conference room. He felt scorched. Shamed and scorched and totally pissed off at her for being unforgiving, and at himself because he had screwed up and created a need for it. He knew better. "Damn it."

Agent Maxwell Grayson stood leaning against the hallway wall. He straightened and then clasped Gibson's shoulder in an unspoken gesture of sympathy. "Rough one, huh?"

"Oh, yeah." Gibson looked back, grunted. "I've got a debrief with Commander Conlee next, and I'm not sure I've got enough ass left for him to chew."

Conlee wouldn't have to chew; Gabby had done a thorough job. But Max didn't mention it to Gibson. Dreading the meeting was a vital part of his training. "You'll probably survive it." Max nodded to add weight to his words. "She's tough—"

"She's a bitch," Gibson interjected with feeling.

Max couldn't disagree. Her unofficial title around the unit was "Queen Bitch." He had caught wind of it, though no one had expressly referred to her by it to him. For that, he was grateful. As her partner, Max would have been obligated to take exception, and since she had earned the name, that wouldn't be easy to stomach.

Rightly or wrongly, Gabby made an all-out effort to be hypercritical of other agents' job performances. Hell, in the last six years, she had alienated everyone in the unit except Commander Conlee and his second in charge, Jonathan Westford. But Max gave credit where it was due, and being hypercritical was only half the story on Gabby. Fairness demanded that Gibson know it. "She's hands down the best active operative in the unit," Max told him. "What she rips you a new one for can— and probably will—save your life down the line. It has others, including mine. That's worth remembering."

"I will." Gibson dragged a hand through his short, spiky hair. "*If* I get down the line without her killing me first."

"There is that." Max stuffed a hand in his pocket.

Resignation flickered over Gibson's face. "She meant it literally, didn't she?"

Max wasn't sure exactly what "it" was, but he could imagine well enough. "I've worked with her for five years. Whatever she said take as fact. I've never known her to make an idle statement or an empty threat."

Gibson's face leaked all its color.

Ah, she'd threatened to kill him, Max deduced. Glad her anger wasn't squared on his head, he nodded. "Better get a move on. Commander Conlee is waiting."

"Wish me luck." Gibson rolled his shoulders, shook off some tension, and then took off down the hall.

"You got it." Not envying him the next half hour of his life, Max watched him go and then walked in the opposite direction, down the hallway, and finally into the conference room.

Gabby stood near the far wall, her arms folded over her chest, her eyes closed, her chin tilted to the ceiling. It was her classic pose for on-the-job meditating to harness her temper.

Max gave her a moment, then spoke up. "Still terrorizing the troops, I see."

"Only when necessary to keep them from killing others, Agent Grayson. Perhaps one day, you." She sat down in one of the hardback chairs and glanced at her watch, clearly pressed for time.

Venting her temper had her face flushed. It looked good on her. Ticked off because he'd noticed, he shifted on his seat and turned his thoughts to business. "You summoned?"

"Yes. Commander Conlee thought it would be a good idea to brief you on the Four Grande operation before I fly back to Florida."

Gabby had been undercover in Florida for the past seven months, investigating judicial corruption claims involving a suspected cell of creative, and unfortunately, extremely effective mercenary assassins known as Global Warriors and their connection to a local judge named Abernathy. The Four Grande operation was a secondary mission she'd taken on. Knowing simultaneous missions were not uncommon to her or to other seasoned SDU covert operatives, Max sat down across the table from her. "Okay. Shoot."

"Succinctly put, Four Grande is in the mop-up stage. I turned it over to the FBI late yesterday. They've handled the arrests."

SDU worked totally behind the scenes. Overt agencies handled the public aspects of all missions. "How many were there?"

"Three. All senior members of Four Grande who were in the country to buy arms through a phony charity they'd set up on the web. That operation has been shut down and the FBI is tracking all transactions back to their points of origin. Homeland Security's all over it, so we're done."

Another success. "Excellent." She might be a bitch, but she was good at her job. Max admired her—not for her devotion, all SDU operatives were devoted—but because as hard as she was on everyone else, she was harder still on herself. He respected that, and all of SDU respected her work. Who could argue with her stats?

Gabby shrugged and a long lock of hair crept over her shoulder. "I would have liked to dig down another layer in their organization to make sure we'd totally disrupted their operation, but they were within forty-eight hours of taking delivery on dirty nukes. Couldn't risk it."

"Good call, in my humble opinion."

She managed a nod. "So we delivered. Close your file on Four Grande."

She had delivered, and *he* never had opened a file on Four Grande. If he had, it would have been empty. This had been yet another mission where she had shut him out and had handled it entirely on her own—failing to mention in this briefing, of course, that she'd nearly been killed by one of the three men arrested and she should have activated Max to protect her back. He should raise hell at her for taking unnecessary risks, but he'd be wasting his breath. Instead, he settled for a resigned, "Great." Yet, sensing something was off, he really looked at her.

Gabby was his age, thirty-five, and five-eight, though she had mile-long legs that made her appear taller. Her hair looked sun-flashed and hung long and loose down past her shoulders, framing her face. She was classic, commanded double takes, and still couldn't be considered anything but beautiful. Taking in the whole package, she was striking. But what made her compelling wasn't the physical package. It was something . . . different.

She had an earthy sensuality that aided her in playing a wide variety of undercover roles and hinted at that "something different." Exactly what it was, she kept private, but Max knew it existed—he sensed it—yet he couldn't, and never had been able to, peg it. That made her a little mystical, and, combined with the deliberate bitchiness he'd decided had to be a protective shield, damned sexy. Not that he'd ever acted on his attraction to her—they were partners—but he understood why men felt drawn to her and compelled to tell her their secrets. Hell, at times, he himself had felt both.

That nebulous something was probably Gabby's greatest professional asset—next to her mind. The woman was incredibly sharp and flexible and fast on her feet. And, blessing or curse, her work was her life.

"I take it your investigation is going well down in Florida?" Max asked, relatively certain it must be since the commander hadn't told him otherwise. Though, with Gabby involved, one couldn't honestly tell. Max wouldn't bet his career that she kept Conlee up to speed twenty-four, seven.

"Complex. Moving at a snail's pace, but fine." She glanced at her watch again and then stood up. "I've got to leave now or I'll miss my flight. Unless something significant breaks, I'll catch you up on developments in two weeks, when I come back to bust Gibson."

She was headed back to Carnel Cove, Florida, to the Global Warrior/Judge Abernathy corruption case. Back to her primary undercover assignment as a judge. "Is Gibson that bad?"

Sparing Max a grunt to signal he should know better, she grabbed her purse, then slung its strap over her shoulder. "No, he's that good."

"Of course." Max bit back a pleased-with-himself smile. He had a lot of faith in Gibson. "You wouldn't waste your time ripping a lousy trainee a new ass."

"I wouldn't?" she asked from the door, casting Max a sly glance back over her shoulder.

"No, you wouldn't." Max revealed his feeble grip on how her mind worked. "You'd just shoot him."

She didn't smile, but she did look tempted. "You're learning, Max." She walked out of the conference room, her heels clicking on the ceramic tile.

The echo grew more and more faint, and Max rewarded himself with a smile. "I'll be damned."

For the first time in five years, Gabby Kincaid had called her partner by his first name.

Did he dare to hope she was thawing?

That wouldn't be a smart move on his part. He seriously doubted she was getting used to the idea of having a partner. She'd been direct about not wanting one, and in five years, she never once had activated him on their joint missions. On those rare occasions where he'd had the audacity to suggest he could be helpful to her, she had flatly reminded him that she *always* worked alone. That rigid stance didn't leave much room for thawing.

Max rocked back on his seat. In the sheen of the copper wall, he replayed their last conversation, where he'd had the temerity—some would say, bad judgment—to offer to help her.

Unless Commander Conlee orders you to put a bullet through my head, don't interfere on my missions. Any of my missions. Actually, it'll be best if you just stay the hell out of my way. SDU missions carry high stakes and higher kill rates. I respect that. And if I die on one, it's going to be because I screwed up, not because some partner got me killed.

Her back being wide open had nearly killed her—a circumstance for which Commander Conlee had blamed Max, until he had reported that "don't interfere" exchange between him and Gabby. Then, despite the commander's assurances, it had taken a while for Max to shake-off the feeling that she had slammed him and his personal worth. Conlee had said that her attitude had everything to do with herself and nothing to do with Max, his skills, or his abilities as a seasoned operative. That when it came to SDU covert operations, Gabby Kincaid was top notch. She knew it, and she trusted no one but herself.

In time, the woman had earned Max's respect and, more than once, his admiration. Somewhere along the way, he had accepted the commander's opinions about her as truth. In SDU, working with a partner without trust marked you both for certain death, which left Max with no choice but to agree with her. Lacking trust, she *did* best work alone.

Even if it killed her.